ONE WYLDE KNIGHT

A MEDIEVAL ROMANCE
PART OF THE DE REYNE DOMINATION SERIES

BY KATHRYN LE VEQUE

© Copyright 2024 by Kathryn Le Veque Novels, Inc.
Trade Paperback Edition
Text by Kathryn Le Veque
Cover by Kim Killion

Reproduction of any kind except where it pertains to short quotes in relation to advertising or promotion is strictly prohibited.

All Rights Reserved.

The characters and events portrayed in this book are fictitious. Any similarity to real persons, living or dead, is purely coincidental and not intended by the author.

KATHRYN LE VEQUE
NOVELS

WWW.KATHRYNLEVEQUE.COM

ARE YOU SIGNED UP FOR KATHRYN'S BLOG?

You'll get the latest news and information on exclusive giveaways, exclusive excerpts, coming releases, sales, free books, cover reveals and more.

Kathryn's blog followers get it all first. No spam, no junk.

Get the latest info from the reigning Queen of English Medieval Romance!

Sign Up Here

kathrynleveque.com

DE REYNE FAMILY MOTTO

Ducibus fidem meam

Faith Guides Me

Dark, sultry, with a hint of fire in his blood from his Visigoth ancestors and a spark in his eye that betray his killer instincts, Thorington "Thor" de Reyne is the son of the Earl of Ashington and one of the greatest knights England has ever seen. His talent is unmatched, so much so that the king himself has demanded Thor's service.

But he has to fight Thor's own father to get him.

Much in demand, Thor has an ego that is fed by the warlords and kings who are fighting over him. But he has own plans that include getting rich, rich enough that he won't have to serve at the whim of a king or an earl.

And the king knows it.

In a strategic move, the king offers a marriage to Thor, to the richest heiress in England, if not the entire world. Lady Caledonia de Wylde is a woman with more money than the king himself and quite possibly more land than any other landholder in England. Not only was she an heiress in her own right, but she married—and was widowed by—a man with roots that went back before the Norman conquest. She's older than Thor, and has three daughters, but Thor doesn't care. He'll get the money he wants and the power he very much craves.

But what he didn't expect was to fall in love with her.

And that's where the tides change.

Lady Caledonia has an enemy, one so dark and devious that he'll do anything to gain her money, her lands, and her very life if he can. Unbeknownst to Thor, he finds himself marrying into an explosive situation where he could very well be the spark that ignites the blaze. Now, he has a wife and an empire to protect, but it's not Thor who ultimately does the protecting.

It's Caledonia.

Hold on for a wylde and passionate ride through Medieval England, where ambition surrenders to lust and the most powerful thing in the world, as Thor and Caledonia discover, is love.

It can save, it can kill… or it can be the ultimate sacrifice.

DE REYNE FAMILY TREE

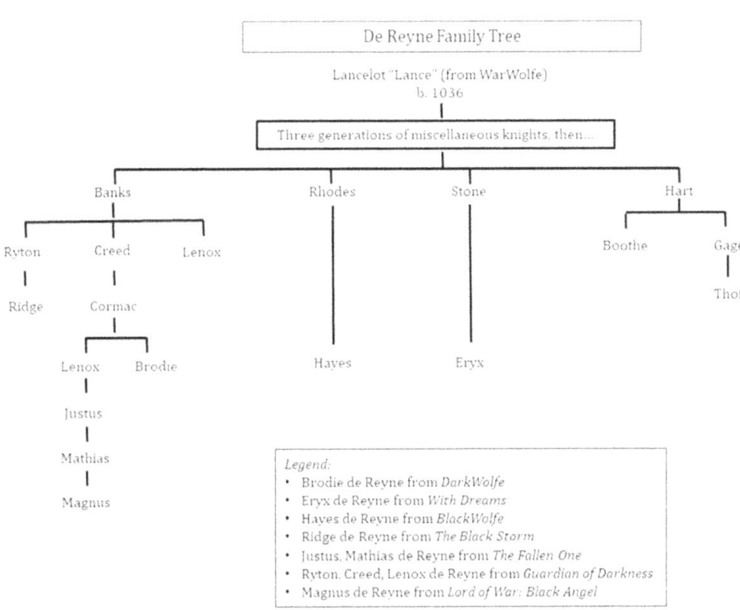

AUTHOR'S NOTES

Here we are with another de Reyne novel!

I really love this family. In fact, they were one of my first favorite families, starting with *Guardian of Darkness*. That was the first de Reyne novel I ever wrote and I absolutely adored the brothers. We saw more of them in *Master of the Dawn*. However, for the purposes of this novel, the brothers from *Guardian of Darkness* are the first cousins once removed of the hero in this tale. Check out the family tree to see more. Something you've probably noticed about the de Reyne family is that the men all have, with some exceptions, one-syllable names. That's their tradition, broken by wives who maybe want other names for their sons. As we know, the de Reyne men are submissive to their wives. Who can blame them?

We've got a few things to talk about before you jump into this book. The first is regarding the heroine and a blend of fact and fiction when it comes to Stafford Castle. Our heroine is linked to Stafford Castle, a real place with a real history. However, in the time period in which this story is set, the history of the castle is unremarkable and not hugely documented, so it's plausible to insert our heroine into that time frame. The de Tosni family did indeed own Stafford Castle, and that's where she gets her married name.

Speaking of the heroine, she's a fan of Gomorrah, that notorious pleasure guild that has popped up in the de Wolfe Pack Generations and Executioner Knights books. What's not to love about an underground guild where one can have—or do—

whatever one wishes? I plan to incorporate more of Gomorrah in future books because it really is a fun place and unique in the Medieval world.

I think you're going to find a lot of interesting characters in this tale, and it's basically split into two parts—pre-marriage and post. We have a few cameos by Roi de Lohr (Lion of Twilight) and Daniel de Lohr (Shadowmoor) and at this period in time, they are getting up there in age—but are still very important to the function of England. Oh, and one last thing—if you've read my novel *Nighthawk*, Patrick de Wolfe's story, then you know that there was a subplot in it where Patrick was supposed to head to London and become the Lord Protector to King Henry. Not to give a spoiler if you haven't read it, but he ends up not accepting the position. Guess who does accept it? That's right—Thor de Reyne, the hero in this story. Patrick turned it down, so Thor accepted.

It all comes full circle!

And with that, the usual pronunciation guide:
Rotri: phonetically sounds like RAW-tree
Domnall: dom-nul
Rhun: Roon

This is a heck of a compact adventure and it starts out hot out of the gate, so hang on and enjoy the ride!

Happy Reading!

PROLOGUE

Year of Our Lord 1271
Westminster Palace

A BATTLE WAS brewing.

A battle so big, so volatile, that everyone in the great hall of Westminster was coiled and waiting. Coiled because they had to know which way to pivot when the battle began. The king, Great Henry as he was called, was on one side, and on the other… Well, the other side was the current Earl of Ashington. A man once known as *El Viento del Norte.*

The North Wind.

One of the greatest mercenaries of his time, an English knight who had spent years fighting with the greatest mercenary army in Aragon under the command of his uncle, a man known as *El Vibora.*

The Viper.

Henry may have been the King of England, but Gage de Reyne, his opponent, was more than a formidable match. Henry had a healthy respect for the man, though he wouldn't admit it. He preferred to stack his side of the battle with great warlords to hopefully show Gage that he wasn't afraid of him.

At all.

Not even a little.

… maybe.

But it had come to this. Years of wrestling for the service of the same man, a man who happened to be Gage's son, but who also happened to be a knight very much coveted by the king. Gage had kept his son in the north, fighting Scots, knowing that Henry was eyeing the man for greater royal duties, and in a moment of weakness, he allowed his son, perhaps the greatest knight his family lines had ever produced, to accompany the king on crusade. The French king was going, and Henry, being pious and semi-delusional, also decided to go. It was an honor for Gage's son to go with him, as Lord Protector. Even kings needed a bodyguard. But ill health had forced him to turn back, and Gage's son right along with him. But the king kept him close, a security shield that he refused to release.

That was when the battle truly started.

The northern warlords, called the Northerners as a group, were a tough band of battle lords because they held the north against the Scottish and, at times, Northman onslaughts. That made them perhaps the toughest of the tough. When there were battles in the south of England or even in France, oftentimes the Northerners didn't participate. They still held the north, like their own little kingdom, and earls such as William de Wolfe, Adam de Longley, Gage de Reyne, and more were, at times, with power that equaled the king's.

And Henry knew it. He knew the Northerners were their own little group, a very strong group, but they were still his vassals. It was moments like this that he was forced to hammer that home. The battle for Gage's son had come down to this day, this moment, and now the final skirmish would unfold. A winner would be declared.

Henry intended to be that winner.

"Understand me, Ashington, so there is no doubt in your mind," Henry said firmly. "I am not requesting the service of your son. I am commanding it. He is not going home with you—he is remaining here with me. Why would you deny your king his wants? Furthermore, why would you deny you son such prestige?"

Gage, his expression lined with displeasure, faced off against a man he'd faced off against before. Henry was old these days. He'd stopped actively participating in battles or even administering the country for the most part. His son, Edward, had taken over most of Henry's duties. As Edward would be king one day, that was perfectly acceptable. In fact, Gage could see Edward behind his father, seemingly remorseful for the man's stubborn behavior against a loyal warlord.

But that remorse didn't change Gage's mind.

It didn't even move him.

"Your grace, it is not prestige you offer Thor, but the role of a nursemaid," he said frankly. "I permitted him to accompany you on the crusade to the Levant. I felt it was important to provide you with his protection. I felt—"

"He *is* my Lord Protector," Henry said, interrupting him stubbornly. "I had a Lord Protector, once, in Patrick de Wolfe, but Patrick chose to marry and remain at his father's holding of Berwick Castle. Thor is the perfect man for the task."

Thor.

Thorington de Reyne, to be exact, Gage's second-born son. He'd been named after his mother's family and had gone by Thor since he was an infant. That was all anyone knew him by. He was also a twin, his older brother by ten minutes being Brian de Reyne, the man who would become the next Earl of Ashington. Brian and Thor had essentially the same facial features and had, as children, been nearly identical, but time and growth spurts had changed that. Brian was dark-haired and big, fair, and freckled, while Thor had the sultry darkness of the de Reynes—wavy, nearly black hair that tumbled to his shoulders and a smoldering handsomeness that he'd acquired the moment he transformed from a youth into a man. But both he and Brian shared shockingly bright blue eyes when no one else in the family had them.

Thor, however, was the fighter.

A war god, just like his namesake.

"I gave my son to you on loan for two years," Gage said, trying to keep his temper down. "He was to accompany you to the Levant and fulfil his destiny as a great and noble knight, but that did not happen. He has returned home prematurely. Did you not think that I, as his father, also have plans for him upon his return? Plans that did not include playing a companion to the king."

Henry's features darkened. "He could only be so fortunate."

Gage could see that he wasn't getting anywhere, so he had to shift tactics. He was dealing with an ill old man, one who was also conniving, and butting heads with him wasn't going to work. He'd known that from the start. Months of missives back and forth regarding the return of Thor to the north had culminated in Gage's presence here at Westminster. Henry had refused him audience for three solid weeks, and Gage knew why.

They were at the crux of that reason now.

Henry didn't want to let Thor go.

"Of course he has been fortunate," Gage said. "But I have

great plans for him also. I expect him to take command of Septentrion Castle, my largest garrison, and a property he will inherit when I pass. It is his. Does a man not have a right to his own property?"

Henry simply looked at him. Then he spoke to Edward, standing behind him to his right, without looking at him.

"Edward?" he said. "Please tell Ashington our intentions for his son. The time has come."

Edward didn't look particularly eager to speak. "Now?" he said. "In front of everyone? Do you not wish to tell Ashington privately?"

"Nay," Henry said in a calculated move. "Tell him now."

Edward grunted, looking to Gage apologetically. "I will clear the hall," he said. "I should not be—"

Henry cut him off, standing up from the chair he'd been planted in. "Nay," he said firmly. "You will *not* clear the hall, Edward. I will tell Ashington what we have planned for his son so that everyone may understand that what I have to offer him is far more prestigious than a little castle somewhere in Northumberland. Let his fellow warlords tell him what a great offer it is."

Gage could hear the condescension in Henry's voice. The man was going to try to use peer pressure to get his wants. "Septentrion is hardly a little castle, your grace," he said. "It is large and strategic."

Henry waved him off. "Compared to what I am prepared to offer him, it is a pittance," he said. Then he pointed at Gage. "Listen to me and listen well, Ashington, because I have a little story for you."

"Go on, your grace."

Henry was moving stiffly, moving for one of the long feasting tables near Gage. He intended to sit, but before he did, he gestured to the men in the hall, men around him.

"Who do you see here?" he asked. "Look at them—do you not see the Earl of Canterbury? Daniel de Lohr?"

Gage's focus moved to the big blond warlord standing off to the side. Daniel de Lohr had inherited Canterbury from his father, David, who passed away about ten years ago. The de Lohrs were legendary in the history of England and particularly during the last sixty or so years.

He acknowledged the earl who was also his friend.

"Of course I know Canterbury," he said, watching Daniel smile faintly. "We are old friends."

"And you know that Daniel's uncle, Christopher de Lohr, gained his fortune through marriage," Henry said. "Who else do you see here?"

Gage spied another Northerner, Edward de Wolfe, son of the greatest knight the north had ever seen. William de Wolfe, Earl of Warenton, was a living legend, and his sons were all a chip off the old block, so to speak. De Wolfe had six grown sons, and while five of them had followed the warring ways, Edward had followed the path of his grandfather and namesake, Edward de Wolfe, and become Henry's counselor and premier diplomat. He was quite young for such a role, but he was excellent because he had been mentored by Henry's greatest chancellor, Roi de Lohr, the Earl of Cheltenham. Roi was Daniel's cousin and a greater statesman had never existed. Roi was here, too, standing with Edward, both of them watching Gage to see how the man was reacting to Henry's bullying.

It was difficult not to feel pity for the man.

"I see de Wolfe and de Lohr," Gage finally said. "I see great men. What is your point, your grace?"

Henry glanced over at Edward and Roi before speaking. "My point is that William de Wolfe married well. That is how he gained much by way of fortune, even if he did marry a Scot. Christopher de Lohr married Arthur Barringdon's daughter and inherited Lioncross Abbey Castle and the Barringdon fortune, which set him up to create his empire. Men *must* marry well, Gage, though I do not have to tell you that, considering you assumed the Ashington earldom through your wife. Do you not think that Thor has the right to do the same, given the opportunity?"

Gage rubbed at his forehead as if to rub away the headache that threatened. "I would appreciate it if you would say what you mean, your grace."

Henry cocked his head in a gesture of agreement. "Very well," he said. "Your son is a great knight, Gage. We both agree on that. You want him in your service and I want him in mine. I can offer him more than you can."

"Such as what?"

"Such as a marriage to one of the greatest heiresses in England."

Gage paused, eyeing him suspiciously. "Of whom do you speak?"

"I will tell you when your son arrives."

That was the first indication that Thor had been summoned by Henry. Before Gage could reply, Henry gestured to someone at the back of the hall and Gage turned to see his son being admitted. Quite tall, and very muscular, Thor was an imposing man wherever he went. He never went unnoticed in any room he entered, for he was a figure that immediately attracted attention. Like now.

The war god had arrived.

Edward de Wolfe immediately broke away from Roi and headed toward Thor, a man he considered a friend because they'd spent so much time together. Gage could see Edward muttering to Thor, who didn't seem particularly perplexed that he'd been summoned, but he did seem surprised when he spied his father.

Surprise that turned to confusion. Whatever Edward was telling him had his brow furrowing, and Thor looked to his father as if to speak to the man, but Henry took control of the situation. He didn't want the de Reyne men to converse before he had a chance to say what he needed to say.

"Sit, Thor," Henry directed. "That's right—on the bench next to where your father is standing. I have something to say to you and I wish for your father to hear it."

Thor was at least a head taller than his father, who was a big man in his own right. He looked at Gage curiously, but all Gage could do was shake his head and indicate the seat on the bench next to him. Slowly, Thor lowered his big body, but he genuinely had no idea what was going on. In fact, he looked to the men around Henry, a group he was usually a part of, and thought he might have missed something.

"Your grace," he said, feeling like he needed to explain himself. "I was not aware you had a conclave. I informed your chamberlain that my horse has been ill and I wished to see to him this morning. I brought a man in from Flanders who swears he can heal what ails him and—"

Henry cut him off. "Nay, Thor, you were not expected to be part of this," he said. "I knew about the horse. How is he?"

Thor visibly relaxed. "He seems to be better, your grace," he said. "He has always had trouble with his lungs, but he is breathing much easier this morning."

"Good," Henry said. "Then we may discuss important matters?"

"Aye, your grace."

Henry nodded and continued. "Thor, it is no secret that your father wishes to take you north," he said, indicating Gage. "He tells me that he has only loaned you to me for my trip to the Levant, and since we have returned early, he wants you to come home. Were you aware of this?"

Thor looked at his father. "I am, your grace."

Henry's gaze lingered on Thor for a moment before he turned back for the big, cushioned chair he always sat in. His bones were old, his joints painful, and the cushioned chair was the closest he could come to something comfortable. He needed to be comfortable so he could think clearly, because he had to plan this out carefully or all would be lost.

He proceeded.

"I think you are a man destined for great things," he said after a moment. "You are not a man who should be relegated to a garrison commander for your father and then for your brother when he inherits the title. You are your father's greatest son, yet you will inherit nothing. Nothing I have said is untrue."

Henry was hammering home something that had been Thor's most disappointing issue. The reality was that he would not inherit anything. Everything would go to Brian. It wasn't something he complained about or lamented because he knew that it was simply the way of things and his brother would make an excellent earl, but those closest to him knew how it troubled him. Perhaps it was something that drove him to be better and faster and stronger than anyone else because he knew he had to earn whatever he gained in life. The king hit him where it hurt. But he kept his chin up as he answered.

"It is true, your grace."

"That is not a life you wish for yourself, is it?"

Thor's gaze had never left Henry. "I have worked hard to earn what I have, your grace."

Henry lifted a thin eyebrow. "And what is that?" he said. "True, you are my Lord Protector and I have paid you well for the past two years, but before that, you served your father at Ashington. Did he pay you well?"

"He did, my lord."

"And before that, you traveled with your father's uncle, Varro de Soto, the Aragon mercenary," Henry said. "The man known as the Viper. Of course I know all about that. You served the man for several years, traveling to a dozen countries, fighting wars for a dozen different warlords who paid you handsomely. What was it they called you?"

"*El Martillo*, your grace."

"And that means…?"

"The Hammer, your grace."

"Ah," Henry said, though he'd already known the answer. "The Hammer. And you have fought many."

"I have, your grace."

"Well paid for them."

"Aye, your grace."

"You are not poor, lad."

"Nay, your grace, I am not."

"But you still have no property, no title, and no future other than what your father and brother dictate."

That was a rather brutal way of putting it, but it was the truth. Thor was still confused as to why he was even here, now struggling not to become annoyed. Had he been brought here only to be made to feel inadequate?

He cleared his throat quietly.

"My father and brother have always been quite generous, your grace."

"But would it not be better not to be dependent on them?"

Thor took a deep breath, tamping down the irritation. "All men are dependent upon each other, your grace," he said. "That is simply the way of the world. May I be so bold as to ask what point you are trying to make?"

Henry knew he had pushed him to the edge, so he backed off. "I am going to change your future, Thor," he said. "All men are dependent on other men, that is true, but almost every great lord you know has been made great, or greater, by a strategic marriage. Your own father was a mere knight until he married your mother. Now he is a great earl because of her. But I am going to make you greater than your father."

"I am not sure that is possible, your grace, but I will ask the obvious—how?"

"With a great marriage."

That hadn't been something Thor expected. His bright blue eyes flickered in confusion, then in shock when he realized what the king meant. He was a man of careful control, but it was threatening to slip at the moment.

"A… a marriage, your grace?" he stammered. "*Me*?"

Henry nodded. "Listen carefully, Thor," he said. "The lady who will be your wife is a lady with a family older than England. Through her father, she descends from the last king of Mercia, Ceowulf Wyldefruth. The House of de Wylde, as it was styled by the Normans when they came to these shores. Lady Caledonia de Wylde de Tosni is the last of her line. A very ancient and powerful line. She was married young to the Earl of Stafford, Robert de Tosni, but they had three daughters. When he died, he was left with no sons and was the last of his line as well. Lady Caledonia not only bears the Mercian line, but the Stafford line also. She is the Countess of Tamworth and Stafford, with more lands, castles, men, and vassals than almost anyone in England. She is an extremely valuable heiress and one I believe would give you the destiny you deserve."

Thor was speechless. He stared at Henry for a moment, unable to look at his father for reasons he wasn't quite sure of. Perhaps it had something to do with Henry saying he would make him greater than his father. Given that he loved his father and admired him, he thought that was rather an insult to him.

But damnation… He could hardly believe what he was hearing.

"I am honored, your grace," he finally said. "Honored and stunned that you should be so generous."

Henry cocked his head, hearing the hesitation in Thor's voice. "But…?"

Thor cleared his throat softly. "But my vocation is my life," he said. "I realize that marriage is a contract and nothing more, but I will widow the woman the day I marry her. I will always be sworn to you and my position as Lord Protector."

Henry nodded. "I know," he said. "And I am grateful. But you deserve this."

Thor wasn't so sure. "And I appreciate that, your grace," he said. "But the truth is that I am not ready for marriage. I've not even considered it. If that is offensive to you, then I apologize, but that is the truth of it. Simply put, I do not think I will make a very good husband."

Henry looked at him seriously. "No one is a good husband at first," he said. "It takes time and effort. Even your father will tell you that. Will you not try?"

Thor shrugged. "As I said, I've not considered it."

"Then think of this," Henry said. "With the power and wealth you would have as the Earl of Tamworth, you would command thousands. Thor, this is a great opportunity for you to position yourself as one of the great warlords in England. As great as any de Lohr or de Wolfe. For that kind of position, you could at least *try* to be a good husband. Do you understand me?"

Thor nodded quickly. "I am not refusing, your grace," he said. "I suppose I am a little overwhelmed, but I am not refusing. I am simply telling you my feelings on the matter."

"But you *will* consider this?"

Thor paused. Drawing in a long, deep breath, he found himself looking to Edward de Wolfe, to Roi standing near him, and even to Daniel and, finally, Prince Edward. They were all in various stages of approval about the offer, nodding faintly at him, silently showing their support. He *did* deserve this. As the second son of an earl, this was an astonishing opportunity, and Thor understood that.

But he also knew something else.

That Henry was trying to keep him loyal to the Crown. Thor had been a point of contention between the king and Gage, each one demanding his service, each one being possessive of his time and skill. Thor was fairly certain that this was a ploy by Henry to make serving him much sweeter than returning to Northumberland and serving his father. This wasn't some altruistic offer with no strings attached, simply because Henry liked him.

This was an offer that came at a price.

Thor understood that plainly.

"I would be a fool not to consider it, your grace," he finally said. "But why don't you tell me what your expectations are of me should I accept?"

Henry chuckled softly. "You are very suspicious, Thor."

"I think I have reason to be."

Henry continued to chuckle. "My expectations are that you will remain loyal to me until the day you draw your last breath," he said. "But since you will outlive me, you will remain loyal to my son. He will need you. Mayhap that is truly why I am offering you this, Thor—Edward will need you when he becomes king. I will go to my grave knowing my son is well supported."

"Even if I returned to Ashington, I would still support you and Edward, your grace," Thor said. "You do not need to bribe me for my loyalty."

Henry shrugged. "It is not a bribe, but a reward," he said. "A reward for your loyalty past, present, and future. It is something you have earned, Thor. It is yours and I want you to embrace it."

Thor thought on that a moment because the way Henry said it gave him an inclination of what the man really meant. He'd been around Henry too long not to know that a command was wrapped up in words that might convey otherwise. Henry was pretending that he had a choice.

But he didn't.

Damn...

"What you mean to tell me is that I cannot refuse," he said quietly.

Henry simply gave him a look that suggested he could draw his own conclusions, and that shook Thor's composure a little more. He'd walked into an ambush and hadn't realized it until this very moment. That power struggle between the king and his father was being brought to a conclusion and Thor would be the one to pay the price. An attractive marriage, that was true. But to a woman he didn't know and had never met. A great heiress with ancient bloodlines. *Caledonia de Wylde*. Thor rolled that name around in his head, thinking he might have heard it before, but he couldn't be sure. The lady wasn't close to the king, that was for certain, and that raised the question—if she was such a great heiress, why *wasn't* she close to the king?

Why hadn't he had dealings with her before?

Thor snorted softly as he stood up from the bench.

"So the marriage is mine whether or not I want it," he said. "Asking me if I would consider it was an empty question because you did not mean it. Not in the least."

Henry shrugged. "It is for your own good, lad," he said. "You may not think so now, but in time you will. In time, you will thank me."

Thor put up a hand as if to stop the man from talking, which was a shocking gesture coming from the king's Lord Protector, a man who was ever-obedient and even subservient to his king. But Thor's irritation was no longer restrained and it was directed at Henry.

"If this woman is such a great heiress, why have I not met her?" he said. "I've never even heard you mention her name in the two years I have been by your side. Where has she been hiding?"

Henry rubbed his hands together, clearing his throat softly as if uncomfortable about what he was going to say. "The lady has been abducted," he said, avoiding answering the gist of Thor's questions. "I have it on good authority that she is being kept at Gomorrah. You know the place, Thor—we all know the place. It is hell on earth and she is being kept there. You must rescue her."

Gomorrah.

That was a name that was only whispered in society, a place so legendary that even discussing it might damage one's reputation. Gomorrah was an exclusive guild where every fantasy a man, or woman, had could come true, founded long ago by a Hessian lord who married an English noblewoman, Lady Camberwell. The enterprising Hessian used his wife's money to buy property from the church to start his notorious guild. Built on gambling and excess, it was a true den of iniquity.

Situated beneath the old St. Dunstan's Church, a Saxon church that burned down every time the Catholic Church tried to rebuild it, they were more than happy to sell the cursed property to the Hessian. In fact, St. Dunstan's was built atop the ruins of an ancient Roman temple, and some said the Romans themselves had cursed the land. Whatever the case, the House of Camberwell made a fortune from it, paying a portion to the Catholic Church every year from the profits. In turn, the church absolved Camberwell of the sin of owning Gomorrah.

A convenient arrangement.

But the mere mention of the name had Thor frowning in disbelief. "Gomorrah?" he repeated in shock. "*Who* has abducted her?"

Henry shrugged as if upset by the situation. "I do not know," he said imploringly. "No one knows. But she is there and she needs saving. Will you save her, Thor?"

Thor's frown grew. "Surely she has family for this kind of thing."

Henry shook his head. "She has no family," he said. "Were you not listening to me? There are no males left in her family.

She is the last of her line. Someone has taken her to Gomorrah and she is being kept there, surely against her will. This is one of the wealthiest women in all of England, Thor. Since she has no one to help her, that must fall on me. I cannot allow another to marry her and control the Tamworth and Stafford fortunes. I want you to take a few of your trusted men, break into Gomorrah, and extract her. Return her to me. Do you understand?"

Thor's frown seemed to be permanent. "Your grace," he said, sighing heavily, "I—"

"That is not a request, Thor. It is a command."

That settled it. Thor had no choice. The frown left his face, replaced by resignation and duty. Still, he knew this entire thing was a manipulated situation, and being a vassal of the king, he was obliged to accept.

But, by damn… he hated it.

"Now I must break into Gomorrah to save this woman from faceless, nameless abductors," he muttered. "Gomorrah is better guarded than the crown jewels. And I am to break into it? And you cannot tell me who holds her, only that she is held?"

"I will go with you."

Daniel stepped out of the shadows, coming to stand with him. He was a middle-aged man but still a skilled fighter, still strong. But more than that, Daniel de Lohr had been a wanderer in his youth, a man who drank and ate and lived a hedonistic lifestyle that had greatly distressed his father. Everyone knew it. Marriage, and age, had mellowed him, but Daniel was still a man up for a good time. Even at Gomorrah. Thor couldn't help the twinkle of mirth in his eye when he looked at him.

"And do what?" he said. "Help me break in? Or do you happen to know how to get in easily?"

Daniel fought off a grin. "What do you think?"

"I think they know you at that terrible place very well."

"How *dare* you insult me."

He couldn't keep a straight face as he said it, which caused Thor to grin in spite of himself. Clearly, Daniel had the password to get through the iron doors that guarded the entry. Thor wasn't surprised. In fact, he was rather comforted by the fact that Daniel knew Gomorrah, and undoubtedly they knew him, so the chances that there was to be bloodshed had been exponentially reduced.

"I will summon True and Bully and Darius," he said. "I will not go into a situation like this without them."

He was referring to his squad of knights, men who had sworn fealty to him when he first assumed the position of Lord Protector. Truett de Nerra, or "True" as he was known, was part of the great House of de Nerra of Selbourne Castle, while Clayne de Becque was his cousin, known as "Bully" because his father had been known as "Bull"—their mothers were sisters. Lastly, Darius de Winter was part of the House of de Winter, otherwise known as the de Winter war machine because of their very large army and unwavering support for the king. It didn't matter who sat upon the throne—the de Winters would support him, and Henry had been particularly grateful for that support during the dark days of Simon de Montfort.

Men that Thor trusted with his life.

Daniel knew this. He'd been a fixture in Henry's court for many years and had come to know Thor de Reyne when the powerful knight assumed the protector role in Henry's entourage. He knew enough of him to know that he was dedicated and serious, almost humorless at times, but the man had a pure heart. He had a strong moral compass, which meant places like Gomorrah either disgusted him or terrified him.

Knowing Thor, it was more than likely the former.

But Daniel wasn't beyond taunting him a little.

"It is understandable that you would want them with you in any given situation," he said. "Including Gomorrah. Do you mean to tell me you have never visited the place?"

"Never."

"Not even with your bodyguards?"

He meant his knights. Thor gave him a half-grin. "Not even with them," he said. Then he tilted his head in the direction of his father standing a several feet away. "And that is the only answer you shall receive from me with my father so close. If he tells my mother I have visited Gomorrah under any circumstances other than the line of duty, she will beat me with a club."

Daniel chuckled. "As would mine," he said. "That is what mothers do, only my mother had to tolerate my father and my son, both of whom are a bit lively, so she had a very worn-out club."

That was an understatement, and Thor flashed his big white teeth. "I miss Chad," he said. "Can we expect him in London anytime soon?"

Daniel shrugged. "Probably not," he said. "He is in command of Canterbury while I am away, but more than that, I do not want him anywhere near a place like Gomorrah. Chad would go in and never come out. We would lose him for sure."

"And not even his wife has soothed his wild soul?"

"He will do anything for sweet Aless, but he still has his wild streak. It cannot be contained."

That brought laughter from Thor because Chad de Lohr was quite possibly one of the most debaucherous men he'd ever met in his life, but the moment was interrupted by Henry.

"Go with Canterbury," he said, sweeping a hand at him. "I am certain your father will approve of your going into a place like Gomorrah with de Lohr by your side, but I warn you, do not be overly long. Find her and get out. Return her to me immediately."

The smile faded from Thor's face as he listened to the last of Henry's command. The whole situation had him rattled and annoyed. He'd walked into the hall a free man and walked out with a betrothal. A glance at his father showed the man to be equally rattled and annoyed. Thor wasn't sure who was feeling it more—him or his father.

"I will, your grace," he said steadily. "Can you at least tell me what she looks like so I know what I am looking for?"

Henry yawned. As an elderly man, conversations like this, most especially as of late, sapped his strength. But this one had been worth it.

He'd gotten what he wanted.

"Look for a woman with white hair," he said. "I've seen Lady de Tosni once and she has very pale hair. As I recall, it was nearly white, so that is all I can tell you. She should not be difficult to find."

Thor nodded, looking to his father in a final gesture to see if the man had anything left to say to him. But Gage was quiet, having been plowed over by the king, and there was nothing left for him to say. He met his son's gaze before shaking his head faintly and looking away.

Defeated.

Henry had won this battle and it was over. Even so, none of them could have anticipated the path that Thor was soon to follow. This moment would mark the drastic change his life was about to take.

If he'd known that, he would have run like hell.

CHAPTER ONE

Gomorrah

MUSHROOMS, HE'D SAID.

One of the men who managed Gomorrah for the Earls of Camberwell had given her a crystal dish containing what looked like dirt, but it wasn't dirt. It was dried mushrooms from the mysterious east.

She'd been seeing colors in the darkness for the past hour.

Colors bounced off the oiled-up skin of the man dancing for her. He was small and muscular, shaved, and quite beautiful. He only had a small piece of cloth around his privates to protect his modesty, but even so, she could see the bulge he had. She'd been to Gomorrah several times and never bedded a man, mostly because she didn't want to catch bugs or a disease they might have gotten from other patrons who were not so clean. Truth be told, the only man who had ever bedded her had been her husband, but the last time had been years ago. She couldn't remember when. The closest she came to a naked man was the one slowly gyrating in front of her.

And he was glorious.

She took another drink.

The wine with the mushrooms had made her head spin a little, so she lay back upon a silk-cushioned couch and waited for the mushrooms to wear off. They were mostly gone anyway. She was in a private room deep in the bowels of Gomorrah, a room that was sectioned off by curtains from the rest of the guild. It was full tonight, as it usually was, and there was music and laughter all around. She was on the level called Sins of the Flesh, as all four levels of Gomorrah had names, and on this level, men or women could live out their deepest sexual fantasies. In the chamber next to her, she could hear a woman groaning as one of the male dancers pleasured her.

To each her own.

To the tune of a man in the corner of the chamber playing a wooden flute, the oiled-skin man dancing for her abruptly lost his modesty panel. A flaccid manhood several inches long now hung proudly and she lifted her eyebrows at the sight, impressed that such a small man could have such a large male organ. Her gaze lingered on it a moment as she wondered what such a sizable manroot would feel like, when the dancer began thrusting his hips at her, moving his hand to stroke his member. When she looked up at him, surprised, he was grinning lewdly at her and licking his lips.

She frowned and shook her head.

The dancer was crushed.

The flute kept playing as the dancer rushed out of the chamber and she could hear a commotion outside. The dancer might have even been weeping. Shortly, the same man who had offered her the mushrooms entered.

"Lady de Tosni?" he said politely. "Forgive me, my lady, but was Dax not to your liking?"

Lady Caledonia de Wylde de Tosni shifted on her cushioned pillows. "Who is Dax?"

"The man entertaining you, my lady. Was he not to your liking?"

With a heavy sigh, Caledonia sat up. "Eros," she said. "Have you ever known me to take a lover while I am here?"

Eros wasn't his real name, but no one went by their real names at Gomorrah. He shook his head. "Nay, my lady," he said. "But I thought—with the right bit of flesh dangled in front of you—mayhap you would change your mind."

"I will not change my mind."

Eros didn't really understand that attitude because everyone came to Gomorrah for pleasure. Those who refused it were oddities. "You know that our dancers and musicians make their money from your generous gratuities, my lady," he said with some concern. "Dax has been dancing for you for two hours. He must make his living."

Caledonia frowned. "Since when I have I not been generous with those serving me?" she said. "Send Dax back in here and tell him I will compensate him. He needn't worry."

Eros nodded. "Very well, my lady," he said. "Thank you. But… but you *do* find him attractive, don't you?"

"He is glorious."

"But not glorious enough to bed."

"Not by me. I do not need any unexpected consequences, including a child or a disease. No offense to Dax."

With a shrug to the odd lady who happened to be a regular customer, Eros headed out of the chamber while Dax quickly returned. He was completely covered up from the waist to his upper thighs now, hiding that skin snake he'd tried to seduce her with. If she wasn't going to bite, he wasn't going to flaunt it. She was banned from the privilege.

It was all Caledonia could do to keep from laughing.

Dax continued his gyrations as Caledonia lay back against the cushions again, drinking the sweet red wine and watching the roll of his muscles beneath his oiled skin. But after two hours of the show, and Dax's little tantrum, she produced a few coins for him and sent him away. A quick discussion with Eros had two dancing women enter her private chamber, and they began to dance to the strains of the wooden flute. It was a beautiful, fluid dance. Caledonia had two left feet when it came to dancing, so she appreciated women who could move so gracefully.

"Lady Callie!" A woman dressed in fine silks poked her head into the chamber. "I heard you were here. Back again, my darling?"

Caledonia recognized the woman who was in charge of all of the other women at Gomorrah and sat up again, smiling.

"Lady Lupa," she said. "A pleasure to see you."

Lady Lupa was an older woman with a Germanic accent and a big gray streak in her upturned hair. She entered the chamber and came to sit beside Caledonia, who took her hand and squeezed it in greeting. Lady Lupa looked like someone's grandmother, but she was much more than that. Savvy, astute, and attuned to business, she managed Gomorrah possibly more than Eros did. She also carried an arsenal of daggers on her belt. If any of the customers veered out of control, Lady Lupa was ready to defend her girls, as she'd done many times before.

Caledonia had a healthy respect for the woman.

"Enjoying Lady Feather and Lady River, I see," Lady Lupa said. All of the female entertainers at Gomorrah were addressed as "lady" followed by a pseudonym. "Two of our finest dancers. You like them?"

Caledonia nodded. "I'm very envious of the way they dance," she said. "I never could dance well. I find it so artistic the way they move."

Lady Lupa smiled, watching Lady Feather and Lady River move gracefully. "They enjoy dancing for you because you appreciate it," she said. "You are not like the men, who only watch them to become aroused. You watch them because of the sheer beauty of the dance."

Caledonia nodded, watching the ladies bend over backward in the course of their dance. "There is something ancient and timeless about it," she said. "I see ancient Roman women dancing when I look at them. I see women before time began, hearing the first strains of primordial music and feeling their bodies sway to it."

Lady Lupa looked at her. "You are a philosopher, my lady."

Caledonia chuckled. "Not really," she said. "My father always called me a deep thinker. I suppose that means my mind wanders more than most."

"He meant you are brilliant."

"Coming from Rhun de Wylde, I do not think so."

"That is your father?"

"Was."

"How long has he been gone?"

Caledonia cocked her head thoughtfully. "Twelve years now," she said. "But he would surely not approve of my coming to Gomorrah, so mayhap it is for the best."

The smile faded from Lady Lupa's face. "You are not our usual customer," she admitted. "But you have been coming to us for a few years now."

Caledonia nodded faintly. "A few, indeed."

Lady Lupa's gaze lingered on her. Lady Caledonia was

something of a mystery to those who managed Gomorrah because, as Lady Lupa had said, she wasn't the usual customer. To begin with, the woman was astonishingly beautiful, clean, and healthy. She had hair so blonde that it was white, with a sweet oval face and enormous, dark eyes with a slight tilt to them. A pert nose and generous lips rounded out the glowing beauty, a highly intelligent woman who never came to Gomorrah for the usual reasons. She didn't gamble and she'd never once paid for the sexual services of any number of men at Gomorrah who would have gladly taken the task.

But she did come to drink.

Lady Caledonia could put away more wine than a man at times. She drank, she closed herself up with burning hemp at times, and she would try anything intoxicating. Today, it happened to be mushrooms that gave one a euphoria. Lady Lupa had heard about it. She also came to watch the dancers, male and female, and she came to listen to the fine musicians Gomorrah had. On occasion, they even had plays or poetry recitations, and she came for that as well. She came for anything entertaining or thought-provoking, anything that opened her already open mind. But it seemed to Lady Lupa that Lady Caledonia was a very lonely woman, in search of something she couldn't yet find.

To satisfy something within herself that needed contentment.

Lady Lupa knew that Lady Caledonia had been married for several years to a man who was much older than she was. He'd died of an illness, and Lady Caledonia spoke of her dead husband without emotion. They'd had three daughters, three young girls who, even now, remained at home while their mother prowled the caverns of Gomorrah. Lady Caledonia wouldn't talk about her daughters very much, but when she did, she drank. There was something painful there when she spoke of her children.

All part of the great mystery that was Caledonia de Wylde de Tosni.

"And I hope you continue to come to us for many more years," Lady Lupa said. She was still holding Caledonia's hand, so she gave it a pat and let it go. "If there is anything more you require, I hope you will tell me."

Caledonia lay back on her pillows. "I will," she said. "I am a little hungry. Could you have someone bring me some food?"

Lady Lupa headed for the door. "I will serve you myself," she said. "We have a wonderful new cook from Athens. He makes a cake with layers of dough and nuts and honey. I will bring you some."

"Sounds delicious," Caledonia said. "And anything with chicken. I do like chicken."

Lady Lupa nodded and rushed out, leaving Caledonia resting back against the cushions. With the wine and music and dancing, it was inevitable that she ended up dozing off. It was dreamy and soothing with the flute music in the background, and as Caledonia drifted in and out, she began to hear something that didn't sound quite normal.

She began to hear screaming.

Yelling was more like it. Things were crashing and there was shouting going on. It sounded like a battle. Startled, she sat up as the flute player stopped and the two dancers came to a halt. Concerned, she looked at the flute player, who seemed frozen, and then to the dancers, who were clearly terrified. More crashing, more shouting, and Caledonia began looking around for a weapon. The closest she came to was a big iron rod used to stir the embers in the brass brazier in the corner of the chamber.

Drunk, and still a little tipsy on mushrooms, she wielded it like a club.

Admonishing the dancers and the musician to remain in the room, she ventured out. The ceilings were low down here, with a passageway that ran from the main stairs, from one end of Gomorrah to the other. There were many smaller chambers on this level and people were beginning to emerge, hearing the same noise that she was. The woman in the chamber next to her was still being pleasured, and Caledonia could hear the woman moaning as if nothing else was going on around them.

She found that rather comical.

But she banged her iron poker on the wall to stop whatever was going on in there, to alert them to the fact that there was trouble. Since her chamber was nearly at the bottom of the stairs, whatever trouble that was overhead would spill down here eventually.

She would be ready for them.

Rushing toward the stairs, she pressed herself up against the wall that was right where the stairs met with the corridor. Anyone coming down the stairs wouldn't see her, and that was exactly what she wanted. Since the stairs were dark and narrow, she would have the advantage. Waiting and listening, she could hear someone barking orders while more people shrieked. Something thumped.

Then they were coming down the stairs.

Lifting her iron rod, Caledonia waited until the first heavily armed knight hit the bottom stair and stepped out into the corridor.

Whack!

She brained the man right on the head and he fell to his knees, pitching forward onto his hands. But she hadn't knocked him out, so she swung again, knocking him to the ground as another knight came down the stairs. Seeing yet another heavily armed man, she began swinging the rod at the man's head and shoulders, but he easily grabbed it. Terrified, she lashed out a foot and kicked the knight as hard as she could in the groin.

He teetered sideways.

By now, people from the other chambers had filtered out into the corridor, seeing the armed knights trying to make their way in and a small woman with long white hair beating them. Gomorrah had guards of its own, and as Caledonia darted away from the knight she'd kicked in the groin, a couple of the big, burly guards came flying down the stairs, crashing into the men at the bottom. More men came crashing down after them and there was a brawl at the bottom of the stairs.

By this time, Caledonia rushed back to her room where the two dancing girls and the musician were huddling fearfully. She focused on the women.

"Is there another way to leave this place?" she asked. "A rear door that no one knows about?"

The women nodded. "In the Sulfur Pit," Lady Feather said. "There is a small staircase that leads to a door. If there was ever a fire, we are told to go to that door."

"Then we must go," Caledonia said quickly, grabbing the silk blanket she'd been lying on because both women were very thinly dressed. "Here—cover yourselves. We must hurry to that door."

The women took the blanket, rushing from the room as the musician and Caledonia followed. She made sure to grab her purse and her cloak, both of which had been lying on the cushioned couch, and tore after the women.

It was dark and chaotic. People were running in all directions. Caledonia could hear screaming and noise behind her and the sound of running feet. That was everywhere, echoing off the stone walls. She followed the women and the musician down some wooden steps to the Sulfur Pit level below. This was the bottom of the guild, the bottom of what had once been a Roman temple. There was a big stone floor down here and stone columns that held up the floor above it. There was also a mosaic on one side of it indicating flowers and wine and birds. Down here was where the most debaucherous things happened, and instead of chambers, there were simply curtains strung up.

But the stone floor and heavy ceiling also kept the sounds of the raid at a distance. Things were happening down here as normal, and as Caledonia rushed by, curtains blew open and she saw a man with three women pleasuring him in every hole in his body. The next curtained section had a man being whipped across his buttocks while a woman had her mouth on his male member.

There were other things going on but she didn't take note. She simply told everyone to stop what they were doing and run. She could see the women and the musician on ahead and a small wooden staircase that led up the side of a wall and disappeared above. People were disappearing up those stairs and Caledonia wanted to disappear up them also, but a young woman tripped and fell in front of her and she was forced to stop running and help the woman to her feet.

That delay was going to cost her.

"You!" someone boomed.

A loud and deep voice echoed off the walls, loud enough to startle Caledonia. She jumped at the sound, instinctively turning around to see two enormous knights a few feet behind her.

Self-preservation kicked in.

She pushed the woman she'd just helped toward the stairs, hissing encouragement to flee, but she didn't try to run after her. She had a feeling she wouldn't make it to the stairs.

"What do you want?" she demanded. "These people have done nothing wrong. They have nothing of value for you."

The knight advanced on her. "What is your name?"

"Why?"

"Are you Caledonia de Tosni?"

That should have made her turn and run away as fast as she could, but she could only manage great confusion.

"Who *are* you?" she demanded. "Why do you want to know?"

The knight kept coming. "Henry has sent me," he said. "Are you Lady de Tosni?"

Henry. She was certain he didn't mean anyone other than the king, because she and Henry had a difficult history together, but that didn't abate her confusion. And she certainly didn't want to give this knight her identity.

"I do not understand," she said. "Why would you even ask me such a question?"

The knight finally came to a halt and looked at her. "Because I was told Caledonia de Wylde de Tosni was being held against her will in this place," he said. Then he flipped up his three-point visor to get a better look at her. "I was told to find a lady with white hair, and you have white hair. *Are* you Lady de Tosni? I require an answer."

She stared at him a moment before looking at the man behind him, hearing screams and commotion in the distance. It was dark on this level and so difficult to see, but she could see people trying to escape in the other direction. But the knight's words were sinking in and her gaze returned to him.

"I am not being held against my will," she said. "Did the king tell you that?"

The knight nodded. "He did," he said. "If you do not tell me that you are Lady de Tosni, I am going to assume that you are and take you with me. If you are not the lady I seek, I would suggest you tell me now."

Even in the dim light, Caledonia could see that he had the brightest blue eyes she'd ever seen. "I am not the lady you seek," she said.

"What is your name?"

"It is no concern of yours."

Before he could reply, a body flew between them, screeching and flashing a dagger. Lady Lupa crashed into Caledonia and nearly sent her onto her bum.

"Do not fear, Lady de Tosni!" she cried, wielding a wicked-looking dagger against the knight. "I will protect you. Run! Follow the others and run!"

Caledonia rolled her eyes as her cover was unknowingly blown. Before she could take another breath, the knight was shoving Lady Lupa out of the way and Caledonia ended up over one of his broad shoulders.

He was heading for the exit.

But Caledonia wasn't going to give up without a fight. She began to twist and kick, managing to squirm off his shoulder enough to ram a finger into his right eye. He staggered but didn't let her go, now helped along by four knights. Caledonia recognized two of them as one she'd brained and one she'd kicked in the groin. She hadn't struck hard enough to keep them down, and the quintet of heavily armed knights hauled her up the rickety wooden stairs to the secret exit that so many people were now aware of.

"Put me down!" Caledonia demanded, kicking one of the knights in the head when he came over to help subdue her. "Put me down or I swear I will kill you all!"

The knight who held her was blinking his right eye furiously, the one she'd jabbed a finger into. "Lady, I was sent to save you, and save you I shall," he said. "I do not know why you are resisting my efforts, but that ends now."

That only seemed to inflame Caledonia, who threw herself sideways and ended up falling onto the ground. He still had her by the hair, however, and he easily picked her up and swung her back over his shoulder. When she began to howl and push at him again, he spanked her.

Hard.

Caledonia gasped at the sting of his swat.

"You *brute*," she spat, now trying throw herself off his shoulder, grabbing what mail she could get a hold of on his back to use as leverage. "How dare you strike me! I will have your head for that!"

She could hear him sigh heavily. "Lady, your threats bore me," he said. "If you had not lied to me, you would not have been removed by force. You chose a path to violence."

She had lied to him, but she certainly hadn't chosen this path. This was all his doing. Using his shoulder to brace herself, she tried to ram her knee into his face. He swatted her again and, suddenly, two knights had hold of her. One had her legs and her abductor had her torso. When Caledonia realized that she was effectively corralled, she fought for another minute before finally surrendering.

"Aye, I lied to you," she said. "What was I supposed to do? Five knights break into Gomorrah and tear the place apart and I'm supposed to give you my name? Of course I'm not going to tell you. I had to protect myself, didn't I?"

A big knight was walking beside her as two of them carried her.

"You have every right to protect yourself, my lady," he said. "My name is Daniel de Lohr. I am the Earl of Canterbury. Do you know my name?"

Caledonia turned to look at the man, whom she couldn't see through his lowered faceplate. "I know your name, my lord," she said. "I know who you are. I am shocked that you are part of this… this raid."

Daniel held up a hand and everyone came to a halt. They were on a small street, a residential area, and there were very few people around. He quietly instructed the men carrying her to put her on her feet, and they immediately did. Offended and shaken, Caledonia straightened out her expensive silk surcoat and smoothed her hair, glaring at the men around her before finally coming to rest on Daniel.

She had a particular glare for him.

"Now," she said. "Let us come to an understanding, once and for all. I am Caledonia de Tosni and I fully resent being treated like a common criminal. I've done nothing wrong in the least."

Daniel unlatched his helm, removing it to reveal a handsome older man with blond hair, graying at the temples. "Nay, you've done nothing wrong," he said. "But we have been sent from Henry and we are under orders to return you to him immediately. By force, if necessary. And you made it necessary."

Caledonia's eyes narrowed. "You never gave me a choice," she said. "One moment I was standing there, and in the next your hired beast carried me out. That was not fair."

"Mayhap not," Daniel said. "But it would have gone much smoother had you not lied to us. Henry wants you, Lady de Tosni, enough to send us to Gomorrah on a pretext, so you may as well accept that we are returning to Westminster."

Caledonia didn't like that at all. "God," she grumbled, shaking her head in disgust. "Do you know why he wants to see me? Do you have any idea?"

"Do *you*?"

Her arched eyebrows shot up. "Of course I do!" she said. "From the missives to the messengers to the courtiers who have come to beat down my door, of course I know what he wants. He was as persistent as a gnat when I was at Stafford Castle, so I fled to London so he could not find me, but he did. He knows I am at Stafford House and has ordered my servants to tell him where I go, which is how he knew I was at Gomorrah. He will not leave me alone!"

She was both angry and frustrated, her cheeks turning shades of red as she spoke. But it was also clear that she was drunk because her movements, and emotions, were exaggerated. She was bloody well furious and didn't care who knew it, not even the very powerful Earl of Canterbury. Truth be told, it frightened her to realize that the king had sent such an important man after her.

That told her that the man meant business.

"Let me counter your statement by asking you a question," Daniel said evenly. "May I?"

Caledonia lifted her hand and let it fall back and slap her thigh dramatically. "Ask," she said dryly. "I cannot stop you, so ask."

She couldn't have possibly known how much he felt like grinning but wisely kept a straight face. "You are the Countess of Tamworth and Stafford, are you not?" he asked.

Caledonia nodded as if everyone knew that. "Of course I am," she said. "Is that your question?"

"Nay," Daniel said. "Tamworth is an old and prestigious earldom, not to mention the added responsibility of Stafford. Since you no longer have a husband, the king has taken it upon himself to ensure your health and safety. He would be a poor king indeed if he did not."

She looked at him as if he'd just said something outrageous. "Is that what you think?" she said. "That he is seeing to my health and safety?"

"Isn't he?"

"He is not," she said flatly. "Do you know what Henry wants, my lord? He wants to marry me to some fool of his choosing so that Tamworth will be managed for the glory of the Crown. Stafford belongs to my eldest daughter when she marries, but Tamworth is mine. I am the heiress. Me and all of my glorious money and property will go to some idiot that the king has chosen and I will have to marry him. Henry has told me that he has already selected someone. Did you know that? Some man I know nothing about will become my husband and manage the earldom. Well, I do *not* want a husband. I do *not* need a husband. I am doing quite well on my own."

Daniel had to put a hand over his mouth so she wouldn't see him smile. "My lady, it seems to me that you are quite capable of managing the property," he said, sounding oddly strained because he was trying not to burst out laughing. "But what about the army? Tamworth has an enormous army, not to mention the army that Stafford has. Do you truly wish to manage two armies on your own?"

She frowned. "I have knights for that," she said. "My husband has three knights who see to Stafford, and my father's knight has managed Tamworth quite well since his death."

"I see," Daniel said. "But what about you? Do you wish to be alone forever?"

She shrugged flippantly. "It would suit me just fine."

"And Tamworth?" Daniel persisted. "What if you die without a son to carry on the Tamworth earldom?"

"What about it?"

"It will revert to the Crown."

"Henry wants it as it is. That is why he is trying to force me to marry his trained dog."

A guffaw bubbled up and Daniel ended up coughing to cover it up. He didn't dare look at Thor, who was hearing all of this. But none of her insults or reasoning was going to make any difference where Henry was concerned. Daniel was going to have to take her to the king regardless of how she felt.

"I would suggest you meet the man you are to marry before you decide he is a fool, and idiot, and a trained dog," Daniel said quietly. "I am sure the king would only choose the finest man for your husband."

She shook her head. "He chose the man who fell at his feet more than any other," she said unhappily. "I know how marriages are made, my lord. I am not a fool. My marriage to Robert de Tosni was a perfect example of that. My father forced me into that marriage when I was only fifteen years of age because Robert's first wife could not produce a son. Did you know that? Then I had three daughters and he blamed me for only bearing female children. As if I could control such a thing."

"I am sure he did not mean it, but desperate men behave irrationally sometimes."

She snorted. "Is that what you call it?" she muttered. "Fine. He was desperate, then. Just like my father was when he married me to him because my older brother, who was set to inherit everything, died of a fever. I was living a life with very few expectations upon me when Constantine decided to let himself die. And that threw me into the maelstrom, my lord. And here I am, waiting to be married to yet another man who will inherit all that is mine. Well, I hope he chokes on it. And I hope he takes my money, goes away, and leaves me alone."

Daniel's gaze lingered on her. "Is that what you want, my lady?" he said. "Truly? To be left alone?"

She pointed back in the direction of Gomorrah. "I want to go back where I came from and enjoy the rest of my evening," she said. "But something tells me that is not going to happen."

"You would be correct."

At that point, Caledonia felt as if all of the fight had gone out of her. Her adrenaline rush from Gomorrah was gone now, replaced by a woozy feeling caused by too much drink and those damnable mushrooms. At least the knights weren't dragging her around any longer, but her destination was clear—she was going to Westminster.

She knew why.

"You are taking me to my new husband, aren't you?" she asked quietly. "Henry wishes to introduce us."

Daniel didn't hesitate. "Aye."

She drew in a long, deep breath, one that signified resignation. "Do you know him, my lord?" she asked. "You have met him?"

"I have."

She looked at him with both surprise and curiosity. "Who is it?"

"A worthy man."

"And you know him?" she pressed. "Personally, I mean?"

"I do."

"But you will not tell me who it is?"

"That is Henry's privilege, don't you think?"

She sighed again, looking away. "I suppose," she said. "Can you at least tell me how old he is? What he looks like?"

Daniel did look at Thor then. The man's faceplate was still up and Daniel could see his eyes, nose, and upper lip. When their eyes met, silent words passed between them—Daniel seemed to be asking for permission to tell her that her betrothed was right in their midst. It really wasn't up to Thor. It was up to Henry. But it might make things easier all around if the lady and her betrothed were introduced to one another without the king's overbearing presence, in a room full of judgmental men.

Daniel's focus returned to Caledonia.

"On that corner is a tavern called the Wren and the Willow," he said, pointing to something behind her. "It is right on the corner. Do you see it?"

Caledonia turned around, spying the tavern immediately. "I do," she said. "I know it well."

Daniel didn't doubt that for a moment. "If you give me your word of honor that you will not run from me, I will send you over to that tavern, where you will sit alone at a table," Daniel said. "I will bring your betrothed to you and you can meet one another before you see Henry. That way, you can decide for yourself what kind of man you are to marry. If he is a fool, an idiot, or a trained dog. Or none of those. He might be someone you appreciate. Would you be agreeable to such a meeting?"

Caledonia looked at him in shock. "You will *bring* him to me?"

"I will."

She turned her gaze to the tavern again, pondering his question, before finally answering. "Give me some money and I will go," she said. "When you wrested me from Gomorrah, I left my purse behind. I require coin."

Daniel dug into the purse at his waist and produced a handful of silver coins for her. As he put them into her palm, he looked her in the eye.

"Deviate from your agreement and I will hunt you down," he growled. "When I find you, it will not be pleasant. My trust is given only once. If you violate it, there will not be another chance."

Caledonia stiffened, preparing a retort, but she ended up simply nodding. Without another word, she headed over to the Wren and the Willow as Daniel and the other four knights watched her go. Once she disappeared into the tavern, Daniel turned to Thor.

"Go," he said. "See if you can convince her that you are not a fool or an idiot."

Thor lifted a wry eyebrow. "Or a trained dog."

Daniel couldn't help it. He burst into soft laughter as the knight standing to Thor's right slapped him on the shoulder.

"You kept your composure, old man." Clayne le Becque, Thor's cousin, was grinning. "I was waiting for you to lay your hand on her backside. You showed more control that I would have."

Thor looked at the man he'd grown up with. He looked very much like his father—shorter, but powerfully built with huge shoulders and arms. It was all he could do not to roll his eyes.

"Trust me when I tell you that physical violence crossed my mind more than once," he said. "I have no idea why I showed such restraint."

"Because neither you nor the lady can refuse Henry, so it would be futile to start off a relationship by beating her," Daniel said. "I do not think she has had an easy time of it."

Thor looked at him in disbelief. "What about me?" he said. "She tried to beat me quite thoroughly when I took her from Gomorrah. The lady tried to gouge my eye out."

Daniel's eyes glimmered with mirth. "I will tell you what was told to me, once, when I met my wife," he said. "This marriage will be what you make of it. If you treat her with a lack of respect and indifference, then you've already set the tone for failure. And Thor de Reyne does not fail, not at anything. Especially not at a marriage that will see him assume the Earldom of Tamworth."

Those were wise words but Thor wasn't convinced. "She is already set against it," he said. "It will be difficult to combat that."

"Then combat it with kindness," Daniel said. "Show her the worth of the man she is to marry. Change her mind."

The last three words were stressed. Thor still didn't think it was that easy, but he didn't argue because Daniel was right about one thing—neither of them had any choice, so unless he wanted to be in a miserable marriage for the rest of his life, he was going to have to make some kind of effort.

But he wondered if the lady would as well.

He would soon find out.

CHAPTER TWO

OH… SHE'D BEEN to this place before.

Caledonia wasn't quite sure why she wasn't completely honest with Canterbury other than the fact that she didn't want him to know just *how* familiar she was with the taverns in London. Most of them, anyway. It wasn't proper for a noblewoman to admit she regularly visited taverns, on her own no less, and most especially not a countess. An heiress to one of the largest and most ancient earldoms in all of England.

That would be her.

Seated near the window facing the street, Caledonia could partially see Canterbury and the knights who had come with him. They were mostly out of her sight, but she could see the tall form of Daniel de Lohr. He was speaking to his men. As she continued to watch, a serving wench brought her a pitcher of spiced, warmed wine and a cup without her even asking for it. That was how familiar most of the taverns on the east side of London were with Lady de Tosni, who traveled alone and had never once, in all that time, been molested or in need of protection.

Mostly because she was quite good with a knife and her

foot-to-groin aim.

Not to say that a few hadn't tried. She was a beautiful woman who reeked of sultry allure, so a few had been foolish enough to approach her. She ignored them until they forced themselves upon her, which had happened more than once, and anything she could use as a weapon would come flying out at them—knives made great deterrents and so did spoons. A cup of wine could be thrown into eyes because they made very effective targets, and when all else failed, a boot to the groin would serve as the final blow. It really wasn't all that difficult and Caledonia was bold enough, and fearless enough, to carry it off. But because she was a good customer, usually the tavernkeeps would get involved and throw out the offender.

Still, she'd never once met a man she couldn't get rid of.

And here she was, yet again, in the Wren and the Willow. They had particularly good stews here because the tavernkeep's wife was a good cook. Even now, Caledonia thought she could smell something delicious in the air. Given that it was nearing sunset, her stomach was rumbling a bit. The mushrooms had worn off but the wine hadn't, and she needed something in her stomach before she drank anything more. She had just whistled to the nearest serving wench when the door to the tavern opened.

A massive knight appeared.

She recognized him immediately as one of the men who came with Canterbury. In fact, it was the man who had hauled her over his shoulder. And broad shoulders they were. There was nothing about the man that wasn't big and intimidating. He stood there a moment, surveying the room like a conqueror surveys his domain, before his gaze finally came to rest on her.

Caledonia sat up straight.

He headed for the table.

As Caledonia watched warily, he pulled off his helm and set it on the table. She wasn't interested in the helm as much as she was interested in the knight—a strikingly handsome knight with dark, wavy hair to his shoulders and a square, firm jaw. When he settled down in his chair and looked at her, she recognized those bright blue eyes. The brightest eyes she'd ever seen. But the whole vision of him was head and shoulders above any man she'd ever seen. Like he had emerged from another place and time, where men were gloriously handsome, like gods. But as she was staring at him, he took her cup, poured out the wine, and, after taking a drink, refused to swallow and sprayed it out all over the floor.

"God's Bones," he said, wiping his mouth with the back of his hand. "What *is* that?"

His disgust in her favorite drink snapped her out of her trance. "Mulled wine," she said, pulling the cup and pitcher in her direction. "Did you have to spit it out like that?"

He eyed her. "How would you have me spit it out?"

"You don't spit it out. You drink it."

He shook his head. "Not *that* stuff," he said. "That stuff is for women and weaklings."

So much for polite behavior. Caledonia sighed impatiently as she poured herself some wine, sipping on the sweet drink while the knight hailed one of the serving wenches and told her exactly what he wanted. Something very manly, undoubtedly. As the woman fled, he returned his attention to Caledonia.

"There," he said. "We'll have something good at this table."

"This *is* good."

She was lifting her cup, and he cocked an eyebrow. "As I said, it is a woman's drink."

He was starting to irritate her. "Why are you here?" she asked. "I thought Canterbury was going to send me the man I am to marry so that I could look him over. Well?"

He simply looked at her. Then he lifted his hands as if she was missing the obvious. Caledonia had to admit that she was so fixated on those bright eyes that it took her a moment to realize what he was telling her.

He *was* the man.

Her face fell.

"Nay," she breathed. "Not you."

"Me."

Her mouth fell open. "*You?*"

"Me."

Her cheeks turned red and it was clear that she was building up to some kind of explosion, so he put his hands up to ease whatever was rising. From what he'd seen, the lady had no trouble rising to anything.

"Before you throw a fit, know that I had nothing to do with this either," he said. "Henry practically bullied me into this arrangement and, in some pathetic attempt to coax forth my husbandly sense of protectiveness, told me that you were being held at Gomorrah against your will and commanded me to retrieve you. That is why I was there. I was hunting for you. But, clearly, you were not being held against your will."

"I was *not*."

"As I said… none of this was my idea, lady, so if you are to become angry, become angry with Henry. I'm a pawn as much as you are."

Caledonia didn't know what to say. She couldn't take her eyes off him, big and strong and handsome, so much more beautiful than her dead husband that she was having trouble believing the man was real. But he, too, was shocked and enraged by Henry's matchmaking, and that meant, to Caledonia, that the man she found blindingly attractive must not find her attractive at all.

Embarrassment filled her.

"I see," she said, her anger dramatically cooling. "What is your name, Blue Eyes?"

He was cut off from replying as a serving wench appeared with his drink and a bowl of something hot. She also had one for the lady. He waited until the servant left before answering.

"My name is Sir Thorington de Reyne," he said. "I will answer to Thor. My father is the Earl of Ashington. My family is descended from the Visigoths, so bloodlust and warfare are in our veins. For the past two years, I have served Henry as his Lord Protector and he sees this marriage as a reward for my services, but he also arranged it to vex my father because those two treat me like a contest. They are constantly fighting one another for my services."

He seemed arrogant, which was typical when it came to English knights, but Thor was clearly an elite knight if he had served as Lord Protector to the king. But what he said, including his manner, told her everything she needed to know. What she didn't know, she could guess.

She could read him like a book.

"Let me see if I understand you," she said. "You are an ambitious knight if you serve Henry directly, and if you have your father and Henry fighting for your services, then you must be well aware of your value. Henry gave me to you so that you could become the next Earl of Tamworth, something your ambitious blood pines for. Now, you will marry a de Wylde and your children will carry not only the line of the Visigoths, but the line of Mercian kings. Surely you know my father was a direct descendant of the last king of Mercia. Did Henry tell you that?"

He nodded slowly. "He did."

He didn't seem impressed by that in the least, and that only fed her sense of embarrassment and shame. The man clearly didn't want her. Taking the pitcher of warm wine, she poured herself a full measure and drank deeply.

"Now," she said, wiping her mouth with her hand. "Since neither one of us can refuse this marriage, I suggest we come to an agreement. I will provide you with the Tamworth title, of course, and should you decide I am worthy of your bed, I will hopefully bear you an heir. I will, of course, surrender Edingale Castle to you, the seat of Mercian kings, and you will allow me to live in Stafford Castle and go about my business as I choose. I will not bother you and you will not bother me. Is that acceptable?"

She was being businesslike, but there was more to it. The embarrassment she had been trying to keep hidden was coming out in her words and actions. She could see that Thor was watching her carefully, tracking her like a hunter would track prey. His gaze never left her. When she was finished speaking, there were a few moments of pause before he replied.

"If that is what you wish," he said, though he didn't sound enthusiastic about it. "I am agreeable to whatever you wish, my lady, but I have some questions."

"What are they?"

He regarded her a moment, toying with his cup. It was obvious that something was on his mind. "I'd like to know something," he said. "If you were not being held at Gomorrah against your will, then why were you there?"

"Because I enjoy the entertainment and the wine."

She hadn't hesitated to answer him, short and concise. He pondered her response, his brow furrowing when he realized she didn't seem ashamed at all about her choice of entertainment establishments. For a woman, that was rather bold and reckless. Certainly not ladylike.

"There are other places you can attend that are not nearly so unsuitable," he said. "Surely you know that Gomorrah's reputation isn't entirely suitable."

"Suitable for whom? For you? For me?" Caledonia shook her head at him. "That is something else we must establish from the start. I will choose my own entertainment, where I go, and whom I see."

"You will not shame me."

"What do you care? You're getting the money and the title. That should be enough to compensate for any perceived shame."

He was taken aback by her attitude. He'd never heard anything so bold or brazen. In fact, it greatly perplexed him. The woman looked like an ethereal goddess with her white hair and dark, intense eyes, but her behavior… He was stumped.

"Are you serious?" he finally asked.

She cocked her head, and her hair, which was unbound and immodest for a widow, fell over one eye when she moved. "What do you mean?"

"I mean your view on how this marriage shall be conducted," he said. "Are you truly so callous about it?"

"How should I be?"

Thor couldn't tell if that was truly her attitude or if she was being defensive because she thought that was what he wanted.

This marriage will be what you make of it.

That was what Daniel had said to him and, truthfully, he was right. But Thor was up against something he'd never been up against before—a woman who was indifferent to him. Somehow, perhaps he'd arrogantly believed she would take one look at him and be agreeable to the marriage. Subservient, even. Fall at his feet like all women did. But that wasn't the case. Was it possible he'd met the one woman in all of England who didn't find him attractive?

That realization was enough to fill him with outrage. If she didn't want him, there was nothing he could to do make the marriage feasible. Perhaps it was best that Henry see what he'd done to two people he claimed to value.

"Come," he said, suddenly bolting to his feet. Reaching over the table, he grabbed her by the wrist. "The king is expecting us and we will not keep the man waiting."

Caledonia stumbled after him as he pulled on her. "Why so rushed?" she wanted to know, looking longingly at the table they'd just left, laden with food and drink. "Can we at least finish our meal?"

Thor didn't answer. He was furious and, if he was willing to admit it, oddly disappointed. Caledonia de Tosni was a seductive beauty if he'd ever seen one and her apathy toward their marriage disappointed him. A woman like that was beyond price. As he pulled her out into the night, his mind wandered to the future, where he had a gloriously beautiful wife as the Earl of Tamworth. He could see sons bearing the blood of ancient Mercian kings, sons who would bear the powerful de Reyne name. Sons that would be the most sought-after knights in England, like their father. He saw so many things now dashed at his feet.

They were going to settle this once and for all.

CHAPTER THREE

H_{E WAS BLOODY} well furious.

Caledonia had been dragged all the way to Westminster Palace, which took over an hour. Down streets with people looking at them strangely, through Ludgate, down Fleet Street to Westminster, where Thor walked in, towing her behind him like a barge, without anyone stopping him. They all knew him. Thor's steed had returned earlier with the Earl of Canterbury and his party, though no one knew why. Thor didn't go anywhere without his silver steed and they'd seen him leave with the animal, but he was walking back.

Pulling a woman with him.

The guards at Westminster were greatly curious about it.

But Thor didn't stop and he didn't offer any explanations. Caledonia was exhausted by the time they'd reached Westminster, but Thor didn't slow down and he didn't stop. He pulled her through the complex and into the great hall, where he began demanding the king. There were men in the great hall who went to meet him, including an older man with dark, graying hair who looked a good deal like Thor. The man kept eyeing Caledonia, trying to find out what the matter was, but

Thor wouldn't tell him. He just kept asking for the king.

Eventually, Henry appeared.

"Thor?" he said, but his gaze soon fell on Caledonia, who was looking a bit disheveled. "Ah! You found the lady. Well done!"

Thor was in no mood for the king's lies. All of this had been a lie. Hunting down the Countess of Tamworth and Stafford under the guise of a rescue had been the biggest lie of all and he had fallen for it. Perhaps not fallen for it as much as he was obligated to obey Henry's order. He yanked on Caledonia, nearly tossing her at the king. She ended up stumbling to her knees, right at the man's feet.

"Aye, I found her," Thor said through clenched teeth. "She was not being held against her will as you had told me, your grace. She was at Gomorrah purely by her own choice. She has insulted me and battled me since the moment I laid eyes upon her and she has no interest in me. I am not to her liking, or not of her station, or any number of excuses, so here she is, your grace. Mayhap you will tell us both why you are demanding a marriage between two people who have no interest in one another."

The chamber was so still, so silent, that a drop of rain against the floor would have sounded like a hammer against an anvil. It was an ugly, dark silence. Even Caledonia was surprised at the sheer vitriol coming from Thor. If she still entertained any doubt that he didn't find her attractive, that doubt had been summarily dashed. She didn't dare look at Thor, or even at Henry, so she simply looked at the ground as she sat there on her knees.

She heard Henry sigh faintly.

"Clear the chamber," he said quietly, motioning to the few

men that were there. "Everyone but Thor and the lady will get out. Now."

The room cleared unnaturally fast, including the man who resembled Thor. But he was the last one out, eyeing Thor severely as if to convey a thousand words of caution and calm. But Thor's focus remained on Henry. Caledonia remained on her knees, seeing the king move away in her periphery.

He was moving toward Thor.

"Sit down," he told him quietly. Then he turned to Caledonia, still on her knees. "My lady, get off the floor and sit here. Please."

He was indicating the bench next to Thor, who had just planted his bulk on the seat. When Thor saw Caledonia coming, he turned away, repressing the urge to roll his eyes. He wasn't in any mood for Henry's matchmaking, but he knew that was exactly what he was going to get. More words to convince him that this marriage would work. It wouldn't, but he would have to listen to it. He had already been as rude to Henry as he intended to be.

He'd let Caledonia and her bold mouth get him out of this.

"Now," Henry said, looking between them. "I am not entirely sure why the two of you are viewing this betrothal as a punishment, but let us get to the bottom of it. My lady, you have the privilege of speaking first. I take it that you do not wish to marry Sir Thor?"

Caledonia had been looking at her hands, but now looked at the king as she spoke. "I would like to know why you told him I was being held against my will, your grace," she said, avoiding his question. "He and his men caused a great deal of chaos on their quest to rescue me."

Henry looked at Thor with interest. "Did you do that,

Thor?"

Thor merely shrugged, as if that was an obvious question, and Henry suppressed a grin. "I can imagine he did," he said, trying not to laugh. "I would like to hear about it, but not now. The lady has asked me a question and I will answer. Why did I tell him you were being held against your will, Lady de Tosni? That should be obvious. You have been avoiding me for quite some time now. You are a very wealthy widow, a valuable commodity, and you must have a husband. Tamworth needs an earl. I have told you this before, yet you ignore me, so I had to be clever in removing you from Gomorrah. Are you surprised that I knew where you were?"

"I know you have had spies following me, your grace."

"Must I truly explain this entire situation to you and why you have been followed?"

Caledonia sighed heavily. "Your grace, I understand everything," she said. "And I've not been ignoring you."

"What would you call it?"

She couldn't give him an honest answer because they both knew what it would be. She wasn't going to admit that she had, indeed, been avoiding him. "The truth is that I do not need, or want, a husband at this time, your grace."

Henry grunted irritably. "When do you suspect you might want one?"

"When I feel the time is right," she said evasively. "I am not entirely certain that—"

"Of course you are not entirely certain," Henry snapped softly, cutting her off. The kind manner had drained out of him because his impatience had taken hold. "You are a woman. You are not meant to rule a great earldom. Between Stafford and Tamworth, you have armies numbering in the thousands. Your husband must command those armies—not you. Like it or not, my lady, you need a husband and I have selected one for you. You *will* marry Thor."

He said it in such a way that there was no doubt that he meant it. Hard and cold, his words reverberated through Caledonia's brain.

You are not meant to rule a great earldom.

Out of all the things Henry said, that was the most stinging.

The statement she resented the most.

"Your grace, you know my family history," she said, trying to keep her formidable temper under control. "You know that I am a direct descendant of Ceowulf, the last king of Mercia. Before him, his great-grandmother many times over was Aethelflaed, the greatest warrior queen of all. She built fortresses and conquered tribes of Saxons and Danes, so much so that she united a great deal of the country. She is *my* great-grandmother, many times over."

Henry nodded his head. "I know of the mighty warrior queen of the Saxons," he said irritably. "Her blood flows through your veins, lady. Bold and fearless. Your husband, Robert, was a weak man. He let you do as you pleased. He let your wild blood boil and did nothing about it."

Caledonia stood up, facing the king as he insulted her. "My blood is royal on *both* sides, your grace," she pointed out hotly. "My mother descended from the last King of Strathclyde, so I have the blood of kings from both sides of my family. Few men can claim that, your grace, so I would say I am more than capable of managing my affairs. I do not need any interference."

Thor was up, putting himself between the angry lady and the king. "Lady, you will not show your king disrespect," he growled. "I suggest you rein in your bold tongue, because it is not helping your cause."

Caledonia found herself looking in the man's chest. He was so tall that she had to crane her neck back to look at him, and even then all she could see were those bright blue eyes, now smoldering with hazard. Before she could reply, however, Henry came around Thor and gently pushed the man away from the confrontation, back to the bench he'd been seated upon. When he was certain Thor wasn't going to rise up and wring the lady's neck, he faced her again.

"I do not dispute that you have more royal blood than most," he said, with less annoyance than before. "But you failed to mention that the kings you descend from were both defeated. They were too weak to hold their kingdoms, so I do not want to hear anything more about them. This is not about your royal bloodlines. This is about a marriage to Thor, who is most deserving of the Tamworth title. If you would only stop throwing a tantrum long enough to speak with him and come to know him, then you might see something pleasant in this association. You will be marrying a man that many women want."

Perhaps mentioning that Thor was much desired was meant to make him more enticing in her eyes, but it didn't work. Caledonia was once again fixated part of the king's statement rather than the whole—on the fact that he mentioned she was descended from *former* kings. It was a low blow as far as she was concerned. More than that, the king was trying to make it seem that if she would only accept the marriage, then everything would be wonderful. They would live a pleasant coexistence and everyone would be happy.

But that wasn't the case at all.

Caledonia suspected the king hadn't told Thor everything

about her situation. All the nasty little details that one didn't like to make known, especially in delicate negotiations like this. Perhaps if the man knew, he might very well put up more of a fight and Henry would have both of them vigorously opposed to the union. Perhaps it would be too much for him and he would surrender.

She was willing to take the chance.

"I understand the situation for what it is, your grace," she said. "What you see is not a tantrum, but genuine concern for Sir Thor. I assume you've not told him of my uncle and cousin? If not, you should have. If he is going to become the Earl of Tamworth, then he should know there are others who greatly covet the title."

As Thor's brow furrowed at the mention of an uncle and cousin he'd not yet heard of, Henry quickly turned to him.

"She is correct," he said. "The lady has an uncle who has been a thorn in my side for years. I was going to tell you of it but the opportunity did not present itself."

It was clear that Caledonia had forced his hand into confessing something he wasn't ready to confess. Not until he at least had a hint of Thor's agreement. But now, Henry was compelled to come clean. If he didn't tell Thor everything, the lady surely would, and Thor seemed to sense that because his gaze lingered on Caledonia for a moment before he turned his attention to Henry.

"What does she mean?" he asked. "Who covets the title?"

"Rotri de Wylde."

Thor's eyebrows lifted in recognition. "I know of him," he said. "Lord Dordon."

"That is correct," Henry said. "Rotri is Robert de Tosni's brother."

Thor nodded as if suddenly remembering that. "I know his son, Domnall," Thor said. "But Dordon and his son fought with Simon de Montfort."

Henry nodded. "Indeed, they did," he said. "While I did not confiscate their lands because Robert asked me not to, and Robert was ever-loyal to me, that does not mean I forgive Rotri or his son for what they have done. Since Robert's death, Rotri has done everything he could to obtain the Tamworth earldom. He has been in London for the past several months, in fact, trying to convince the church to issue a papal dispensation to allow Domnall to marry Lady de Tosni, thereby assuming the Tamworth earldom."

Thor was starting to catch on. The entire reason Henry wanted him to marry Lady de Tosni was now blatantly obvious. "And that is why you pledged her to me," he said. "To prevent this."

Henry simply cocked his head in a gesture that conveyed Thor was correct. The implication was clear and now… *now*, the betrothal was starting to make more sense. Thor thought it was something that Henry had abruptly decided, but he could see by the expression on the king's face that it wasn't.

The man had a reason for it.

To keep it away from Dordon.

"Now I understand," Thor said. "Rotri must not have found a prince of the church willing to issue such a thing, and you fear that he might. With enough money, even a papal representative can be coerced."

"He tried to gain my consent right after Robert died," Caledonia said, sounding far more like a reasonable woman than she had since Thor had met her. When Thor and Henry turned to look at her, she seemed almost calm about it. "Rotri has always coveted what my father had. He was my father's heir until my brother was born and, oddly, he didn't seem to covet the earldom when Constantine was alive. I suppose he was resigned to the laws of inheritance at that point, but when Constantine died and I became the heiress, he became quite… strange."

Thor looked at her seriously. "Strange?" he said. "How?"

Caledonia pondered his question as she sat down, rather heavily. The alcohol and the mushrooms had given her a headache and reality was starting to set in. She didn't like reality much.

But at the moment, she had to face it.

"I was married to Robert when my brother died," she said. "That meant Robert was to be the next Earl of Tamworth when my father passed away because of his marriage to me, the Tamworth heiress. At first, Rotri was vocally opposed to it. He was angry and told anyone who would listen that he should be the next earl. He tried to get close to Robert and become an ally, but Robert did not trust him. That offended him greatly. When Robert died, however, Rotri was back—this time, to try to convince me that I needed to marry Domnall. When I refused, for I would not marry Domnall if he was the very last man in England, Rotri tried to find a priest who would petition for a papal dispensation. It would be a consanguine marriage because we are cousins. So far, Rotri has not found a priest who will support his quest but I am certain he will not stop until he does."

So there it was, concisely outlined. It put a different cast on the situation, to be sure. As Thor digested the information, Henry turned to him.

"Now you know everything," he said. "Rotri de Wylde covets Tamworth, so when you marry the lady—the lone de Wylde heiress—I am certain you will become his mortal enemy."

Thor snorted softly. "That matters not to me," he said. "If I were Rotri, I would worry about provoking my wrath if he angers me."

As Henry nodded sincerely, Caledonia spoke quietly. "Robert was positive that Rotri tried to kill him at least twice," she said. "My uncle is a man with no conscience. He is not beyond murder to get his wants. You should know that if you and I are wed, he will consider you a target."

Thor gave her a half-grin. "If he thinks he can hit this target, I invite him to try."

"Then it does not concern you?"

"Hardly," Thor said. But his smile quickly faded. "You have been the sole heiress for some time now, since your husband's death. Has he tried to move against you?"

She shook her head. "Nay," she said. "He would rather I marry his son. Rotri is a believer in bloodlines."

Henry seized on the moment. "Would you not rather have Thor as your husband than your pimple-faced cousin, Lady de Tosni?" he said. "Clearly, Thor would be able to defend you against your uncle. Rotri would have no chance at all against Thor de Reyne, the man once known as *El Martillo*."

Bewilderment washed over Caledonia's features. "What does that mean?"

"The Hammer," Thor said hesitantly. "I served with a mercenary army years ago—my uncle's army, Uncle Varro—in Navarre. I was given the name by his men."

Strangely enough, she seemed interested in that. "The Hammer," she repeated. "Because of your prowess in battle?"

Thor nodded. "There were a few reasons," he said, not

wanting to divulge that one of the reasons had to do with his sexual adventures with willing maidens. "It is because of my skill in warfare, but also because Thor is the god of the Northmen who carries a hammer in battle."

Caledonia let her gaze linger on him a moment, nodding, but kept silent. For the first time since their introduction, she seemed to be interested in him. "I know," she said. "I studied with a priest who was fond of the history of gods in different cultures. I remember Thor and Odin and the rest. But you have no Northman blood, so you are not named after the god?"

Thor shook his head. "As I told you, my bloodlines are Visigoth," he said. "Mayhap there is some Northman mixed in there, but my name, Thorington, is my mother's maiden name."

As she nodded, Henry chimed in. "He has a twin," he said. "Did he tell you that he has a brother who looks just like him?"

Caledonia shook her head. "We've hardly spoken, your grace," she said. "He has not had the opportunity to tell me everything about him."

Henry simply nodded, his gaze fixed on her, but there was something in his expression that suggested he wasn't finished with this conversation or this situation. Not in the least. The lady was calmer now, which was a blessing, and Thor seemed to have returned to his normal cool demeanor. Henry was grateful. But he had something to accomplish here and wasn't going to stop until he had.

"Thor," he said, "send Peregrine to me."

Peregrine was Henry's favorite servant. The man did any-thing that was asked of him and probably wielded more power than almost anyone in court, much to the distress of Henry's more official courtiers. Without hesitation, Thor went to the main entry doors, opening them and sticking his head out. He didn't see who he was looking for, so he went to a secondary pair of doors. There, he found the man he'd been seeking and Peregrine de Grasse entered on Thor's heels. He was a tall man, older, with thin white hair. He moved swiftly toward Henry, who looked at Thor and pointed to the lady.

"Take Lady de Tosni to the other end of the hall and wait for me," he said. "Go."

Thor did as he was told. He went to Caledonia, who was sitting down, and indicated the other side of the hall. With resignation, she rose and moved with Thor to their destination. There was a table that contained a bowl of fruit—small green apples, green pears, and fat plums—and a pewter pitcher with the king's seal on it and several small, and dirty, cups. There were also chairs, but neither one of them sat down. They were watching Henry as he engaged in a quiet conversation with Peregrine, who was nodding eagerly.

"What do you think he is telling him?" Caledonia finally asked.

Thor was watching the pair. "I am not certain," he said. "But it is possible he is arranging for some kind of celebration on the event of our betrothal."

Caledonia looked at him. "But I've not agreed to this."

Thor was still looking at Henry. "Henry does not need your agreement," he said. Then he looked at her. "Nor does he need mine. This is what he wants, and we will obey."

Caledonia geared up for an argument but all that came out was a loud hiss. "God's Bones, man," she said in an irritated burst. "Must we really go through with this?"

Thor took a deep breath because he didn't want to rise to her anger, which was evidently easy to do when it came to her. He was a man of supreme composure, but she had sorely tested that today.

"Lady, I apologize if you do not find me to your liking," he said. "I am sorry if you do not find me attractive or appealing, but railing against the king's wishes is not going to change things, so I suggest you find one thing about me that you find tolerable and focus on it. Mayhap it will make this marriage easier for you to swallow."

She scowled, her mouth popping open. "Don't you dare turn this on me," she said. "You are the one who cannot stand the sight of me."

His brow furrowed. "Who told you that?"

"It's obvious in everything about you!"

He shook his head slowly. "I do not know what you think is obvious, but my lack of interest in you isn't one of them," he said. "You are quite beautiful. I've never seen finer."

That stopped Caledonia in her tracks. Her scowling expression moved to one of surprise. "You think so?" she said with shock.

"I think so."

All of the rage and irritation in her manner abruptly stopped. It was like throwing water on a fire. She stood there, dumbfounded, as she pondered his words.

"But… but you think I do not find anything attractive or appealing about *you*?" she finally said.

"That is clear."

"It is *not* clear," she said. "I thought you did not find me attractive."

"And I thought you did not find *me* attractive."

She rolled her eyes. "God's Bones," she said, snorting. "In case you do not yet realize this, which I suspect you do, your name also describes you. You *look* like a god. Men like you are not real, Blue Eyes."

She'd called him *Blue Eyes* more than once. A smile tugged at his lips. "I'm real enough, I promise."

Caledonia looked him over for a moment. *Really* looked him over. Then she shook her head as if bewildered by the entire situation. "I just spent the past several hours in Gomorrah watching a young man dance for me," she said. "He was muscular and oiled and quite enticing. But he cannot hold a candle to you. If you were to work at Gomorrah and dance for the wealthy women who come there, you would make a fortune."

Thor did the unexpected then. He burst out laughing, and the sound echoed off the stone walls of the hall in a chorus of resounding booms. His laughing was so infectious that Caledonia ended up grinning at him. That stalwart, serious knight had the most unrestrained laugh she'd ever seen.

"What is so humorous?" she demanded, but it was lightly done. "I am serious. You would be richer than Midas. Rich women pay a good deal to get a look at men like you."

Thor had to wipe the tears from his eyes. "Christ," he muttered. "That is the best thing I've heard in a very long time. Me—a dancing boy?"

"Can you dance?"

He started laughing again. "As a dancer, I have five feet and all of them going in the wrong direction," he said. "Do not count on me to dance, lady. I would fail you miserably."

"What's this?" Henry had scurried over to them when he heard the laughter, but there was concern on his face. "What has happened? Thor, why are you laughing?"

Thor was still wiping the tears of laughter from his eyes. "The lady has informed me that I can make more money if I were to become an entertainer at Gomorrah, your grace," he said. "She said that wealthy women pay a good deal to be entertained by a man like me. Rest assured, I am not considering it."

Henry was a bit shocked at the lighthearted nature of the conversation. Thor's laughter had been most unexpected. He looked at the lady, who also seemed to be smiling.

Barely.

"A man like Thor," he repeated. "You mean… a big man? A knight?"

Caledonia shook her head. "I mean that he is a comely lad," she said. "Rich women would pay well to be entertained by a man of such beauty."

Henry's old face lit up. "Then you do find something redeemable about him?"

Realizing she'd been caught praising the man whom she had been vehemently opposed to, her cheeks flushed and she lowered her gaze. "I have no way of knowing," she said, trying to sound as if she wasn't in awe of him. "I wonder if his character is as handsome as his appearance. If he is your Lord Protector, then I hope he would be a fair and just man."

"Thor?" Henry said, incredulous. "Lady de Tosni, there are few men in England who are as fair and just as he is. But you shall find that out for yourself, very soon. I have summoned a priest and you shall be married before the day is through. Then you will have plenty of time to come to know him."

Caledonia's eyes widened as she looked at the king. He seemed happy about it, as he should, because he was having his way in all things. Then she looked at Thor, who had stopped laughing and now had an impassive expression on his face. She couldn't tell if he was pleased with it one way or the other.

Speechless, she simply sat down and turned away from them both. The decision had been made and the battle was over.

… or was it?

She wasn't going down without a fight.

She wasn't ready for this!

"May… may I be excused?" she asked, feeling an overwhelming need to break free of the oppressive atmosphere, one that was forcing her into something she wasn't ready to be forced into. "I should like to find the garderobe."

Thor looked at Henry, who shrugged and moved away, leaving the decision to Thor. Being a polite man and always willing to agree to a lady's polite request, he nodded and silently indicated for her to follow him. Caledonia stood up, following him through a smaller door and into a corridor.

As soon as they entered the long, dim walkway, she could smell the garderobe even though the servants had tried to mask the smell with vinegar. There was no way to mask a smell of that magnitude. Thor took her down the corridor, made a turn, and then went all the way to the end. The garderobe was little more than a small chamber with three open holes carved into stone seats set into the wall. There was a curtain for privacy from the corridor outside, but that was all. Most people attending the garderobe would have had their servants stand in the doorway to keep others away, but she had no servants. Only that damn curtain. When she stepped in, Thor thankfully closed the curtain and moved away from the opening to give her some privacy to do her business. But the question was whether or not he'd moved far enough away for her to do what she must do.

She didn't want him to hear her.

Because they were on the ground level, the windows that allowed light and ventilation into the garderobe were high on the wall behind the stone seats. All Caledonia had to do was stand on the seats to gain access to the window. It was simply a matter of pulling herself through and leaping to the opening. Down below, she could see the sewage canal that ran to the Thames, which was right next to the palace. She knew exactly where she was and, with little effort, leapt through the window and into the small area below.

Once her feet hit the ground, she began to run.

CHAPTER FOUR

I T WAS AN apartment near Aldgate, adjacent to St. Botolph, comprising of the entire top floor of a three-storied manor home that had once belonged to the Earl of Lincoln. The family lost the home to a debt they'd owed to the church, who turned around and sold it to a man from Paris who broke it up into apartments and sold each one for a princely sum.

Rotri de Wylde, Baron Dordon, had been given the apartment by his brother. His older brother, Rhun, had inherited everything else, including the castles and the title and the vast army, but Rotri had come away with a small garrison castle, Dordon, and a dingy little apartment in London because his brother hadn't wanted it. At least that was what Rotri believed, even though his brother had insisted he simply wanted Rotri to have something that belonged to him.

But Rotri deserved so much more.

In his opinion, anyway.

He was an ambitious man, an intelligent man, and one that believed himself to be an astute political player even though the past several years had seen him support Simon de Montfort, who had been defeated in the battle for the English throne.

Rotri tried to make himself indispensable to Simon, more loyal than any of his other followers, but Simon seemed to think that Rotri wasn't a man of integrity. He seemed to think that all he was working toward were the rewards that could be given to him by a new king. Simon had even gone so far as to voice that concern, but Rotri had denied it vehemently. He only wanted to serve, he'd said, and he tried to make it sound as if he would be loyal no matter what the cost.

No matter if he never received any reward for his loyalty.

Rotri thought he'd been convincing enough, but Simon didn't seem to think so and Rotri never received any gifts from Simon. Once de Montfort had been killed, Rotri knew that was the end. He would still have his small outpost castle at Dordon and he would still have his dingy apartment in London, although the apartment wasn't entirely dingy. It did have lovely, big windows that let in the light, but any fine furnishings had long been sold to keep Rotri and his son living in the manner to which they were accustomed.

The truth was that Rotri wasn't completely destitute. In his barony, there were several villages that he collected taxes from. The land was good and the crops were usually abundant, so the money he received was a decent amount of coin. The unfortunate fact was that both Rotri and his son simply liked to spend money and live well. They spent it on fine wine or fine horses or even women. Rotri's wife died long ago and Rotri hadn't seen a need to remarry considering he already had an heir, but he very much wanted that heir to marry well.

That was where his niece came in.

That was exactly why he was in London.

His lovely, intelligent niece was the heiress to one of the wealthiest earldoms in all of England. The Tamworth earldom had made its money from mining coal and lead deposits because the entire area around Tamworth was full of valuable minerals. In addition to the ore, there were also great forests of good English oak on Tamworth lands, and the wood had been harvested for decades for furniture and other things.

More money coming in.

But that was simply for the last few generations. Before that, no one was quite sure where the earldom got its vast wealth—but there were rumors that a few ancestors were nothing short of pirates. Since the de Wylde ancestors were descendent from Mercian kings, some thought that those kings had plundered other kingdoms and stolen their wealth, so there were many theories as to how and why the Tamworth earldom had become so wealthy.

Wealth that one solitary woman controlled.

Rotri had never seen such a travesty in his life. A woman with that kind of money and that kind of control was an abomination. That was the argument that Rotri used to several bishops, princes of the church that he hoped would see his point. The Bishop of Nuneaton didn't. The Bishop of Birmingham actually ordered him away. However, the Bishop of Oxford took him seriously enough to send him to London with a letter of introduction to the Archbishop of Canterbury, but that meeting hadn't happened yet.

And Rotri was going to remain in London until it did.

It never did any good to speak to the lesser priests, the ones who had no real power in this matter. Since his son and Lady de Tosni were first cousins, Rotri needed a papal dispensation for a marriage with bloodlines that were this close. The truth was that he was racing against the clock when it came to a marriage between his son and his niece because Rotri was a cunning man.

He knew that his niece was a hot commodity, and he further knew that the king thought so as well.

Henry had entered into the situation shortly after Robert de Tosni died.

That was when Rotri realized he would be fighting an uphill battle. The king wanted Lady de Tosni, and Rotri had to know of the king's plans so he could make his own. He wasn't beyond paying for information and certainly wasn't beyond paying for a few spies. There were always those close to men of power willing to divulge what they knew for a few coins, and Rotri had paid dearly for information from Westminster that told him Henry was trying to find Caledonia a strategic marriage.

But Caledonia, evidently, wasn't so eager.

There was information that she was as elusive with the king as she was with her own uncle. Caledonia had always been something of a free spirit, even a wanderer, who wasn't content to remain at home. There was news that she was spending a good deal of her time in the taverns and gambling dens of London. A serving wench at a tavern on the eastern side of London had even told him that the lady was a devoted visitor to the most notorious guild in all of London, Gomorrah.

Rotri didn't find that hard to believe.

He knew a little something about his niece. He knew that she had virtually been ignored as a child because her father and mother focused all of their attention on her older brother. Constantine de Wylde had been a stellar young man who received the finest education available. By all accounts, he was of good character and would have made an excellent earl, but an ailment that settled in his lungs one winter destroyed all of that and he died before he'd had a chance to fulfill his destiny. The loss had devastated his parents and both of them had passed away within a year of their son's death. That left their sole surviving child as the heiress to the great Tamworth empire.

The daughter that was an afterthought.

Caledonia had been formally educated and followed the path that all noble young women follow in their life. She had been taught to dance, to paint, to speak more than one language, and everything else that a fine young lady should know. But everyone knew that Caledonia de Wylde lived up to her name because she had a wild streak in her that no one could seem to tame. Not the nuns who tutored her nor the fine households where she fostered. Caledonia was bright and beautiful, but as wild as an untamed stallion. She'd always had a penchant for parties and doing any number of things that well-bred young women simply did not do. Her father, a strict and humorless man, had married her at a very early age to Robert de Tosni, hoping that her much older husband would be able to tame that wild streak.

Robert tried at first, but soon lost interest.

The Earl of Tamworth had been a good man, at least in the beginning. He tried politeness and understanding with his young wife. But his patience wasn't endless, and within the first couple of years of their marriage, he realized that he wasn't going to be able to control Caledonia, a woman full of life and vigor who liked to escape the castle to prowl the taverns in the surrounding villages. He'd caught her gambling with his soldiers more than once, but the final straw was after the birth of their eldest daughter when she went into town, not even a week after the birth, to celebrate at one of the taverns without him.

After that, Robert decided that she was not to be trusted.

The young woman who had been ignored all of her young life went back to being ignored by her husband. They had two more daughters, which was a miracle in itself because Caledonia didn't particularly like to be bedded by her older husband, but he very much wanted a son and, surprisingly, she knew it was her duty to produce one. Additionally, childbirth had proven very easy for her. But two more daughters came, and no sons, and Robert was at his wits' end.

His final stroke was perhaps the cruelest.

Robert employed his former nurse as a caretaker for his own children, and the woman had final say on how his daughters were raised. Not even their own mother had any control. Everything was given over to Madam Madonna and Caledonia was pushed out from the lives of her own children by that woman, whom Robert fully supported. He had told Caledonia once that he would rather have his daughters raised by a nun than by a wild hare of a mother. Rather than fight with him about it, Caledonia returned to her taverns and her gambling dens while her daughters were raised by a strict and loveless woman.

Aye, Rotri knew all of this because in order to gain a papal dispensation, he'd had to investigate every aspect of his niece's life. Most of the information had come from her father before he died, while some of it was just rumor. Still, the Bishop of Oxford told him that if he could produce proof that Caledonia was reckless and sacrilegious, it might be possible for such a marriage on the grounds that the lady was incapable of managing her own affairs and therefore incapable of managing an entire earldom. Rotri had even forged a document from a servant who used to serve the Earl of Tamworth, a servant who had never existed, declaring that Lady Tamworth was irresponsible and godless, so irresponsible that her own husband charged the raising of their children to someone else.

Now, all Rotri had to do was gain an audience with the Archbishop of Canterbury and produce his forged document. He had been waiting for almost four months for the opportunity and, quite frankly, was becoming impatient. As he stood at the window in the small solar of his apartment, gazing over the smoke-hazed skyline of London, he began to think that perhaps he needed to simply appear at the archbishop's door every single morning until the man finally agreed to see him. He was growing weary of waiting because he knew Henry wasn't waiting.

And that was what he was hoping for right now.

News about Henry.

Domnall, his son, had been trying to infiltrate the servants at Westminster Palace. Rotri was cunning, but Domnall was clever with a conscience. That meant he didn't exactly agree with his father's methods sometimes, but he was convinced that he deserved to be the next Earl of Tamworth because he carried the same noble blood that Caledonia did. Their fathers were brothers, after all. The only difference was that his mother was from a minor noble family, no one of note, and the only reason his father had married her was because they had met at a feast and he managed to compromise her during a tryst in the darkness. What Rotri thought would be a simple conquest of a daughter of an unremarkable family turned into an unexpected pregnancy, and he was forced to marry her.

Domnall was the result.

Even now, his son was over at Westminster because he was convinced there would be a breakthrough today. He'd had it on good authority that a servant he'd been paying well for the past several weeks was about to come forth with information because Henry had several nobles in town and there was to be a great meeting. Great meetings usually covered a variety of subjects and it was possible that Lady de Tosni and her rudderless earldom might be one of them. The same servant had mentioned that Henry had spoken of Lady de Tosni before, with frustration because she seemed to be good at eluding him. The hope was that she would be discussed again. If she was, Rotri needed to know about it.

So he waited.

It was nearing the nooning hour when he finally heard the door to the apartment open. He heard voices, including those of his son, as the young man removed his cloak and handed it off to a hovering servant. Footsteps approached the small solar where Rotri was pretending to wait casually when the truth was that he was on pins and needles. When Domnall's bushy red head finally came through the door, it was all Rotri could do not to run at the man.

"Well?" he demanded. "Is there any news?"

So much for being composed. His anxiety was written all over him. Domnall cast his father a long glance on his way to a wooden pitcher of wine. He didn't bother with a cup, but rather drank it straight from the neck. Some trickled down his chin, leaving a purple streak, before he finally lowered the pitcher and wiped his mouth with the back of his hand.

"Plenty," Domnall said, struggling to catch his breath. "The servant I met at the marketplace those months ago serves in the halls of Westminster. You remember the one? One of our own servants knew him and knew he served at the palace. He serves the king personally. The man has cost me a fortune but today, it has finally come to fruition."

Rotri's eyes widened in anticipation. "What has happened?"

Domnall sighed heavily, wiping at his mouth again. "Callie has been found."

Rotri had expected more than that. "I see," he said impatiently. "So she has been found. We know she is in London. She has been residing at the Tamworth townhome, so that is not news. Why do you think I am in London? When Canterbury agrees to seek a papal dispensation, we know where she is and we will immediately collect her and force her to remain here, with us, until the dispensation is received. Canterbury will support this action."

Domnall cocked an eyebrow. "Will he?" he said. "Papa, you know I want Tamworth more than you do, but holding Callie hostage until we receive word from the pope… She will not be a submissive hostage. You know that."

Rotri waved him off. "We'll chain her to the wall if we have to," he said. "What else have you discovered?"

"That she is to be married to Thor de Reyne."

That brought a big reaction from Rotri. "*What*?" he gasped, eyes wide. "Henry has found her a husband?"

"Aye."

"Are you certain?"

Domnall nodded. "Certain enough," he said. "The man I have been paying said that the Earl of Ashington was at Westminster today and he and Henry were arguing over Thor. You remember him, don't you? He fought with Prince Edward against de Montfort, but we've met him before. At a feast at Bowes Castle years ago. His father is Lord Ashington and Thor serves the king as his personal protector."

Rotri was beside himself at the news. "Of course I know him," he said. "I knew his father's brother, Boothe, many years ago. Gage de Reyne is an ambitious bastard. Married the Ashington heiress and assumed the earldom."

Domnall cocked an eyebrow. "Sound familiar?"

He meant the current situation they were trying to manipulate, and Rotri scowled. "Tamworth is your right, lad," he insisted. "With my brother dead, and Constantine gone, it would be logical that the earldom would go to you."

"You and I may think so, but no one else seems to. Now, Callie is betrothed."

That was devastating news to Rotri. Raking his fingers through his silver hair, he turned away, trying to think of a way to salvage the situation. But he couldn't get past the disappointment he felt.

"Damnation," he muttered. "I knew she had Henry's attention. I should have moved more swiftly with this. I should have gone to Rome myself for a dispensation."

"That would have taken months, if not years," Domnall said. "What we should have done was abduct her, and I would have married her by force. Not even Henry could have dissolved a consummated marriage."

Rotri glanced at him. "And you know she is betrothed for certain?"

Domnall nodded. "The servant heard it for himself."

"Who is this man?"

"His name is Peregrine."

"And he is close to the king?"

"Very close."

Rotri considered that as he sat down in one of the remaining chairs in the chamber, one that hadn't yet been sold. A servant very close to the king could still be useful. Perhaps there was still a way out of this.

"Then if he is close, he can tell us when the marriage is to take place," he said after a moment. "Mayhap there is something we can do to prevent it."

"Like what?"

Rotri rubbed his chin. "Mayhap there is something the church can do," he said. "Knowing we have staked a claim on Caledonia, mayhap they can intervene and prevent the marriage until word is received from the pope."

"We do not have a claim on Callie."

"We have a better claim that de Reyne does," Rotri snapped. Then he cooled as an idea came to him. His eyes widened. "Wait… a claim… a *claim.*"

Domnall eyed his father, who seemed to be in the throes of a striking idea. "What claim?" he said. "What are you talking about?"

Rotri held up a finger as he tried to put his thoughts into words. "A claim—a legitimate claim—might be the only thing to stop the marriage," he said. "Something I should have done long ago."

"What *are* you talking about?"

He looked at his son. "A *claim*," he said urgently. "I had it within my grasp the entire time but did not think of it. I suppose that I did not think it would be so difficult to obtain a dispensation and simply forgot about it. But now… it may be our salvation!"

Domnall sighed impatiently. "I do not know what you mean."

Rotri held his hands up, shaking them like a madman. "Listen to me," he implored. "I have a missive from my brother that asks me to manage Callie's affairs, but it is a very old missive from when she was a young girl. If Rhun died while she was still young, he would need someone to manage her. He asked me to do it."

Domnall was starting to catch on. "And you are just remembering this?" he said, aghast. "Do you still have it?"

Rotri nodded wildly. "I do!" he said. "It is back at Dordon, somewhere in my solar. I've not seen it in years, but it must be there. I will send a servant for it immediately!"

Now, Domnall was excited like his father was. "If this is true, then it could be what we have hoped for all along," he said. "At the very least, it will delay whatever Henry is intending. Rhun was her father and, as a widow, she would fall back under his wardship with no other man to take charge of her."

Rotri shook his head, looking at his son with more delight than Domnall had seen in a very long time. "Not under Rhun's wardship," he said. "Under *mine*. And I would have to give permission for any marriage."

It was as if a curtain was drawn back and the sun of possibilities was now blazing brightly upon them. Rotri wanted to keep Tamworth in the family and Domnall knew he'd go to great lengths to do it, but the sudden remembrance of an old missive from Rhun was unexpected. However, given that the mighty war machine of Ashington was involved, that might set up an epic struggle. If they were keen on Caledonia, too, then they would surely not want to relinquish her, not even for her father's wishes from long ago.

If they could prove it.

A servant was riding for Dordon before the day was out.

CHAPTER FIVE

AFTER WAITING OUTSIDE of the garderobe for about fifteen minutes before he was impolite enough to check on the lady, Thor really wasn't surprised to find her missing. Windows were open and she was gone. He was simply angry at himself that he'd let her trick him.

It didn't take a genius to figure out where she had gone.

Henry was nowhere to be found when he charged back into the hall, so he informed the nearest servant that he was going to retrieve Lady de Tosni. In fact, no one seemed to be in the hall, his father included, so he headed out to collect his horse, which had been returned to Westminster by Daniel when Thor had gone to the tavern with the lady after the chaos at Gomorrah. But now, Gomorrah was once again Thor's target as he headed out of the stable, only to be stopped by his men, who had seen him from the palace where they'd been waiting for his meeting with Henry to end. After a brief explanation as to where he was going and why, Clayne, Truett, and Darius were more than ready to return to Gomorrah with him.

While Thor's men collected their horses, Thor went to the gatehouse to question the guards about letting a woman with white hair slip through. The main gates to Westminster weren't normally kept closed because of the administrative offices at the palace, so it wouldn't have been difficult for a solitary woman to leave. No one was stopped going out, only coming in. The guards remembered her but there hadn't been anything remarkable about her other than someone mentioning that the woman was flushed, as if she'd been running.

Not running so much as escaping.

That only made Thor angrier.

His men joined him at the gatehouse shortly and the group of them thundered into London, through the Ludgate entrance and on to the eastern side of the city where Gomorrah lay buried beneath the ruins of an old church. Rather than beat the door down like they did before, Thor was subtler this time.

He went in through the secretive secondary entrance.

As he'd hoped, they'd not barred the door after the initial breach earlier in the day. Perhaps they hadn't realized it, or perhaps they didn't care, but in either case, Thor and his men descended into the depths of the guild, down where it was dark and dank and smelled of rot. They could hear people talking in the distance and even some musicians striking up a tune, but no one stopped them as they came in the back way. It was quite a contrast to the resistance they'd encountered earlier in the day, and Thor had his men split up and hunt for the white-haired lady. No punching or kicking or fighting this time. They were moving in stealth, in the shadows. He had no idea where the guards were, the ones they'd encountered the first time, but he didn't hunt for them.

He was hunting for something else.

Some*one* else.

In truth, the lady wasn't difficult to find. She was on the

next level down, sitting at a table with drinks spread out before her and deep in conversation with an older woman. Several feet away, couples danced to the strains of a citole. Thor sat down across the table from her but it was a full minute before she even took notice of him.

Any hint of pleasantness vanished. Her eyes widened and the battle lines were immediately drawn as she picked up the nearest weapon, which happened to be a dull knife used for butter.

"I am *not* going back," she declared. "I do not care how many men you've brought with you this time. I will not go back, and if you try to force me, I'll give you more of a fight than you expect."

Thor didn't move a muscle. He simply watched her face as she spoke. Truly, she had quite a face. Her lips curved in a most alluring way and her pert nose had an arrogant tilt to it. But the defiance in her voice was undercut by something else. He thought it was fear.

She's afraid, he thought.

Fear and desperation.

He could smell it in everything about her.

"Is that why you ran?" he asked. "Because you are afraid?"

Her brow twitched in confusion. "Afraid?" she repeated. "Afraid of what? You?"

He remained cool. "You tell me," he said. "I can see it in your face."

"You see nothing. You do not know me."

He cocked an eyebrow. "I know enough about you to know that you are foolish," he said. "Only a fool would run from the king's directive."

That took her down a peg or two but she was still indignant.

"What you call foolishness, I call self-preservation."

"What are you preserving yourself from?"

Her gaze lingered on him. "Another miserable life," she finally said. "I've already had two. I do not need a third."

"How do you know it will be miserable?"

She didn't have a quick answer for him. She simply turned away, eyes averted, as the older woman next to her continued to watch the situation carefully. Mostly, she was looking at Caledonia, perhaps to get a sense of what was going on and if she needed help. After several long moments, the older woman turned her gaze to Thor.

"You were here earlier," she finally said to him. "With the knights that entered. You were with them."

Thor glanced at her. "Mayhap," he said, but it was all he would say. His attention, and the conversation, was on Caledonia. "My lady, what makes you think a marriage to me will be miserable? Am I not given the opportunity to prove otherwise before you condemn me?"

"You killed two of our guards," the older woman said before Caledonia could answer. "You had no reason to do that. Why did you come here?"

Now, Thor turned his gaze on her in full. "Woman, if you do not go away and leave me to this private conversation, you will not like my reaction," he said, his voice rumbling like thunder. "You are not part of this. Leave this table. I will only tell you once."

The older woman's jaw moved as if she wanted to reply but thought better of it. Sanity was in control and not a death wish. Standing up, she left the table without another word, leaving Thor alone with Caledonia. She was watching the older woman walk away.

"You did not need to be rude to her," she said.

Thor's gaze was fixed on her. "You will answer me," he said. "Am I not given the opportunity to prove that you will not be miserable before you condemn me?"

Caledonia finally looked at him. "What do you want me to say that I have not already said?" she said. "You know I do not wish to marry you. I do not wish to marry anyone."

"You do not have a choice," Thor said. "As the heiress to Tamworth, you must marry. It is your duty."

Her delicate jaw twitched faintly. "And you have come to force me back to Westminster."

"If it was my intention to force you, we would already be halfway back to the palace," he said. "It is my intention to bargain."

That had her interest, but only slightly. "Bargain?" she repeated. "What bargain could you possibly make?"

Thor glanced at the table, at the empty cups. It gave him an idea. Clearly, the lady was unlike any woman he'd ever met. She wasn't the sweet, delicate, obedient type. Not that all the women he knew were like that, but all of them, to varying degrees, were at least obedient. But not Caledonia—she had another level of stubbornness tucked down inside her. It was almost a mannish type of stubbornness. She had no fear and seemingly did not care what people thought of her. She was an enigma, but one he intended to crack.

Now, it was a matter of principle.

"Do you gamble, my lady?" he finally asked.

She nodded slowly. "I have been known to."

"And if you lose, do you keep your end of the bargain and pay your debts?"

"Always."

"Then you consider yourself a woman of honor."

"Honor is all I have left, Blue Eyes. What is your point?"

Oh, but she was bold with the apparent nickname she had for him. *Blue Eyes.* She had such an unrestrained and bold way of speaking. It was in her manner. It was in everything about her, this boldness that let everyone know she was strong and sharp and more than a formidable opponent. Thor had to admit that he was appalled by a woman like that, but he was also strangely fascinated.

"My point is that we can settle this matter now," he said. "Until this moment, I have put up a weak fight. I will admit that I am conditioned to obey the king, no matter what, and my resistance to this betrothal had been strong at first but I quickly succumbed to the inevitable. That is why you've not seen me put up more of a battle, my lady. I have more to lose than you do, so obedience is my only real choice. However, you do not have the same conviction. You continue to fight, but you cannot keep it up forever. Henry will win in the end if you fight alone."

She was puzzled. "What do you mean by that?"

"I mean that I can fight with you. Or not."

A flicker of interest came to her eyes. "Explain."

"We can wager on it," he said. "A fair game can decide if I fight with you or against you."

Her eyes narrowed as she realized he was approaching her on level ground, on terms she could understand. They were in a gambling guild, after all. He'd found her here, and when she escaped, she'd come back. Clearly, she was comfortable here.

He wanted to bargain, did he? If she had him on her side, the king might forget this scheme, indeed. Surely the king couldn't force two people to marry who vehemently opposed the union. Perhaps they could put up such a fight that the king would grow weary and move on. But if he didn't, Caledonia needed Thor on her side.

Running from him hadn't worked.

Perhaps gambling with him would.

"Very well," she said after a moment. "I am listening. What do you propose?"

He pointed to the cups in front of her. "That we drink together."

Her eyebrows lifted. "Is that *all*?"

He shook his head. "It is not all," he said. "We will ask the servants to bring the strongest drink they have and pour it into cups. We will each have one. You will ask me a question, any question at all, and if I answer it, you must take a drink. If I refuse, then I must take a drink. We will do this until only one of us left standing and whoever is left wins the wager. If you win, I will fight with you against this marriage."

Caledonia was much more interested in this than anything he'd said since they'd first met. "And if you win?"

"Then we marry immediately."

She puffed out her cheeks, blowing out a long breath as she considered his proposal. In truth, it wasn't unfair. It was actually *quite* fair. It would be a decisive victory for one of them, and only because she could drink most men under the table was she considering it. He didn't know she had a great tolerance for wine and ale.

He was playing right into her hands.

She was so confident that she could hardly keep the smile off her face.

"Very well," she said. "I accept."

"Good."

"And you give me your word that you will hold up your end of the bargain?"

"You have my oath, lady. There is no stronger vow than that."

It was evident from her expression that she believed him. Not that she had a choice, but she was willing to go on a little faith if it would get her out of this predicament. With that in mind, she turned around and shouted like a barmaid to summon a servant. Thor had never heard anything like it, this ethereal creature shouting like a common fishwife. As he fought off a grin, the older woman whom he'd chased from the table appeared and Caledonia ordered something called *gorzalka*. He'd never heard of it. As the older woman nodded and turned to leave, Thor stood up.

"I will see to this drink to ensure she does not put anything in it to poison me," he said. "What is it that you have asked for?"

Caledonia watched him as he moved toward the older woman, who happened to be Lady Lupa. "It comes from far to the east," she said. "It is the strongest drink I've ever known, but smooth. You do not know how strong it is until you've had too much and you cannot get up from the floor."

He simply nodded, his gaze lingering on her for a moment, perhaps suspiciously, before he motioned the older woman on her way.

He followed.

Once Caledonia was left alone, she thought about running again. It was her first instinct. But she'd given her word that she'd wager with him, and if she did, she'd get him off her back forever. That was the deal. She was willing to see it through to be done with this betrothal nonsense once and for all.

Finished.

Oddly, there was a small part of her that was disappointed. Thor de Reyne was quite handsome to look at, young and enormously strong. Far more handsome than Robert had been. Thor would be a husband any woman would be proud of. But here she was, eager to get rid of him because she didn't want to marry again. Ever. And she knew, as she lived and breathed, that it was a stupid stance.

Did she really want to be alone for the rest of her life?

That was the reality of it. She was fighting to be alone when the truth was that she was a valuable commodity as a widowed heiress. Thor said that if he won, they would marry immediately. She was certain that was out of greed to claim the title and not some misplaced desire to marry her, personally. She had nothing to do with it.

Only ambition.

He only wanted what she had.

With that lingering thought, she waited. Thor returned shortly with Lady Lupa, who was carrying a tray with a large pitcher and two cups on it. Thor indicated for the woman to set the tray down on the table between him and the lady.

"I had her pour it out of a bottle I opened myself," he told Caledonia as he sat down. "The wine is pure enough. I even made her take a drink, which seemed to make her eyes water. If she isn't dropping dead, then it must be fit for our purposes."

Caledonia silently waved the older woman away as she picked up the pitcher and began to pour full measures for them both.

"I would be remiss if I did not warn you about *gorzalka*," she said. "I feel that I should—"

"You've already warned me."

He had cut her off with his arrogant reply and she looked at him, possibly in amusement, as she handed him a full cup.

"Very well," she said as if he was sure to regret this bargain. "Shall we begin?"

Thor nodded. "You may ask the first question."

Caledonia had to choose her question carefully. If he answered it, she would have to drink. If he refused, he would have to drink. She wanted to get the man drunk so her question had to be pointed. Uncomfortable, even.

But she had to be perfectly clear.

"This is not my question, but may I ask about the rules so I understand completely?" she said.

He nodded. "What is it?"

"May I ask *any* question?"

"Any question."

"Even a question you may not like?"

"I said any question. But that means I also get to ask you any question."

So she couldn't badger him too much or he would badger her in return. Now, there was some strategy involved because he could do to her what she wanted to do to him.

The lines were drawn.

"How many women have you bedded in your lifetime?" she asked.

It was the first volley in the battle and it was a heavy one. She came charging out on the offensive, like any good opponent, and Thor had to seriously keep from laughing at the question. She was trying to shock him, but it wasn't going to work. He needed to get the woman sauced so they could be over this nonsense and get on with their lives together.

Such as it was.

"Nineteen," he said without hesitation, though he was certain it wasn't that high. Frankly, he didn't even know what the number was, so it was the first number he could come up with. "I answered you. You must drink, my lady."

Eyeing him, Caledonia took a swallow of the stuff, wincing as it went down because it was so strong. "What is your question for me?" she asked.

Her voice sounded tight, as if the alcohol had burned her throat, and Thor had to think of a good question.

"How many men have *you* bedded in your lifetime?" he asked.

Caledonia coughed. She coughed again. She suffered through a coughing fit before she spat out an answer.

"Forty-nine," she said hoarsely, still coughing. "You must drink now."

He did, a big swallow, and it damn near burned a hole in his throat. Now he knew why she was coughing, but he wasn't going to give her the satisfaction of knowing that he found the drink almost unbearable. The most he did was clear his throat.

"Christ," he muttered. "How is it that you can even walk if you've bedded so many?"

"Is that your next question?"

He shook his head quickly. "Nay," he said. "It is your turn."

She coughed one last time before taking a deep breath and thinking carefully on her question. She wanted to hit him hard, so there was no backing off what she'd started.

"Because you have bedded so many women, do you have any diseases of the male member that I should be aware of?" she asked. "Do you have the French pox?"

That did cause him to cough, and cough loudly, because he had to cover the laugh that came belting out of his mouth.

"I do not think so," he said, wiping his mouth with the back of his hand. "Do you want to inspect me to find out?"

"Is that your question to me?"

"It is."

Caledonia realized he'd cornered her quickly. If she refused to inspect him, he might consider it a refusal to answer. It was difficult to tell with him. But she wondered if he was prepared to drop his breeches for her inspection were she to agree to it. Perhaps he didn't expect her to and was willing to take the chance.

She was going to turn the tables on him.

"Thank you, I would like to inspect you," she said. "Lower your breeches. Let me see what nineteen other women have seen."

The blue eyes began to crinkle at the corners. God help him, it was all Thor could do not to burst out laughing. She was being bold and reckless and entirely inappropriate, and he had to admit that he was impressed. When he should have been appalled, he was actually impressed. The woman was fearless as few people were. Without hesitation, he stood up and began to untie his breeches, but he abruptly came to a halt.

"Wait," he said. "I answered your question. You must drink."

She frowned. "I answered *your* question, so *you* must drink."

One hand on his breeches, Thor picked up the cup and took another drink of that liquid lightning. Caledonia did the same, tossing back a healthy swallow and sputtering because of it. He was about to slide his breeches down his hips when she put out a hand to stop him.

"Wait," she said. "You do not need to show me. I believe

you."

He cocked an eyebrow. "Are you certain?"

"I am?"

He inched one side of his breeches down. "It would be no trouble."

"Pull your breeches up, de Reyne. I do not want to see your flesh sausage."

He couldn't help it then. He started laughing. By the time he fastened his breeches and sat down, he was crying with laughter.

"Where did you hear such a thing?" he said. "No lady should say such words."

Caledonia was smiling. His laughter lightened what could have been a truly embarrassing moment, but more than that, he had a positively delicious smile, one that changed the entire shape of his face.

It was astonishing.

"In case you've not realized it, I am not an ordinary lady," she said. "What would you prefer I call it? Your gospel pipe? Your staff of delight? Your—"

He cut her off. "I understand clearly enough," he said, wiping the tears of laughter from his eyes. "You needn't prove your vocabulary to me, though I find it somewhat shocking that you should know such things. But along those lines, now it is my turn to inspect—I want to see what forty-nine men have already seen. Lift your skirts."

Her smile vanished unnaturally fast. "I will *not.*"

"Then you must drink."

Angrily, she grabbed her cup and took another big swallow, nearly choking on it. Thor sat across the table from her, a smile still on his lips as he watched her struggle with the strong drink.

"It is your turn," he said. "Ask me anything."

Caledonia wiped her mouth with the back of her hand, eyeing him unhappily. Unfortunately, she'd been drinking most of the day, and even though the drink, and those damnable mushrooms, had worn off for the most part, the three big gulps of the *gorzalka* were quickly catching up with her. Her throat was on fire and her head was beginning to swim a little as she faced off against the excruciatingly handsome man across the table.

Truth be told, he was looking better by the moment.

"You do not really want to marry me, do you?" she asked.

He shrugged. "A man should marry sometime."

He'd answered her, so she took another drink. It was going down easier with each successive gulp. Thor watched her, seeing that she was quickly becoming inebriated. With the strength of that liquor, it was little wonder. She was heading in the direction he wanted her to go, but even so, he took some pity on her.

He hoped it wouldn't cost him.

"Where do you get your unusual name?" he asked.

She pushed her hair back, uncovering her right eye, because up until that point the front of her hair had hung down over half her face. She blinked, trying to focus on him as she struggled against the drink.

"My mother descended from the kings of Strathclyde," she said. "Her name was Alba and she named me Caledonia, after her home. It is the Roman name for Scotland."

He nodded faintly as he collected his cup, making it look like he was taking a big swallow when, in fact, he took a very small one. He, too, was already feeling the sting of that drink and wanted to keep his wits about him as much as he could.

"It suits you," he said.

Her brow furrowed. "What do you mean?"

He shrugged. "It's a lyrical name," he said. "It's ethereal and beautiful. Like you."

Caledonia widened her eyes, shocked by the compliment. She wasn't sure how to respond with the man actually being nice to her. "Everyone calls me Callie," she said. "Only my mother and Robert called me Caledonia."

He shook his head. "Caledonia is much better suited to you," he said. "Do you have another question for me?"

Caledonia had to think about it. "How old are you?"

"I have seen forty summers."

Her mouth popped open. "You are that old?"

"You forgot to take a drink."

She did, quickly and sloppily. "You are *that* old?" she said again.

He grinned before taking a drink, letting out a cough because the stuff was burning holes in him. "How old are you?" he rasped.

She stared at him a moment before slumping in her chair and averting her gaze. After a moment, she reached for the pitcher and poured more of the clear liquid into her cup. Then she refilled his.

"Old enough," she muttered. "Old enough to have given birth to three children I never see. Three children I'm not *allowed* to see. Did the king tell you that?"

The mood quickly shifted from adversarial to conversational. That terrible drink was clearly loosening Caledonia's tongue because Thor was quite certain she wouldn't have said such a thing otherwise. She'd been determined not to let him in, not to show him any interest or understanding, but those softly uttered words had his smile fading.

He looked at her seriously.

"Nay," he said. "Why not? Why can you not see your own children?"

She grunted, taking yet another drink of that potent liquid. "Because it was what Robert wanted."

He was confused. "Your own husband did not want you to see your own children?"

Caledonia shrugged. "He decided I was not someone he wanted raising his daughters," she said, finally meeting his eyes. She shrugged again. "A nun is raising my children. A nun Robert engaged, a woman who will not let me see my own daughters. I am a stranger to them. Their own mother."

Thor thought that was a tragic tale, indeed. "Where are they?" he asked.

"Stafford Castle," she said. "That is the Stafford seat, you know. Edingale is the other castle, but that belongs to Tamworth. Both will be yours when you marry me. *If* you marry me. That bitch raises my daughters and refuses to let me see them. I cannot stay at Stafford if I cannot see my own children because it is like torture, so I come to London. In case you were at all wondering why I run and why I come to Gomorrah, it is because it is the furthest I can get and not think about my children."

Those few pathetic sentences told Thor a great deal about the lady and her behavior. Now, it was starting to make some sense. He couldn't understand why the Countess of Tamworth refused to rule the earldom in dignified widowhood, but rather chose to live a life of drink and debauchery. Always running, pretending she had no responsibilities...

She was a woman who was bleeding inside and trying to

hide it.

"Did Stafford tell you to go away?" he asked quietly. "Did he send you away from your children?"

"He did not stop me if that is what you mean," she said. "I will tell you a secret, de Reyne. Robert de Tosni only wanted sons and all I gave him was daughters. I was useless to him. He never wanted me as it was, but to bear him only girl children… Well, you can imagine how disappointed he was. He thought I did not know that he sent my father missives about it, but I knew. He would tell my father what a terrible mother I was, what a terrible wife I was. Then my brother died and my father shortly thereafter. And now who controls both Stafford and Tamworth? That failure of a wife and mother. *Me!*"

The alcohol had the better of her and she was running off at the mouth, but Thor was understanding a great deal about her thanks to that powerful drink that had fed her demons. Now, they were coming out.

"Were you trained to manage it?" he asked.

She grinned and lifted her cup. "Is that another question?" she asked drunkenly. "Because I'll answer it. I was tutored by Lady d'Umfraville of Prudhoe Castle, who believed all young women should know how to read and write and do sums, among other things. I was very good at my lessons. She trained me well. But my father managed his own empire and Robert would never let me near anything he did. I was chased away and left to feel useless. That was Robert's name for me, you know— *Déchet*. It means waste. Rubbish. That's what he considered me—rubbish."

Thor shook his head, disgusted by what he was hearing. "And he said that right to your face?"

Caledonia nodded. "He meant me to know," she said. Then

she took another drink, a big one, and nearly fell over as she tipped her head back to drain the cup. "He told the knights commanding Stafford Castle what he thought of me, and they do not care for me. Edingale was a little different because they understand I am the heiress, so those knights show a little more respect than the Stafford knights do. And now the king intends to chase me away from managing Stafford and Tamworth by marrying me to you. You will manage it and I will, once again, be *Déchet*. Rubbish."

She made a grab for the pitcher, but he moved her cup away when she tried to pour. It was no longer his intention to see her drunk and compliant because the drink in her veins had taken their conversation, and possibly their wager, in an entirely different direction. Getting her drunk wasn't funny anymore. Not after what she'd just told him. Undeterred by his actions, Caledonia drank from the neck of the pitcher, two big swallows, and slammed the vessel back down again. Shortly thereafter, she tipped over, face-first, onto the table.

She was out.

Thor sat there for a moment and simply watched her to see if she'd snap out of it, but she didn't. Face against the table, she was already snoring heavily. But he realized he had what he wanted—she'd passed out and now he could take her back to Westminster. But after hearing how she viewed herself and the torment the woman had been put through, he felt strangely protective over her. He came from a wonderful and loving family, but she hadn't. He was sure there was more to the story, but what he'd heard was enough.

Caledonia de Wylde de Tosni had to be at least twenty-five years, if not more. She was a mature woman, with three children, and a mess of a life. He should have been extremely wary of marrying a woman like that. He didn't want a mess of a wife. But something told him that, deep down, there was more to her. He wasn't sure why he felt that way, but he did. Perhaps all she needed was a chance, an opportunity to not feel like rubbish. He had no idea why he should feel compelled to take on a woman with more demons than most, but as a man of compassion, he knew he couldn't walk away from her. It would have been easy for him to tell Henry he hadn't located her and use that as leverage to break the betrothal, but he couldn't seem to do it. This night had been eye-opening in many ways and he'd made his decision.

He hoped he wouldn't live to regret it.

CHAPTER SIX

"PEREGRINE SAID THAT she was brought back to Westminster last night," Domnall said. "It cost me nearly every coin I have, but he told me that the wedding is planned for today at Westminster. What will we do? We do not have Uncle Rhun's document yet."

Rotri had been seated, eating his morning meal of bread and wine, when Domnall burst into the apartment. Startled by the news, he tried to swallow the bite in his mouth but ended up spitting it onto the floor so he wouldn't choke.

"Today?" he sputtered. "When?"

Domnall shook his head. "Near *sext*," he said, naming the noon liturgy of the hours. "If that is true, there is not much time."

Rotri was already up, brushing off his tunic and wiping at his mouth for any remnants of crumbs. "We must go now," he said. "We must be there when Callie and de Reyne arrive. I am not entirely sure we can stop the marriage without the document in hand, but we can try. I can plant the seeds of doubt, mayhap enough to cause a delay."

He was heading for the wardrobe where his cloak was hanging. The apartment had six big chambers, not including two smaller chambers on the sublevel of the building where the servants slept near the kitchens. An older servant who had been with Dordon for many years rushed in to help Rotri don his cloak as Domnall already headed for the entry door. Rotri pulled his cloak on, heading for the door after his son as the servant followed after him, straightening it out and brushing off any visible dirt.

Down the stairs and they were out into the cluttered yard behind the manse.

Domnall's horse was already waiting, so it was simply a matter of preparing Rotri's horse, an aging animal that he'd had for almost thirty years. All of the fine horses he'd purchased over the years had been lost in gambling games, including one to his son, who was riding that prize today. A young beast, blond and strong, and Rotri eyed his son as he mounted the animal. He was still peeved that Domnall managed to wrest the horse away from him. He loved his son, but he hated losing to him.

Soon enough, Rotri's horse was brought around and Rotri mounted the beast, heading out to the Lombard Street with Domnall beside him. There were crowds out today, as it was market day, so they had to slow down or risk running people over. The weather was warm, with dust kicking up in the air and children and dogs running through the street. One dog ran up to Domnall's horse and barked, causing the horse to nip at it.

Domnall chased the dog away.

"You still have not told me how we are going to prevent this marriage," he said to his father. "You do not have Uncle Rhun's missive in your possession, so it will be your word only, and I doubt that de Reyne or Henry will stop their plans simply because you say so."

Rotri knew that but was clinging to the hope that his convoluted logic could postpone this wedding. "It depends on how convincing I can be," he said. "Mayhap if I create enough of an argument, they will at least delay the wedding until the missive in question can be presented. The king knows I have staked a claim on Callie. I will bring the document to the Archbishop of Canterbury and let him decide the intent of my brother. If he agrees, then approval of her marriage will be given to me and, of course, I will not approve."

"And you will proceed with the dispensation."

"Exactly. Time will be on our side."

Domnall lifted his eyebrows. "You really should have remembered this missive sooner," he said. "It could have saved us a good deal of time and effort to prove Uncle Rhun's intent when it came to Callie."

Rotri grunted. "As I said, I did not think it would be so difficult to gain our wants," he said. "Moreover, how am I supposed to remember a missive I tossed aside nearly the moment I received it? Constantine was alive, as was Rhun, and the chances that Callie would not have anyone to take charge of her and her fortune were very small. I put it aside and forgot it."

Domnall didn't reply. It wasn't the first time his father had forgotten something important. Forgetfulness had been increasing as Rotri got older, but so did his agitation at small things. The man was volatile in the best of times these days, and forgetting something as important as Rhun's missive requesting Rotri's management over his daughter should it come to that wasn't surprising. Disappointing, but not surprising.

But Domnall let it go. There was no point in harassing his father over it. Rotri seemed moderately convinced that their interference would work in spite of the lack of the document, but Domnall wasn't so sure. He, too, hoped it would be enough.

They would find out soon enough.

Westminster Palace loomed ahead, sitting on the banks of the Thames like a great, rambling beast. The spires of Westminster Cathedral could also be seen, shrouded in the faint smoky haze that hung about London these days. Smoke from cooking fires, from dust, clouded up in the hair and created a layer of murk that clung to the entire city. Sometimes, the breezes from the ocean to the east blew it out, but today was not one of those days. Everything looked smoky and dirty.

But that wasn't what had Domnall or Rotri's attention.

That enormous cathedral up ahead did.

They could only hope they were in time.

෮

"ARE YOU AWAKE?"

Caledonia wasn't entirely sure that she was. She thought she might have been dreaming. She'd been staring at an unfamiliar ceiling for an indeterminate amount of time before she heard a soft, deep voice ask the question.

Are you awake?

She recognized the voice.

Her heart began to beat a little faster.

Slowly, she turned her head and the hammers started. Hammering her skull, her brain, her eyeballs, and even her teeth. Everything seemed to hurt.

Her hands flew to her head.

"I think I am dead," she muttered.

She heard a snort. "You are not dead, though you might wish you were, given the pain you are now experiencing."

She grunted, eyes scrunched closed. "Nay, I *am* dead," she said. "Send every physic in London to me now, please."

"You think that multiple physics can cure your ache?"

"I think it will take that many to carry my giant head out of this chamber for burial, because it feels as if it weighs more than a horse." She peeped an eye open, catching sight of Thor as he came into view. "Why are you grinning at me? Where am I?"

His big arms were folded over his chest as he gazed down at her, a hint of a smile on his lips. "At Westminster," he said. "I did not know where you were staying in London, so I brought you here. This is my chamber."

Her other eye popped open and she stared at him a moment before lifting her head slightly and looking around at what was genuinely a grand chamber. The ceilings were soaring, the walls paneled and painted, and five enormous arched windows were overlooking… something. She couldn't see what was beyond the windows, but she could hear men and birds and the sounds of a morning.

She laid her head back down again.

"I do not remember coming here," she said, closing her eyes against the surging ache.

He unfolded his arms and moved to the edge of the bed. "I am not surprised," he said. "That drink you ordered was… powerful. It put you to sleep."

She put her hands over her eyes. "It has never done that to me before," she said. "I usually tolerate it."

"Not this time."

She uncovered one eye and looked at him. "Did you poison me?"

He shook his head. "Of course not," he said. "When did I have the chance?"

"I do not know. I do not remember."

"What is your last memory?"

She had to think on that. "You told me I had a lyrical name," she said. "You said it was beautiful."

"Like you."

Both hands came away from her eyes and she propped herself up on her elbows, glaring at him as much as her red-rimmed eyes would allow.

"If you think sweet words will convince me to marry you, then you are sadly mistaken," she said. "I do not want to hear them."

He lifted a dark eyebrow. "I would not use sweet words to coerce you," he said. "I am not manipulative by nature. Moreover, I do not need to coerce you. You lost our bargain and that means we shall be married today."

Caledonia almost argued with him, vehemently, but she remembered the part of the conversation where she had agreed to a wager. She thought she could out-drink him, but he, in fact, had held his own. More than that, he had bested her. Given that she had told him she was a woman of honor, it would do no good to continue the fight. Looking around, she could see that she was in a very big bed.

She thought she knew why.

"I see," she muttered. "And you brought me back here to consummate a marriage that will take place today. Is that it?"

Thor shook his head. "I did not touch you," he said. "You snored like a drunkard all night. I do not take advantage of women who are not agreeable to something as serious as that."

Somehow, she believed him. He'd never given her a reason not to believe that he was a man of honor, and, as she'd told him, honor meant something to her. It was practically the only thing she had that preserved her dignity. After a moment, she smiled ironically.

"So you have your bride," she muttered, tossing back the covers to see that she was still in the clothing she'd been in the night before, down to her shoes. "I lost and you won."

"That is the gist of it."

"And you expect me to go quietly?"

"I expect you to honor your word."

She swung her legs over the side of the bed, but she was moving slowly because of her aching head. "I fully intend to honor it," she said. "But I also told you that I would give you the title and the wealth and we could go our separate ways. I do not expect you to treat me as if my position matters. You are free to do as you please."

Thor watched her a moment before lowering his bulk into the nearest chair. His gaze remained fixed on her.

"*Déchet*," he said. "You expect me to treat you like your husband did?"

She looked at him sharply. "Where did you hear that?"

"You told me all about it last night."

She blinked, realizing she probably had in her drunken state. She didn't get drunk often but knew that when she did, she talked. Somewhat embarrassed, she averted her gaze.

"So you know," she mumbled. "Robert called me rubbish and useless. I assume you will do the same."

"Then you assume wrongly."

She glanced at him. "Is that so?" she said. "That would be… different."

"Given that is all you know, I am sure it will be."

She tried to stand up but was hardly able to get to her feet. "You needn't pretend that I will not be a wife in name only," she said. "And do not think that it bothers me—as long as you provide me coinage to do as I please, I will not trouble you. Edingale shall be yours along with the armies of both Tamworth and Stafford, but not Tamworth Castle. It belongs to the de Marmion family because an ancestor of mine made a bargain with the Duke of Normandy to keep his lands except for Tamworth Castle and some surrounding land, which the Norman family de Marmion control. The rest belongs to me."

He watched her as she gave up trying to stand and simply sat there. "I am going to ask you a question, my lady, and you will be perfectly truthful with me," he said. "Will you do that?"

She shrugged. "I have nothing to hide."

"Do you like living the way you do?"

It took her a moment to register what he had asked her. Brow furrowed, she looked at him again. "Having my freedom?" she said. "What else is there for me? I seek entertainment every night. I eat in fine taverns. Do I like it? It is my life. It is what I do."

"Does it make you happy?"

She had to think about that. "Happy?" She snorted softly. "I suppose. I do not know what being happy means. Am I content? I am not un-content if that is what you mean. I have had to make my life any way I can."

It still wasn't a straight answer, and Thor continued to watch her. That white hair was a shiny, silky mess, all over her head and face and shoulders as if a tempest had brushed it, and she was pale this morning, indicative of the fact that she didn't feel very well. He also noticed that when she spoke, she had the slightest lisp, which he found rather sweet. She looked like such an angel.

But she led a devil's life.

"I have had the night to think about this marriage and I would like to make a proposal to you," he finally said. "Will you listen?"

She sighed heavily. "Speak, then. It cannot be worse than what I have already endured, so do your worst."

He leaned forward in his chair, elbows on his knees and his hands hanging. "I do not know why Robert did not utilize his wife in the proper manner, but that is not a mistake I intend to make," he said. "I have a few questions before I make the proposal, if you will indulge me. As the Earl of Tamworth and Stafford, I will assume control of Stafford Castle and Edingale Castle. Is that correct?"

She nodded, yawning as she pushed some of that hair away from her face. "You will," she said. "There is also Amington Castle, a small garrison on the northern edge of the Tamworth earldom," she said. "There is also a London townhome."

"Is that where you have been staying?"

"Aye," she said. "It is on Coleman Street, near Moorgate. It is called Basinghall House. It is a de Wylde property that belonged to my father, and when you marry me, it will become yours."

He motioned to her clothing, which was rumpled and stained. "Is that where I should send for something appropriate for you to wear to our wedding?"

She looked down at herself. She was wearing a surcoat and shift that was sloppy at best, but she liked it that way. "I do not have anything better than what you see," she said frankly. "I do not like attracting attention to myself. If I wear fine clothing, some might think I have money, and that could lead to unwanted confrontations. I do not travel with guards, so it is best that I appear as if I do not have wealth."

He pondered that for a moment. "You are one of the wealthiest women in England, yet you travel unnoticed and live like a peasant," he said. Then he shook his head. "Remarkable."

"Why?"

"Because someone has done you wrong, my lady. Very wrong."

She frowned. "Why do you say that?"

He gestured at her dress in general. "I am going to say something, and I hope this does not offend you, but you have been treated poorly your entire life to the point where you do not know how to behave or how to act," he said. "I assume it started with your father, who favored your brother over you, and then it continued when you wed de Tosni. Has no one ever told you that you deserve to live like a countess?"

Caledonia wasn't sure how to answer him because it was clear that no one had ever said that to her. "I am what you see," she said. "What do you want me to say?"

Thor shook his head with regret. "My lady, I am going to tell you how our marriage is going to be and what I say may shock you," he said. "It may come as a surprise for you to hear that I do not intend to give you coinage and send you on your way."

That puzzled her thoroughly. "You're not?"

"Nay," he said. "Because I will need you."

Her eyes widened and she leaned away from him. "You… you *what*?" she said, suddenly uncertain. "Why do you need me?"

He lifted his big shoulders. "Because I do not know Tamworth or Stafford," he said plainly. "You do. You know everything. You will be extremely valuable to me as my wife, as my chatelaine, and as my advisor as I learn about the earldoms.

If you think for one moment I want you away from my side, you would be wrong. De Tosni was a fool to discard you the way he did. Mayhap he did not need you in any capacity, but I do. Will you help me?"

That was a question Caledonia had never heard before. Ever. Thor could see the wheels of thought turning in her eyes, those dark eyes that, as he'd discovered last night, weren't actually brown. They were simply the darkest shade of green he'd ever seen, with brown around the edges. He could see in her expression that this was a woman who had never been told she was wanted in her entire life, and as a man who had a mother he loved and several sisters, Thor found that incredibly cruel.

Had she truly been treated so poorly?

"My lady," he said quietly when she didn't answer right away. "*Caledonia*. May I call you that? I hope I am not being too forward when I tell you that last night, I had some insight into the life you have led and I do not think anyone has ever shown you the respect you deserve. I would like to change that if you will let me. My parents have an excellent marriage, and I had always hoped for the same. I do not want the kind of marriage that you and de Tosni shared. I want a wife who will work with me, who will help me, who will tell me when I'm wrong, who will laugh at me when I stumble, but one who will also reach out a helping hand to pull me to my feet if I do. Does... does anything I've said sound appealing so far? Or do you truly want to live a drunken life in the vaults of Gomorrah?"

Caledonia was watching him with an expression he'd never seen on her features before. Her face had always been hard. So very hard. But at the moment, he thought he saw something hopeful there. He saw... warmth? Joy? He couldn't tell because when she realized that he was studying her, she averted her gaze and looked at the floor.

"It is a fantasy," she said quietly. "Marriage is not like that."

"My parents would beg to differ."

"Then they are an exception to the rule."

"Would you not want our marriage to be an exception to the rule?"

She sighed heavily, still looking at the ground. "I… I do not know," she said. "I must think. Let me… think. Please."

Thor knew it had been a lot to take in, especially for someone who had come from a marriage where she had been treated like an annoyance. What he was offering her was foreign at best.

A fantasy? Maybe.

But it was a fantasy he wanted.

"You can think all you wish," he said. "I simply wanted to tell you what my expectations were. However, what I do want to settle is the fact that when I go to Stafford, you will go with me because I really do need your help. Will you at least accompany me there?"

She hesitated a moment before nodding. She didn't speak, but she nodded.

That was all Thor needed.

Standing up, he headed for the chamber door. "Good," he said. "You have my thanks. Now, I will summon a bath for you and find some ladies to help you dress for the day."

Her head came up. "Did you not hear what I said?" she said. "I do not have anything finer than what you see."

He paused by the door, winked at her, and opened it. After stepping through the panel, he shut it quietly behind him, leaving Caledonia feeling disoriented, confused, but also the slightest bit… giddy. She'd never had a man wink at her.

You idiot! she thought to herself.

But that didn't stop her from smiling.

The day, as Thor had planned it, was in motion.

CHAPTER SEVEN

"THERE IS SOAP in my eye!"

Caledonia squeezed her stinging eye shut as a maid poured water all over her head and face, rinsing off the slimy soap that smelled of lavender and rose, something that had been scrubbed into her skin and hair until everything was fresh and tingling.

All of it under the direction of a rather dictatorial young woman.

After Thor had left Caledonia with a wink and a smile, he'd returned a short time later with a beautiful young woman at his side. She was petite, with luxurious red hair and the same bright blue eyes that Thor had. It didn't take a genius to figure out they were related, even before Thor introduced her as his youngest sister, Lady Nicola de Reyne.

It was Nicola who took charge of preparing her brother's bride, from dresses she brought with her to a bathtub that had been filled with hot water and floating rose petals. Nicola had brought three servants with her, women who moved efficiently to their mistress' orders, and that had included stripping Caledonia of what she was wearing and nearly drowning her in the bathtub she currently sat in. Lots of soap, lots of scrubbing, and the final insult was rinsing her hair with flat ale that stung her eyes and did nothing to help her aching head.

Meanwhile, Thor must have been standing outside of the chamber door, because Nicola kept going to the panel and talking through it. It seemed that they were debating about what dress Caledonia should wear, as if she didn't have a say in the matter, and when she was finally scoured within an inch of her life, she was pulled out of the tub and plopped in front of the hearth that had a steady fire in it. The wood crackled and popped as she was vigorously dried, all of which aggravated her aching head, until Thor passed something through the door to Nicola, who brought it over to a table near Caledonia. It was a basin that contained some kind of liquid, and Nicola made a compress out of the rag that was in it. She had Caledonia lean forward as she put a cold compress smelling strongly of mint on the back of her neck.

It was enough to elicit a groan of relief from Caledonia.

After that, she didn't much care what Nicola did to her. Her head was forward, the compress was on her neck, and the servants went about drying her hair in front of the heat. Nicola gave the order to remove the tub, and it was promptly withdrawn as Thor stood in the doorway and supervised. But his gaze soon moved to his betrothed as she sat in front of the fire wrapped in several towels. It wasn't improper because she was covered up, but Nicola kicked him out and shut the door in his face once the tub was removed.

She could hear her brother complaining through the closed panel.

"He asked me to help, so I am helping," Nicola said as she approached Caledonia. "Now he wants to come in and bother us, but we do not need his help. He can wait until the final product is presented."

Caledonia's head was still down, but she assumed that Nicola was speaking to her. "You have been most helpful, my lady," she said, though she felt as if she'd been beaten on a rock like a pile of laundry. "I hope it was not too much trouble for you."

Nicola knelt on the ground next to Caledonia so she could look her in the eye. "It was no trouble at all," she said. "I was already at Westminster."

Caledonia could see her from the corner of her eye, as it was difficult to turn her head with the compress on her neck. "Are you visiting?"

Nicola shook her head. "I serve at court," she said. "My mother sent me to the queen two years ago. I do not think I have ever seen you, my lady. I hear you are the Countess of Tamworth and Stafford."

Caledonia's initial impression of Nicola, aside from her being rather bossy, was one of kindness. Strangely enough, it was. The woman was decisive and gave orders, but she also had an easy manner about her. Even now, in speaking to a woman she didn't know, she smiled and seemed very interested in her. That put Caledonia at ease somewhat.

"I do not travel in the same social circles that you do because my husband was not part of that crowd," Caledonia said after a moment. "Do… do you like it at court?"

Nicola shrugged. "Mostly," she said. "These days I help Lady de Dreux with her children, and I do like being around the children."

"Who is Lady de Dreux?"

"Beatrice," Nicola said. "The king's younger daughter. She and her children have been at Westminster for some time and I have been tutoring the older children."

Caledonia smiled politely. "How clever you must be," she said. "Are you married, my lady?"

Nicola grinned, but it was an embarrassed gesture. "Not yet," she said. "I am the youngest of eight children and the youngest daughter, so my parents are in no hurry for me to marry even though there is someone I am sweet on."

One of the servants took away the cold compress to refresh it, and Caledonia sat up straight as another servant continued to dry her hair. "Ah," she said. "Then I wish you well, my lady. I hope he is sweet on you, also."

"He is," Nicola assured her. "At least, he'd better be. A de Winter is very hard to tame, you know. They are notorious for dodging matrimony."

"De Winter?"

"Aye," Nicola said, rising from her kneeling position. "The House of de Winter. They are great supporters of the king, you know. They have an enormous army."

"Where are they from?"

"East Anglia."

"I do not know them," Caledonia admitted. "But I also do not travel in military circles."

Nicola's gaze lingered on her. "When you marry my brother, you will," she said. "But do not worry. I will help you all that I can so you know who people are and who are friends and who are foe. You will not be alone in this, I promise."

Caledonia found those to be comforting words. She wasn't used to anyone comforting her, or even being kind to her, so Nicola de Reyne was a new experience altogether. Long ago, when she fostered at Prudhoe Castle, she had friends there, young ladies she trusted, but once she married Robert, those friendships faded away. She didn't stay in touch with them like she should have, mostly because her attention was on Robert and their turbulent relationship. Sometimes she wondered what became of Lady Carina and Lady Estelle, but in a way, she was glad they couldn't see what had become of her.

It occurred to her, however, that her direction in life was changing. She was marrying a de Reyne, a man who said he wanted her by his side. He needed her help. That was still an astonishing concept to her. No one had ever needed her. No one had ever wanted her, but Thor evidently did. And Nicola, his sister, was being quite kind to her.

Was it possible her life really *was* changing?

Or were these people only pretending until the marriage was completed?

Caledonia pondered those very things as Nicola smiled at her and headed over to the bed where all of the dresses she had brought with her were laid out very neatly. Caledonia remained by the hearth as the servants finished drying her hair, but she could see the dresses on the bed. She could see yellow and blue and orange and even a red one as Nicola pawed over them. Nicola held up the yellow one, which was silk and quite lovely, but she evidently didn't think that one was good enough because she picked up the blue one that was right next to her.

"Blue symbolizes purity," she said, holding it up for Caledonia to see. "But that is usually worn by women who have never been married before, so mayhap this isn't the right one for you."

Caledonia was precluded by responding because Nicola was making the decision that the blue dress simply wasn't appropriate. It was a very pretty dress, but it was off the table as the yellow dress and the orange brocade were held up for inspection. After a few moments of consideration, those dresses were put aside with the blue dress. That left the red dress, but when that was picked up, Caledonia could see another dress underneath it.

That dress was silver.

"This one," Nicola said with confidence, picking up the silver dress that, upon closer inspection, was more an icy shade of blue than actually silver. "This is exquisite and very nearly matches your hair. I think you should wear this one."

Yet again, Caledonia had no say in the decision-making process. Nicola seemed to know what was pretty and what was appropriate, so Caledonia let her select the wedding dress. Truth be told, she really didn't care. As Nicola had said, she had already been married once. She had already been through a large wedding mass with hundreds of guests and had already been through an enormous wedding feast that her parents had paid for. Robert had only been mildly attentive to her for the duration, spending a few moments at the start of the feast with her, but he quickly retreated to his group of friends and proceeded to get drunk.

That had led to a disappointing wedding night.

As Nicola laid the silver dress back on to the bed and begin to hunt around in the jewel box she brought with her for the appropriate adornment, Caledonia's thoughts turned toward her wedding night with Robert. He had been married before and had therefore taken little time with his new bride, who had gone to his bed a virgin. She'd had no idea what to expect because the only thing she'd been told about it had been by Lady d'Umfraville when she fostered at Prudhoe, but also by the silly gossip and speculation of her fellow wards. At that age, girls were curious about the act of intercourse and most of them tended to listen to the servants, who had spectacularly misin-formed tales to relay. It had made the marriage night both terrifying and titillating, but in her case, it had been uncomfort-able and embarrassing.

It occurred to her that she was about to face that again with Thor.

That very realization put Caledonia in a rather quiet and apprehensive mood as Nicola went about dressing her for her wedding mass. She remained wrapped up in the linen towels even after her hair was dry, because Nicola and the servants wanted to dress her hair before she donned her clothing. Caledonia sat and brooded in front of the fire as Nicola went to work.

The first thing Nicola did was heat up a hair iron in the hearth. That was used to roll Caledonia's thick, rather straight hair into curls that were then gathered up and piled on the top of her head, like an enormous bun. Nicola had set aside a section of hair that was braided and wrapped around the base of the bun. The result was absolutely elegant because it looked as if Caledonia was wearing a silver crown. Nicola made it look clean and chic by rubbing a slight amount of fragrant pomade on her hands, made from almond oil, and ran that over the hair that was leading into the bun to tamp down any stray hair. The result was a very groomed appearance with a beautiful smell from the almonds.

After her hair was finished, Nicola focused on Caledonia's face. Caledonia had never worn cosmetics in her life, but Nicola had brought some with her. Fashionable noblewomen wore rouge and lip stain, and plucked their brows. Caledonia had beautifully shaped brows with a natural arch, so there wasn't much to do with them, but Nicola did put a bit of tint on her cheeks and on her full lips. Just a hint, enough to give her a bit of a glow.

After that, it was simply a matter of putting on the dress, so Nicola had Caledonia stand up as the servants peeled away the drying towels. A shift went on first, sleeveless and soft, and over that went the silver dress, made from the finest silk and embroidered with silver thread. It had a daringly low neckline, lined with white rabbit fur, and the long, belled sleeves were lined at the ends with the same white fur. Because of the silver embroidery around the neckline and bodice, Nicola put silver earrings on Caledonia's earlobes that dangled, with a sapphire in the center surrounded by small pearls. After that, she stepped back to admire her handiwork.

"There," Nicola said, smiling. "Now you look like the Countess of Tamworth and Stafford. Let me ask my brother to see if he thinks you look like a bride."

With that, she sent one of her servants to the door to summon Thor, who was still standing right outside in the corridor. He immediately entered, taking about five steps into the chamber before his gaze fell on Caledonia. She looked at him, he looked at her, and the man came to a dead stop.

He simply stared at her.

"Well?" Nicola said. "What do you think? Does she look like a bride?"

Thor couldn't answer her right away. His gaze was riveted to a woman in silver that, he was positive, was a figment of his imagination. He'd never seen anything so exquisite in his entire life. Lifting a hand, he pointed at her.

"Caledonia?" he said in disbelief. "It is truly her?"

Nicola laughed softly at his reaction. "What do you think?"

He shook his head in amazement, coming a little closer as

his eyes drank in the sight. "I think she looks like an angel," he said honestly. "She's the most beautiful thing I've ever seen."

Caledonia had been holding her breath when he came into the chamber, fearful of his reaction, but his unbridled response had her blushing furiously. She was suspicious of it at first, but from the expression on his face, she could see that he meant it. Having never been praised in her life, not by her mother or father or dead husband, hearing someone compliment her beauty was a new experience entirely. Embarrassed, she lowered her head so he wouldn't see her flaming cheeks.

"Lady Nicola is to be praised," she said. "This is all her doing."

Thor came forward, a smile playing on his lips. "She had quite a bit to work with," he said. "How do you feel?"

Caledonia shrugged. "My head feels a little better."

"I meant about your appearance. How do you *feel*?"

Caledonia was going to shrug again until Nicola put a hand-held mirror in her grip. That forced Caledonia to look at herself, to see what Thor and Nicola were seeing, and she found a woman she hardly recognized staring back at her.

Thor was right.

She *was* beautiful.

And it scared her to death.

"This… this isn't me," she finally said, tossing the mirror aside and backing away from Thor and Nicola. "People will laugh!"

The smiles faded from Thor and Nicola's faces. "Why would they laugh?" he asked. "Caledonia, you are an exquisitely beautiful woman. You should dress like this every day. It would make me the proudest man in England."

Caledonia was becoming increasingly distraught. "Why?"

she said. "This is not what I look like."

"It is exactly what you look like."

"People will think I am pretending to be something I am not!"

She was starting to tear up, and Nicola wasn't sure why, but Thor did. He'd had a glimpse into her world and suspected what the trouble was.

It was going to be difficult to convince her otherwise.

"I do not think so," he said with quiet firmness. "Caledonia, listen to me. You are the Countess of Tamworth and Stafford, only no one has allowed you to shine before now. They've kept your light dimmed, your beauty hidden behind those peasant clothes you wear, but that is going to stop now. You deserve to wear the finest clothing. You deserve to be respected, and I swear to you that I will do just that. You needn't fear that people will ridicule you because that will not happen."

"It will!"

"It will not because you are finally assuming the position you were born to assume. This *is* you."

The tears were falling from her dark eyes as she looked at him, trying to determine if he was really telling her the truth. She felt terribly uncomfortable, but she also felt as lovely as she'd ever felt in her life. Wiping at her eyes, she picked up the mirror again with a shaking hand, studying herself in it. But after a few moments, she closed her eyes and set the mirror down again.

"God's Bones," she whispered. "I am so uncomfortable."

Thor took a few steps in her direction and ended up standing next to her. "Why?" he murmured.

Caledonia shook her head, bewildered. "I… I am not sure," she said. Then she snorted ironically. "Believe it or not, when I fostered, my mother made sure I had lovely clothing. I had some very pretty things. But once I married Robert, he did not want to spend any money on my clothing and there did not seem to be a need. I was never head of my own home, or the hostess of a great feast. There was no reason to have fine clothing, so I suppose seeing myself like this… It is a shock."

Thor couldn't help it. Reaching out, he put a couple of fingers under her chin and forced her to look up at him. When their eyes met, he smiled.

"You were born to look like this," he said softly. "You are magnificent, and if I must tell you that every day for the rest of your life until you believe me, then I will."

Her cheeks flamed again; she could feel it and he could see it. But she couldn't manage to tear her gaze away from those piercing blue eyes.

"And this… this pleases you?" she asked, running a hand over her sleeves. "You do not mind that I dress like this?"

"After we are married, we will go into London immediately and I will commission a dozen dresses just like this for you," he told her. "Then I am going to take the peasant clothing you wear and burn it."

He chuckled. She chuckled. As they lost themselves in what was perhaps their first true moment of warmth, Nicola invaded their space and put her arm around Caledonia's shoulders.

"I will go with you," she said. "I will help you pick out the styles that are fashionable right now. We will spend all of my brother's money!"

She said it so gleefully that Caledonia laughed softly. "I do not wish to make a pauper out of him," she said. "I can pay for it."

Thor shook his head. "You will do no such thing," he said.

"As your husband, it will be my pleasure. I will have the most beautiful wife in England, much to the envy of everyone. Let me be proud."

Caledonia didn't know what to say to that. Nicola hugged her, reassuring her that she *was* beautiful and that it was fine for her to feel beautiful, and Caledonia simply went along with it. Kindness had lowered her defenses, and she could feel herself being swept away by people who seemed genuinely interested in her.

It was an amazing feeling.

"Do you know that no one has ever asked me how I feel?' she said, looking at Thor. "You are the first man that I can ever recall asking me that."

He snorted softly. "It will not be the last, I am certain," he said, his eyes glimmering. "Are you ready to be married? To me?"

For the first time since she met him, Caledonia felt confident in her reply. No hesitation. If this was to be her destiny, then it was time to get on with it.

She was ready.

"Aye," she said after a moment. "I am ready. Are you?"

His answer was to extend an elbow to her. With a smile on her lips, Caledonia accepted. With Nicola trailing after them, they made their way over to Westminster Cathedral.

⁜

"Wait! Stop this marriage!"

Thor, Caledonia, and Nicola had barely stepped into the vast cathedral when someone was shouting. Thor wasn't even sure it was meant for them until Caledonia came to a halt and hissed.

"Damnation," she muttered. "It's them."

Thor's brow furrowed as he looked at the men coming out of the shadows, heading in their direction. "Who?" he asked.

Caledonia's eyes never left the approaching pair. "My uncle and cousin," she said with disgust. "Lord Dordon and his son Domnall."

That had Thor's expression cooling. It was nearing the nooning hour, when Henry had declared that a priest should bless their marriage at the noon mass, but they'd arrived a little early, so the king wasn't present. His father wasn't there, either.

Now, he had to face Caledonia's uncle and cousin alone.

"Nica?" he said to his sister. "Take Caledonia away from here. Take her into the nave. Go, now."

"Wait," Caledonia said, grasping his arm. "I should be present. Please do not send me away."

Thor looked at her, realizing he was about to do what her former husband had done—pushed her aside so he could deal with something he knew nearly nothing about. He'd asked for her help as he assumed the earldom.

Perhaps it needed to start here.

"Very well," he said, putting his hand over hers as it grasped his arm. "We shall face this together, then."

He could see that his response surprised her. She'd been prepared for him to deny her, to shrug off her worth. But he didn't. She continued to grip his arm as Rotri and Domnall came to within a few feet of them. Before Thor could speak, she put out a hand to stop them.

"Come no closer," she said. "You are not welcome here, Uncle. What do you want?"

Rotri and Domnall came to a halt, looking between Caledonia and Thor, but they were mostly looking at her.

"Praise the saints that we have this moment to speak," Rotri said, sounding sincere. "We've not seen each other in a long time, dear niece. I've sent word to you, but you have never responded."

Caledonia was hard. "There is a good reason for that," she said. "I do not wish to speak with you, Uncle. I want you to leave me alone. Do you not understand that?"

Rotri extended his hands imploringly. "How can I leave you when your father asked me to watch over you?" he said. "It was your father's wish that I become your guardian should anything happen to him. That is what I must speak with you about."

Caledonia's brow furrowed in confusion. "What *are* you talking about?" she said. "I am a grown woman. I do not need a guardian."

"You are a young woman with a vast fortune," Rotri said. "Of course you need a guardian to help you manage it."

She cocked an eyebrow. "You mean that you've found another way to try to get your hands on my money," she said. "It will not work. I do not need a guardian and you cannot make me."

"What's this?"

The question came from behind Thor and Caledonia. Everyone turned to see people coming in through the cathedral entry, with Gage de Reyne leading the group. The question had come from him, but Henry and his courtiers, including Daniel de Lohr, were behind him. In fact, many people were coming in and Rotri looked a little startled by it, but the moment he realized the king was approaching, he began to call out to him.

"Your grace!" he said. "Your grace, I must speak with you! This marriage between my niece and this… this knight must not go forward. I have the right to forbid it!"

"He does not," Caledonia said flatly, shouting because her uncle was. "He is only trying to gain control of the Tamworth fortune through his lies."

"I am not lying!" Rotri shouted at her.

But Caledonia waved him off. "My father knew you were a liar," she said. "Why do you think he kept you at arm's length and only gave you a small allowance at the death of your father? You and Domnall spend everything you have and then some. And now you want the Tamworth fortune!"

"Me?" Domnall entered the conversation. "Why am I being dragged in?"

Caledonia turned on him but Gage was there, putting himself between her and her pestering relatives.

"Enough," he said, putting out his hands in a gesture of silence to both parties. "You will not behave like common rabble in front of the king. Now… what is this all about?"

Rotri started to speak but Gage shut him up, turning to Caledonia instead. "My lady?" he said politely. "Would you enlighten us?"

Caledonia eyed her uncle angrily before replying. "When Thor and I entered the cathedral, my uncle and cousin were here," she said. "I do not know how they knew we would be here, but they must have been waiting for us."

Gage lifted a dark eyebrow. "And they ambushed you?"

Caledonia nodded briskly. "In a sense," she said. "They have been trying to force a marriage between my cousin and me and have done everything in their power to push the issue. This is just another tactic in their latest war to gain the Tamworth wealth."

Rotri started to protest, but Gage shut him up with a pointed look. "You will have your turn, de Wylde," he said before returning his attention to Caledonia. "Why did they come this time, my lady? To stop the marriage between you and my son?"

Caledonia's eyes narrowed as she looked at Rotri. "With more lies," she said. "My uncle says that my father wished for him to be my guardian, but that is simply not true. My father would have never requested such a thing."

Daniel came to stand next to Gage, listening to the situation. He knew Dordon distantly, but he'd never had any direct interaction with him. What he'd heard about him, however, wasn't flattering.

"You are a little old for a guardian," Daniel said, interjecting an unbiased opinion into the mix. "Women your age and older usually do not have guardians, so even if your father requested such a thing, it is a ridiculous suggestion. Moreover, your uncle would have to show proof. Does he have proof?"

"I do!" Rotri would no longer be silenced. "I have sent a servant to my seat to retrieve the missive. Until it can be brought back here and examined, there must be no marriage."

"How old is this missive?" Daniel asked. "When was it sent to you?"

That had Rotri showing the first signs of hesitation. "A few years ago," he said evasively. "But it clearly states my brother's wishes when it comes to the Tamworth properties."

Daniel and Gage looked curiously at one another. "A few years ago and she would have been married to de Tosni," Gage finally said, returning his attention to Rotri. "It makes no sense that her father would have asked you to become her guardian if she was already married."

Rotri was being backed into a corner by the logic. "I… I do not know why he sent it, but clearly, those were his intentions," he said. "That means that she cannot be married without my permission, and I will not give it.”

“But she can be married with mine.” Henry, who had been listening to the argument, stepped forward, eyeing Rotri with disdain. “Go away with your false claims, Dordon. Be glad that I not have you arrested and thrown in irons.”

That seemed to settle it, but Rotri was nearly beside himself. He thought he’d had such a strong argument but the king didn’t seem to think so.

“This is unjust, your grace,” he pleaded. “The Tamworth wealth must be properly managed, and my brother wished for it to be managed by me.”

Henry turned to the guards behind him. “Take him and his son away,” he said. “I do not wish to see them again.”

To the symphony of Rotri and Domnall’s loud protests, both men were hauled from the cathedral by guards who were a bit rougher than they should have been, but Rotri and Domnall put up a bit of a fight. When they were clear of the cathedral, Henry turned to Thor and Caledonia, smiling weakly.

“Fool,” he muttered. “Now, shall we commence? I have arranged for a feast tonight to celebrate the uniting of de Wylde, a very old family, and de Reyne, one of my most powerful supporters. This is a moment to be celebrated. A moment that almost did not arrive.”

He meant the litany of vehement protests from both the bride and groom, who now seemed to be oddly agreeable. Caledonia looked like a goddess, and Thor seemed content about it. Even Gage seemed puzzled by the evidence before him but didn’t argue it. He was done with that. Henry got what Henry wanted and his son would become the next Earl of Tamworth. It wasn’t a bad deal, at least for Thor, and with all things considered, Gage knew he was gaining a powerful new ally in his son. Lose a knight, gain an ally.

He could live with that.

"But a moment that is here," Gage continued, smiling at his son and the thoroughly radiant lady beside him. "My lady, welcome to our family. We are honored to be tied to the House of de Wylde."

He took her hand and kissed her on the forehead, gently leading her toward the nave where everyone was starting to gather, including the Archbishop of Canterbury, the very man that Rotri had been trying so hard to see. William Chillenden was a former monk who found himself in a very powerful position after the long tenure of Boniface of Savoy. Henry wanted William, but his son, Edward, wanted another man, so there had been a bit of a power struggle going on between father and son. Therefore, William was more than willing to do anything for his king, including this marriage.

As he prayed over the couple and intoned the wedding mass, Lady Caledonia de Tosni became Lady Caledonia de Reyne.

Much to the surprise of Henry and Gage and perhaps even Thor, she didn't seem sorry about it in the least.

CHAPTER EIGHT

Westminster's great hall

"I UNDERSTAND THAT you wish to see your new property, but I would like you to remain in London for now," Henry said. "There will be all the time in the world to visit Stafford and Edingale and survey your empire, Thor. For now, I want you here."

That wasn't what Thor wanted to hear. He had been the Earl of Tamworth and Stafford for about nine hours and very much wanted to see his lands and property. He wanted to visit the villages and meet the people. All of the things he'd watched his father do, a man whom he very much wanted to emulate as a good and right earl. There was responsibility with that position and he wanted to give it his best effort.

But Henry had his own wants at the moment.

"Your grace, forgive me for speaking up, but there are reasons why I would like to go north now," he said. "The lady has been away from her properties for quite some time, leaving the management to knights sworn to her father and to her former husband, and it is very important that I make my presence known and inform them that these are now my properties. I fear that men left to their own devices like that may be stealing me blind, or worse."

"You cannot know that."

"That is true, I cannot," Thor said, his manner more impassioned than usual. "But keep in mind that these properties have been without a man in command for years. Tamworth died several years ago and Stafford has been gone for two. I feel that it is crucial to make my presence known as soon as possible because there is no knowing what the Edingale or Stafford knights are doing with my lands, my villeins, or anything else that belongs to me. They may have taken everything for themselves, especially with Caledonia away in London. Do you at least understand my concern, your grace?"

Henry did. He nodded reluctantly. "I do."

He still didn't seem willing to capitulate, but Thor wasn't giving up. He went for the throat. "You may want me in London at this time and I respect that, your grace," he said. "Nothing has given me more pleasure than serving you as your Lord Protector. But you know, and I know, that there is nothing happening in London at this time that *requires* me. Everything is peaceful and there are no pressing matters. I am simply asking for a month or two to survey my new lands and establish my earldom. I will return to you once I have done this."

Henry eyed him, sighing heavily before taking a sip of the tart red wine that he had provided for the feast that he was currently the center of. Not the new Earl and Countess of Tamworth and Stafford, but the king. As it should be, at least in his world. The feast had been going on for about two hours at this point and they'd eaten seven courses so far. More were coming. He'd had Thor by his side nearly the entire time, a man who was supremely obedient to his king, even to the point of taking him away from his bride. Now, he was demanding more of Thor's service when Thor rightfully wanted to see the properties he'd acquired. Not that Henry blamed him.

Moreover, the man was right.

He sighed heavily.

"Very well," he said, realizing he couldn't fight him any longer. "If that is your wish, then go north and establish your dominance over any foolish knights who believe your properties belong to them."

"Thank you, your grace."

"But once that is done, I expect you back at Westminster immediately."

"Of course, your grace." Thor hesitated a moment before continuing. "I intend to take my men with me. I have a feeling I will need their assistance in whatever I am facing."

Henry nodded, noting de Reyne's knights at the table just to the left of the dais. Clayne, Truett, and Darius were a powerful trio, one Henry liked to have at his disposal, but he supposed it wouldn't be too much trouble to allow them to go with Thor. The new earl had earned the right to have men sworn to him by his side. Besides… Henry had pushed hard enough for this marriage, so it made him look foolish to resist Thor's requests now that he had what he wanted.

"Take them," he said. "And I will send you with five hundred royal troops to infiltrate your armies. That way, they cannot revolt against you if they are diluted with men loyal to me."

Thor scratched his head, knowing that was a possibility. "Let us hope they will swear their allegiance to the new earl and that will be the end of it, your grace," he said. "But I thank you for the additional troops. It is much appreciated."

Henry gestured to the knights off to his left. "Those three will help you settle your earldom," he said. "They are quite formidable. But I want them back, too."

Thor looked over at his men, who lifted their cups in his direction. "The four of us have been together for a long time," he said. "As I said, I will need them. And we will all come back."

"Can I not at least keep de Winter with me?"

"I am nothing without Darius commanding my armies."

Henry made a face and looked away. "Then take him," he said. "Leave me without anything at all, Thor. You are taking the best men with you, including yourself."

"But only for a short time, your grace," Thor said, fighting off a smile at the incensed old man. "I promise we will return. We will always be sworn to you."

Henry shrugged and turned to complain about the situation to Gage, who had no sympathy for him, and Thor was finally able to breathe a little and speak to his new wife. But he knew Caledonia hadn't been lonely. She and Nicola had been chatting like magpies the entire time, and Thor watched his new wife as she giggled with his sister, a side of her he'd not seen before. She was… lighthearted. Her expression was very nearly joyful. Was that the same woman he'd drunk with the night before? The woman who traveled in the shadows and did as she pleased? The change was truly astonishing. Caledonia was whispering something to Nicola, and he heard his sister gasp.

"And he was *nude*?" Nicola was saying. "Dancing in front of you, he was nude?"

"Who was nude?" Thor wanted to know. "What are you talking about?"

When Caledonia and Nicola realized he was listening, they tried to stifle the giggles but couldn't quite manage it.

"I was telling your sister about Gomorrah," Caledonia said. "I was telling her about the time I—"

Thor put a hand up. "Stop right there," he said. "You will not tell my maiden sister about that den of debauchery. My father will be quite unhappy if he finds out Nicola knows something of Gomorrah."

Nicola was quite titillated with stories of the most notorious guild in all of London. "Did you know that you can pay for anything at Gomorrah?" she said, clearly enraptured by the very idea. "*Anything?* Men will dance for you and women will feed you. Callie says that—"

"I told you to stop," Thor warned. "Another word and I will tell Papa, and he will have something to say about it."

Nicola turned her nose up at him. "Don't you dare tell him anything," she said. "There are plenty of things I could tell him about you, but I never have. Are you willing to betray that trust?"

Thor wasn't. He and Nicola had a special bond and he loved her dearly. But she was also annoying and petulant at times, and his palm fairly ached to spank her.

He pointed a finger at her.

"Fine," he said impatiently. "But no more stories about Gomorrah."

"I promise."

She was lying. He knew she was lying. *She* knew that *he* knew that she was lying. But Thor let it go, giving her a final glare before turning to his wine as Caledonia watched the interaction between brother and sister.

It reminded her of her relationship with her own brother.

"Do not trouble yourself, Blue," she said. "I will not tell her anything more, I promise."

He looked at her, puzzled. "Blue?" he repeated. "Why did you call me that?"

Her dark eyes were glittering at him. "Because you have the bluest eyes I have ever seen," she said. "All I can think to call you is Blue Eyes."

"My name is Thor."

"As you wish, Blue."

He snorted softly and shook his head at her impudence. "Have it your own way," he said. "But I have just been given permission to go north and survey my new earldom. That is good news, don't you think?"

Caledonia's smile faded. "Home?"

He could see that she didn't have the same enthusiasm as he did, and his joy at the situation faded. "Aye," he said. "Why? Do you not want to go?"

She nodded. But her eyes teared up and she lowered her head, struggling with her composure. That wasn't like her, this bold and fiery woman, so concern swept him. He instinctively put an arm around her shoulders, leaning into her so no one could hear their conversation except his nosy sister, who leaned in also.

"Will you tell me why this troubles you?" he asked softly.

Caledonia was so used to keeping her feelings and thoughts to herself that to have someone ask her—actually ask her—was quite new. It was also embarrassing. She wasn't used to having so much attention on her, but she quickly realized something— she liked having Thor so close. He was big and powerful, yet there was a gentleness about him. At least, when it came to her there was. He'd been that way from the start. It was a warm trap of human kindness, but a trap that filled something in her life that had been lacking.

A most tender trap.

"Truly, it is nothing," she said, struggling to shrug off his concern. "I… I simply have not been home in a while. Will we be going to Stafford Castle, too?"

Thor nodded. "That is where your children are, isn't it?"

As she nodded, Nicola gasped. "I did not know you have children," she said. "How many do you have?"

Caledonia was trying to discreetly dab away the moisture around her eyes. "Three," she said. "Three daughters."

Nicola sighed in delight. "How very lovely," she said. "What are their names?"

"Jane, Janet, and Joan."

Nicola was delighted by the idea of three daughters. "Such pretty names," she said. "Very fashionable."

"I was not allowed to name them," Caledonia said, showing little interest in Nicola's compliment. "Their father named them in accordance with his mother's wishes."

Nicola didn't quite understand that. She and Caledonia hadn't really discussed her marriage to Robert beyond the fact that she had once, indeed, been married to the Earl of Stafford, so she wasn't sure how to respond. Looking to her brother for direction, she could see him shaking his head faintly. That told Nicola it wasn't a good subject to be on, but she wanted to give the woman comfort.

"I… I am sure they are beautiful and intelligent," she said, trying to sound positive and helpful. "Won't it be good to go home and see them? How long has it been?"

That was the wrong question to ask. Caledonia lowered her head even further and the tears came again. Nicola had no idea what she'd said wrong. But Thor had an inkling; he gave Caledonia a gentle squeeze and spoke softly and reassuringly.

"If you are worried about the old nun who is their guardian, I will send her away if you wish it," he murmured. "I will chase her away the moment I set foot in Stafford and you will never see her again. Would you like that?"

The tears were forgotten. Caledonia's head came up and she looked at him in shock. "You… you would do that?"

"If you wish it. Do you?"

Did she? Since the day the girls were born, she had wished it. She had prayed for it, hoped for it, but Robert had been determined to keep the old hag who had raised him in charge of his own children. The nurse who'd poisoned Caledonia's own children against their mother and there had been nothing she could do about it.

It never occurred to her that Thor would.

If her marriage to him only brought her the removal of that beastly woman, then it was well worth it.

"Aye," she said hoarsely. "I wish it. Very much."

He winked at her and leaned back, removing his arm from her shoulders. "It would be my pleasure, Lady de Reyne," he said, using her new title for the first time. "Therefore, there is no more trouble. We are eager to return and see to your children. I suppose they will become mine, too. I should like to meet them."

Caledonia couldn't keep the tears at bay after that. Thoughts of seeing her children and perhaps actually being a family with Thor undid her. She stood up quickly, rushing from the hall as Nicola tried to follow her, but Thor held her back. Instead, he went after his new wife because, to be perfectly truthful, he wasn't entirely sure that she wasn't running from him again. He just wanted to make sure. She'd been quite compliant since he brought her back from Gomorrah, so he wanted to make sure she hadn't lulled him into a false sense of security. He didn't want to say he didn't trust her not to head back to Gomorrah if it all became too much for her, but…

Fortunately for both of them, Thor found Caledonia out in the corridor. She was standing near one of the big windows that overlooked a small courtyard that was enclosed on all four sides. There was a small garden in the center of the courtyard and he walked up behind Caledonia, lit up by the moonglow. When he looked at her, he could see her profile. She was looking at the moonglow, too.

He could see the tears on her face.

"If I said something to upset you, I apologize," he said. "Mayhap I am behaving clumsily, though I do not mean to."

Caledonia was shaking her head before he finished getting the words out of his mouth. "You are not clumsy," she said, turning to him. "I am. Clumsy and disoriented and over-whelmed. I've spent so much of the past ten years alone, without any comfort or support, that when I am show such regard—as your sister has, as you have—I feel as if this entire situation is unreal. How can any of this be real? Am I lying in a stupor at Gomorrah, dreaming all of this? I fear that I am."

He shook his head. "If you are, then I am dreaming right along with you and my mother would box my ears if I went to Gomorrah for entertainment," he said, watching her smile weakly. "Therefore, the answer is nay—you are not dreaming. This is real."

"And you are always this kind?"

He fought off a smirk. "Not always," he said. "But for you, I will make an exception. But while we are on the subject of Gomorrah, what were you telling my sister about a nude dancing man?"

Caledonia snorted softly and wiped the tears from her face. "Yesterday, when you came to Gomorrah with your men, I had been watching a young man with fine muscles dance for me," she said, watching him frown in disapproval. "Have no fear; I never touched him, or any of them, and they never touched me. I did not go to Gomorrah for the touch of a man. I went because there was always something to drink or eat or smoke to inhale that changed my reality. It took me away from this life I live and, for a brief moment, made me forget. That is all."

He could understand that. "And I do not judge you for it," he said. "But I want to make it clear that from this day forward, I do not want you to go to Gomorrah. If it is adventure you seek, I will give it to you. If it is excitement, I will provide it. I will provide whatever you desire, my lady. But I do not want you returning to Gomorrah again. Please."

He spoke the last word as sort of a plea, one Caledonia took seriously. He didn't order her not to go. He was asking, and because he asked, she would comply. She'd told him she didn't want another marriage like the one she had with Robert—and based on her experience with him so far, she didn't think Thor would be another Robert. Perhaps he would provide something solid and meaningful, something she wouldn't have to fill with hazy days at Gomorrah just to forget her terrible life.

She was willing to take that chance.

"As you wish," she said.

He smiled faintly. "Thank you," he said. "And I hope that if something is troubling you, you will tell me. I have never been very good at guessing women's thoughts, so you would be doing a me a great favor if you simply tell me what you are thinking or feeling."

She cocked her head, looking at him seriously. "Do you

mean that?"

"I never say anything I do not mean."

She lifted her eyebrows, baffled by his request and subsequent answer. "Forgive me for asking, but are you *always* this understanding?"

He chuckled at her bewilderment. "I have two sisters and a mother, women who are greatly revered in my family," he said. "I also have three aunts and a variety of female cousins, so I have grown up with women. My father always impressed upon my brothers and me that women were to be treated carefully and kindly. I also have a grandmother who would thump me on the head if she felt I was being rude, and I do not like to be thumped on the head."

She smiled because he was. "I will not thump you on the head," she said. "But I will tell you that I grew up with men who cared nothing for what I felt or thought. My brother was a little different, however. He was kinder to me than most. Losing him was quite devastating, to be honest. Constantine's death changed everything in my life. There were days when I both wept for him and cursed him. So… if I ever seem overwhelmed or confused by a kindness, know that I will try to become accustomed to it. It has simply been a long time since I have experienced it from those close to me."

"I will become easier with time," he said. "When you realize that you will be a true wife to me, and that I will do my best to be a good husband, you will learn to trust me. We will build that trust together."

She took a deep breath, squaring her shoulders with summoned confidence. "I hope so."

"Will you tell me something?"

"If I can."

"Why did you cry and leave the hall? Was it something I said?"

She nodded. "It was, but not in the way you think," she said. "You cannot know the times I have prayed for the guardian of my children to drop dead or go away and never return. I had resigned myself to her outliving all of us. But what you said… sending her away… Those are words I have only heard in my dreams."

He could see how emotional she was about it. Lifting her hand, he kissed it. "Then may all of your dreams become reality," he said softly. "I will admit that I am somewhat surprised that we have come to an agreement so quickly. Given the fact that we were both opposed to this marriage at the first, I thought we would be in for more difficulty."

Caledonia had never had anyone kiss her hand like that. She could feel his hot breath against her flesh and her heart was beating furiously. It was difficult to breathe much less keep a coherent thought in her head, but she understood what he was saying. Truth be told, she was a little surprised, too.

"You mean that you thought I would give you more trouble," she said. "Mayhap I had planned to, but you are convincing when you want to be, Blue."

He shook his head at her nickname for him. "Blue?" he repeated. "You could not come up with something more original than that?"

She started to laugh. "What, for example?"

He shrugged as he lowered her hand. "Who knows?" he said. "Handsome? Hercules? Dolt? I have an uncle who is addressed as Bull. That is manly enough."

She laughed softly. "Let us not forget *El Martillo*."

He pointed a finger at her. "Exactly," he said. "Why can you not call me the Hammer?"

"Hammerhead?"

He rolled his eyes as her laughter grew. "Nay," he said flatly. "Not that. Forget I even brought it up."

She had her hand over her mouth to soften the laughter that was coming forth. "Were you truly a mercenary?"

He nodded. "A very good one," he said. "So was my father before he married my mother. There is excellent money to be made in fighting other men's wars."

"What made you stop?"

He shrugged as the laughter faded. "I missed my home, I suppose," he said. "I came home and served my father for a while until Henry offered me the position of Lord Protector. That has also been lucrative."

"Will you continue as Lord Protector?" she asked. "Even after assuming Tamworth?"

He nodded. "For now," he said. "But at some point, I would simply like to manage my earldom and live my life for me and not for the king. Speaking of such things, you will have to educate me on Edingale and its functions. I should like to know all I can before we arrive."

Caledonia nodded. "I can tell you more about Edingale than I can Stafford," she said. "Robert kept things to himself, so we will have to examine his ledgers when we arrive. I can tell you very little about Stafford Castle, but remember that it belongs to my eldest daughter. When she marries, the title goes to her husband."

He nodded. "I recall," he said. "But until that time, I will do my best with it. What about the knights who are now in command? Will I have trouble with them?"

Caledonia shrugged. "The Edingale knights will be easier, I

think," she said. "A pair of brothers who served my father and grandfather. They are quite old, but they are obedient."

"What about Stafford?"

She sighed. "That may be more difficult," she said. "I never had any control over them. They only had interaction with Robert."

"How many are there?"

"Three," she said. "The captain of the army and two subordinate knights. I know that the captain was with Robert's father and the two subordinates are his relatives. Cousins, I think."

Thor considered that for a moment. "Then we will return to Stafford first," he said. "I think we should settle that location first before moving to Edingale."

"I agree," she said. "But… but I think whatever you do, you will succeed with them. You are an elite royal knight, after all. How can they possibly contest you?"

He smiled, hearing praise in that statement. She hadn't been free with it other than to tell him that he had the bluest eyes she'd ever seen. But there was a rapport starting between them that was warm and friendly. The defenses she had kept up against him since their introduction had come down, little by little, and they were both starting to feel comfortable. He was grateful. The last thing he wanted to do was keep up a running battle, so he would settle for her being overwhelmed and disoriented as their new life began. It was better than the alternative.

But he was very much hoping the warm and friendly mood would continue.

Speaking of warm…

"I suppose it is growing late," he said, looking around to the torch-lit corridor. "The feast will go on through the night whether or not we are in attendance. Are you weary? Do you wish to retire for the night?"

It didn't occur to Caledonia what this night truly meant until she realized it was her wedding night. He was suggesting they retire. *Together.* She knew what that meant. With that awareness, she averted her gaze as she nodded her head.

"If that is your wish, of course," she said. "I suppose I am a bit weary. I've not recovered from the *gorzalka* completely."

Thor lifted his eyebrows. "Nor have I," he said. "I will probably still be woozy from it for days to come."

She grinned. "I would not be surprised," she said. "I do not see me drinking that terrible stuff again for a very long time, if ever."

Thor reached out to take her elbow. "The next time I wage war, I'll bring some of it. It will surely defeat whomever I am fighting without any bloodshed."

"Your secret weapon?"

"I will conquer the world with it."

With a grin, Caledonia let him turn her around and together they headed for the door that would dump them out into a smaller section of the bailey. Thor's chamber was across the compound and beneath a blanket of brilliant stars, they headed away from Westminster's great hall and toward the beginning of their marital life together. Quite differently from even a day ago. Or so Thor hoped.

He hoped it would be like this for them, always.

Little did he know what lay in store.

CHAPTER NINE

"WHO ARE YOU looking for?"

Nicola gasped as the voice came from behind her. She'd been peering from the doors where Caledonia and Thor had disappeared, trying to catch a glimpse of them, and someone had snuck up behind her. Whirling around, she came face to face with Darius de Winter.

"It's you," she said, hand on her chest to ease her pounding heart. "I was looking for Thor."

Darius threw a thumb in the general direction of the gate-house and apartments. "I am certain he is gone by now," he said. "If I had a new wife, I would not spend my time in a hall talking to other men. I would be with her. Always with her."

The mood rapidly turned into something warm and wistful. Painful, even. Nicola's gaze drifted over the big, handsome knight, a man she'd been in love with for the past two years, if not longer. She'd only been sixteen when she fell for the brawny, dark de Winter son, a man who served her brother, but she hadn't hinted to her mother about him until about a year ago, mostly because she knew that her parents would say she would have to wait because her older sister, Diara, wasn't betrothed yet. Happily, Diara was now betrothed to a d'Avignon son, a marriage that was to take place in the autumn when the leaves turned colors.

That left the path open for Nicola now.

"I know you would," she whispered. "I've not spoken to you in two days. I've missed you."

"And I've missed you," Darius said in that sweet, low voice. "You look beautiful tonight."

Nicola looked down at her blue silk dress. "This is your favorite dress."

"It is."

"I wore it for you."

"And it is much appreciated."

She looked at him again. "Do you suppose you can meet me tomorrow?" she said. "I can break away from the princess for a short time. Mayhap you can meet me by the river in our usual place?"

He nodded, but his expression was serious. He took a step toward her. "I shall, but seeing your brother marry has made me realize that I no longer wish to waste time," he said. "I have done as you have asked. I have refrained from speaking to your father. But you were eighteen years of age last month, Nica. I want to ask your father's permission to marry you. May I, my dearest? Is there any reason we must still wait?"

Nicola went to him, wrapping her hands around his as he held them against his broad chest. "He may be feeling senti-mental with my brother getting married," she said softly. "And my sister is marrying in a few months. I've always felt we should wait until Diara marries before we speak with him."

Darius wasn't happy with that answer. "I fail to understand why," he said. "It is not as if our feelings are any secret."

"I know."

"Your father knows I am going to ask for your hand."

"I *know*."

"Then why the delay?"

"Because she is my youngest daughter and I am a selfish man."

It wasn't Nicola who replied, but Gage. He stood just a few feet behind them, but they'd been so wrapped up in one another that they never heard him approach. They were tucked over in a darkened corner of the hall and the ambient noise had masked his movements. Nicola gasped and yanked her hands out of Darius' grip, but her father had seen them. He knew they had been holding hands. In fact, he'd seen Darius approach Nicola as she peered from the doors, looking for her brother, and that was when he'd left the dais and headed for them. He had to chuckle at a daughter who thought he hadn't seen the obvious.

"Christ," he muttered, looking at Darius. "Did you get rope burn on your palms with the speed with which she removed her hands?"

Darius smiled weakly, holding up both hands, palms out. "Am I bleeding, my lord?"

Gage pretended to peer more closely. "Not that I can see," he said. Then his gaze moved to his daughter. "Nica, surely you do not think I am oblivious to this. I've known for a while now. You needn't pretend any longer."

Nicola tried not to look guilty. "I am sorry, Papa," she said. "I wasn't pretending anything. At least, I wasn't trying to."

"But you think I did not know?"

"Did Mama tell you?"

He pointed to his face. "I have eyes, lass," he said wryly. "I would have had to be blind not to see what is going on between you and de Winter. When I asked Thor if there was something I should know, he said that it was not his secret to tell. And your mother did mention something, but very little. Of course I figured it out. I am not a fool."

Nicola went to him, putting her hands on his arm. "Are you angry?"

Gage shook his head. "Angry? Nay," he said. "But I would have been angry if either one of you had spoken to me about this before you came of age. Darius, the time has come to be plain. Am I to assume you have intentions toward my daughter?"

Darius wasn't prepared for this conversation. Not really. He'd been planning it in his mind for nearly two years, ever since he became aware that the flame-haired de Reyne sister couldn't take her eyes off him, but she had been adamant that they must wait until her older sister was married. Now that the sister was planning her nuptials, Darius was more prepared to move forward, but he hadn't expected it at this very moment. He'd been caught off guard. Yet the moment was here and he stood straight, focused on the mighty Earl of Ashington.

His future father-in-law.

He hoped.

"I do, my lord," he said with as much bravery as he could summon on such short notice. "Lady Nicola has forbidden me to speak to you until she came of age, and—"

"That was wise."

Darius nodded even though Gage had cut him off. "Indeed, my lord," he said. "When Lady Nicola told me the time was right, I planned to approach you and ask for her hand."

"And?"

Darius took his eyes of Gage long enough to look at Nicola,

who was gazing back at him with a hopeful expression. But not just any hope.

Hope for a future for them both.

Darius smiled faintly at her.

"I am not asking for just any hand," he said quietly, returning his attention to Gage. "I am asking for the hand of a woman who is as kind as she is wise. Who is as beautiful outside as she is in character. The hand of a woman I would die for a thousand times over and cherish forever as my wife. The hand of a woman I will love with all my heart until the end of all things. That is what I wanted to say to you. Should you grant me permission to marry her, know that there is no moment in my life, now or evermore, that will be as important to me as this moment. The moment that the woman I love becomes mine."

By the time he was finished, Nicola was teary-eyed and Gage had a smile on his face. It had been a powerful and touching speech, articulated by a man who had spoken from his heart. In fact, Gage chuckled softly.

"Good God, Darius," he finally muttered. "Is *that* what you were going to say?"

"It is, my lord. Every word of it."

Still smiling, Gage looked at Nicola, who beamed up at him with the anticipation that all young women in love had. He could read it in her eyes.

It would be difficult to refuse, in any case.

"And this is what you wish, sweetheart?" he asked. "This would make you happy?"

Nicola nodded, flicking a tear from her eye. "Look at him, Papa," she said. "Is he not the most handsome, most wonderful man in all of England?"

Gage laughed softly, kissing her on the cheek. "He is fairly wonderful, aye," he said. "If you are terribly sure, then I see no reason to deny him. Darius, you have my permission to marry Nicola. But let us wait until after her sister is married, please. Let this be Diara's year. You two can marry next spring."

With a shriek of delight, Nicola threw her arms around her father's neck, knocking him sideways. He barely had time to recover his balance before she let him go and rushed at Darius, hitting the man so hard with a flying hug that he grunted at the impact. All the while, she was squealing with happiness. Rubbing his neck where she'd hit his throat, Gage chuckled at the unbridled display of joy.

"Nicola, show some decorum," he admonished her, but he knew it was futile. "You nearly smashed your betrothed into the ground with that display. Did she break any ribs, Darius?"

Darius had one arm around Nicola as she danced around, trying to calm down as her father requested but being unable to do so. "If she did, they will heal," he said, rubbing his sternum. "Thank you, my lord. From the bottom of my heart, thank you."

Gage nodded, watching the two of them beam at each other. "Be happy together," he said. "That is all the thanks I require."

"I will do my best, my lord," Darius said. "You have my word."

"That is good enough for me," Gage said. "But I am afraid I did not come here to only discuss a betrothal. I have come with some news that will see you two separated for a time."

Both Darius and Nicola looked at him with concern as she stopped dancing about. "What is it, Papa?" she asked.

"My lord?" Darius said, overlapping her.

Gage could see how upset they were, right on the heels of having been so deliriously happy. He felt rather sorry for them.

"It is not terrible," he said, holding up a hand to ease them, "but Thor wants to go to his new properties in the north and, Darius, you will be going with him. Henry has given his permission."

Darius looked at Nicola to see her reaction before returning his gaze to Gage. "For how long, my lord?"

Gage shrugged. "I do not know," he said. "As long as it takes Thor to survey his properties, I suppose. It will not be forever."

Nicola reached out to take Darius' hand, holding it tightly with both of her small, warm mitts. The poor woman looked as if she wanted to cry.

"Thank you for telling us, Papa," she said. "And thank you… for your permission to marry. It means so very much to us."

Gage smiled faintly at his struggling daughter. "He will not be gone forever, sweetheart," he assured her. "You are to marry a knight. You must become accustomed to him leaving you from time to time. Lord knows I've left your mother enough times that I'm surprised she remembers me when I return. It is simply part of the profession."

They were encouraging words, but Nicola wasn't willing to give in to them. She was looking at Darius with sad eyes, and he wasn't sure how to comfort her. They'd been separated before, but this was different. They were newly betrothed.

He didn't want to leave her, either.

"Even if I must go, it will not be tonight or even tomorrow," he told her. "Shall we go back into the hall with your father?"

Nicola nodded, but she still held his hand tightly. "Aye."

It wasn't exactly proper for her to be holding Darius' hand as they returned to their seats, so Gage held out his hand to her, encouraging her to come with him.

"Let us return and see what course is next," he said. "Henry told me that there were at least fourteen courses for the feast, so let us see what delicacies are in store for us."

But Nicola shook her head. "Not at the moment," she said. "Will you let me have a few moments alone with Darius, Papa? Please?"

Gage looked at Darius, who seemed rather hopeful about having a few moments alone with her, too, so he relented.

"Just a few," he said. "And when you come back in, do not be holding hands, please. A proper distance, at least until the betrothal is announced."

"When will that be, Papa?" Nicola asked.

"Soon," Gage said. "We will have a celebration just for the announcement, as befitting the House of de Reyne and the House of de Winter. This will be a great union."

Nicola snorted. "I am marrying a man, not his family."

Gage snorted softly. "You think so, do you?" he said. "I will let Darius explain that one."

With that, he headed back toward the dais, leaving Darius and Nicola alone in the shadows. When he was out of earshot, Nicola turned to Darius.

"I am going with you when you leave with my brother," she said.

Darius frowned. "You cannot go with me."

"I can," she insisted. "The new Lady de Reyne has no ladies-in-waiting. She will need my guidance, so I am therefore going with her. I will convince my brother that it is necessary. It is simply coincidence that you are going, too."

He grinned. "You are a clever little devil, Nica."

She smiled arrogantly. "I know," she said. "But you like me

that way."

His smile softened. "I love you that way," he murmured. "And you cannot possibly know how happy I am right now."

She squeezed his hand. "I do," she whispered. "Because I feel that way, too."

"Shall we return to the hall?"

"With pleasure."

Standing a few feet apart, they came out of the shadows and made their way through the hall and the crowds of men as the next course was brought out, which happened to be fish in a sweet sauce. Perhaps it wasn't their betrothal feast, but it would do. Their love, and their joy, would finally come to fruition.

For Nicola and Darius, it was the best night of their lives.

03

"WHAT DID YOU say?"

"I said it has been one of the best nights of my life."

Caledonia stared at Thor a moment before breaking into a grin. "I thought that was what you said," she said. "I suppose I had to hear it twice to believe it."

"Why?"

They had reached Thor's chamber, the one with the windows that overlooked part of Westminster's outer bailey, and Thor was in the process of lowering the oilcloth blinds that would keep out the light and dust and weather as Caledonia stood awkwardly near the end of the bed.

"Because you speak of our wedding night," she said. "It is true that tonight has been quite pleasant. Surprisingly so. But my only experience with a wedding night, with Robert, was hellish. It is difficult for me to think of any night that has to do with a wedding as a wonderful thing."

Thor smoothed down the end of the oilcloth he was working on. "Given how de Tosni treated you, I can only imagine how bad it was," he said. "If you wish to tell me, that is your choice. I will not force you to."

She lowered her gaze. "I feel as if all I do is complain and tell you horrible things, but the reality is that everything I tell you is the truth."

"Then what is the truth about your wedding night with de Tosni, if only so I do not make the same mistake?"

She drew in a long, pensive breath. "You will not," she said. "But the truth is that my father sold me to Robert. I was a bride for a price."

Thor secured the bottom of one of the oilcloths to the nail on the windowsill. "He *sold* you?"

She nodded. "De Tosni had been married before," she said. "His wife died and he had two daughters, who also died, so he offered my father a high price for me—and my father, being greedy, accepted. Instead of Father paying Robert a dowry, Robert paid a groom's dowry that went straight into my father's coffers. On our wedding night, Robert got drunk and wanted a son so badly that he insisted the priest who married us pray over us as we consummated the marriage. I lay on my back as my husband forced himself upon me, and all the while a priest stood over us and prayed that I would conceive a son. Our eldest daughter was born exactly nine months later."

Thor was looking at her in horror. After a moment, he shook his head in disgust. "God's Bones," he muttered. "I am so very sorry that happened to you, Caledonia. You did not deserve that."

There was something vindicating in his sympathy, something that made her feel comfortable in telling him the horrors of what she'd experienced. She'd never really spoken of them to anyone, and Thor was so easy to talk to that it simply came out whether or not she wanted it to.

"That is not the worst of it," she said, trying not to feel ashamed. "My husband bedded me six times during our marriage, and each time, he had the priest come and pray over us. Every single time. Once I conceived, he would not touch me again until he wanted another child."

Thor grunted in revulsion. The more he heard about Caledonia's life, the more pity he felt for her. He was a man with a heart, something he'd struggled with as a mercenary those years ago because mercenaries were men who were, by definition, heartless in most cases. They were only in it for the money. It was true that Thor had been driven by coin because, as a second son, he had to earn his way in life, but he struggled with the unconscionable things that mercenaries sometimes did. He endured it for a few years before he finally came home, eager to return to a position that was more honorable than fighting for money and not faith or loyalty. But even in all of the situations he'd experienced in his life, some good and some bad, Caledonia's tales of woe were difficult to hear.

The demons she had went deeper than he'd thought.

"I am glad that you feel you can tell me these things," he said after a moment. "I cannot imagine it is easy for you to remember them, much less speak of them. You honor me."

She looked at him. "I tell you because I think you should know," she said. "We are married and you should know that right now… What we are about to do… I am so terrified that I want to run. It is taking a great deal for me not to."

He went to her, reaching out to take her hand. "You have been, since I have met you, one of the most courageous people I have ever known," he said. "You are fearless as few people are. You speak of horrors from your past without breaking down and screaming about them, and I cannot imagine how much control that takes. But I want to promise you that although we must consummate this marriage, I will make sure you are comfortable with it."

She looked at him, contemplating his words. They were strong and sincere. "Are you *truly* this kind?" she finally asked.

He laughed softly. "You have asked me that before," he said. "Would you prefer I push you around and shout at you?"

She grinned. "Not particularly, but I keep waiting for you to lose your temper or do something unsaintly," she said. "Truly, you are too good to be true. You are an angel. Mayhap I should call you that instead of Blue."

"I'm no angel," he assured her. "Remember—I was a mercenary. I kill on command. And a host of other unsavory things I will not discuss."

"But you will not have a priest stand over us tonight when we… as we…?"

He shook his head so she didn't have to finish. "I'd throw him out the window if he tried," he said. "What we do tonight should only be between the two of us. We do not need an audience."

That seemed to give her comfort. At least she was convinced that this wouldn't become a spectacle. She looked at the chamber, at the dresses that were still lying on the bed where Nicola had left them, at shifts and shoes and other things that were lying about.

"Then I suppose I should pick up these things your sister brought so we can clear the bed," she said, moving to collect the yellow and blue and red garments. "I like her, by the way."

"Nicola?"

"She's very sweet."

"She's a pest and should be swatted away," he said sternly, but he saw her grin. "But… she is kind when she wants to be."

Caledonia put the garments on the nearest table and began picking up the shoes on the floor. "Thank you for sending her to me."

"You are welcome."

"Does she live in London all the time?"

"Mostly."

"A pity," Caledonia said. "I feel as if we could be friends. A pity she cannot go with us to Edingale."

He was standing over by the bed, loosening his belt. "Would you like that?"

She looked up from the table of clothing. "That would be impossible," she said. "Your sister serves at court."

He shrugged. "I can speak with my father," he said. "It might help you to have Nicola around while we are settling in. She could be of great assistance."

Caledonia didn't want to get her hopes up. "Do you think she would be willing to leave court?"

"She has been here for a few years," he said, removing his belt and slinging it across the nearest chair. "It's possible she would be pleased with a change of duties and a change of scenery. Besides… Darius is going with me. If she knows he's going, she'll want to come."

"Darius?"

"The man she is in love with."

Caledonia nodded in understanding. "She mentioned there was someone special," she said. "From the House of de Winter?"

"A very powerful family that mostly resides in Norfolk," he said, moving to remove his heavy tunic. "Do you know of them?"

"I confess that I do not."

Thor loosened the laces on the blue tunic. "A big family with several branches," he said. "Most families are like that. Mine certainly is. But de Winter has two main branches—Davyss de Winter, son of Grayson, who was Henry's champion years ago, and then Hew de Winter and his sons, Darius and Dirk and Rafe. Hew and Grayson were brothers. There are more de Winters scattered about, but those are the main branches of the family."

As he was talking, he'd pulled the tunic over his head, exposing his naked torso. Caledonia found herself staring at him, hearing his voice but not hearing his words. Everything seemed to get fuzzy and her face suddenly grew quite hot. He had a magnificent chest, broad and powerful, and his arms were heavily muscled. Even his shoulders and neck had muscles. The man was, quite honestly, one of the most perfect specimens she'd ever seen—and given her regular visits to Gomorrah, she'd seen plenty.

"Caledonia? *Callie?*"

It occurred to her that he was calling her name. Speaking to her. She'd been so consumed with staring at the man's naked flesh that she hadn't heard him at first. Sheepishly, she tore her eyes away from his chest and looked him in the eye.

He grinned.

"Did I bore you too much with the de Winter lineage?" he asked.

She shook her head. Then she nodded. Flustered, she turned back to the garments on the table. "I am sorry," she said.

"I suppose I'm simply weary. It has been a long day and, I swear to you, I think I'm still a little drunk from last night."

He laughed softly. "As I said, I think we both are," he said. "But the way you were looking at me… you're not going to ask me to dance, are you?"

Her cheeks flamed at the question but she couldn't help but giggle. "It had not occurred to me," she said. "But I will say that the last time a man in your state of undress danced for me, he removed everything and tried to seduce me. I assume that is what you are going to do, too?"

"Was he one of the forty-nine men you've taken to your bed?"

She burst out laughing, turning to look at him. "I really have not taken forty-nine men to my bed," she said. "I only said that because you said you'd taken nineteen to your bed. I wanted to shock you."

He was grinning. "I have a confession."

"What?"

"I really have not taken nineteen women to my bed."

"Then how many?"

His eyebrows lifted. "Do you really want to talk about now?"

She cocked her head curiously. "Why?" she said. "Are you ashamed?"

He shook his head. "Nay," he said honestly. "But I shouldn't think the subject of my past lovers would be of any interest to you."

Caledonia pondered that statement for a moment. "I suppose it is not," she said. "But I do want to know one thing."

"What is that?"

"Will I be competing with a memory of a former love?

Someone who has marked your heart?"

"Will I be competing with the same?"

"I asked you first."

Thoughtfully, he sat down on the bed. "When *El Martillo* was in Zaragoza, he met a woman named Lenore," he said, speaking of his alter ego. "Lenore was the daughter of the man who had paid us a good deal of money to destroy a neighbor. Lenore was fiery and lovely and, in fact, reminds me of you a little. She was strong, like you. I admired that. But she was meant for another and that was disappointing. Did she mark my heart? She did. But I did not give it to her. I've not given it to anyone."

Caledonia appreciated the honest answer. "Thank you for telling me," she said. "I can truthfully tell you that there was one man in my life that I loved madly when I was fostering, but I was only eleven years of age and he was at least forty years, with a wife and sons and grandchildren, so there was no hope for me. I had so little love from my own father, and Sir Roland was so free with his hugs and kindness that it was natural I should love the man. I imagined we would marry someday in spite of his already having a wife, but his life was cut short when I was about thirteen years of age in a skirmish with some outlaws. It was an inglorious ending to a glorious man. It still makes me sad to think of it sometimes."

Thor had a gentle smile on his lips. "But you honor him every time you think of him," he said. "I promise you, a man who is well remembered will never die. He lives on as long as you speak of him."

"Then he will live as long as I have breath in my body."

Thor grinned. "That is a fine tribute," he said. "But I must say I am glad he did not marry you. If he had, you would not be here now."

"True," Caledonia said, watching him pull both boots off and set them by the bed. "Should I undress now, too?"

He looked at her. "Would you like me to help you?" he said, indicating the garment she wore. "The ties are in the back."

She nodded and turned around. He stood up from the bed and came up behind her, unlacing all of the careful ties his sister had put in place. He could see the elegant nape of her neck, her alabaster skin, and his attraction to her was nearly overwhelming. He didn't want to seem overeager and scare her, not when she was already spooked, so he gently untied the back of her gown when he really wanted to yank it off her and explore what he had before him.

Damn, but the woman was fine.

"Would you like me to take the lead?" he said softly. "If you simply want to experience this moment and not do any of the work, I am happy to do what needs to be done. If you are comfortable with that."

She turned around to look at him, the dress coming loose as she did. "I know you are trying to be considerate," she said, appearing a little nervous now that her clothes were coming off. "I appreciate it, truly, but I have done this before. But I will be honest when I tell you that I took no pleasure with it."

"Would you like me to show you pleasure?"

"*Can* you?"

His lips twitched with a smile. "I can," he said. "I will if you will let me."

She took a deep breath and squared her shoulders. "Very well," she said. "What do I need to do?"

His smile broke through and he moved so that he was standing in front of her, gazing down at her. "You need to promise me that whatever I do, you'll simply let me do it," he said. "I promise that I will not hurt you and if you are uncomfortable, you can tell me to stop, but if you are brave—and willing—just let me do what I want to do."

It didn't seem unreasonable. Considering this had been a dreaded duty her entire married life with Robert, she wasn't entirely sure that Thor could show her any pleasure, but she was willing to let him try. He'd not lied to her yet, but more than that, she was quite attracted to him. His close proximity made her cheeks heat up and her heart race. That had never happened with Robert, so perhaps this would be different.

It was yet one more chance she was willing to take with him.

With resignation, she nodded.

Thor didn't hesitate. He grasped her arms and steered her toward the bed, laying her back on the mattress with incredible gentleness. Once she was flat on her back, looking up at him with some apprehension, he slanted his mouth over hers—gently at first, but with growing passion when he realized how sweet she tasted. True to her agreement, Caledonia simply lay there and let him kiss her.

She might have even kissed him back.

That emboldened him.

The dress had to come off. With his mouth fixed to hers, he pulled it down in one big yank, pulling it off her feet and lowering his big body on hers. She still had a shift on, a thin linen sheath, and his hands stroked her arms, her shoulder, before moving to her breasts. They were round and full, quite succulent under the shift, which was nearly transparent because it was so fine. His mouth left hers, blazing a trail of kisses down her neck, to her chest, before he moved to her left breast. He kissed it through the fabric before finally clamping his hot mouth on her taut nipple. Suckling her through the fabric nearly brought her off the bed, but not because she was frightened.

Because she liked it.

Their passion was gaining momentum by the moment. The more he suckled and probed her breasts, the more she writhed beneath him and the more aroused he became. Her response was innate, inexperienced, and honest. It only served to excite them even more.

At some point, she stopped simply lying there and letting him do as he wished. Her arms came up, going around him as he suckled her. He could feel her hands timidly touching him, knowing she was feeling what he was feeling, and he smiled as he continued to suckle. He'd hoped to awaken her a little and could see that he was succeeding. Caledonia's apprehension seemed to be gone as she arched shamelessly against his mouth, her body wanting to experience all he had to offer. It was everything she had been denied for all of these years. She had no idea that a touch could be so sweet, a kiss so tender.

She wanted more.

Thor wanted her so badly he could hardly think straight. He'd expected this experience to be slow and pleasant, but it was quickly turning into a roaring blaze. The more she responded, the more forceful he became. At some point, he stopped feasting on her breasts long enough to remove her shift and his breeches with it. Then they were nude on the bed, their limbs intertwining, flesh against flesh.

Thor was on fire.

He pushed his knees between her legs, pulling her knees apart. He trailed his fingers to her inner thighs and heard her moan softly, but he slanted his mouth over hers again and the sounds were muffled. Slowly, his hands moved up to the dark curls between her legs and delicately roved over the outer flesh.

Caledonia startled when she felt his fingers caressing her. He did not probe her, merely touched her, and it gave her the opportunity to become accustomed to his touch. Robert had never touched her there, except with his male member, so to feel Thor's hand down there was a new and arousing experience. She wasn't afraid.

In fact, she liked it.

Shockingly, she liked it.

Thor's fingers finally probed her, gently at first. Given the fact that she had given birth to three children, she'd had her share of midwives between her legs, and it wasn't a completely foreign feeling, but the way Thor was touching her most definitely was. He kept on with his forceful kisses, inserting his finger into her carefully and hearing her gasp at the penetration.

"Did I hurt you?" he whispered raggedly.

She shook her head. "Nay."

"Are you uncomfortable? Should I stop?"

All Caledonia could do was shake her head, winding her arms around his neck and timidly slanting her lips over his. Laughing low in his throat, Thor pushed two fingers into her, mimicking the thrusting rhythm that would soon be taking place. Her body throbbed and pulled at him and he could no longer wait to claim her. Removing his fingers, he placed his manhood against her.

Slowly, he thrust into her because he wanted to measure her reaction. Would it be too much? Would she resist? But Caledonia showed no signs of breaking, opening her legs wider for him in a gesture that had him on fire. Two full thrusts and he was fully seated, and then the primal rhythm took hold. He thrust into her again and again, feeling his climax approaching faster than he had believed possible. Beneath him, Caledonia moved with his body, wrapping her legs around his hips, pulling him down into her. Her hands, so still when they had begun, were now moving over him—his chest, his torso, his hips. When she touched his buttocks, however, it was his undoing—he released into her with a growl of satisfaction that shook them both.

Caledonia felt his member throbbing within her and knew what it meant. It was the only thing Robert lived for and then he was quickly gone. But she had actually been enjoying this moment with Thor so much that she was disappointed that it was over so quickly. Or so she thought.

Thor wasn't done yet.

Even after he climaxed, he continued to move within her, still full and hard. Thor wanted her to enjoy this as much as he had and moved his hands under her hips, holding her against him as he continued to thrust into her. Caledonia's body was responding, the heat in her loins like liquid fire that was blooming in intensity. Every time their bodies came together, sparks flew. She could feel them. More sparks and she was quickly approaching… something. She didn't even know what it was, but it was as if her entire body was lifting. Rising out of the bed. Then his last, hard thrust threw her over the brink and she experienced her first release.

Caledonia pealed a cry as her entire body stiffened with rapture. Thor's mouth descended swiftly on hers to muffle the cry as he felt her heated walls pull at him. Her first release was monumental. Her body was electrified by it. Given her reaction, he was fairly certain she'd never experienced one before.

He was glad it was with him.

Caledonia wasn't sure what had happened. All that she knew was that she had never before felt such rapturous pleasure. It came from the junction where their bodies joined, and she put her hand down there, curious and exploring, but was so sensitive that she immediately had another release as soon as she touched herself. Realizing where it came from, and how good it felt, she rubbed herself again and more ripples coursed through her. Thor, still embedded in her, remained where he was, feeling her body adjust to something it had never had the pleasure of experiencing before. He gently kissed her neck, her shoulder, her earlobe, as Caledonia fondled them both.

And then he grew hard again.

Thor didn't know how long they spent in a clutch, making love, fondling one another, acquainting themselves with something that was beyond simple pleasure. It was shocking and delirious and erotic. Caledonia's curious hands played with him long into the night.

And he let her.

CHAPTER TEN

Birmingham
Seven days later

CALEDONIA HAD TRAVELED this route many a time, but never like this.

Never like this.

When she had been quite young, she had traveled this road from Edingale to London with her family because of the London properties they held. Her father tended to like London in the spring and also in the autumn because the weather tended to be good. Summer in London was a sticky affair, with the humidity rising off the river that flowed gently through the city, and winters could be particularly brutal. Her father liked his own hearth and his own bed at Edingale during the winters because he was a man of creature comforts as he grew older.

Caledonia remembered traveling with her parents between London and Tamworth, never particularly exciting affairs, but simply something they did from time to time. They passed through a dozen villages that looked the same, with people that looked the same and cottages that were arranged mostly the same way, and none of them had ever stood out in her mind.

She considered the route to be unspectacular, and even when she married Robert and they would sometimes travel to London, she still considered the road between Stafford and London to be boring at best.

But this time, it was different.

This time, she was traveling with Thor. He had borrowed a small carriage from the royal livery so that she didn't have to ride on horseback for several days. Caledonia had only actually ridden in a carriage when she was a child because Robert wouldn't entertain the thought of providing any comfort for his wife when it came to travel, so as an adult, the only way she'd ever made the journey had been on the back of a horse.

Not this time.

Traveling with someone she actually wanted to be with was a different experience altogether. Somehow, the bumpy road didn't seem so bumpy and the drab villages didn't seem so drab. The food that they ate seemed to have more flavor and the daytime passed slowly while the nights passed too quickly. Since their wedding, Caledonia had spent every subsequent evening exploring him as she had on that first night. The day she married him was the day her life completely changed, and something she had once viewed as an unpleasant duty was now something she looked forward to.

Her duty in the bedchamber.

And Thor was the reason.

He really was too good to be true. In her opinion, there wasn't one thing about him that was imperfect. His manner, his appearance, his character... All of it was perfect as far as she was concerned. And she clearly wasn't the only one who thought so, because everyone he encountered, and everyone he worked with, seemed to have the highest regard for him. He was well liked by those who knew him, including his own wife, who even now was leaning her head out of the carriage to try to catch a glimpse of him toward the front of the escort. It wasn't as if he wasn't straining to catch a glimpse of her, also, because every time she sought him out, he seemed to be looking in her direction.

She waved, and he waved, and all was right in the world.

As this flirtation was going on, day after day, it was also true that Caledonia wasn't alone in the carriage. Nicola had somehow managed to attach herself to the escort heading to Stafford. As Thor had explained it, he felt that his sister could be a great deal of help, as they had discussed on their wedding night, to the new Lady de Reyne, and Nicola seemed more than willing to accompany her brother and his new wife to their new life. Caledonia had to admit that she was very glad because she genuinely liked Nicola, but it didn't take her long to figure out that she wasn't the young woman's focus.

A certain handsome knight was.

It took Nicola less than a day to confess that her father had given permission for her to marry Darius, but they were not going to announce it until after her sister's wedding. They didn't want to steal attention away. But given the fact that Nicola liked to talk, Caledonia suspected that everyone would know about the betrothal well in advance of the sister's marriage. In fact, all Nicola could talk about was Darius and their wedding—she spoke of where they would live and how they would live, and what names they would give their children. She had her whole life planned out, which Caledonia thought was rather sweet. She had spent an entire week listening to Nicola plan out her future.

It certainly was a different way of life than what she was

used to.

Spending so much time with Nicola had taken her back to the days at Prudhoe Castle and her friends that she had been so attached to. That had been a good time in her life, so the memories were pleasant and she was feeling happier than she had been in a very long time. In fact, she could never remember being quite so happy, which was completely foreign to her. But she also knew that she was about to face something at Stafford Castle that she wasn't sure she was ready to face.

Three little girls who thought she was a monster thanks to a certain nun.

They would be reaching Stafford Castle tomorrow, so tonight was their last night on the road and Thor had called a halt to the escort in Birmingham, which was about a day's ride south of Stafford. Caledonia knew Birmingham well, because both Stafford and Tamworth conducted their business there, including the bankers, so she was well acquainted with the city. She recommended they stop at Ye Olde Oak, a very old tavern that was quite well known and quite large. It was single-storied, but spread out in a group of cottages with a large common area in the middle where drink and food were served in any weather. It could accommodate many. There was also an enormous barn that had been converted into the tavern's common room and could easily shelter a few hundred people.

Thor sent Truett ahead to secure chambers for the night while he and Clayne headed back to the carriage where the ladies were riding. Caledonia stuck her head out just in time to see her husband approach.

"We'll settle in at Birmingham for the night," Thor said. "I've sent True ahead to secure rooms."

Caledonia smiled up at him as he rode atop his dark brown

horse with the gray mane. He was in full battle regalia, from the top of his helmed head to the bottom of his booted feet, a big man bearing big weapons. She recalled seeing him like this the moment they'd met in the darkness at Gomorrah and how frightening he'd been.

Fortunately for them both, she no longer found him frightening these days.

"Have you been to Birmingham often?" she asked.

Thor shook his head. "Nay," he said. "I think I have only been here twice, and that was passing through."

Caledonia looked up ahead, shielding her eyes from the afternoon sun. "It has an excellent market on Thursdays," she said. "And there is a large merchant district. People travel from all over to attend it."

"Good," he said. "So shall we."

She looked at him. "What do you mean?"

He gestured at what she was wearing, yet another borrowed dress from Nicola because her clothing was plain and she wanted to put some thought into her appearance for her new husband. He seemed pleased when she did.

"Because we can purchase fabric for you to have more dresses made," he said. "Is there a seamstress in town? Mayhap we should pay her a visit."

Caledonia nodded reluctantly. "There is a seamstress," she said. "A few that I know of, but..."

She trailed off and he lifted a dark eyebrow. "But *what*?"

She sighed, looking at her lap. "But the expense of all of this," she said. "Fine dresses are not inexpensive, angel."

Angel. She'd gone from calling him Blue Eyes or simply Blue to angel. It wasn't exactly a term of endearment for a man, but she thought it summed him up perfectly and he wasn't going to argue with her. He liked hearing her call him by a pet name, something that was a new experience for him. It made him feel special and adored.

Loved, even.

He'd been responding to it for days now.

"We have been over this," he said patiently. "You cannot go on wearing my sister's clothing for the rest of your life. More than that, you are my wife. I should like you finely dressed. What you wear is a direct reflection on my ability to provide for you."

She chuckled softly. She never could hold out long against his wishes. "Very well," she said. "If you are going to cry about it, I will have some new clothing made."

"I want to go!" Nicola leaned over, pressing on Caledonia as she looked at her brother. "I want to help pick the fabric."

Thor turned his head, looking on ahead as Birmingham loomed. "Speak with my wife," he said. "It is her decision whether or not she wants your help. But do not pester her if she does not."

"Of course I do," Caledonia said, smiling at Nicola. "I need your help. I have never had much of an eye for clothing."

"And jewelry," Nicola said, knowing her brother could hear her. "The Countess of Tamworth and Stafford should have magnificent jewelry. Darius said that Tamworth is wildly rich and you should look the part, don't you think? Make my brother buy you jewelry."

Thor did look at the carriage then. "And I am going to sew your lips shut and make you walk home," he said. "Do not push her if she does not want to."

"Who says she does not want to?"

They started to argue, and Caledonia threw up a hand to

stop them. "Jewelry would be very nice," she said to Nicola. Then she looked at Thor. "But I do not wish for you to spend too much. I would not get much use out of coffers full of jewels."

He flipped up his visor, smiling sweetly. "You should," he said. "If any woman in England could do them justice, it would be you."

Caledonia grinned like a silly fool at his compliment before glancing at Nicola. "Is he always like this?" she asked.

Nicola was giggling, too. "Always like what?" she said. "Like a stabbing pain in my backside? But aye, he is always like that. He can get around our mother with sweet words and smiles, just like he does with you."

Caledonia broke down laughing. "I meant to ask if he is always so kind."

Nicola eyed her brother, who was smirking at her, waiting for a typical sister's answer when it came to a brother.

"Aye," she said begrudgingly. "He is always so kind. I have several brothers, you see. Brian is the eldest and he looks like Thor, except that he had an accident several years ago, so he walks with a limp. He does not fight. Did Thor tell you that?"

Caledonia shook her head, looking at Thor. "Nay," she said. "We've not spoken much about his siblings, so I did not know."

"Brian can still fight," Thor said. "He broke his leg in battle and it never healed correctly. He is not agile in a fight, but he is an excellent commander."

"And this is your twin?" Caledonia asked.

"Aye," Thor said. "My mother said that I was holding on to Brian's foot when we were born. It is only by fate that he was born first."

"If you were holding on to his foot, it seems that you were

trying to hold him back."

Thor snorted. "Probably," he said. "But he is my brother. I adore him."

"We have other brothers, too," Nicola said. "Taite serves with the de Winters of Narborough Castle, but John and Hart serve at Ashington with our father."

"You have five brothers?" Caledonia asked.

"Six," Nicola said. "Keats is the youngest brother and is a trainer at Kenilworth Castle. He is Blackchurch trained, like Thor and Taite, and commands a high price as a trainer. Papa is very proud of him."

Caledonia looked at her curiously. "Blackchurch?" she repeated. "I do not know what that is."

"A training guild for elite knights," Thor said. "They only train the best of the best. I was trained there along with Taite and Keats, but John and Hart did not make it. Brian's injury prevented him from the intense training of Blackchurch."

"What do you mean, John and Hart did not make it?"

"They failed. If you fail at Blackchurch, they banish you."

"Is it terribly difficult?"

Thor nodded. "Blackchurch knights command a very high price because they have been so intensely trained," he said. "We can withstand anything. We know everything. We can accomplish anything. Why do you think I was so successful as a mercenary?"

On the road ahead, someone was shouting that that took Thor's attention. Caledonia watched him charge up to the front of the escort, unable to take her eyes off him. She had no idea that, beside her, Nicola was watching her. When she felt Thor's sister grasp her hand, the spell was broken and she looked at Nicola only to see that the woman was grinning at her.

"I think you are starting to look at my brother the way I look at Darius," Nicola said.

Caledonia cocked her head. "How is that?"

"You look at him as if you adore him."

Caledonia's cheeks flamed in an instant and she lowered her gaze, away from Nicola's probing eyes. "He… he is one of the only people in my life who has ever been truly kind to me," she said. "Sometimes I still cannot believe he is real."

"He *is* real."

"And you are not just saying that because he is your brother?"

Nicola giggled. "What would you have me say?" she said. "Do you want to know the truth? I was born when Thor was twenty years of age. I was a very late baby for my parents and my mother told me that I was attached to Thor, even as an infant. Of course, he was training and doing things that knights do, so he was not home a good deal of the time, but when he was, he and I were inseparable. I love all of my brothers, but Thor has always been my favorite. You ask if he is real… He is very real. And very kind. But I will warn you—it takes a good deal to anger him, but when his temper is unleashed, you do not want to be anywhere near him. He is positively terrifying."

Caledonia tried to catch another glimpse of him. "He has had ample opportunity to become enraged at me, but he has not," she said. "The man has the patience of a saint."

"He does," Nicola agreed. "But he does not for people who cross him. Or his enemies. I have heard my father tell tales of *El Martillo*."

"He told me about his life as a mercenary."

Nicola didn't reply. She fell silent as Caledonia continued to peer from the window, catching sight of Thor up near the front of the escort in conversation with another knight. But the few moments of silence were broken by Nicola's soft voice.

"Callie," she said quietly, "we have spent a week together and I like you a great deal. But the truth is that I do not know you well. I have never seen my brother so happy, so I will say this to you—thank you for making him so. Thank you for bringing joy into his life because he deserves it. I pray that the two of you always know this happiness. But I swear, by all that his holy, if you betray him or hurt him in any way, I will kill you myself."

Caledonia looked at her, sharply, only to see that she was completely serious. It was a hard expression, something Caledonia had never seen on Nicola's face before. Rather than become offended by her statement, however, she was touched by it. She knew it was from the heart, from a sister who loved her brother, so she took it very seriously.

"I have made mistakes in my life," she said softly. "I have not been as kind as I could have been, or attentive, or even thoughtful. You know that my life has been… difficult, and I will not explain things to you again, but suffice it to say that I would not knowingly hurt Thor. Not when he has shown me a side to life that I did not know to exist. I will always try to make him happy, I promise. I hope you believe me, because it is true."

Nicola smiled weakly. "I believe you," she said. "But I had to say it. My brother means a good deal to me."

"And to me."

"I can tell."

Caledonia smiled bashfully. "Mayhap you can, but can he?"

Nicola laughed. "Have you not seen the way he looks at you?" she said. "Callie, he is positively smitten. He is probably already in love with you."

Those words hit Caledonia hard. *He is probably already in love with you.* No one had ever been in love with her before. To her knowledge, no one had ever loved her before except for Constantine. And maybe her mother.

But no one else.

She wasn't sure there was anything about her to love.

"How would you know that?" she asked in surprise. "We've only known each other a matter of days. How is it possible to know you love someone in so short a time?"

Nicola shrugged. "Think about it," she said. "Does he fill your every waking thought?"

"Aye."

"Do you long for the sound of his voice?"

"Aye."

"Would you do anything for him, anything in the world?"

"Anything he asked and more."

"Then mayhap you are in love with him, too."

Caledonia's eyes widened. That was something that had never occurred to her—and having never been in love, she had no idea what it would feel like. But she did know that her heart skipped a beat when she saw Thor and that she craved the man's touch. She craved the sight and smell and sound of him. Was it love?

It was certainly *something.*

She was distracted from her thoughts as Thor rode up to the carriage again, indicating the city up ahead.

"The crowds on the street of the merchants are starting to wane," he said. "They are planning on closing their shops soon, so if we are going to purchase goods, we must go now."

With that, he instructed the soldier driving the carriage to pull it forward at a brisk pace. The conversation between them was forgotten while Caledonia and Nicola held on as the carriage lurched over the road, making a right turn into the city. They passed through the gates, and immediately the bustle of the city came into view.

And what a city it was.

Birmingham had big buildings, both businesses and residences, built from classic wattle and daub or the occasional stone. Caledonia felt at home here, a city she'd been in many times. She had good memories here, of going to market with her mother and of the relatively carefree life she led as a child. She remembered Constantine buying her sweets here. Birmingham was one of the few places that didn't harbor any difficult memories for her, so she wasn't distressed as the carriage came to a halt and the door opened.

Darius was standing there, smiling at Nicola.

The woman practically jumped into his arms, and Caledonia chuckled as Darius tried to peel Nicola off him for propriety's sake. She could see Thor standing behind Darius, giving his sister a deeply disapproving expression as Darius was trying desperately to force her to behave properly. But Nicola wasn't listening to Darius and didn't care what her brother thought. She ended up winding her arms around Darius' left arm and sticking to him like glue as he pulled her away from the carriage so Thor could remove Caledonia. When he stepped up to the cab door, Caledonia paused before exiting.

"Should I jump on you like Nica did to Darius?" she asked. "I want to make sure I understand your expectations."

She was jesting. Thor rolled his eyes. "It would be more appropriate than what she just did," he said, eyeing his sister unhappily. "Christ, that girl has no sense of decorum at all. You'd think she was the only woman in the world who had ever been betrothed."

Caledonia grinned. "She is very happy," she said. "I've been listening it to it for seven days now. I can tell you exactly *how* happy she is."

"I have no doubt that you can," Thor said. "But my question would be how happy are *you*?"

Caledonia's smile faded as she gazed into those bright blue eyes. "Can you not tell?"

A smile tugged the corners of his mouth. "I never want to assume."

"You can assume," she said. "If I do not look happy, then I will tell you plainly. This week with you has been the happiest week of my life. I feel as if I am living in a dream."

He reached out and took her hand. "No more thoughts of running off to Gomorrah?"

"I cannot even remember the place."

"Are you sure?"

"I am."

With a grin, he lifted her hand, kissed it, and tucked it into the crook of his elbow.

Proudly, Thor led his wife through the column, picking up Darius and Nicola as they went. Clayne joined also, leaving Truett in charge of the escort now that the man had returned from securing rooms for the night. As the group headed toward the long but narrow street of the merchants, Clayne began sniffing the air.

"Smell it?" he said. "The roasting meat. The bakers' ovens are roasting beef for suppers all over the city."

It wasn't uncommon for the ovens of the bakers to be used for things other than bread. They roasted meat for families who didn't have the ovens or facilities to do it, and at this time of day, the ovens were going full steam for families all over the city.

"It smells like venison," Caledonia said. "Slightly sweet."

Thor looked at her. "How do you know that?"

"Because I like venison."

Clayne took up pace on her other side. "It *is* beef," he insisted. "I would know that smell anywhere. When I was young, my mother would make a mixture of finely chopped beef, spices, and mushrooms and bake it in a pie. Then she would cover it with gravy. My brothers and I would have to fight my father for it, but I always won. No one beats me when it comes to food."

He was grinning as he said it, and Thor chimed in. "His mother is my mother's sister," he told Caledonia. "His father was a knight sworn to my father, many years ago. A fiercer man you will never meet."

"Then you are telling me that he is family," she said seriously.

"He is," Thor said. "We call him Bully. It is a long story, but suffice it to say that his father is known as Bull and Clayne is just like his father. Little Bull."

She understood. "And I am free to treat Bully like family?"

Thor suspected she had something in mind from the way she asked the question so he nodded, a smile playing on his lips. "I wish you would."

With a playful glance at her husband, Caledonia turned her attention to Clayne, who didn't look anything like her beauteous husband. He was fair, muscular, and short, and he had an aggressive manner about him, so she thought the name Bully suited him. She hadn't spent much time around him during their journey because he was usually busy carrying out Thor's commands, but she'd seen enough to know that the man was stubborn, loud, and easy with his laughter.

Truth be told, he reminded her a good deal of Constantine.

"I will make you a wager," she said to Clayne. "I will bet you that my nose is sharper than yours. It *is* venison and it is coming from the next street over. Go and see for yourself if you do not believe me."

Clayne frowned. "Beef!"

"Venison."

"Go and find out," Thor told his cousin irritably. "Buy some while you are at it. I am hungry."

That was enough to send Clayne through the alleyway between the main streets, heading for the bakers and the smell of beef. Or venison. That left Caledonia and Thor, with Nicola and Darius following, on the street of merchants that was quite vast.

It was a small city unto itself.

It was less crowded at this time of day because most people had already done their shopping, so they were able to find a shop that carried fabric. A seamstress was next door and had pre-made garments, loosely basted, to be finished when a lady purchased them. Thor and Nicola were particularly interested in those while Caledonia wasn't entirely sure about them. She didn't really know fashion, although Nicola had done her best during their week of travel to educate her. Still, Caledonia hung back, looking at the tables of silk scarves, as Nicola made contact with the merchant.

The pre-made dresses began to come off their pegs.

Beautiful surcoats and complete dresses made from elaborate fabric were laid out on one of the merchant tables. In some cases, the dresses were quite detailed, with different types of fabrics on the bottom of the surcoat than on the top. There were embroidered bodices, silk panels, and brocade skirts. Then there were simpler gowns made from linen or lamb's wool or fabrics from faraway lands. There were many to choose from, many that Nicola pored over, and Thor eventually brought Caledonia over to the table to look.

"Well?" he said. "Nica has picked these out. Do you like any of them?"

Caledonia was uncomfortable selecting clothing like this. Nicola had spent time at court so she knew what was popular and fashionable, but Caledonia knew nothing.

"They are all very pretty," she said hesitantly. "It is difficult to choose."

Nicola held up a ruby-red silk, putting it against Caledonia to see how it would look on her. "This is very pretty," she said. "Do you like the color, Callie?"

Caledonia looked down at it. The dress was magnificent with gold thread, but it was so unlike anything she ever wore. As she tried to think of something kind to say to Nicola, who was genuinely trying to help, Thor could see her reluctance. She didn't seem particularly at ease.

"Nica," he said. "Put that dress aside and find something blue. I like blue."

As Nicola turned around and went in search of a blue garment, Thor grasped Caledonia by the arm and gently pulled her back over to the scarf table, away from his sister and the merchant as they pawed over the clothing.

"What is wrong?" he asked softly. "Why do you not seem excited about this?"

Caledonia took a deep breath, forcing a smile. "It is not that I am not excited," she said. "But those dresses..."

"What about them?"

Caledonia was reluctant to say, so she tried to be tactful. "I have never had elaborate dresses like that in my life," she said. "I am not comfortable dressing like a queen. I am sorry to say that because I know you liked to see me well dressed, but I would much prefer something simpler."

Thor well remembered what she was wearing when he met her. He knew that all of her clothing was like that, so much so that she'd been borrowing gowns from his sister so she could be more properly dressed. But he'd come to see over the past week that, in spite of her incredible beauty, Caledonia had rather simple tastes. She didn't like to spend money, didn't want to wear fine silks or jewelry or even pretty lady's slippers. She dressed very nearly like a peasant and was happy that way.

He could see that this was going to be a delicate dance with her.

"I would be very happy to find you simple clothing," he said. "But will you at least honor your husband's wishes by choosing simple clothing with finer fabrics? Truly, Caledonia, you are far too beautiful to wear broadcloth. You were made for gorgeous clothing and it does my heart good to see you dressed well. Will you at least consider it?"

Caledonia nodded, but reluctantly. "If it will make you happy, I will," she said. "And I will even select an elaborate gown for those times when the situation calls for it."

"Good," he said, kissing her. "Thank you. Would you like me to help you pick them out?"

"Do you want to?"

He shrugged. "To be honest, I know nothing about fine clothing other than whether or not I like the color."

Caledonia could see, in that moment, that he wasn't any more comfortable picking out dresses than she was. Probably less so. It must have been emasculating for him to be in the merchant stall, but he was doing it for her, so she took pity on him.

"Go," she said. "Your sister will help me. Why not go and find your cousin? Make sure he does not cheat by telling me the roasting meat we all smelled was beef and not venison."

Thor lifted his eyebrows in agreement. "Knowing him, he would try to sew cow hide on the venison just to prove a point."

"Then you must save my honor."

He smiled at her, leaning down to kiss her sweetly. "Always," he whispered.

With a wink, he was gone, heading out of the merchant stall as Caledonia stood there and grinned.

Does he fill your every waking thought?

Do you long for the sound of his voice?

Would you do anything for him, anything in the world?

Those were the questions Nicola had asked of her as the definition of love. They were like listing the symptoms of a disease—did she have all of them? She was fairly certain she did.

And it didn't distress her in the least.

Still smiling, she turned back to the garments.

☙

DARIUS HAD BEEN standing outside of the merchant stall when Thor emerged, for the man had flatly refused to enter or have anything to do with what he considered women's duties. Thor left him at the mouth of the stall as a guard for his wife and sister as he headed back the way they'd come. His destination was the street of the bakers because he was quite hungry and, knowing him, Clayne would eat everything and forget to bring him something. Stomach rumbling, he headed down the avenue.

Nearing the end of the street, he happened to glance at the shop on the corner, which was small and cluttered, but in the open window he could see several exotic-looking daggers that were chained together and locked so no one could make off with them. Curious, he went to look at them, seeing that they were all shapes and sizes and clearly not forged in England. As he peered at a particularly large dagger with a metal blade that seemed to be discolored, the merchant came up on the other side of the window.

"Good day, my lord," he said. "You are inspecting my Levant daggers."

Thor glanced at him. "Is that where these are from?"

The merchant nodded as he unlocked the chain and pulled the larger dagger free. He handed it carefully to Thor.

"Damascus steel," he said. "The most prized steel in the known world."

Thor held it up in the light. The steel of the blade had wavy lines, beautifully mottled. "I've heard of it," he said. "I've never seen it, though. Are all of these daggers like this?"

The merchant nodded and handed him another one. "I have four of them," he said. "I went on a buying trip last year to Paris and Venice and Rome. I found them in Rome along with many ancient treasures. Would you like to see them?"

Thor shook his head. "Not now," he said. "But I am very interested in the dagger. How much do you want for it?"

"Ten pounds."

"That is a good deal of money."

The merchant conceded the point. "It is, but it is an exquisite weapon," he said. "That steel will cut through anything. It will cut flesh as easily as a knife through butter. Surely a knight such as you would want to have such a magnificent weapon at your side?"

Truthfully, Thor wanted it. Like a child wants a toy, he wanted the dagger. It really was beautiful. As he pondered the extravagant purchase, the merchant reached over to one of his nearby tables and brought forth a box filled with trinkets and jewelry.

"Buy the weapon and I will give you something for your wife," he said. "You have a wife, do you not? A comely man like you should have a dozen."

Thor gave him a half-grin. "I do not think my wife would let me," he said, weakening as the man flashed the jewelry box at him. "What do you have for her?"

The merchant held up a gorgeous gold and citrine necklace. "I got this in Rome along with the daggers," he said. "I was told that an empress wore this."

"Lovely."

"And this," the merchant said, putting the citrine necklace aside as he picked up another with a long gold chain and what looked like a big jewel at the end of it. "I was told that a Roman Caesar gave this to his wife. It is a blue lapis lazuli and a star has been carved into it. See it? Under the star is the word *Uxorious*."

Thor could see the star and the Roman letters. The lapis was surrounded by diamonds, uncut, but the entire necklace was quite beautiful.

"What does *Uxorious* mean?" he asked.

"It is the Roman word for glorious wife or revered wife," the merchant said. "Give this to your wife and she will never become angry at you again."

As Thor took the necklace from the man to inspect it, the merchant dug into the jewelry box again and came up with a gold ring. It had a row of diamonds in it, glistening in the light.

There was scrollwork in the gold, making it a truly lovely ring. The merchant held it out to him.

"And this," he said. "Would your wife like this? It is made for a beautiful woman. Does she not deserve it?"

The man was quite a salesman, and Thor finally snorted, taking the ring and both necklaces from him.

"Give me the dagger, too," he said. "Ten pounds for every-thing."

"Of course, my lord."

"I need to get away from you before you sell me this entire shop."

The merchant chuckled and scurried away, returning with a silk-lined box for the jewelry. Thor paid him his money and took his treasures, quite happy with the dagger. It was most impressive. But he was even happier with the jewelry. It wasn't much, but it was well made and beautiful. He hadn't thought of buying Caledonia a wedding ring until the merchant produced the gold band, and the necklace—*Uxorious*—was something he hoped she would like. It summed up how he felt about her, this woman he'd chased down, fought with, drank with, and made love with.

Glorious wife, indeed.

When he gave it to her, she wept.

CHAPTER ELEVEN

ROTRI WASN'T EXPECTING Peregrine.

Humiliated and furious after their defeat at Westminster, Rotri and Domnall had retreated back to their London apartment to regroup. They'd been there for a week. The marriage they'd tried to prevent had gone ahead and there was nothing they could do about it.

Nothing short of murder.

That was Rotri's next step, as he saw it. Caledonia was married to a de Reyne knight, but knights were warriors. They went to battle and got themselves killed every day. All Rotri had to do was make sure Thor de Reyne was killed. Somehow.

But he wasn't exactly sure how.

He needed to know more about the man.

That was where Peregrine came in. As the king's most trusted servant who wasn't an advisor or someone who held a formal title, Peregrine had access to men like Thor de Reyne without really being noticed. Surely Peregrine could tell Rotri something about Thor that could help him in his quest to rid himself of the man who currently held the title that belonged to

Domnall, but Peregrine wanted coinage for his information. Domnall paid him the remainder of the money he'd brought with him to London, so Peregrine was growing rich off two greedy and conniving men.

Rotri intended to get his money's worth.

"Thank you for coming," he said as Peregrine sat down in his solar and Domnall poured him a measure of wine. "I am glad we finally have the opportunity to meet. You have been quite helpful to me and my son and we are appreciative."

Peregrine, who was usually well dressed, had on rather plain clothing for the journey to the Dordon apartment because he didn't want to be noticed. It had taken Domnall days to convince him to come, and even then he only did it when Domnall paid him well. But he wasn't here for a social call. He'd figured out that Dordon and his son would pay him well for any information from the palace, specifically about Thor de Reyne or Gage de Reyne, and he was going to milk them for all they had. Some of the information he gave them wasn't even truthful, but he'd tell them anything for the coins Domnall seemed to want to throw at him.

He was only here today for more money.

"You want something and are willing to pay for it, my lord," Peregrine said. "Let us be honest—this is not a friendly visit. You want something from me, so ask your questions and be swift. I am expected back at Westminster soon."

So much for pleasantries. Rotri sat down across from the man.

"I like a man who gets straight to the point of his visit," he said, still trying to be polite in spite of Peregrine's not-so-friendly attitude. "I want to know where Thor de Reyne is. I will assume he has gone back to Westminster? Do you know if he is living there, or is he elsewhere?"

Peregrine took a long drink of the cheap wine. "He is not at Westminster," he said, smacking his lips. "The Earl of Tamworth and Stafford has gone north to inspect his properties."

That was news to Rotri. "When did he leave?"

"About six days ago."

"How long will he be there?"

"I do not know."

"Did his wife go with him?"

"As far as I know," Peregrine said. "I heard Ashington speaking of their marriage and the journey to visit the properties."

Rotri passed a concerned look at Domnall. "He has *left* London."

Domnall nodded. "Indeed," he said. "Then mayhap we should leave as well."

Rotri pondered that a moment before returning his attention to Peregrine. "Is there anything else you can tell me about him?" he asked.

"What else do you want to know?" Peregrine asked, unhappy that he had been provided terrible wine. "Before you ask, know that I do not know the man personally. He is above my station. I am a mere servant and nothing more, so anything I tell you is rumor or observation."

Rotri understood. "As I said, we are appreciative," he said. "Has Ashington left, too? Or does he remain in London?"

Peregrine was looking at his wine cup, barely full, and the inordinate amount of dregs collecting at the bottom. *Cheap wine,* he thought. "Ashington is still here," he said. "My lord, all I can tell you is that Tamworth was married to Lady de Tosni. That night, the king held a feast in their honor with fourteen courses, and the couple seemed content. They left London two days later. That is literally all I can tell you unless there is something more you have in mind."

He seemed impatient. Rotri watched the man's restless movements before shaking his head. "There is not," he said.

Peregrine downed the rest of the cup and slammed it back to the table before standing up. "Good," he said decisively. But he paused, looking between father and son. "I am not entirely sure what your obsession is with Thor de Reyne, but you must know that the man is unbreakable. He is a Blackchurch-trained knight, an elite warrior, who not only holds the title of Lord Protector to the king, but now he is the Earl of Tamworth and Stafford and commands thousands. More to the point, his wife, a lady who is your niece, is now under his protection. I know you have been trying to see the Archbishop of Canterbury for quite some time, and I know you showed up at Westminster Palace with a tale of some document that proves you have guardianship over the former Lady de Tosni, but I would strongly suggest you forget about her. Pursuing whatever you are pursuing with Thor and the lady will only get you killed."

Rotri didn't want to burn his only contact in Henry's court, but he didn't like the advice. It was difficult for him not to bite back.

"Thank you for the information," he said through clenched teeth. "You may go now."

Peregrine's gaze lingered on the man before he snorted wryly and headed for the door. It was clear that he thought Dordon was ridiculous. When the man was gone, Domnall turned to his father.

"He is right," he said quietly. "This is at an end, Father."

But Rotri shook his head. "It is *not* at an end," he said. "It will never be at an end until I have what I want. There is a way. We simply have to discover what that is."

Domnall had never been as enthusiastic about this scheme as his father had been. He was more rational than Rotri, a man who believed God had played a bad joke on him by making Rhun his older brother. Domnall believed he was due the family fortune, but that was mostly because his father had impressed it upon him. Rotri had wanted it for himself, but knowing that he couldn't marry his own niece, he would foist that responsibility onto his son.

But the obsession with it all was becoming irrational.

"And what would you hope to discover?" Domnall asked, struggling not to show his impatience. "You have spoken of killing de Reyne, but I will tell you that it is a futile plan."

Rotri frowned. "Why is it futile? With no de Reyne, Callie will once again be a widow."

Domnall shook his head. "You are not thinking this through to the logical conclusion," he said. "If de Reyne is dead, then Callie is once again a prized widow and the king will simply marry her to someone else."

"But I have a document that says—"

"Father, *stop*." Domnall finally raised his voice. "Do you not understand? That document will not hold up. You are simply delaying the inevitable. You know this."

"I do not!"

"The king is not going to make you a guardian of a grown woman with a large fortune, especially since that fortune now belongs to her husband!"

They were shouting at each other now. Frustrated, Domnall turned away, raking his fingers through his hair, while Rotri sat there and scowled. They often had these little tempests between them but they usually blew over. Knowing that they would never get anywhere if they continued to argue, Domnall struggled to compose himself.

"Father, you seemed to be focused on things that will not help this situation," he said. "You are fixated on this document. You have started to speak of killing de Reyne, but you must know how impossible that will be. As Peregrine pointed out, he is a Blackchurch-trained knight. You cannot kill him. You cannot force the king to make you Callie's guardian and you cannot kill her husband. How *else* are you going to gain the title and the money? You must think of something else."

Rotri didn't want to admit that his son was possibly right. Rotri was a schemer and a dreamer, always the one to come up with a plan. But that wasn't happening with his niece. What he wanted was slipping through his fingers.

Domnall was correct.

He had to think of something else.

"If there is another way," he muttered, standing up to pour himself some of that cheap wine. "*If* there is another way, what would it be? If I cannot gain control of Tamworth through that document or through marriage, how else can I gain it?"

Domnall leaned back against the wall. "You cannot," he said flatly. "Unless she is going to simply give it over to you, which she is not, there is no way you can gain control of Tamworth."

Rotri nodded in resignation. But then he came to a halt. His brow furrowed as an idea came to him and, suddenly, he wasn't so resigned anymore. He looked at his son as if a bolt from God had just struck him, infusing him with the greatest idea of all time.

He set his wine cup down without drinking any of it.

"We must make her *give* it to me," he hissed as the ideas

rolled through his mind. "We must make her *gladly* give it."

"How?"

"A ransom."

Domnall looked at him in confusion. "What ransom?"

Rotri was onto something. "You know as well as I do that knights are often ransomed in battle," he said. "I've heard of men gaining kingdoms through ransom. It was done quite frequently during Richard's quest to the Levant. De Montfort did it with Prince Edward when he captured him in battle several years ago. If I could capture de Reyne, the ransom would be the Earldom of Tamworth. An earldom for Callie's husband."

Domnall was starting to catch on. "That is possible," he said. "Though I am not sure she could give you the earldom, not without Henry's permission. But she could give you the wealth."

"Exactly," Rotri said. "We will capture de Reyne somehow and ransom him back to his wife. And given that he is Henry's Lord Protector, I am certain the king would do anything to ensure his safety."

"Even agreeing to giving you Tamworth?"

"I may get more than Tamworth," Rotri said excitedly. "The king may give me anything I want in exchange for his Blackchurch-trained knight!"

Domnall thought on the scheme, which was probably the most feasible one his father had come up with. Instead of focusing on something that was out of his control, like the marriage between his son and Caledonia, he was focusing on something he *could* control. The capture of a knight. True, it wasn't just any knight, but with proper planning, it could be done.

After a moment, he nodded his head.

"Very well," he finally said. "We capture de Reyne and hold him for ransom. But the fact remains that we must catch him first. How will we do that?"

Domnall shook his head. "I do not know yet," he said. "Mayhap we pay a call on the new couple to apologize for the scene in the church and congratulate them on their marriage. Mayhap we offer a truce and pretend to be one happily family. Mayhap that will be his downfall—we will pretend to be loving relatives and his guard will be done. If de Reyne does not suspect we are coming for him, how can he prepare for us?"

"True."

"Then we must return home immediately," Rotri said, a sense of urgency in his tone. He picked up the old pewter bell he used to summon his servants and rang it loudly. "We must pack the household and go as soon as possible. Peregrine said they had departed six days ago, so they are well ahead of us by now. We must hurry."

Domnall didn't need to be told twice. As he headed down to the stables to make sure the escort was prepared, Rotri whipped his servants into a frenzy to pack the house so they could return to Dordon Castle.

Now with a new scheme to carry out.

Thor de Reyne's days as a free man were numbered.

CHAPTER TWELVE

Stafford Castle

T HEY WERE WAITING for them.

The morning they had left Birmingham, Thor had drafted a missive to be sent to Stafford Castle announcing his approach. He was clear in the missive about who he was and what he was, and he was clear that he was returning with his new wife, the former Lady de Tosni. He sent the missive ahead with a swift messenger from among his escort, a very young man, skinny and spry, riding a skittish horse that probably ran faster than a bolt of lightning. Therefore, by the time they reached Stafford Castle toward sunset, the entire house and hold was waiting for them in the bailey.

Thor had never been to Stafford Castle before, so it was a new experience for him. Not only was this an unfamiliar castle, but it was now his holding. There was something infinitely satisfying about riding through the gatehouse of his very own castle. He glanced at his fellow knights, men who had been with him for years, and he could see the approval in their eyes.

He felt puffed up like a peacock.

But that was tempered by his concern for Caledonia's reaction to returning to a castle that she had presided over in theory, yet a place that held no fond memories for her. She had mentioned that all of her children had been born at Stafford Castle because Robert had insisted on it, so in that respect there was some sentimentality attached, but that was all. Nothing more. Thor made sure to ride next to her carriage as they came in through the gatehouse because he wanted her to know that he was with her. He would always be with her. He wanted her to know that he was thinking about her even as he entered his new property.

This was an important moment for her, too.

Stafford Castle was a large but unspectacular fortress. The stone castle sat on a tall motte in the center of a vast village-and-castle complex and was built in the shape of a cloverleaf. It had four big towers on all four corners with a small bailey in the middle of it. But even if the fortress on the hill wasn't too terribly impressive, the complex of Stafford Castle as a whole was.

The entire campus, with the motte in the middle of it, was surrounded by a moat encircling another bailey that included stables and outbuildings. There was a wall that surrounded the moat and butted up against that wall, and a village spread out toward the south. Interestingly enough, the village seemed to be one big fortified facility of cottages, businesses, and outbuildings that were directly related to the castle. However, the wall built around the castle proper was stone while the one built around the village was made of wood. Giant logs that had been harvested from local forests were rammed into the ground, with the tops of them carved into a sharp point. Anyone trying to mount the wall could very easily impale themselves on the point, which was good for defense. In all, Stafford was built for protection and had been well designed.

Thor found it all quite fascinating.

As his party entered the upper bailey at the top of the motte, he could quickly see that it was too small to hold the hundreds of men he had brought with him from London, so he had Truett take the bulk of the escort back to the lower bailey, where there was more room for them to assemble. Thor remained with about twenty men from his escort, his remaining knights, and the carriage. As the bulk of the army cleared out, he happened to notice the messenger he had sent with the announcement of his approach. The young man was hovering near the gatehouse at first, but quickly rushed to blend in with the royal army when it entered the compound. He didn't think much of it until the soldier approached him and tried to get his attention.

"My lord?" the young soldier called. "Lord Tamworth?"

Thor heard him. He'd just dismounted his horse, perhaps a little wearily, and he removed his helm before answering.

"What is it?" he said.

The young soldier seemed nervous. His eyes kept shifting around, looking at the gathering Stafford soldiers, but also at three knights who had just emerged from the keep. They'd been on the roof of the structure, watching Thor and his party enter, but now they were in the bailey.

The messenger was mostly focused on the knights.

"They are not happy you are here, my lord," the young soldier whispered. "They have opened Stafford to you, but the knight in command—he calls himself Cristano de Lucera—has said that he requires proof you are the Earl of Tamworth and Stafford. He says that marrying de Tosni's widow is not enough for him and, if you do not prove it to him, he will order you out."

Thor's expression cooled. "Did you hear him say that?"

The young soldier shook his head. "Nay, my lord," he said. "But I have been confined to the gatehouse and heard those men speaking of it. The other two knights who serve de Lucera have the same family name, but they are known as Adan and Benedicto. Be careful of them, my lord—the rumor is that even if you can prove that you are the new earl, they will try to kill you."

"Have you been threatened at all?"

"Nay, my lord, but they forced me to stay at the gatehouse. I could not wander."

"Do we know anything more about these knights?"

"Only that they rule Stafford as if it is their own private domain. Everyone says so."

Thor nodded as if it meant nothing to him. His manner was completely unruffled at such critical news. Truthfully, he wasn't at all surprised, given that the knights had had the run of Stafford since Robert died. As he feared, they viewed the castle as their own private kingdom. God only knew what they'd stolen from the Stafford coffers. Holding out a hand to tell the young soldier not to move, he casually went over to the carriage and leaned inside.

"Stay here," he commanded softly. "Do not move until I tell you to. Do you understand?"

Caledonia didn't know why he was being so mysterious, but she didn't like it. It made her more nervous than she already was. But she nodded without hesitation.

"Of course, angel," she said. "We will remain here."

Thor winked at her and moved to the remaining escort, muttering something to the sergeant, who immediately nodded and then moved to the next man, muttering something to him as well. Whispers began going through the ranks of royal soldiers as Thor reached Darius and Clayne at the end of the escort.

"Do you see the knights who came from the keep?" Thor asked in a casual manner.

Darius and Clayne nodded. "Aye," Darius said. "Why?"

"Because I am told that the two younger knights will attempt to kill me," Thor said. "Send someone for True and bring him, and about a hundred men, back here immediately. Meanwhile, you two will disarm the two younger knights. I will take the older one. Show no mercy."

Darius and Clayne understood their assignment. They began to head up through the escort, aiming for the three knights who were standing about twenty feet away. There were Stafford men on the battlements and in the gatehouse, but there were more royal troops in the bailey. Thor moved up on one side of the carriage while Darius and Clayne moved up on the other. Together, the trio headed toward the three knights who were watching the incoming party through critical eyes.

"Who is Cristano de Lucera?" Thor asked.

Two of the knights looked to the third, an older man with face like leather. He didn't seem even moderately respectful of Thor as he looked him up and down, like he was inspecting a side of beef.

"I am," he said, refusing to address him as "my lord." "Are you de Reyne?"

Thor didn't answer. He walked right up to the man and punched him squarely in the face with a ham-sized fist. Meanwhile, Darius made short work of Adan. Benedicto, a bigger man, put up more of a fight with Clayne. But it was a short fight.

Clayne was called Bully for a reason.

With the two younger knights subdued, Thor stood over Cristano.

"I am Thor de Reyne, the Earl of Tamworth and Stafford," he told the half-conscious man. "I understand that you intend to throw me from my property if you are not convinced it is mine. Therefore, let me convince you."

With that, he reached down and grabbed de Lucera by the front of his tunic. He dragged the bleeding man back across the bailey, straight to the carriage where Caledonia and Nicola had watched the confrontation. They were looking at Thor with big, startled eyes as he pulled his victim up to the cab.

"Sweetheart," he addressed Caledonia calmly. "There is a satchel under your seat. My satchel. Will you please find it and open it?"

Caledonia quickly did as he asked. She knew he'd kept a leather satchel in the cab, unwilling to put it in the provisions wagon where the knights usually kept their possessions, so she found it under her feet and pulled it forth, untying the straps at the top.

"Thank you," Thor said, giving de Lucera a brutal shake when the man tried to weakly push him away. "Now, inside you will find several pieces of folded vellum, but I am looking for the one with the royal seal on it. It is rolled. Will you please pull it forth?"

Caledonia rummaged around in it, as quickly as she could, with Nicola helping her. In fact, it was Nicola who found the scroll with the royal seal and handed it out the window to her brother.

Thor took it and dropped de Lucera back into the dirt.

"Here is my proof," Thor said to the man, who was bleeding from a ruptured nose. He held up the scroll for the knight to see. "A decree by Henry granting me title to the Earldom of Tamworth and Stafford. You also know the former Lady de Tosni—she will tell you that we were wed and that the property is mine. Are you still uncertain about this?"

De Lucera was blowing blood out of his mouth, lying at Thor's feet. "Nay, my lord," he said. "I am no longer uncertain."

"Good," Thor said. Then he looked to Darius and Clayne. "Put all three of these knights in the vault until I decide what's to be done with them. Put our men on guard. Once they are in the vault, I want you to gather every Stafford soldier down in the lower bailey."

"Aye, my lord," Darius said. "Where is the vault?"

Thor looked straight at de Lucera, who was afraid he'd receive another punch if he didn't answer. "Gatehouse," he said, then quickly added, "My lord."

Darius reached down and yanked de Lucera to his feet. The older knight was still so woozy that he was having difficulty walking, but that didn't stop Darius and Clayne from shoving him and his two beaten cousins all the way back to the gatehouse with the help of about fifteen royal soldiers. Already, the gathering of the Stafford soldiers was beginning as Truett returned with about a hundred men flooding into the bailey behind him. Darius relayed the commands and Truett went to work. Shouting could be heard all over Stafford Castle as Thor's orders were in motion. Troops were being separated and de Reyne was taking control. Satisfied that he would have Stafford secured very short, Thor finally returned his attention to Caledonia.

"Well?" he said, smiling at her as if he hadn't a care in the world. "Would you like to see your children?"

He pulled the door open and she moved to climb out, but she was still looking at him in shock over what had just happened.

"You… you *hit* de Lucera," she finally said. "My God… You actually struck him!"

Thor helped her out of the cab. "What of it?"

Caledonia seemed genuinely stunned. Dressed in one of the garments that they'd purchased yesterday in Birmingham, an exquisite blue silk, she looked over the castle, the bailey, before finally returning her attention to Thor.

"He had it coming," she finally said. "God's Bones, Thor. You have no idea what a bully of a man Cristano de Lucera is. A horrible dictator who breathes cruelty like men breathe air. It is part of him. He deserved what you did to him."

Thor took her hand, feeling that it was clammy. She was nervous. "You told me that you had nothing to do with the knights," he said. "But you know de Lucera's character?"

She shrugged. "I have lived here for many years," she said. "Of course I am going to know something of the people here, even if Robert did control everything."

"You should have told me of de Lucera and his cousins."

She looked at him seriously. "When we first met, there was so much turmoil," she said. "We were building trust. We are still building trust. I felt that if I told you what I knew about de Lucera, *truly* told you, that you might think I was trying to discourage you from taking possession of Stafford. I was afraid you might think it was one more ploy to talk you out of the marriage."

He could see her point. "Very well," he said. "But you must tell me everything. I could have walked into an ambush with the de Lucera family."

Caledonia shook her head. "I do not think so," she said. "They are men of talk, not action. They are arrogant and nasty, but cowards at heart."

Thor took the hand he held and tucked it into the crook of his elbow. "But I am not," he said quietly, a smile on his lips. "But tell me next time if you know something, even if you think it is not significant. Will you do that?"

She leaned against him affectionately. "Of course I will," she said. "I apologize that I did not."

"You are forgiven," he said. "But what about this nun? What can I expect from her?"

Caledonia's warm expression faded. "She is a tyrant," she said. "Her name is Madam Madonna and she was Robert's nurse. A former nun. He has always surrendered to her, in every way. Whatever she wanted, he gave it to her. She not only supervised the children, but she was chatelaine as well. I was told it was her duty, not mine. I am certain she is inside the keep somewhere. She would not leave that which she commands."

"Then Madam Madonna is about to meet someone she cannot command."

"She will more than likely try."

"Shall we find out?"

Thor said it with some enthusiasm, as if he was looking forward to it, and Caledonia broke down in a weak smile. She was about to reply when she happened to glance at the carriage and saw Nicola still sitting inside, looking frightened and lonely. She held out a hand to her.

"Come, Nica," she said. "We are going to go inside now. Will you come with me? I will need you."

Nicola climbed out of the carriage and scurried over to them. She had seen her brother pound the hapless knight and was just a little fearful now. She latched on to Thor's other arm.

"Where is Darius?" she asked her brother. "Where did you send him?"

"He is handling the men," Thor said. "Have no fear. He will return to you shortly."

Nicola kept looking around, hunting for Darius, but Thor began to walk, pulling the women along. They were heading for the square keep, three stories in height, with a flight of stone steps leading to the entry with the biggest door Thor had ever seen. It was a small, compact keep, and as they approached the stairs, a figure abruptly appeared at the top.

A woman had emerged, followed by other women. Servants, perhaps. She stood at the top of the steps and held out a hand.

"Come no closer until you announce yourself."

The three of them came to a halt, looking up at a woman dressed in brown woolen robes. She had a tight wimple covering her hair and her face was rosy and wrinkled and completely hairless. But her expression…

That was the stuff of nightmares.

With her eyebrow-less eyes, she stared down Caledonia as if beholding her worst enemy. There was something in the very air that swirled about her, a dark miasma of wickedness. Other than those few words, she hadn't said a thing, but she didn't need to. The animosity radiating out of her spoke for her.

As Caledonia looked at the woman, something in her snapped.

It was because Thor was with her and she was feeling brave. After all these years, she'd finally have the voice that Robert never allowed her to have. She'd never liked Madam Madonna, not from the moment she first met her, because the old woman had made her feel inferior and stupid. She'd only been a breeding mare, the woman had said. Madam Madonna had a gift for making people feel stupid.

And Caledonia had let her.

But no more.

Thor gave her courage.

"You know who I am," Caledonia said, her gaze fixed on the woman as she let go of Thor. "I am the Countess of Tamworth and Stafford, and this is my keep. Where are my daughters?"

Mother Madonna's eyes narrowed. "Lady Stafford," she said imperiously. "You've decided to return, have you? There was no need. You are not required here. I thought that was made clear to you."

It was a nasty thing to say in a long line of nasty things that Madam Madonna had said to her over the years. In times past, Caledonia would have simply taken it. She would have lowered her head and kept her mouth shut because Robert forbade her from talking back to the old nun. That had been established long ago.

But no longer.

"*Where* are my daughters?" she repeated.

The old woman looked at her curiously. "They are of no concern to you," she said. "Why have you returned? And who are these people you have brought with you?"

Before Caledonia realized it, she was marching up the steps, right up to the woman who was a little taller than she was and about twice her weight. All of those years of pain and anguish at being separated from her daughters came rushing upon her, and the very barrier that had caused her all of that agony was standing right in front of her. Without thinking, she shoved the woman back by the shoulders, so hard that Madam Madonna toppled sideways, ending up down on one knee.

Enraged, Caledonia loomed over her.

"Listen to me, you arrogant bitch," she snarled. "*I* am Lady Tamworth and Stafford, descendant of Ceowulf and the kings and queens of Mercia. Robert is dead and I have brought my new husband, the new Earl of Tamworth and Stafford, home. This is *his* castle now. Not yours, not Robert's, but his. You will never again speak to me in that manner or I will have him cut your tongue out. Do you understand me?"

It was a violent, brutal threat. When Mother Madonna tried to get up to challenge her, Caledonia kicked the woman in the knee and sent her onto her arse. Mother Madonna tried to kick her, to fight back, but Thor came up the stairs and grabbed the old woman by the arm.

"Anyone who moves against Lady Tamworth will suffer my wrath," he said, pulling the old woman down the stairs and to the dirt below. When she tripped into the dust, on her knees again, he simply stood there and watched her wallow without sympathy. "Look at me, madam. My name is Thor de Reyne and I am the Lord Protector of our king. I am not Robert de Tosni and I have no respect or regard for you. Am I making myself clear? Your days at Stafford are finished. My wife will be the mother to her daughters now. You are no longer required."

Mother Madonna's expression was full of shock and horror. "My-my lord," she stammered, throwing a finger at Caledonia. "She attacked me. I am allowed to defend myself!"

Thor could see simply by the woman's arrogant stance that everything Caledonia had said about her was true. All of it. There was no remorse, no hint of understanding, no clue that her reign of terror was over and she was no longer in control.

Though he hadn't been particularly brutish with her, as he simply wasn't the type to be brutish with a woman—*any* woman—it was difficult for him to keep from becoming angry with her. Once he was enraged, anything could happen.

Therefore, he kept his composure.

"You are not allowed to do anything, not anymore," Thor said evenly. Then he looked to his sister, who was watching the scene with a good deal of surprise. "Nica, go back to the carriage and find the sergeant. You know Alastair, don't you?"

Nicola nodded hesitantly. "Aye, Thor."

"Find him and tell him to send me four soldiers. Hurry now."

Nicola was gone, scurrying back the way they had come. Thor then turned to Madam Madonna, still sitting in the dirt, and reached down to pull the woman to her feet. As this was going on, Caledonia turned for the keep and bolted inside, off in search of children she'd not seen in a very long time. Children she hadn't been allowed to see alone. Not ever. Her visits had been supervised by the old woman in dirty robes who was now standing in front of Thor, her head down in submission. But now, that barrier was removed.

Once and for all.

She had to find her daughters.

☙

"WHAT IS THAT child doing?"

The question came from Darius. He'd just come from securing the de Lucera knights in the vault and now he was sweeping the upper bailey, per Thor's command, so he could send every Stafford soldier down to the lower bailey where they were being gathered. He had two royal soldiers with him, both of them older, seasoned men he'd served with for a few years, so he trusted them. He knew them.

His question was directed at them.

But they didn't have an answer. They were in the kitchen yard, which was quite large and cluttered, and directly ahead of them were three little girls. One was sitting at the edge of what looked like a fishpond, her feet in the water, while the smaller one seemed to be eating dirt. But the third one, who was probably eight or nine years of age, was standing in front of a corral of goats and speaking loudly to them.

Words Darius and the soldiers recognized.

"I… I think she is preaching, my lord," one of the soldiers said. "She is reciting something from the Bible. I've heard it before."

Curious, Darius stepped into the yard with the soldiers alongside. The girls at the fishpond noticed him. The one with her feet in the water, who was probably six or seven years of age, even waved to him, but the youngest one, who was no more than three, was still stuffing dead grass and dirt into her mouth.

"For I know that my Redeemer lives and at the last He will stand upon the earth," the oldest girl was saying to the goats. "It is important to do the will of God, to know… know what he wants. He wants us to obey him. Like you will obey me when I tell you to do something."

The goats kept eating. The girl tried to force a couple of them to look at her but they were more interested in their feed, so she moved her position so she would be in front of them. In doing so, she caught sight of Darius and the soldiers and, after a moment of surprise, followed by a little fear, curiosity took over and she walked over to them, focusing specifically on Darius.

"Who are you?" she asked.

"My name is Darius. Who are you?"

"I am Jane," she said. "Darius, did you know that Christ loves us all?"

As Darius gazed down at the girl, who was quite pale and slender, he began to suspect who she was. She looked very much like a woman he'd traveled with recently, one with white hair and dark eyes who had married Thor. Truth be told, Darius only knew that Caledonia had children at Stafford because Nicola had told him, so he didn't know much more than that.

He was fairly certain he had found them.

"I've heard that He does," he said, gesturing to the pair around the small fishpond. "Friends of yours, my lady?"

Jane looked at the girls he was referring to. "My sisters," she said with disinterest. Then she reached out and took Darius' hand, pulling him with her. "They do not believe in God. They are not going to heaven. Come, and I will tell you about God."

Darius found himself being dragged away by a small girl so he had to be gentle about refusing her because she seemed most ardent.

"My lady, I would like nothing better, but I have duties to attend," he said. "Mayhap… mayhap another time."

He tried to walk away, but Jane wouldn't let go of his hand so he ended up pulling her with him. "Where must you go?" she asked. "Why are you here?"

Darius was forced to peel her hand off his, as carefully as he could. "I have come with the Earl and Countess of Tamworth and Stafford," he said. "Your mother, I believe. Are you not the daughter of the Countess of Tamworth and Stafford?"

Jane looked at him as if she didn't quite understand what he was asking. "Madam Madonna is my nurse," she said. "I have no father or mother."

Darius wasn't quite sure why the child would say such a thing, but the truth was that the subject of Caledonia's children had never really come up. The entire trip north had been spent supervising the army, and he'd spent little time with Nicola. When he did, the last thing he wanted to talk about was something other than the two of them, so the child's response was strange.

He looked at the pair around the fishpond.

"Can you tell me their names?" he asked Jane. "And I do not think it is very good for the youngest child to be eating dirt. Mayhap we should stop her?"

Jane shrugged. "She always eats dirt."

"Why?"

"Because Madam Madonna tells us we must suffer."

That sounded quite strange to Darius. He didn't know who this Madam Madonna was, but he was fairly certain that a young child shouldn't be eating dirt. He began to look around.

"Where *is* Madam Madonna?" he asked.

Jane shook her head. "I do not know," she said. "Will you not come with me so I can teach you the word of God?"

Darius realized she had found his hand again and was holding on to him with a death grip. "Not now," he said. "As I said, I have duties… Mayhap you should come with me so that we may find your mother. She has arrived."

"No need, Darius."

The voice came from the keep, and Darius looked over to see Caledonia standing in the doorway that led to the kitchen yard. But she was simply standing there, not moving, and although Jane looked at her, the child didn't seem to care that her mother had returned. At least, she didn't react as if her mother had returned. But she walked over to the doorway and gazed up at a woman she resembled a great deal.

"Would you like for me to teach you the word of God?" she asked.

At the sound of her eldest child's voice, Caledonia's eyes welled. It was such a magical moment, something she'd thought would never happen, but here it was. Here *she* was.

She still could hardly believe it.

"Greetings, Jane," she whispered tightly. "You've grown so much since I last saw you."

Jane was looking at her mother with some confusion. "Who are you?"

"I am your mother."

Jane blinked. Then she stumbled back and held up her hand to Caledonia. "My… mother? But I have no mother!"

"Aye, you do. It is me."

That seemed to terrify the girl. "You will come no closer!"

Caledonia didn't look surprised by the child's reaction, though Darius was. He watched with some concern as Caledonia came out of the kitchen door and faced her daughter.

"Don't be afraid," Caledonia said as gently as she could. "I promise that my appearance is a good thing. I will not hurt you, I swear."

"Nay!" Jane cried. "The… the devil is within you!"

"The devil is not within me," Caledonia said steadily. "If Madam Madonna told you that, it was a lie. She has been lying to you."

"Don't say that!"

"I am sorry, Jane, but she has," Caledonia said, realizing that she was only seeing a hint of the damage that Madam Madonna had caused. "She has been lying to you all along so you would not love me."

Jane slapped her hands over her ears. "The devil is speaking to me!" she shrieked. "Go away, devil! Go away from me!"

With that, she fled the kitchen yard through the postern gate, running out behind the keep. Caledonia didn't try to stop her. She simply stood there, looking at the gate as tears streamed down her cheeks. With a heavy sigh, she wiped off her face and turned back toward the fishpond where the girl who had her feet in the pond was still sitting, now looking at Caledonia curiously.

The other child was still eating dirt.

Two more lost waifs, manipulated by the evil that was Madam Madonna. Caledonia knew she had an uphill battle ahead of her, which had been shockingly evident with her eldest. Jane had been exposed to it the longest. But now… now, she was facing her younger daughters, who didn't seem as terrified of her as Jane had.

She took a deep breath, composing herself.

She wondered how badly she was going to frighten child number two.

"Greetings, Janet," Caledonia said to the girl with her feet in the water. "You have grown a good deal, too. Do you know me?"

Janet de Tosni stared at her mother for a moment before taking her feet out of the pond and standing up. She was dressed like a servant, in dirty clothing that was torn. She wore no shoes, nor were there any around that suggested she might have taken them off to put her feet in the pond in the first place. The child was so skinny that surely a strong wind would have blown her away.

"Mother," she said. "You're Mother."

At least she wasn't running from her. That realization nearly brought tears again. "Aye," Caledonia said softly. "I am your mother. And you have grown very big since the last I saw you."

Janet was looking at her with open curiosity. She walked up to her mother, looked at her fine dress, the way her hair was pulled back, and even lifted up the hem of her gown to inspect her shoes. Scrutiny complete, she simply stared at her mother expectantly.

Caledonia wasn't sure what to say to her. Janet wasn't fleeing, but she wasn't welcoming, either. Caledonia crouched down to bring herself more to Janet's level when she noticed that someone had joined them. The youngest child, with dirt in her mouth, and all over her face and body, had wandered up and was looking at her as if she had no idea who she was. There was simply naked curiosity and nothing more.

Caledonia forced a smile at the child who had turned three years of age this month.

"Greetings, Joan," she said, looking at the filthy, angelic child. "You have grown just like your sisters. You have become a big girl."

Joan uttered a sound, possibly a word, but it was difficult to tell with the dirt still in her mouth. She reached out to touch her mother's hair, getting dirt on it, but Caledonia didn't care. At least the child was showing some interest in her. In fact, Caledonia thought that it was a rather magical moment, but she couldn't understand a thing the child was saying.

"My apologies," she said. "I cannot understand. What did you say?"

"She always talks like that," Janet said. "She has her own words."

Caledonia looked at her. "Her own words for what?"

Janet took her little sister by the hand and pointed at the pond. "Blake," she said. "Blakey? What's that?"

Joan looked at the water. "Boty!"

Janet looked at Caledonia. "See?" she said. "She calls water 'boty.'"

Caledonia's brow furrowed. "But why?"

Janet shrugged. "She screamed too much when she was a baby," she said. "Madam Madonna told us not to talk to her until she stopped screaming. She still screams, but she cannot talk."

Caledonia was horrified to hear that. "She cannot talk... at all?"

Janet shook her head. "Madam Madonna said she had too much of our mother in her and we weren't to talk to her until she learned to be obedient."

The child didn't even seem to care that she was telling her own mother what Madam Madonna said about her. She was speaking very matter-of-factly.

Caledonia's horror was only intensified.

"But... but she's only a baby," she said, looking at the dirty child. "How is she to learn words if no one speaks to her?"

Janet shrugged. That was as much as she knew. Caledonia felt so much sorrow that she lowered her head so the children wouldn't see the tears in her eyes. She'd known that coming to Stafford would be difficult, and this was as bad as she had feared. Probably worse. As she wiped at her eyes, she caught sight of Darius' legs in her periphery. Turning in his direction, she could see him over by the yard gate along with two royal soldiers. By the expression on his face, she could see that he'd heard everything.

"Go about your duties, Darius," she said quietly. "There is

no need for you to remain here."

Darius nodded but didn't move. "Would… would you like me to remain, my lady?" he said. "Mayhap I can… help."

Caledonia shook her head. "Thank you, but nay," she said. "Please go about your duties."

Darius and the soldiers left the yard without another word. When they were gone and the gate was secured, Caledonia returned her attention to the two moppets in front of her.

For a moment, she simply looked at them.

Janet was more like Robert. Her hair was pale, like her mother's, but she had blue eyes like Robert had. She had his height, too. She was tall. The youngest, Joan, was more like her, but Caledonia thought she saw a bit of her mother in the child. Honestly, it was difficult to tell what she looked like because she was covered with filth.

It was truly baffling.

"What were you and your sisters doing out here?" she asked Janet. "Do you not have lessons? Or tasks to complete?"

That meant nothing to Janet. "What tasks?"

Caledonia shrugged. "I do not know," she said. "Helping in the keep? Learning to sew? What does Madam Madonna tell you to do?"

"Nothing," Janet said as her sister stuck a dirty finger up her nose. "She tells us to go to bed and when to wake up, but then she goes away."

Caledonia frowned. "What do you mean by that? Where does she go?"

Janet shrugged. Then she yawned and looked around the yard as if uninterested in the question. "She just goes," she said.

"But who feeds you? Who conducts your lessons?"

"We do not have lessons," Janet said. "If we want food, we

go to the cook. Sometimes she gives us bread in the morning, but sometimes she has none. Blakey eats the dirt because she is hungry. My chicken lays eggs for us to suck, but not always. At night, when the men are feasting, sometimes we are given a bowl with food. We share it."

Caledonia's horror reached new heights as she heard of her children's daily life. "But… but no one takes *care* of you?" she asked.

Janet didn't even know what that meant, so there was no answer to give. Caledonia was so overwhelmed that she didn't even know what to say. Her children were pale, thin, dressed in rags, and eating dirt.

A mother's worst nightmare.

She was precluded by asking further questions when Thor made an appearance. He came through the yard gate, from the bailey, and Caledonia immediately saw him. She rose from her crouched position, where she had been speaking to her younger children, watching him approach her. He looked at her, at the girls, and seemed almost apprehensive.

"Are these—?"

He was gesturing to the two young girls. Caledonia nodded. "They are," she said, her voice trembling. "That is Janet and Joan."

Thor smiled at the girls, who stared up at him without a reaction. He couldn't help but notice how dirty and bony they were. His smile faded as he looked at his wife.

"They're beautiful, like their mother," he said softly. "But I just saw a young girl running wildly around the bailey screaming that the devil had appeared to her. That couldn't be the eldest… could it?"

Caledonia nodded. "It is," she said, looking sick. "I told you that Madam Madonna had poisoned my children. The younger two do not seem to be too terribly affected, but Jane… The moment I told her who I was, she accused me of being the devil and ran away."

"Ah," Thor said in understanding. His gaze inevitably moved to the small, malnourished children standing a few feet away. "Madam Madonna is in the vault along with the de Lucera knights. The Stafford soldiers are being gathered and informed of the new command change as we speak. Therefore, the girls are yours, my love. Take them in hand. Take this entire keep in hand and let them know that the rightful chatelaine of Stafford has taken her place. I know you will excel at whatever you do."

She looked at her as if the thought hadn't occurred to her. She was so focused on seeing her children that the thought of actually assuming control at Stafford—any kind of control— wasn't something she'd contemplated. She just stood there, looking uncertain, and Thor put his hand on her arm in a comforting gesture.

"What is it?" he said softly.

She blinked, trying to stave off the tears. "I… I am not sure," she said. "I feel as if… You must understand that I was never permitted to take my rightful place here, so I feel as if I need permission in order to do anything at all."

Thor smiled. "I am the Earl of Tamworth and Stafford," he said gently. "You have my permission, Callie. You have my permission to do whatever you want, to whomever you wish, and however you wish. This is ours, my love. But at this moment, you need to make it *yours*."

He was right. Caledonia had to shake off every doubt, every fear, every shred of uncertainty. She was strong. She knew she was.

But this was a monumental task.

"Every servant here was taught to disrespect me," she said. "Look at my children—they are filthy and starved. Madam Madonna evidently did not care for them at all. Janet told me that she simply let them do as they pleased, and they are hardly fed. Look at them, Thor. They are like wild animals. Joan cannot even speak because no one would teach her."

Thor could hear the anguish in her voice. It would have been one thing to come to Stafford to find her children well tended and educated. At least her mind could be at least a little to know they were being cared for. But that evidently hadn't been the case. Even Thor could see how dirty and skinny her children were, which he found quite disturbing.

He could only imagine how heartbreaking it was for her.

"Then your arrival is a sign from God," he said. "He meant us to come here, at this moment, so you can save your children. I will find the eldest one, but you must take the little ones and tend to them. They are in desperate need, Callie."

She nodded even before he finished speaking. "I know," she said, looking at them. Then she put her hand over her heart, her lower lip trembling. "Is this what I left them to, Thor? Abuse? All the while I was in London, trying to forget about everything… here… Is *this* what was happening to my children?"

He could feel the guilt rolling off her in waves, like the pounding of the ocean, and he didn't want to add to it even though he could very much understand her torment. "You could not have known," he said. "You were chased away by that wicked woman. Your spirit had been broken by Robert. You cannot blame yourself for staying away. You had to do what you felt best when there was nothing left but pain."

She sniffled, looking at him. "Pain," she murmured. "My pain at being kept from my children. But I stayed away when the truth was that was that Robert was dead. I *am* the Lady of Stafford. I could have come here and sent Madam Madonna away. But… I didn't. Was my spirit so broken that I did not understand that my power had been returned to me with Robert's death?"

She was becoming distraught, and he leaned over and kissed her temple. "You will not think of that now," he told her softly but firmly. "Do not think of yourself. Think of your children. Take those two inside and bathe them and feed them. I will find the eldest one."

She returned her attention to the girls as she quickly wiped away her tears. "You are correct," she said, squaring her shoulders and trying to shrug off that crushing guilt. "But I fear I need your help."

"Anything you wish, my love."

Her dark gaze moved to the keep. "The servants," she said. "Will you gather the servants and tell them that I have returned and they are to obey me? I fear they will not listen to me, since Robert told them not to. As the new lord, you have that power."

Thor nodded. "Of course," he said. "I will do it immediately."

"Thank you," she said. "And I want the cook dismissed."

"Why?"

"Because Janet told me that she would hardly feed them, even though she knew they were in distress."

His jaw twitched faintly. "I will do what is necessary to ensure you are obeyed and comfortable in your own home," he said. "I will send Nicola to you. She can help."

"Thank you."

"It is my pleasure," Thor said with an encouraging smile. "I will return to you shortly."

With that, he kissed her and left the kitchen yard, leaving Caledonia standing with two children she'd given birth to but who didn't know her at all.

She was determined to change that.

God help her, she was.

CHAPTER THIRTEEN

THE CLEANING AND feeding of Janet and Joan de Tosni was a monumental task.

Caledonia struggled to put aside her emotions, her innate guilt, and focus on the duty at hand as she took her daughters inside to begin reversing the process that Madam Madonna had started. Entering the keep itself was an interesting experience because she had always been limited as to the rooms she could visit. She and Robert had separate bedchambers, and hers was on the top floor with the servants and quite possibly the smallest chamber in the entire keep, while Robert had the large chamber on the next floor down and Madam Madonna had the room next to his.

The old nurse was still watching over her charge.

The daughters slept in what was essentially an alcove in Madam Madonna's large and spacious chamber. Caledonia figured this out when she took the girls inside and wanted to know where they kept their clean clothing. As it turned out, they didn't have any clean clothing. They only had the clothes on their back. Janet took her to Madam Madonna's chamber, which was lavishly furnished, and then showed her mother the small alcove that had three little mattresses on the ground. There weren't even any blankets. The saving grace was probably the fact that the alcove was next to the hearth, so even in cold weather, the girls wouldn't freeze. But seeing how her children had been raised not only increased her guilt—it fueled a fire of rage in her that seemed to be gaining intensity by the moment.

Nicola eventually found her in Madam Madonna's chamber, and when Caledonia explained the situation to her, Nicola was suitably outraged. However, she had one thing that Caledonia didn't have—the fact that she was somewhat emotionally detached from the situation. She had a better perspective on what needed to happen and how it needed to happen, and as Caledonia convinced her daughters that they needed to take a bath, Nicola swung into action.

The first thing she did was rummage through Madam Madonna's personal possessions looking for soap or anything else that could be used for a bath. Mother Madonna, in spite of being a former nun, seemed to have a plethora of personal possessions, including bathing implements, oils, and soaps. The woman had enough loot to start her own merchant stall because she also had combs, perfumes, and even some cosmetics. The more Nicola dug around, the more she found.

It was all quite surprising.

Handing Caledonia the oils and the soap, Nicola went on the hunt for a tub. She had absolutely no fear as she searched through the halls and chambers until she finally came across a copper tub that was kept near the kitchens. At this point, Thor had all of the servants rounded up and out in the bailey, where he could explain to them who was now in charge. In fact, the entry door was open and Nicola could hear her brother speaking rather sternly to the servants from the keep. There were at least fifteen of them that she could see, all of them listening to the new Earl of Tamworth and Stafford.

Her brother.

She was actually quite proud of him.

Unwilling to wait for the servants to be dismissed, Nicola went through a kitchen that smelled heavily of smoke and yeast, and out into the kitchen yard in search of some royal soldiers because she needed help lugging the water and the tub up to Madame Madonna's chamber. Because she was a resourceful young woman, she was able to convince Darius to give her a hand even though he had his own duties given to him by Thor. Nicola wouldn't be put off, however, and being that he was in love with the woman, Darius simply obeyed her. He grabbed several soldiers, and the group of them headed back to the keep so they could bring the bathtub up to the upper floors.

As was usual in almost all castles, there was an enormous iron cauldron of hot water boiling over the open flame. It was a staple in most kitchens so any hot water needs could be fulfilled, including baths. Darius and the soldiers found buckets, and the bathtub, along with the hot water, was hauled up to Madam Madonna's chamber. As they entered, they found Caledonia cutting off the bottom on a pair of shifts she had found. Given the fact that the children had no clothing, she had little choice unless she wanted her daughters to run around naked, so she'd commandeered two shifts she found in a trunk and, using scissors she found in a sewing kit in the same trunk, cut them both to fit her daughters. They were a little big, but they would have to do until she could make real clothing for the girls.

One problem at a time.

Once the tub was half-full of steaming water, Caledonia and

Nicola coaxed the little girls out of their filthy and tattered clothing. Janet argued that she liked what she was wearing and intended to go back down to the kitchen yard and play with her pet chicken, but Caledonia managed to convince her that taking a bath would be more fun. According to Janet, she'd never taken a bath in her life, and given the state of her skin and clothing, Caledonia was willing to believe it. However, she didn't seem to be afraid of the water and, in fact, climbed in happily when she realized it was warm. But Joan, the baby, was positively terrified of the water and screamed as if she was being murdered as Caledonia lowered her into the warm bath.

As Nicola scrubbed Janet, Caledonia scrubbed the little one. Joan stood up in the bathtub, screaming at the top of her lungs as her mother washed her with soap that smelled of lavender and rosemary. The wash also included washing out her mouth because it was still full of mud and dirt. The areas between her teeth were black with dirt, and Caledonia used some of the fabric that she had cut off the shifts as a rag to clean the child's teeth. There was even dirt in her nostrils. For the dirt-eating child, the grit was literally everywhere.

In fact, the baby was so dirty that they considered this bath just the first rinse. Nicola sent down for the soldiers again, and they returned to empty the bathtub and bring fresh water. The second bathing was a little better, and didn't leave the water nearly as dirty as the first, but Joan still screamed through the entirety of it. Caledonia soldiered through, however, scrubbing and rinsing a child who seemed to feel that she was genuinely being murdered in the process. Once it was all done, and the girls were clean and dried and put into the makeshift clothing, Joan promptly fell into an exhausted sleep on Madam Madonna's bed. It took Janet a little longer, but once everything was said and done, she fell asleep next to her sister.

Warm and clean for probably the first time in her young life.

Caledonia would have rather liked to have joined them.

Standing over her daughters, she felt as if she'd been through a battle. Which she had. But they were both clean and the baby's hair was drying into soft white curls in the warm air. To see them like that eased Caledonia's heart a little, but it would be a long time before the guilt of leaving her children in such a horrible state left her. But, as Thor had said, it was time for her to focus on her children and not her own guilt.

It was time to *do* something about it.

She'd gotten a good start.

"God's Bones," Caledonia muttered. "I've never been so exhausted in my life."

Nicola was still sitting on the floor where she'd dressed Janet. She couldn't seem to get up. "I think I've lost my hearing in one ear," she said, sticking her finger into it. "I've never heard a child scream so long and so loudly before."

Caledonia nodded in agreement, gazing down at her sleeping daughters. "They're like feral animals," she said. "No discipline, no rules or love or guidance. Joan screamed as if she'd never seen water in her life."

"She probably hasn't," Nicola said, wearily rising to her feet. She spied the girls on the bed, sleeping so sweetly, and chuckled. "But look at them now. They are angels."

"For the moment."

"Where is the eldest one?"

Caledonia's attention turned away from the bed and toward the windows. She could hear the sounds of the bailey outside.

"That," she said thoughtfully, "is a very good question."

CƷ

HE WAS ON the hunt.

Thor was on the trail of Jane, who had been screaming in the upper bailey about a devil, but now had conspicuously vanished. Thor knew that the servants and the Stafford army had been gathered and that they were waiting for him in the lower bailey to address them, but he had promised his wife that he would find her eldest daughter, and find her he would.

But she was elusive.

Not for long if he could help it. He had been following her trail, being directed by royal soldiers who had seen the child run past them, until he ended up in the stables where the grooms were settling the warhorses after their journey from Birmingham. He was down in the lower bailey now, following the signs, and ended up just inside the stable door. The stables of Stafford were quite large, a long building that stretched along part of the motte. It made sense because all of the filth from the stables was easily dumped into the moat right behind it. As he cautiously entered the structure, which still had servants inside as they tended to the animals, he began to hear a small, high-pitched voice.

He wasn't sure where it was coming from, but he happened to glance at one of the servants who was filling a feed bucket, and the man pointed to the eastern side of the stable block. Thor didn't even ask him why he pointed because he already knew.

There was someone in the stable who shouldn't be there.

Therefore, he headed off to the eastern portion of the stable block, where he immediately caught sight of a slight, white-haired child. Her hair was to her knees, matted and dirty, and she wore tattered clothing that was too small for her frame. There were several horses at this end, including his own warhorse, and the child seemed to be standing just in front of his stall. The horses were facing inward as they munched on their grain, but that didn't stop the little girl from talking to big horse arses.

She seemed quite intent.

"And that is why Christ has saved you from your sins," she was saying. "Whenever you disobey your master, you are disobeying God. All creatures need salvation, and I am here to make sure you understand the spirit of God."

Thor couldn't help the confused furrow of the brow. He thought he hadn't heard right with the first sentence he was able to make out, but then he realized that the child was trying to preach to the horses. She seemed quite serious about it. Given that she wasn't hysterical at the moment and screaming about devils, he took the opportunity to approach her.

Carefully.

"My lady?" he said, trying to catch her attention. "My lady, are you Lady Jane?"

She stopped looking at horse buttocks and turned to him. Thor hadn't gotten a good look at her before, when she'd run through the bailey, but now he could see that she was the exact image of Caledonia. She had the same dark, dark green eyes and white hair, the same upturned nose, the same lips. It was like looking at his wife when she'd been a child, such a beautiful, ethereal child.

A child who was looking at him curiously.

"Would you like me to teach you the word of God?" she asked.

He smiled, gesturing to the horses. "Is that what you were

doing?" he asked. "Teaching them the word of God?"

She nodded. "Even the animals must know," she said. "How else are they to get into heaven?"

"How else, indeed," Thor said. "But you *are* Jane, are you not?"

The child eyed him before nodding and turning away. "You can listen to me as I teach them," she said. "Do you know that God loves you but if you disobey Him, you will go to hell?"

She was going back to the animals. Thor watched her closely. "Do you know that if you disobey your mother and father, you will go to hell also?"

Jane stopped and looked at him. "I have no mother or father," she said. "My father is dead."

"But your mother is not," he said. "Before you start screaming that she is the devil, who told you that? Because saying that your mother is a devil when she is not is a sin."

Jane's eyes widened. "But she *is* wicked! She is the devil!"

"Who told you that?"

"Madam Madonna!"

Thor already knew that, but he wanted to hear it from her. He knew it wouldn't do any good to deny it. He wondered just how bright she was and if he could possibly reason with her, because they certainly couldn't have her running all over the castle screaming that Caledonia was the devil.

He crooked a finger at her.

"Come here," he said. "Sit down."

He was indicating a clean spot of hay near one of the empty stalls, but Jane was confused by the request. "Why?" she said.

"Because I am asking you to. Please, my lady."

"Who are you?"

"I am the new Earl of Tamworth and Stafford," he said.

"Your father held the title before I did. Now it belongs to me because the king granted it to me. Do you understand?"

She nodded, but he wasn't entirely sure she really understood. Still, his explanation had her moving over to the spot he had indicated. When she sat down, he sat a few feet away from her, facing her.

For this conversation, he needed to get down to her level.

"My name is Thor," he said, looking into those dark eyes. "As I told you, I am the new earl. That means you will be living in my home from now on. Do you understand me so far?"

Jane nodded. "All of us?" she said. "Me and my sisters and Madam Madonna and the servants?"

Thor wasn't sure he should tell her about Madam Madonna yet, but on the other hand, he wanted to be completely truthful with her from the start. Lies or hiding information wouldn't do well when building trust, and he wanted to build that very much.

"Lady Jane, do you know what a lie is?" he asked, avoiding her question.

She nodded solemnly. "Aye," she said. "Lies displease God."

"But *what* is a lie?"

"When you say something that is not true."

"Exactly," he said. "Well done. Now, do you think God is displeased when people are cruel?"

"Aye."

"I think so, too," Thor said. "My lady, how old are you?"

Jane shrugged. "I am not of age yet," she said. "Madam Madonna said I will be of age in a few years and then I will marry someone of her choosing."

That was an interesting bit of information, but he didn't pursue it. "May I ask if Madam Madonna is good to you?" he asked.

She nodded without hesitation. "She prays for us," she said. "She prays that God will let me go to heaven. My sisters will not go to heaven, but I will."

"Did Madam Madonna tell you that?"

"Aye."

"Do you love your sisters, my lady?"

That was a question Jane had never considered before. Perhaps no one had ever asked her. It seemed to confuse her.

"They are my sisters," she said.

Thor phrased it another way. "I know," he said. "But if they were to get hurt or die, would you be sad?"

She had to think about that. "I would miss them."

"Because you love them," Thor said. When she still looked rather blank, he elaborated. "If they were to become ill, would you help them?"

"I have helped them when they are ill."

"Because you are the eldest, you must protect them," he said, watching her still-blank expression. "If someone was trying to hurt them, would you protect them?"

She cocked her head thoughtfully. "Once, a soldier tried to take Joan," she said. "I screamed and he was stopped."

Thor smiled. "You see?" he said. "You are a very good sister because you love them, and that makes God very happy."

She didn't look so blank any longer. Hearing that bit of praise from Thor made her smile. "And I will go to heaven!"

"Of course you will," Thor said. "But that brings me back to what we were originally speaking of. Do you believe it is wicked when someone lies? Does it displease God?"

She nodded eagerly. "Aye, it does."

Now, Thor had her understanding what he wanted to speak

to her about. At least a little. He forged ahead.

"I am going to tell you a story because I want to explain something to you," he said. "Many years ago, a lady had a baby. A lovely daughter that she loved very much. God was very happy with the birth. But someone wicked took the baby away. Told the baby lies about her mother. The mother was not wicked, and it was very sad for her to be kept away from her baby. God was no longer pleased. He was displeased with the wicked person. Would you be displeased, too?"

Jane had to think about that. "But why would the wicked person take the baby away and lie?"

"Because she wanted the baby," Thor said. "The wicked person took the baby away because she did not want her mother to have her. She told the baby anything she could so she would hate her mother. That surely must displease God very much because it of the lies. One of the commandments is to honor your father and mother, after all."

Jane nodded but wasn't sure what to say to it all. Thor could see that he was close to overwhelming her with his conversation because she was young and clearly wasn't very adept in the art of conversation. It occurred to him that everything she'd said to him about the word of God sounded as if she was mimicking someone.

Perhaps that was all she knew.

The only human contact she'd ever had.

"I am telling you this for a reason, my lady," he said quietly. "You were the baby in my story. Someone very wicked has kept you from your mother and has told you lies about her. God is not pleased about that. He is not pleased that you called your mother the devil."

Now, Jane was starting to catch on to what he was saying

and why. Her breathing started to quicken.

"Where is Madam Madonna?" she said, her eyes welling. "I want to speak to Madam Madonna."

Thor could see that he was about to lose her. "My lady, listen to me for a moment," he said. "It is important. With Madam Madonna, all you knew was poverty and suffering."

"Nay!"

"Are you hungry?"

"God wants us to suffer!"

"He does not," he said. "Madam Madonna wanted you to suffer. She wanted you to be hungry and cold. But your mother has come to help you and you will never be cold and hungry again, I swear it. You will go to bed with a full belly and awaken to food and warmth. She will love you and you will be happy. Would that not be better than living in rags as you do?"

Jane was starting to weep. She lurched to her feet and ran off before he could stop her. But he let her go, standing up and brushing the chaff off his breeches, hoping he hadn't made the situation worse with her. The child had clearly been conditioned to believe only what Madam Madonna told her.

It was a sad situation.

Pondering his next move, Thor wandered from the stable, heading out into the large lower bailey where soldiers and servants were gathered. He'd brought around eight hundred men with them, and at this moment, his men were on the battlements, at the gatehouses, and guarding de Lucera and Madam Madonna in the vault. Given that he needed to speak to those sworn to Stafford, he pushed aside thoughts of Jane and headed toward the gathering. Truett was bringing in several more errant Stafford soldiers and saw him coming. As his herd of soldiers mixed with those already gathered, Truett went to

Thor.

"That is all we can locate, Thor," he said. "We are fairly certain that this is everyone."

Thor looked at the collection. "Excellent," he said. "How many Stafford soldiers?"

"We can only find about seven hundred," Truett said. Part of the de Nerra family, he was big and dark and intimidating. "It seems that there were twice that many, but after de Tosni died and his wife fled to London, no one wanted to remain under the de Lucera knights. I'm hearing tale that they stole from their own soldiers and treated them rather poorly."

Thor grunted. "Then that will work in our favor," he said. "When was the last time they were paid?"

"When de Tosni was alive, from what I can gather."

"What about the servants?"

"The same, I would imagine, but I've not spoken to any of them."

Thor paused and turned to Truett. "It simply proves my theory," he said. "I said that it was possible de Tosni's knights were ruling over Stafford as if it was their person domain, and you are the second person who has confirmed that theory. I intend to have an honest conversation with these men about it, but one thing is increasingly certain."

"What is that?"

Thor cocked a dark eyebrow. "That de Lucera, his cousins, and Madam Madonna are to be exiled from Stafford permanently," he said. "In fact, I see no reason to wait. True, will you see to it?"

Truett nodded. "Of course," he said. "What do you want me to do?"

Thor turned in the direction of the gatehouse with the vault hidden below it. "Take twenty of our men," he said quietly. "Escort them to collect their belongings, but they are to take nothing of value with them. No coin, no weapons. They can only take what they can carry, and you will have them escorted out of here and left at Penkridge. That was the village just south of here. Give them two pounds each and tell them that if they ever show their faces at Stafford or Tamworth that I will cut their heads off and feed them to the pigs. They're damn lucky I'm not keeping them all in the vault for the rest of their lives. But… I want to be fair. Fairer than they've treated anyone around here, from what I'm hearing."

Truett fought off a grin. "I will happily do it, my lord."

"Do it today."

"Aye, my lord."

With that, Truett was gone, preparing to throw the de Luceras and Madam Madonna out on their ears while Thor went to the head of the gathering of Stafford soldiers and servants and told the entire group who he was, whom he stood for, whom he had married, and the fact that every individual who served Stafford was to listen to Lady de Reyne as if God Himself was speaking to them.

He left little doubt.

Some would say that Stafford Castle was saved that day.

CHAPTER FOURTEEN

One Week Later
Dordon Castle

WHEN ROTRI AND Domnall returned to Dordon nearly a week later, they were in for a surprise.

Rotri was relieved to see the pale walls of Dordon Castle come into view. He felt as if he'd been away forever when the truth was that had only been a few months. When he had first received Dordon from his brother upon the death of their father, he had complained so much about it that everyone thought he hated it. The truth was that he loved the place.

He simply wasn't satisfied with "only" Dordon.

Big dreams, big wants, big aspirations. That was everything Rotri was. But over the years, Dordon had grown on him, and as he watched his very own fortress come into view, he felt as if he was finally home. The entire journey back from London had been uncomfortable at best because they had spent most of their ready cash on bribes for Peregrine. That meant they had to save what money they had left so they could at least eat. Eating meant no money for beds, so they had found shelter in liveries or simply under the trees at the edge of a village. But now that they were home, Rotri was looking forward to sleeping in his own bed.

The creature comforts of home.

It was nearing sunset as they approached the drawbridge of Dordon Castle. The structure didn't have a conventional gatehouse, but it had a drawbridge that was quite effective in keeping marauders and enemies at bay. There was a deep trench dug around most of the castle, a trench that the drawbridge spanned, but the entire north side of the castle was built on the edge of a cliff that overlooked a waterway that tended to fill up in the rainy season. The moat connected to the waterway, creating a seasonal lake surrounding the castle.

The result was that Dordon Castle was solidly protected on all sides. It was technically a Tamworth garrison against the Welsh who were known to venture this far into England, but Rhun had let his brother run the garrison as he saw fit. He never really imposed anything on Rotri, knowing that the man wanted to be in charge of his own domain.

Rhun had simply let him do as he pleased.

A domain that welcomed him back with open arms as the sun lay low in the west. The birds were gathering over the water way behind the castle, flocking up into the sky with their cries drifting upon the wind. But Rotri didn't notice because he was completely focused on the drawbridge and his men who were waiting there to greet him. The small contingent from London traveled over the drawbridge and into the belly of Dordon Castle, welcomed as if they were kings.

But it was all an act.

The truth was that Rotri was not well liked by his people, but he expected them to welcome him with open arms, so they did. Men rushed out to meet the escort, helping to unload the wagon and taking the horses away to the stable. Everyone pretended they were glad to see him, but they weren't. No one particularly cared. Rotri had left his major domo in charge when he left for London, and that man was one of the first people to meet him as he approached the small keep.

Rotri lifted a hand in greeting to the man.

"I see my castle is still standing, Duns," he said, sounding as if he were a conqueror who had returned to his empire. "I trust that everything has been well here."

Duns, a Scotsman with bushy white hair, an enormous beard, and foul-smelling breath, nodded. "Aye, m'lord," he said in his thick accent. "All has been well. Welcome home."

"Thank you," Rotri said, raking a weary hand through his head. "But I must confess that I am exhausted. I want food and sleep and nothing more until tomorrow. Then we may discuss what has gone on in my absence."

"Aye, m'lord," Duns said, following Rotri as he headed for the keep. "But… we have visitors, m'lord."

Rotri came to a halt, frowning at him. "What visitors?"

"Cristano de Lucera is here," Duns said. "He is with his cousins and an old woman who wears the robes of a nun. He wants to speak with ye."

"De Lucera?" Rotri said, puzzled. "Who is that?"

"A knight at Stafford Castle, my lord."

Rotri knew he'd heard that name before but couldn't place it. Now, he remembered at the mention of Stafford. "What does he want to talk about?" he asked.

"He would not tell me, m'lord."

That made no sense to Rotri. His bed was calling him, but something made him pause. *Stafford Castle. The man is from Stafford Castle.* The fortress where Caledonia and Thor were at this very moment. At least, he assumed they were there, given they'd departed London for de Reyne's new properties. Stafford was one. Therefore, he couldn't imagine that this visit was a coincidence.

Something told him to talk to the man.

"Very well," he said. "Where is he?"

"The great hall, m'lord."

That had Rotri turning for the great hall, which was positioned across the bailey. It wasn't a big hall—perhaps only able to seat seventy or eighty men—but it did the job. Rotri was focused on the old wooden entry doors when Domnall called to him.

"Where are you going?" his son yelled. "I thought you were exhausted!"

Rotri didn't stop in his march toward the hall, but he lifted a hand to catch his son's attention. "Come with me," he said. "Hurry!"

That had Domnall breaking in his direction, across the dusty bailey to catch up with his father about the time he entered the dark and dank hall, with what windows there were placed high in the wall for ventilation and a firepit in the center of the room. Rotri entered with Domnall on his heels. Immediately, they caught sight of four people sitting near the firepit, which was lit at this time of night. The entire hall smelled of smoke. As Rotri approached the table, all of the men seated around it stood up.

"My lord," de Lucera said. "I do not know if you remember me, but I am Cristano de Lucera. I was the captain to the Earl of Stafford, Robert de Tosni, when he was alive. Your niece, Lady de Tosni, is his widow."

"I remember you," Rotri said, but there was great suspicion

in his expression. "It has been a long time, but I remember you."

"I am honored, my lord," Cristano said. "We have been here for a few days, waiting for your return. I hope that does not displease you."

Rotri shook his head. "It does not," he said. "I was told you wished to speak with me. It must be important if you have waited for days."

Cristano nodded. "It is, my lord," he said. Then he indicated the two younger knights standing next to him. "These are my cousins, Adan and Benedicto."

Rotri didn't care about them. He brushed off the two dark, rather dirty younger men because he only cared about what Cristano had to say. "Well?" he said. "Why are you here? Why aren't you at Stafford?"

Cristano indicated for Rotri to sit. "You must be weary, my lord," he said. "Sit and we will send for food."

Rotri was at the end of his patience. "I do not want food," he said, slapping the tabletop. "I want to know why you are here, and you will answer me. Why aren't you at Stafford?"

So much for pleasantries. It was clear that Cristano had been trying to create some kind of social atmosphere, but Rotri was having none of it. Cristano eyed his cousins apprehensively before continuing.

"Because I no longer serve there, my lord," he said frankly. "That is why I have come. I hope it is not too much of an imposition to inquire if you are looking for the service of strong knights. If so, my cousins and I would like to submit our experience for your consideration. We are excellent knights, my lord. We are seeking a liege, and I thought—since Dordon is part of Tamworth—that you could use knights who are familiar with Stafford and the surrounding area. We would like to remain where we know the land and the politics, my lord, and it seemed logical to come to you since we had nowhere else to go. Will you consider it?"

That statement made no sense to Rotri. "No longer serve at…?" he repeated, baffled. "But you have been a Stafford for years."

"Several, my lord."

"And you have been dismissed?"

"Aye, my lord."

"But why?"

Cristano's jaw twitched with emotion. "Because the new Earl of Stafford and Tamworth brought his own knights," Cristano said. "He has bitterly and without cause exiled us from a castle we have taken great care of for many years. Two of those years have been since the death of Lord Robert. But still, we were given no consideration. We were dismissed as if our service did not matter in the least. We beg you to consider our fealty."

Rotri was struggling to process it all. He looked at Domnall, who seemed equally surprised. "Is *that* why you have come?" he said. "Because de Reyne threw you out?"

"Aye, my lord. Most unfairly, I might add."

Oh, but this was a surprising bit of news. When Rotri had entered the hall, he hadn't expected this. So Thor de Reyne had taken possession of Stafford Castle and dismissed de Tosni's knights, had he? That was an extremely interesting development, but it was also fortuitous one.

Very fortuitous.

For the entire journey from London back to Dordon Castle, Rotri and Domnall had been discussing how they could create a situation that would see Thor fall into their hands. If they wanted to ransom the man, they had to get their hands on him, and as Rotri looked at the three knights in front of him, he could only see men that had been wronged by de Reyne. Slandered, even. They were clearly bitter about it.

Perhaps they were men who would jump at the chance to get even.

That brought about Rotri's ideas that he and Domnall had come up with on the journey north. They'd had nothing but time on their hands to scheme. After much discussion, they had decided to carry out a raid to draw Thor out of the castle, which was most important if they wanted to get a clear shot at him. If Thor remained holed up in that fortified castle, there was no way they would ever be able to get to him. No way they could touch him. But if they were able to draw him out in some kind of skirmish, that might be their only opportunity to abduct him. But now, with the appearance of de Lucera and his cousins, it was as if God was confirming his scheme by way of these cast-out Stafford knights.

He couldn't believe his luck.

"You say that you were unfairly dismissed?" Rotri said.

Cristano nodded. "We were not even allowed to take our possessions," he said. "I had to leave most of my expensive weaponry behind, along with my money. My cousins, too. This woman was cast out without anything at all, and she tended the de Tosni children since birth. We are all victims of de Reyne's greed and unjust ways. Will you not help us, my lord?"

He was indicating the woman sitting next to him, wrapped up in brown robes, but Rotri didn't give her a glance. "Of course I will," he said, trying not to sound too eager. "It just so happens that de Reyne has been unfair to us, also. In fact, my son and I have been discussing ways to exact justice on the man. Now that I hear your story, I would assume you might be interested in the same, eh?"

Cristano didn't even seem surprised by the suggestion. It seemed to perk him up. "Justice against de Reyne?" he said. "Those are sweet words, my lord. What did you have in mind?"

Rotri told him.

CHAPTER FIFTEEN

"**P**UT YOUR HAND here," she whispered, putting his palm against her breast. "Let me feel you against me, your flesh to mine."

Thor didn't need to be told twice. It was early in the morning, and he'd already made love to her twice the night before, but she tended to like it in the morning, too. This woman who had looked at intimacy with a husband as a duty and a horror now couldn't get enough of it when it came to Thor. Not that he minded. With a growl, he picked up his wife and carried her to their bed, a very big bed that had once belonged to Robert.

But no one thought about that.

Now, it belonged only to them.

Once on the mattress, he loosened the fastenings on her surcoat, pulling at them as she helped him. There was eagerness in her movements and in his. When he yanked the bodice down, he tore her shift a little in his eagerness and snorted as she giggled, but it didn't stop his momentum. He yanked again, freeing her breasts, and his mouth clamped down onto a warm and tender nipple.

As he suckled her furiously, Caledonia cried out softly,

holding his head to her breast as if he were a starving child nursing against her. She hadn't been allowed to nurse her own children, so there was something innate and intimate and satisfying for Thor to suckle her. She never knew she liked it until he did it, and these days, he took great delight in her breasts. As if they belonged to him, personally.

Perhaps they did, just a little.

Pushing her back on the bed, Thor continued to nurse hungrily at her breasts as he caressed her buttocks and stroked her inner thighs. She took his hand and put it against the dark fluff of curls between her legs, thrusting her pelvis forward and trying to entice his fingers into her body. Thor knew that and responded by slipping a finger into her tight, wet sheath, feeling her gasp with pleasure. When she began pushing her woman's center against him, mimicking the pelvic thrusting he would soon be doing, it was all he could take. Unfastening his breeches, he put the tip of his hard, throbbing phallus against her warm and wet folds.

"Tell me you love me," he murmured, gently kissing her chin, her mouth. "Tell me that I am your everything."

Caledonia was bucking against him, trying to force him into her body. "I love you," she whispered, something she had been doing for a few days now. "Give me your seed, angel. Let me bear your son and I shall never ask for more."

I love you. Those words drove Thor wild. He thrust into her, listening to her gasp with the sheer glory of it. She cried out softly as he thrust again and again, seating himself to the hilt, feeling her tight wetness around him. It was bliss. Caledonia clung to him, wishing he could bury himself deeper. Thor was hung like a bull, something she reminded him of nightly, and it made him feel powerful and virile. He satisfied her every time, but she was so desperate for the man that she always wanted more. As he thrust into her, he was so forceful that she ended up nearly sliding off the bed on the other side. With soft laughter, he had to pull her back onto the mattress so they could continue. Caledonia wrapped her arms around his neck, kissing him passionately as he made love to her. With every thrust, he rubbed his pelvis against hers, and she could feel sparks when their bodies met. Those sparks always ignited a wildfire, and even though neither of them wanted this to end quickly, it was difficult staving off the blaze.

As usual, the blaze flared and Thor couldn't hold back his release. Caledonia put a hand down between them, feeling him as he climaxed into her body, but in doing so, she touched herself and climaxed along with him. Thor held her tightly, feeling her curious and loving hands between them, touching him, caressing him.

It was a magical moment.

"I love you," he murmured into her ear. "I cannot remember when I haven't loved you."

Caledonia pulled her face from the crook of his neck, smiling at him. "I remember when you did *not* love me," she said, teasing him. "I remember being thrown over your shoulder and hauled around like a sack of grain."

"You deserved it."

"And dragged away to face Henry."

"You very *much* deserved it."

She giggled as he moved his body weight off her, lying down beside her with his arms still around her.

"I am sure that I did," she said. "But I am glad you did not give up. Your persistence has given me more happiness than I can comprehend."

He gave her a half-grin, looking at her beautiful profile. He loved the way her nose tilted upward, and there were times when he would gently drag his finger down the slope of her nose, tracing the outline of it. There were times when he watched her sleep and couldn't believe his life had turned out the way it had. Everything had happened so quickly. A marriage, a title, a castle, and a love he wouldn't trade for anything on this earth.

It had been thirteen days since their arrival at Stafford Castle. Thirteen days of coming to know his wife, his wife's daughters, of becoming familiar with his property. Thirteen days of watching Caledonia realize she was no longer the outcast and finding her role amongst people who wanted her to succeed.

It was amazing what a little love and support could do.

But it was also thirteen days of discovering just how badly the inhabitants of Stafford Castle had suffered under the de Lucera cousins and Madam Madonna. Thor really hadn't planned on remaining at Stafford because he wanted to visit Edingale Castle, but it seemed that Stafford needed him at the moment.

For the first few days, servant and soldier alike had been afraid to speak up, to tell of their experiences under Cristano de Lucera, but once they started to, terrible stories came out. Stories that had Cristano stealing from his men, selling off servants to other castles for the money it would bring him, of selling the fine horses that Robert de Tosni had collected, and of relegating the soldiers and servants to eating gruel or anything they could hunt and kill while he and his cousins and Madam Madonna lived like kings.

But Thor was determined to change that.

The Stafford soldiers had lived so long with the de Lucera cousins that having a liege who actually cared about them was a shocking concept. But Thor was very much like his father, a man who was concerned for those he commanded, so as the days passed, the soldiers seemed to grow more comfortable with him. He and Clayne and Darius and Truett formed a powerful quartet, and together they worked to convince the Stafford soldiers that not all commanders were terrible men. Some of the soldiers even sent word to those who had abandoned their service to Stafford, and over the past couple of days, former soldiers began flooding back to Stafford Castle, eager to return to their posts and willing to give the new Earl of Tamworth and Stafford a chance. Since no one had much liked de Tosni or de Lucera, Thor didn't really have to worry about their loyalties.

They were willing to go on a little faith.

The same could be said for Caledonia's daughters. At least the two younger girls had quickly warmed up to their mother, who had spent the vast majority of her time sewing clothing for them and initiating lessons. Nicola had been a great help when it came to the clothing and the lessons, and even though she had been a rather flighty student herself in her younger years, she was very smart and helped Caledonia tremendously.

Janet, the middle child, was the one most eager to learn. The child had spent thirteen days being bathed and fed on a regular basis, having her hair combed and braided so that it was nice and neat, and spending a few hours every day learning letters and also words from the Bible. That was the way both Caledonia and Nicola had been taught, learning words that were printed in the Bible and then translating them to a language they all spoke. Janet had learned quickly and already could write her name and several other words. She was also learning her numbers and could already write the first five. After that, she still got a little fuzzy, but it had only been a few days.

Caledonia was very proud of her progress.

Joan, the youngest, was a little more of a challenge. Since Madam Madonna had forbidden anyone from talking to her, she was a little more than an infant when it came to communication. Caledonia had been trying for thirteen days to break her of eating dirt and grass, hoping it wasn't just a habit but simply because she had been hungry enough to eat anything. That meant that the child always had a piece of bread or cheese in her hand, for if she wanted to eat something, it would actually be food and not foliage. As a result, she was getting quite a happy, round belly on her, which, given how skinny she was, was wonderful to see. She was starting to fill out, and as of the past couple of days, as long as she had bread or cheese or some other type of food in her hands, she wouldn't resort to eating the dirt.

But both Caledonia and Thor watched her closely to make sure of that.

Jane, however, had proven to be the real challenge. She had been so conditioned by Madame Madonna that it had been difficult to break through. Both Caledonia and Thor tried, but she was still quite wary of her mother. Darius even tried because she seemed to like him quite a bit, and he was under the impression that the child had been so frightened by Madam Madonna and her doom-and-gloom message that she was torn between wanting to disbelieve what she'd been told and terrified of what would happen if she did.

It was heartbreaking for Caledonia to not be able to break

through to her own child, but they were all working on it and trying to help the little girl understand that her mother was not a devil and that Madam Madonna had been lying to her. Nicola spent time with Jane in an attempt to break through to her, and out of all of them, she probably had the best chance because she was young and slightly immature and seemed to be able to understand Jane better than the rest. She had more patience with her, and Jane was starting to respond to that.

Slowly as it was.

In all, Thor and Caledonia felt as if their thirteen days at Stafford Castle had been productive and eye opening. Everyone was learning what their new role at the castle would be, and when Caledonia wasn't with her daughters, she was learning the ins and outs of how the castle was run. She caught on quickly. One of the biggest problems at Stafford was the filth factor—it was everywhere because no one had taken decent care of the keep in years—so several days ago, Caledonia had instructed the house servants to start scrubbing floors and cleaning out cobwebs. It was a major task that was still going on, even today. In fact, that was where she was heading when she had been sidetracked with her magnificent husband.

Not that either one of them minded.

That was what Thor thought as he gazed at Caledonia's profile. Reflecting over the past thirteen days made him smile. It was as if he'd been thrust into another world, one where he was wildly happy. Happier than he'd ever been with a woman he'd never wanted to marry.

There was a hell of a lot of irony in that.

"Are you truly happy, Callie?" he asked softly. He'd long since softened his stance on only calling her by her full name. "Honestly?"

She turned her face so that she was looking at him as they lay there, side by side. "Of course I am," she murmured. "Can you not tell?"

He reached out, gently stroking her cheek. "I can," he said. "I just need to hear it. I do not know about you, but I feel as if this entire marriage has been something of a dream."

She smiled weakly. "It feels like that to me, too," she said. "But a very happy dream. I'm here, with you, and I am coming to know my daughters. There is nothing that could make me happier."

He smiled in response, gently rubbing her chin with his thumb. She had an enormous dimple in it, and he loved that. "I was thinking of something," he said. "Something that may shock you."

"What is it?"

"Let me ask you a question first," he said, propping himself up on one elbow. "You are the last de Wylde, correct?"

"Aye," she said. "For the Tamworth branch of the family. There are others, but they are not nearly as important socially as my father was. I am the last of the Ceowulf branch of the House of de Wylde."

"A very old and very prestigious name."

"It is," she said. "But that happens sometimes. Old families die out, or at least the males who bear the name do. My daughters are de Tosni, but they bear de Wylde blood."

"What would you say if I wanted to take the de Wylde name?"

She looked him in shock. "What?" she gasped, sitting up. "Why would you do that?"

He sat up alongside her. "It is not unusual for a man, from a family of lesser nobility, to take the name of his wife if she is of a higher social station," he said. "It has happened before, many times. If I take the de Wylde name, our sons will be de Wylde. The line will continue through them. Tamworth has belonged to de Wylde for hundreds of years until now. Until me. I do not wish to break that continuity."

She could see that he was very serious, and it touched her deeply. "Oh… Thor," she breathed, reaching out to cup his face. "What a remarkable thing for you to consider. But what on earth will your father say?"

He shrugged. "My father married my mother to inherit the Ashington earldom, you recall," he said. "I do not know why he did not take on the de Thorington name, but he named me after the family. I am the last vestige of a great line. My brother, Brian, will inherit the earldom, as you know, and I have four other brothers who will carry on the de Reyne name. But there is no one to carry on the de Wylde name. Your great bloodlines must not be diminished, Callie. I am willing to take your name and continue the de Wylde tradition. Become a de Wylde knight, as it were."

Caledonia was stunned. It was the most selfless thing she'd ever heard of. "I… I do not know what to say," she said. "That you should give more thought to your wife's bloodlines than your own… Thor, that is incredibly generous."

He smiled faintly. "We do not have to decide today," he said. "But I wanted you to know what I was thinking. I want to discuss it with my father, too. I think he will approve."

"Aye, you must discuss it with your father," Caledonia said firmly. "You must have his blessing."

Thor nodded. "I will," he said.

Then he heard shouts floating in from the bailey outside and stood up, pulling up his breeches as he went and peered from the window.

"Darius has some returning Stafford soldiers out there," he said. "He says they are hardly trained at all. We are going to have to start running a training school for those men. I cannot have soldiers who have no idea what to do in battle."

Caledonia was up, pushing her skirts down and pulling up the top of her bodice, including the torn shift. "As I recall, Robert never worked with his army, and I do not think the de Luceras ever trained them," she said. "I cannot remember ever seeing any organized teaching."

He straightened out the top of her bodice, waggling his eyebrows apologetically when he saw where he tore it. "That is about to change," he said. "And you and your sweetness have made me late. I must go."

With that, he bent down and kissed her before heading for the chamber door. Caledonia scooted after him, collecting her slippers and pulling them on as she tried to walk.

"I must speak to you about the meat stores," she said. "Evidently, there is very little, as we have discovered the servants and soldiers were being fed gruel. We must discuss what we are to do about bulking up the meat. I have some ideas, if you will listen."

He paused at the door, his hand on the latch. "Of course I will," he said. "But let me see to my duties this morning and I will meet you in the solar in the early afternoon if you wish."

She smiled. "Good," she said. "Thank you."

He winked at her. "Thank *you*."

With that, he opened the door, only to find two young children standing there. Thor nearly tripped on them. Janet and Joan gazed up at him with their bottomless eyes.

"What are you two doing out here?" he asked after he

caught himself on the doorjamb. "I thought you were with Lady Nicola?"

They had been dressed by Nicola, that was clear. They were clad in adorable dresses made from the fine shifts left behind by Madam Madonna, garments that Caledonia and Nicola had worked hard on altering. Their hair was braided and tied back with a strip of the same material of their dresses. Nicola had been taking great delight in brushing and braiding their hair, so it was obvious his sister had been involved with them at some point that morning.

"I want to bring my chicken inside and Lady Nicola says no," Janet said seriously. "My chicken is lonely outside."

The chicken again, Thor thought. They'd been dealing with that damn chicken since the moment they arrived, an enormous black hen that Janet claimed as a pet. The thing was as big as she was and surely weighed as much, but she carried it around from time to time, or it followed her around mostly. Several times, they'd found it in the bedroom that the girls now shared, the big bedchamber that had once belonged to Madam Madonna. Those three little mattresses in the alcove had been burned and now Jane slept on her own small bed that Darius had made for her, while Janet and Joan slept on the big bed Madam Madonna used to occupy. Sometimes that chicken ended up between the girls in the bed.

But Thor tried to be patient about it.

"I do not think your chicken is lonely," he told Janet, stepping out into the landing while the girls followed him. "She has friends in the kitchen yard to keep him company. Why not go down and see her?"

Janet frowned, looking a good deal like her mother in that gesture. "Her name is Mary," she said flatly. "Mary is obedient.

Why can't she come inside?"

"Because she is a chicken," Thor said patiently. "Chickens do not live inside. People do."

"But she is my *friend*."

"I understand. But she is still a chicken."

He'd told her that a dozen times, but still, she continued to ask. He was fairly certain that she was trying to wear him down, hoping he'd give permission because he was either annoyed or finally took pity on her. Truth be told, it was difficult to look into that little face and not want to give in, but Caledonia most emphatically didn't want a chicken in the bedchambers, so Janet was going to have to accept it. In fact, as Thor stood there and tried to reason with her, Caledonia emerged from their bedchamber.

"It is time for lessons, ladies," she said, extending an arm to herd them toward the stairwell. "And stop asking about your chicken. Mary will be fine in the kitchen yard, where she has always been."

"But she is lonely," Janet said, starting her sob story on her mother.

"Not for long," Caledonia said evenly. "You will see her soon."

"If she cannot sleep with me, can we at least give her a bed?"

"She has a nest to sleep on."

"She *needs* a bed."

Thor was grinning, watching the interaction between Caledonia and her somewhat manipulative middle daughter. They were still becoming accustomed to one another, but they were learning quickly and bonding beautifully. The littlest daughter even slipped her hand into Caledonia's without prompting as she began to lead them down the stairs. He thought it was all rather sweet and had to admit that he enjoyed being a parent more than he'd thought he would. He let Caledonia take the lead in all things, of course, but he liked having the baby fall asleep on him after supper, or Janet climbing into his lap because she wanted to talk more about her chicken.

A shockingly domestic life for a man who had never even considered such a thing.

But no more shocking than his suggestion to assume the de Wylde name. He had no intention of shirking the de Reyne name entirely, merely adding de Wylde to it. As he'd told Caledonia, it wasn't unusual for a man to take his wife's family name if she was of a higher station and he assumed what was largely considered a family title. He'd been thinking about doing it for a few days now, ever since this life he'd undertaken had become something delightful. He still couldn't believe he had such a beautiful, brilliant wife, and already he was falling in love with her daughters.

Even Jane.

"Let us attend to our lessons now and we will discuss the chicken later," Caledonia was saying as she went down the stairs with a little girl in each hand. "For now, we have tasks to attend to. So does Thor. My angel?"

He was right behind them as they came off the stairs with the keep entry directly in front of them. "I certainly do," he said. "You attend your lessons, and mayhap I will speak with Darius about a… bed… for a chicken. Mayhap he can build one."

Janet ripped her hand from Caledonia's grip and threw herself at him, trying to hug him and grab him all at the same time in her excitement.

"Will you?" she nearly yelled. "Will you ask him?"

Thor had to steady her before she tripped and fell on him.

"I will ask," he assured her, but then he caught sight of Caledonia's disapproving expression, and that cooled his own enthusiasm. "But… mayhap we should ask for your mother's approval first. My love?"

Caledonia couldn't very well deny the child. She thought a bed for a chicken to be quite ridiculous, but perhaps this was all part of gaining her daughter's trust. She was building something here and wanted to make her child happy, so perhaps she needed to relent on this.

Even if it was with a bed for a chicken.

"If Darius will build such a thing, I suppose it is acceptable," she said reluctantly. "Thor, why not take Janet with you to ask Darius? You can join us in the solar once you have spoken to him."

Janet seemed wildly excited about a chicken bed. Fighting off a smirk, Thor winked at his wife and took the child with him, holding her hand as they headed from the keep. Caledonia watched them go, smiling as they faded from view. Then she looked down at the child still in her grip, noting that Joan was looking up at her. She smiled at her and squeezed her hand.

"Shall we go to our lessons now?" she asked, not really expecting an answer. Joan was bright, but speaking was still beyond her capabilities. "Lessons? *Lessons?*"

As she nodded, the child nodded. Caledonia wasn't sure if she was simply mimicking her or if she really understood her, but it didn't matter. She took the little girl into the solar, where they had an entire corner set up with a table for their lessons. Today, they were working on letters. Caledonia sat down, pulled Joan onto her lap, and wrote the letter *A* on a piece of vellum. They had been working on *A* and words associated with the letter *A* for the past week. That was how Caledonia had been taught long ago, so she simply repeated the lessons Lady d'Umfraville taught her.

Nicola joined them shortly and, soon enough, Janet returned. Nicola took over part of the lesson and spoke of all of the words that started with the letter *A*. She even gave the girls small green apples because the word apple started with an *A*. Janet was very good at writing the letter, and Joan could write it so that it was semi-legible, which was a big step for the little girl.

She was praised appropriately.

Toward the nooning hour, Nicola pulled out small pieces of vellum and a few paints they had made with berries and grass. There were only four colors, but that didn't matter. With a frayed water reed as a brush, Janet and Joan could paint pictures as part of their lessons. They seemed to like learning to paint best of all, so Nicola helped them with their pictures while Caledonia headed off to the kitchen to bring them back something to eat for the midday meal. The door to the solar was closed, and when she opened it, a small body fell through, onto the floor at her feet.

Jane pushed herself off the ground.

"I am so terribly sorry," Caledonia said, helping the child up. "I did not know you were there. Are you injured?"

Jane eyed her mother. "Nay," she said bravely, rubbing her right elbow. "I am not. It does not hurt in the least."

Caledonia could see that wasn't true but didn't argue with her. Frankly, she was surprised to see the girl at all. Jane made it a policy to avoid her mother at all costs, but more than that, Caledonia had come to see over the past several days that Jane was simply a loner. She was an odd child thanks to Madam Madonna's care and spent several hours every day preaching to the animals in the stable. They'd all seen her do it. Darius even tried to talk her out of it, but she was firm. It was something she needed to do. Therefore, it was a distinct surprise to see her here.

But Caledonia wasn't the only one who saw her.

From inside the solar, Janet piped up.

"Summer!" she cried. "Come! We are painting!"

Jane didn't react at first. She seemed quite indecisive. Caledonia opened the door wider.

"You are most welcome," she said softly. "We have been having lessons. We would like for you to join us."

Jane looked between her mother and sisters, unsure what to do. She couldn't even announce why she'd come in the first place, but she was here. She'd been eavesdropping on her sisters and mother and knew they were having fun and learning. She'd heard about it and even caught glimpses of it, like now. Darius had even tried to talk her into coming, but she was stubborn. This was so very foreign to her.

She couldn't be part of it.

… could she?

"Nay," she finally said, backing away. "I… I must go."

The smile faded from Caledonia's face as she watched her eldest child back up. "Go where?" she asked.

Jane didn't have a quick answer because she was nervous. Nervous and scared. She wanted to go in with her sisters, but she knew that was wrong. "I must spread the word of God," she said. "They must know that Christ loves them. I must go."

"Jane," Caledonia said as she began to follow the girl. "You do not have to spread the word of God any longer. You are safe, lass. No one is going to hurt you. We want to love you if you'll let us. Won't you join us?"

"Nay!" Jane said as she bumped into the entry door, grabbing for the handle. "I must teach about Christ!"

"Why?" Caledonia was suddenly on her, dropping her knees and grabbing the girl by the arms so she couldn't get away. "Why must you do this? You are preaching to animals, Jane. Animals who do not understand you, who will never know the love of Christ. I know you must understand this. Why do you do it?"

Jane was trying to pull away, but not too strongly. "Because… because I must!"

"*Why*, lass?" Caledonia pleaded. "Did Madam Madonna tell you to do this? Did she tell you that you must do this?"

The tears started to come as Jane began to resist more strongly. "Let me go!"

"Not until you tell me why you feel the need to preach to animals," Caledonia said steadily, though it was becoming a struggle to hold on to her squirming daughter. "Jane, if Madam Madonna told you that you must preach, then she was wrong. It is right that you should love God, but you do not need to preach. You are not a priest or a nun. You are a young girl and, right now, should be learning how to be a woman. You should be learning your letters and how to sew and how to paint. You should be learning things that all girls should learn, and that does not include preaching to the animals."

Jane managed to get one hand free and began beating on the hands that were holding her. "Let me go!" she demanded, weeping. "You are wrong! I must preach if I am to go to heaven! Madam Madonna said so!"

"Madam Madonna was *wrong*."

"Nay!"

Caledonia managed to grab Jane's free hand and yank on the girl, forcing her onto her knees in front of her, where she couldn't get leverage to pull away. Caledonia was afraid that if she ran, she would hide forever. The child had been so conditioned by Madam Madonna that she didn't know right from wrong, love from hate, or anything else. She only knew fear. Caledonia prayed she could break through to her because if she couldn't, Jane was lost.

And Caledonia wasn't going to lose her.

"Listen to me," Caledonia said softly but firmly, mere inches from Jane's red face. "Jane, I want you to listen to me carefully because I believe you are a bright lass. I believe you can understand what I am saying and not surrender to your fear of Madam Madonna. Listen to me carefully, please. Did Madam Madonna ever show you love?"

Jane was yanking to pull her hands free from Caledonia's grip. "Let *go!*"

"Not until you answer my question."

Jane was growing frustrated and terrified. She wasn't going to answer. She was stubborn, and Caledonia knew that must have been something she got from her mother because Caledonia was stubborn, too. Realizing her child wasn't going to answer her, Caledonia attempted to break through.

"Love is good," she said quietly. "God loves you and is happy when we show love to others. Especially our family. I love you, Jane. I have loved you since you were born. Madam Madonna tried to kill that love you have for me by telling you lies about me. None of it is true. I only want to love you and make you happy. I want to hug you and feed you tasty food and teach you how to paint and how to write. I want to see you grow up happy and find a good husband who will love you, too. I am not the devil. Sometimes, the devil tells lies, and that is all Madam Madonna told you. Lies. *She* was the devil, Jane. Only the devil would take a child from her mother."

Jane shrieked. "That is not true!"

"It is," Caledonia insisted. "If you continue to do as Madam Madonna wished, then you are allowing the devil to control you. Do you understand me? Do not let the devil win!"

Panicking, Jane bit the fingers that held her. With a yelp, Caledonia released her with that hand, but when Jane went in to bite the other hand, Caledonia slapped her across the mouth to stop her from doing it. Jane was behaving like an animal and Caledonia's reaction was instinctive. The slap shocked Jane, who tripped back onto her arse as Caledonia released her.

"You will not bite me again," Caledonia said sternly, though she was shaken. The entire conversation had shaken her. "Jane, you are my daughter and I love you. I want to show you that I love you, but I cannot do that if you are going to behave terribly. God is not happy with children who disobey their parents. One of his commandments is to honor thy father and thy mother. I would suggest you follow His commandment and stop your ridiculous behavior."

With that, she turned for the solar as Jane sat there a moment, watching her, before scrambling to her feet. Caledonia slammed the solar door with such force that it echoed in the entryway.

Jane turned and ran. She ran until she ended up in the stables, in front of her equine audience, weeping and praying and preaching. She didn't know anything else.

And that was how Thor found her.

CHAPTER SIXTEEN

H E THOUGHT HE'D seen a shooting star blast through the bailey.

As it turned out, it was only Jane.

He had no idea why the child was running from the keep, but he could guess. When it came to Jane, and Caledonia for that matter, there was always volatility involved. Thor had considered himself merely an interested bystander for the first couple of days at Stafford, but he'd shared a conversation with Caledonia one night that forced him to realize that he wasn't simply that. He was Caledonia's husband and, by default, now had three daughters through that marriage. Three little girls who had been emotionally starved and abused by those entrusted to their care.

That was when he ceased being a bystander.

He followed Jane's trail.

She'd run into the stables, which seemed to be her favorite place. She could hear her sobbing as she preached to the horses yet again, her preferred congregation because they didn't question her or try to engage her in conversation, something she was also afraid of. The child had many fears that they'd all been trying to help her with, but she was very much a solitary creature. Fearful of living, fearful of dying.

The truth was that he felt rather sorry for her.

"She went in here."

A voice came from behind him, and he turned to see Darius walking up. "I know," he said quietly. "I've been following her from the keep."

Darius nodded, coming to a pause beside Thor as they both looked over the darkened innards. It didn't take long before they heard open sobbing, intermittent between bouts of preaching. Carefully, Thor and Darius entered the stable, peering around a corner to see Jane standing in front of a row of stalls that housed the knights' horses. Big horse butts were facing her, but she was crying and quoting the Ten Commandments. Something about honoring parents. As they'd found out, she couldn't actually read, but simply repeated what she'd been told.

Thor stepped out of the shadows.

"Jane?" he said quietly. "What's amiss, my love?"

She turned to him, startled by his appearance. It took her a moment, but she began to point at him.

"G-go away," she wept. "I d-do not want to talk to you."

Thor kept coming, with Darius emerging from the shadows behind him. "You do realize that I am here because I am concerned," he said. "I saw you run out of the keep and came to see why. What happened?"

Jane was wiping furiously at her eyes, streaking dirt down her cheek. Unlike her sisters, she hadn't allowed her mother to bathe or dress her, so she was still in her rags—only her rags were growing tight on her because the one thing she would accept was the food she was given during the day. Like the other two, she was eating constantly.

But she was a confused little girl.

"Sh-she told me that I am sinning," she sobbed. "I am breaking a commandment."

It made sense to him now that he'd heard her speaking about honoring her parents. "Aye," he said evenly. "That is a commandment from God, and you have been breaking it since your mother arrived."

Jane's eyes widened and she burst into a fresh round of sobs. "I am not going to heaven!"

She was so dramatic that Thor had to fight off a smile. "If you continue to break the commandment, God will be displeased," he said. "But if you ask for forgiveness and begin being kind to your mother, God will see that you are sincere. He will forgive you. Do you understand?"

She sniffled, nodding as she wiped her eyes. Darius came to stand next to Thor, a sympathetic smile on his lips as they both watched the child struggle. She was such a confused little thing.

"You are very bright, so I know you understand that we must always be kind to your mother and father," Thor went on. "If you return to the keep and apologize for your actions, I know your mother would forgive you. She will always forgive you, Jane, but you must ask her. She loves you."

Jane had stopped the hysterical sobbing, now rubbing her eyes with her dirty hand. "If she loves me, why did she go away?" she asked.

That was one of the first intelligent questions he'd heard come out of her. She spent so much time regurgitating Madam Madonna's poison that the child could hardly think for herself. Therefore, for her to ask why Caledonia had left the family home was a milestone of sorts. It meant that she could, indeed, think for herself.

He took it seriously.

"I will answer your question," he said. "But first, I want to ask you one of my own. Will you listen?"

She was still rubbing her eyes, but she nodded. "Aye."

"Do you know what a knight is?"

She stopped rubbing and looked at him with red-rimmed eyes. "A warrior for God."

"Indeed," Thor said. "That is a good answer. But part of being a knight means that we always tell the truth. It is called honor. That means that the king trusts us because we never lie to him. Do you understand that?"

Jane nodded. She was actually making eye contact with him and not in an hysterical fashion, as was usual with her. "Madam Madonna told me that knights are bound by God," she said. "You are like angels."

Thor glanced at Darius, who smirked and looked away, before continuing. "In a manner of speaking, I suppose," he said. "But the point I am making is that I will never lie to you. You can always trust me to tell you the truth, even if it is unpleasant. You have asked me why your mother left you and I will tell you the truth—because your father sent her away. Your father did not love your mother because she did not give birth to a son, so he sent her away. That is the only reason she left, Jane, I swear it. It was not because she did not love you. She does. But she was forced to leave."

She continued to stare at him with those dark green eyes. It was a magnificent color, a subtle green, and when the light hit it, one could see flecks of gold and brown. He'd gazed into Caledonia's eyes enough to know, and Jane's eyes were the same color. Eyes that seemed to be churning with what he had just told her.

"I have two sisters," she finally said. "My father never told me that he wanted a boy."

"He would not have told you that. Why would he?"

She shrugged. "I would try to talk to him sometimes, but he did not want to speak to me."

Thor smiled faintly. "You can speak to me anytime you wish," he said. "Darius, too. If you have questions or an issue, you may tell us and we will help you with it. We will always be here for you, Jane. I wish you would believe that."

Her gaze moved from Thor to Darius, who was smiling at her. Her focus returned to Thor. "Why did Madam Madonna not bring my mother back?" she asked.

He lifted an eyebrow. "Can we discuss Madam Madonna without you weeping and running away?"

That was the usual way those conversations went, but Jane nodded and Thor continued.

"Because if your mother came back, then Madam Madonna would no longer have charge of you and your sisters," he said. "She felt that she was the only one capable of tending you. She did not want your mother back because she was jealous of her. Madam Madonna wanted all of the control and did not want your mother interfering. Madam Madonna used to be your father's nurse, in fact. Did you know that?"

Jane nodded. "He called her 'mada.'"

"Did you also know that your father was married before he married your mother?"

Jane cocked her head. "He had two wives?"

"Two at different times," Thor said. "His first wife died, and so did her daughters, so he married your mother in the hope that she would have sons to inherit the title. But your mother only had daughters. Madam Madonna was brought to help tend you and your sisters because she had once been your father's nurse, only your father did not want daughters, nor did he want a wife who only bore daughters. He sent your mother away and told Madam Madonna to raise you and your sisters however she wished. When we arrived, we saw your sisters in the garden, dirty and hungry. I asked you once if Madam Madonna took care of you, and you grew upset with me. Do you remember?"

Jane nodded. "Aye."

"Will you answer me?"

"Will you tell her my answer?"

"Of course not," he said. "Lass, she's never coming back, not ever."

Jane had to think on that. Once, when she had been told that Madam Madonna had been sent away, she'd grown hysterical. Given that the nun was the only mother figure she'd ever had, right or wrong, she was attached to her. But the more time passed and the more she listened to Thor and Darius and even her own mother, the more she began to question Madam Madonna. With her, Jane only knew one kind of life. Now, with the arrival of Caledonia and Thor and even Nicola and Darius and the others, she was starting to see another way of life, one of kindness and caring and food and warmth and love.

Yes, even love.

It was an entirely different world.

And maybe not such a bad one.

"I don't know what to do," she finally said, her red eyes welling again. "Madam Madonna told me that I must preach the word of God and I would go to heaven. She told me that's what I must always do, but I feel afraid when I do it and afraid when I don't. No one listens to me. Do you think God will truly forgive me if I ask forgiveness for breaking his commandment?"

Thor nodded. "He will, I am certain of it," he said. "Jane, did Madam Madonna always tell you what to do?"

"Always."

"From now on, the only people who are going to tell you what to do are me and your mother," he said, bending over so he could be more on her level. "And we will tell you to learn your lessons, play with your sisters, and be happy. You do not have to preach any longer, I promise."

She nodded, her lower lip trembling as she started wiping her eyes again. *Poor, confused lass,* Thor thought. He also thought their conversation might have been the least bit overwhelming to her, so he patted her gently on the shoulder before pointing to Darius.

"Darius is going to make a bed for your sister's chicken," he said, nodding his head when Darius rolled his eyes at the ridiculous request he'd been roped into. "It seems that Lady Janet wants a bed for her chicken to sleep in, and since Sir Darius is so good at building things, he has agreed to the task. Mayhap you would like to help him build it."

Darius knew that Jane wasn't one for groups. She was a lonely child. But having her help him build a bed for a chicken, as foolish as that sounded, might help her feel more comfortable with the people who now lived in her home. It might help her even want to participate in other things, including lessons with her mother. Perhaps it was a small step, this chicken bed, but it was a step to bigger things. Hopefully.

Darius held out his hand to her.

"Come along, my lady," he said. "Help me find some wood so we may fashion a bed for your sister's chicken."

Still sniffling, Jane went with him. Thor watched them go,

hearing Darius ask her how big she thought the bed should be and her hiccupping reply. But it was a start.

A new start for Jane.

And for Caledonia.

With a smile on his lips, he went back to his duties.

☙

"Here you are. I've been looking for you."

In a small outbuilding in the kitchen yard, Darius looked up from the small cradle he was building to see Nicola standing in the doorway. Jane was standing next to him, handing him nails, but when he saw Nicola, he immediately came to a halt.

"I have been here," he said. "Lady Jane and I are building a bed for a chicken."

Nicola stepped into the shed, smiling. "Ah," she said. "For Mary. I heard."

Jane had her head down, focused on what Darius was doing. She was terrified to look at Nicola, whom she knew to be a friend of her mother's. Darius could see the child's discomfort.

"Lady Jane has been an excellent apprentice," he said. "We have been speaking of England and all of her great cities. Have we not, Jane?"

Jane nodded, once, but kept silent. Darius fought off a smile.

"In truth, I have been doing most of the talking," he said. "I fear that Jane is missing her tongue and does not know how to speak. She has been quite silent, though I know she does speak to the animals, so she must have a tongue that magically disappears and appears when she needs it. Is that true, Jane?"

Jane looked at him with big eyes, and Darius laughed softly. So did Nicola. Darius bent down and peered at her mouth.

"Well?" he said. "Has your tongue magically disappeared?"

Jane shook her head almost frantically, but Darius didn't believe her.

"Show me," he said. "Stick your tongue out."

Jane did, but Darius pretended not to see it.

"Well?" he said. "Where is it?"

Jane's wide eyes grew wider. "Here!" she said, sticking it out again. "Don't you see it?"

Darius pretended to suddenly see her tongue as she pointed to it. "Now I do," he said. "'Tis a great relief. I thought it was missing and would not return."

Jane frowned. "That is silly," she said. "Tongues do not magically disappear."

"Yours does," Darius said, a twinkle in his eye as he turned back to the half-finished chicken bed, which was really no more than a square frame of wood at this point. "Let us continue our conversation about the great cities of England. One of my favorite cities is York. It has an enormous cathedral that is quite elaborate. God must be very pleased that the English have built such a great house for Him."

He held out a hand for a nail, and Jane handed it to him, but she was trying to envision the church he had mentioned.

"Is it made of gold?" she asked.

Darius shook his head. "Nay," he said. "Only stone. Gold is very soft and would collapse under its own weight. Stone is better. I think God prefers stone."

"Why?"

"Because it is strong, like He is."

That fascinated Jane. As she pondered the great stone walls of York's cathedral, Nicola caught Darius' attention and silently motioned for him to send Jane away. Darius finished nailing the leg of the chicken bed before complying.

"I need more nails," he said. "Lady Jane, will you fetch more nails? They are over in the smithy shack."

Jane looked indecisive. "But how will I know which nails you want?"

"Bring me a handful. I will pick the ones I want."

Quickly, she dashed off. Darius was practically the only one she did anything for, so she was diligent about it. As she rushed away, he turned to Nicola.

"You have very little time before she returns," he said. "She is very fast."

Nicola cocked an eyebrow. "Should I be jealous?" she said. "It is clear that she thinks the world of you, though I cannot imagine why she thinks you are so wonderful."

She said it dramatically and he knew she was jesting. In all the years he'd known Nicola, he'd never known her to be the jealous type, and most especially not with a child.

"That is because I *am* wonderful," he said, pointing the hammer at her. "You would do well to remember that."

"I remember it every day, my sweet."

He chuckled, returning his attention to the bed. "What did you want to say now that she is gone?"

Nicola's smile faded. "Try to convince her to return to her lessons," she said quietly. "She and Callie had words earlier because Jane was being very difficult, so can you please speak with her? You seem to be the only one she listens to."

He inspected the leg he had just nailed down. "I will try," he said. "She is a very confused young lady."

"I know. But allowing her to remain in this state does her no good. We must help her."

"I will do what I can," he said. "Provided you promise me

something."

"What?"

He eyed her. "That you will meet me here after supper," he said. "I've not held you in my arms for an entire day."

She grinned. "Do they ache?"

"For you, they do."

She was about to comment when Jane suddenly reappeared, her hands full of iron nails. "Here," she said, carefully putting them on the table he was using. "Are these good?"

Darius began to sort them out. "They are perfect," he said. "Can you pull the small ones out, please?"

They were returning to the bed, and Nicola caught his eye, winking at him, before heading back toward the keep. That left Darius alone with a skittish girl, one he hoped he wouldn't chase away with talk of lessons. But, as Nicola said, he was practically the only one who could do it.

He began inspecting the small nails.

"These are very nice," he said again. "You are smart, my lady. Do you wish to learn how to make a chicken bed? Are you watching what I am doing so you can do it someday if you need to?"

Jane was still pulling out the shorter nails. "I would rather help."

"You do not like to build?"

She shook her head. "Nay."

"What do you like to do?" he asked, inspecting a nail closely and blowing on it to dust off the rust. "What I mean to ask is: what brings you joy? Drawing? Singing?"

He was trying to be very careful with how he led into the conversation. He wanted it to be natural, organic. She didn't seem defensive as she continued to sort the nails.

"I do not know how to draw or sing," she said. "I spread the word of God."

"Do you like it?"

She nodded. "I will go to heaven."

"You will go anyway," he said. "You do not need to preach in order to go to heaven."

She set aside a few nails into the short nail pile. "That is not what Madam Madonna says."

Darius picked up one of the smaller nails in preparation for using it. "There are many good men who do not preach but still go to heaven when they die," he said. "I think Madam Madonna meant that knowing the word of God is good and keeping it close to your heart is good, but you do not need to preach. Living a good life and honoring God's commandments are a better way to get into heaven, I think. I do not preach, but I know I am going to heaven."

She looked at him then. "How do you know?"

He glanced at her, smiling. "Because I have followed his commandments," he said. "I do not envy. I do not lie. A knight must take his vows of knighthood before God, so in a sense, I have sworn to uphold God and those He loves. That means I will go to heaven. As I said, many men who do not preach will go to heaven. There are better ways to get there."

That had Jane thinking. Having lived such an insulated life for so long, new ideas were strange to her. Intriguing, but strange. Over the past several days, she had shown some interest in learning what others knew and thought, but the innate fear that Madam Madonna had instilled in her was difficult to overcome.

"How… how else can I get there if I do not preach?" she asked.

Darius shrugged before placing another leg against the bedframe and giving it a few whacks. "It makes God happy when you are obedient and strive to do the right thing," he said.

"I am obedient."

He glanced at her. "Are you?" he said. "I heard that you and your mother had strong words today. Were you being disobedient to your mother?"

Jane appeared horrified that he knew about their argument. She quickly lowered her head and refused to answer, so Darius stopped hammering. He had a feeling he had just ruined what he had started, so he kept his voice low and calm as he spoke.

"What did you argue about?" he asked gently. "Jane, one of the things that displeases God is a stubborn attitude. If I ask you a question, then it pleases Him if you answer. Tell me what you argued about."

Jane began blinking rapidly as her eyes filled with tears. "She said that Madam Madonna lied to me."

"She did. We have all told you that."

Jane's head shot up, her expression full of distress. "But why do you say so?"

He set the hammer down and came around the table, pulling up the stool next to her. "My lady, would you say that you and I have become friends?" he asked.

Jane nodded hesitantly. "Aye."

Darius reached out, taking her little hand. "Janie, do you feel safe with me?"

She nodded, but the tears were still threatening. "Aye."

"And you know that I would never lie to you."

Again, she nodded, wiping her nose. "Has… has everything I've been told been a lie, then? *Everything?*"

That was such an astute and painful question, one Darius

was surprised to hear. That kind of question took great reasoning powers, but it also took a willingness to understand that everything she knew in life might not have been true. Everyone had been telling her the same thing, and now she was starting to question. She was starting to think.

Darius gave her hand a squeeze.

"Not everything," he said. "Madam Madonna instilled a strong love of God in you. That is a good thing. But what she told you about preaching and your mother were lies. I know you are afraid of what to believe, but I promise you that if you believe what we tell you and allow yourself to at least come to know your mother a little, I think you will see what is truth and what is a lie with your own eyes. You are old enough to make that decision. All we are asking is that you not let Madam Madonna make it for you. She has no power over you anymore, Jane. It is time for you to find your voice and learn and grow."

Jane looked at him, unable to stop the tears now. It was difficult to comprehend, but that was exactly what she was trying to do—comprehend. She wiped at her eyes with her free hand.

"But what should I do?" she asked, sniffling.

Darius smiled and kissed her small hand. "You should go into the keep and have lessons with your sisters," he said. "You should be obedient to your mother. She is a kind woman, Janie. She only wants to love you. It would make me happy if you tried. Will you try?"

Jane looked at him, at the table, and at the half-built chicken bed. "But who will help you build the bed?" she asked.

He shrugged. "I will stop right now so you can go inside to your lessons," he said. "When you are finished, I will resume and you can help me. I would not think of building this bed without you."

He was nodding his head as he spoke, encouraging her, and Jane finally broke down and nodded with him. "If you think I should go," she said.

"I think you should go," he responded. "Would you like for me to walk to the keep with you?"

She nodded, wiping at more tears, and Darius set the hammer down. Still holding her hand, he led her out of the shed, through the kitchen yard, and to the keep. He led her right into the solar, where Caledonia was helping Janet write the letter *A* over and over. When Caledonia looked up and saw Jane, she stood quickly and went to her. Because Darius was holding her hand, Jane felt brave, but she also felt sad that she had behaved so poorly the last time she saw her mother.

"Greetings, Jane," Caledonia said hesitantly. "Would you like to watch?"

Jane looked up at Darius, who took pity on the child and replied for her. "Jane would like to join the lessons," he said. "She was helping me build a chicken bed, but we have decided that this is more important. Do you have a place where she can sit and join in?"

It was all Caledonia could to not to hug Darius. She was fairly certain he was instrumental in Jane's change of heart, knowing how the girl had built a trust with him. After the harsh words with Jane earlier, Caledonia wasn't honestly sure she would see her eldest daughter anytime soon.

But here she was.

And Caledonia was overjoyed.

"Of course," she said. "Jane, you may sit next to Janet. We are writing our letters. Would you like to try?"

Jane nodded, but she didn't let go of Darius' hand. He was

forced to walk her over to the table, and even when she sat down, she didn't let go. Eventually, she did, but Darius and Caledonia decided it would be a good idea for him to remain. If he stayed, maybe she would, too.

It was a big step for Jane.

And a big step for Caledonia.

But one they were both ready, and willing, to make.

CHAPTER SEVENTEEN

OURTEEN DAYS AFTER being summarily dismissed from Stafford Castle, Cristano and his cousins, along with Rotri and Domnall and about fifty men from Dordon Castle, were ready to move.

Those fourteen days had been full of planning, of discussions, and in the end, the scheme they came up with was a solid one. The only person not actively part of the scheming was the woman who called herself Madam Madonna, and she was more concerned with finding another position as a nurse or tutor to children of nobility. She didn't seem to have the same sense of vengeance that the knights had. To be truthful, Rotri could see that there wasn't any love lost between the knights and the old woman.

Hearing them discuss their respective positions at Stafford Castle led him to believe that there might have been a power struggle between Cristano and the woman. Now that Cristano was determined to seek vengeance, she didn't seem interested. It was evident that she would rather look for another opportunity than try to reclaim what she had, so twelve days after her arrival at Dordon, Madam Madonna departed with a small escort for Whitby Abbey, where she had served as a postulate long ago. Whitby had connections with every noble family in Northern England, and she wanted to find another family through them.

And with that, Madam Madonna was gone.

Rotri didn't care one way or the other. He sent the woman on her way, leaving him with the de Lucera cousins, who were more determined than ever to stage an ambush a means to their end. Their target for the action was the village of Millford, to the east of Stafford but in sight of the castle. The plan was to burn all they could, raise a ruckus, and then wait for the garrison at Stafford to come to the rescue of the villagers. Thor would undoubtedly be leading them and would walk right into an ambush.

It was a simple plan, but one that had to be carefully orchestrated because Stafford would roll out hundreds of soldiers while Dordon didn't quite have those numbers. They didn't want to be massacred, so the men had been instructed to burn and flee—run circles around the Stafford men and try not to actually engage them. Most of the Dordon soldiers hadn't seen a battle in years because Dordon had been peaceful for that long, so the raid confused them. Rotri assured them that it was a necessary task, so they asked no questions.

They simply prepared to ride.

There was great anticipation in the air as they prepared for their night raid. Rotri wanted to make sure that there was nothing on the soldiers to identify their loyalty, so the men were instructed not to wear Dordon standards as they usually did. They were only to wear clothing that had no identification on them at all, another thing that confused them, but another thing they simply didn't question. Rodri had told them that if they saw something they wanted that they could simply take it, so there was a little more enthusiasm when they realized they'd be getting something out of this.

Still, no one knew why they were really doing this, but most of them thought it had something to do with the new knights Rotri had acquired.

No one recognized the men who had come to visit a few days earlier until an older soldier mentioned that they had seen them at Stafford Castle. That rumor ran through the ranks like wildfire, but they still couldn't make heads or tails out of the new knights and the event of a raid on a Stafford Castle. It seemed quite odd, but Rotri was quite odd, so it was simply in line with the man's strange and demanding behavior.

Shortly before dawn on the following day, the men were satisfactorily dressed and prepared for the coming skirmish. Although Dordon was a functional castle and theoretically at the ready for any attempts made against it, the truth was that many of the men had dull swords and hadn't used a shield in years. Even their crossbows were only marginally functional. That meant that the entire day before the raid had seen the smithy forge blazing at full steam as swords were sharpened. As the horizon turned shades of pink, the Dordon men had very sharp blades, and more than one man had cut himself as a result. Blood was already being spilled and the men laughed nervously about that. They hoped it wasn't a bad omen. But the moment came when the column was formed and Rotri led the charge across the drawbridge and out into the road beyond. They would reach the village in two days—or less—and the madness would begin.

Rotri was counting on it.

It took the Dordon men a day and a half to reach Millford

because Rotri had driven them so hard and, truthfully, the raid was like taking candy from a baby because the villagers of Millford hadn't seen an attack in many years. The area had enjoyed years of peace and tranquility, so the inhabitants were caught completely off guard as the Dordon men rolled in. They were beginning to close up shop for the night as farmers returned from their fields and merchants returned to their home. Wives who were waiting for their dinners to cook stood in their front doors and gossiped with other wives simply to pass the time, and they paid little notice to the group coming in from the southeast. They were unarmed and unprepared when Rotri gleefully gave the command to charge.

But all did not go as planned.

The first thing that happened was Domnall charging into the village and taking a corner too quickly. He was caught off guard by the overhang of a two-story shop that was located on the corner. His head slammed into the protruding second story and he was knocked off his horse, unconscious, as his men continued on their raid. There had been so many men rushing in that no one really noticed he'd fallen. To make it more difficult, night was falling and people were running. It was chaos.

No one bothered to check on Domnall as he lay in the gutter.

It was instant confusion. Rotri's men lit up the main avenue of the village, setting fire to businesses as the merchants and owners tried to take their inventory out of the backs of the shops. One of them came out of an alleyway with a heavy cart, full of anything the man and his family could grab, and they charged around the corner right where Domnall was lying, crushing him under the weight of the wheels.

But no one could see him because it was dark.

Rotri, in fact, was at the other end of the village, keeping an eye on the distant castle of Stafford. It wasn't so far that he couldn't see the torches on the wall of the structure, and he knew he'd see the approaching response because they would all be bearing torches on their way down the hill. Having no idea that his son was dying in the street on the other side of the village, he told his men to continue burning and gave them permission to take anything they could carry.

As far as Rotri was concerned, it promised to be a glorious night.

But it was a costly one.

The entire village was in flames by the time Rotri and Cristano caught sight of the torch-laden army that was coming down the hill from Stafford. Knowing that Thor was approaching gave them the time to plan for the moment he arrived, so Rotri had his men hide away from the avenue, tucked into dark corners of the village, away from the burning as they awaited the arrival of the Stafford response. Rotri began to think it strange that he hadn't seen Domnall since they entered the village, but he didn't think much of it. He assumed his son was handing the south end of the village.

He couldn't have been more wrong.

As he was about to find out.

⁂

"It's *what*?"

"Going up in flames," Thor said quickly as he started grabbing for his battle protection. "The entire village to the southeast is going up in flames. Our sentries can see it from the wall, so I can only assume it is either under attack or someone's cottage caught on fire and is burning down the rest of the village. In either case, I must go and do what I can. What can you tell me about that village?"

Caledonia was dumbfounded by the suggestion of disaster at a nearby village. "There are two of them on the road south," she said. "We passed through them. One is Millford and the other one is Rugeley."

"Which one is closer to Stafford?"

"Millford."

"Then it must be Millford because it is quite close," he said, pulling a heavily padded tunic over his head. "I must get to the armory and dress, my love. Since I am not entirely sure what the trouble is, I would ask that you stay in the keep. I will put men on guard and we shall lock up the gatehouses, but you and the children are to remain in the keep. Have you ever been at a castle on alert before?"

Caledonia shook her head. "Never," she said. "This is a first."

He smiled and kissed her forehead as he headed for the door. "Then I will tell you not to worry," he said, opening the panel. "It is more than likely a cooking fire out of control, but we must make sure."

She nodded, following him as he went out onto the landing. "I know," she said. "You are the earl and these are your vassals. You must ensure their safety."

"Exactly."

She looked at him a moment, a smile on her lips, before shaking her head in a wry gesture. "Robert would have simply let them burn," she said. "He would not have cared. I find it remarkable that you do."

He smiled and kissed her again, this time on the lips. "I'm

sure I will not be long," he said. "But do as I tell you. When I leave the keep, throw the bolt and lock it up. You will also secure the shutters on the windows."

Caledonia followed him down the stairs to the entry level below. "I will," she said. "Please be cautious, angel. Remember that there are those who would rejoice if you were injured or worse."

He looked at her, frowning. "Who?" he asked, but the question was barely out of his mouth when he realized what she meant. "Ah. Those two. Well, I will be happy to disappoint your greedy uncle."

He was nearly to the entry door when it flew open and Nicola rushed in. She almost smashed into her brother in her haste.

"There is a villager at the gatehouse," she said quickly. "Darius sent me to tell you that someone is raiding Millford!"

That settled the question of what, precisely, was happening, and Thor could feel himself tensing for battle. Determination filled him as well as a sense of duty. He'd been through this more times than he could count. But he knew his wife hadn't and she had heard the news. He suspected that she was frightened now. He turned to Caledonia to find Nicola standing next to her, holding her hand.

"Then *El Martillo* rides," he said, smiling at his wife as he said it. "I cannot imagine who is attacking my property, but they had better prepare themselves. This hammer is deadly."

Caledonia wasn't amused. "It is my uncle," she said, frightened. "It has to be. They are trying to harass us."

Thor put his hands on her face and looked her in the eye. "Or it could be outlaws from the forest to the north," he said seriously. "We know they are there. The Stafford soldiers have told us as much. I will not know anything until I get there, so do not jump to conclusions yet."

He didn't seem concerned that he was facing a battle in the least. If anything, he seemed oddly happy about it. *El Martillo*, indeed.

The mercenary was ready to fight.

Reluctantly, Caledonia nodded in agreement, and he kissed her one last time before quitting the keep. Caledonia and Nicola shut the door and bolted it, calling to the servants because the shutters needed to be closed as well. Soon enough, several house servants were closing up the shutters in every chamber as Caledonia and Nicola went upstairs to the level above, shutting the heavy door on the stairs and bolting it as well.

Now, all they could do was wait.

CHAPTER EIGHTEEN

ROTRI HAD DOMNALL in his arms.

The man was hysterical.

"My son," he wept, spittle dripping from his lips. "My son is dead!"

As the village of Millford burned around them, the men from Dordon were facing a difficult scene. Domnall had been discovered near the southern edge of the village, crumpled and smashed in a gutter because he'd evidently been trampled. Even his head was smashed. When Rotri was notified, he's rushed to the southern end of the village as men gathered around the corpse, only to see his son lying in a pool of his own blood.

It had been a gruesome scene.

Cristano, Adan, and Benedicto were standing around, watching Rotri mourn his son, the only one out of all of them who seemed to show any common sense or reason. It was true that he went along with his father's plans in whatever the man wanted to do, but he wasn't a fanatic about it like Rotri was. How he'd been killed was anyone's guess because no one had seen it happen, but it was clear that he'd been trampled or run over, because his entire body was broken.

And so was Rotri.

"My lord," Cristano said, "I realize this is a terrible moment for you, but the Stafford army is coming. We can see them along the road. Are we to follow the plan we discussed at Dordon? Are we still to go through with it?"

Rotri was sobbing openly, holding his son, feeling how broken he was. "Oh, God," he breathed as if he was losing his mind. "God help me. Please, God help me!"

Cristano had lookouts on the northern end of town, watching for the Stafford approach. The entire situation was working as it should have and he didn't want to lose this opportunity. Domnall's death was unfortunate, but that didn't change facts. Cristano wanted revenge against de Reyne. He wanted his money and possessions back, everything he'd been forced to leave behind at Stafford Castle. All of this he wanted, but he wasn't going to get that if Rotri fell apart.

They had to stay the course.

"My lord, please," he said, trying not to be insensitive because it might turn Rotri against him. "We… we must not let your son's death be in vain. If we lose this opportunity to capture de Reyne, then Domnall would have died for nothing. We must hurry because the Stafford army will be upon us shortly. May we continue to follow the plan?"

Rotri's head came up. Every orifice on his face was leaking something. He was beyond grief at the moment, but not so far gone that he didn't hear Cristano's words. The only thing he could think of was blame. He had to blame someone for this.

Someone was going to have to pay.

"I want you to kill him," he spat. "Kill de Reyne when you see him!"

That hadn't been part of the plan. "If we kill him, we cannot ransom him," Cristano said evenly. "We were going to ransom him, my lord. Lure him into an ambush and abduct him. That was our plan."

"Nay!" Rotri shouted. He jabbed a finger at Cristano. "I will give you everything I have, pay you every coin I possess, if you will kill de Reyne. This is *his* fault! He is to blame for my son's death!"

Cristano looked at his cousins, who were gazing back at him with expressions that could have been taken as agreement. Benedicto in particular seemed highly agreeable because he didn't like the fact that one of de Reyne's knights had bested him in a fight. He had a score to settle with de Reyne, and the knight who bested him, so he was perfectly agreeable to kill them. Either way, revenge would be exacted. When he made eye contact with Cristano, he nodded. Just once.

But it was enough.

"Very well," Cristano said, more to his cousins than to Rotri. "Find the crossbows and secure positions around here. Quickly. Get a clear shot at de Reyne and take it. I will do the same. But tell the soldiers to continue with their original orders—they are not to engage the Stafford men or the knights. They are simply to run about and make chase."

"At some point, de Reyne will end up in front of us," Benedicto said with satisfaction. "I could take that man out and sleep like a baby afterward. My conscience would be clear. He deserves what he gets for the way he has treated us."

Cristano waved a hand at him. "Go," he said. "Find your vantage point and stay out of sight. If de Reyne or his men see us…"

Benedicto was already on the move, grabbing Adan as he went. Together, the two of them headed off, shouting to the

Dordon men who were gathered, discussing the death of Domnall and the situation in general in hushed tones. But the shouting knights had them moving. As the entire Dordon contingent began to move, Cristano returned his attention to Rotri.

"My lord," he said. "Let me help you move your son. You must not be sitting out in the open when the Stafford army comes. They will want to know why you are here."

Rotri was still weeping, still holding Domnall. "I want them dead," he sobbed.

"I know," Cristano said steadily. "And we shall make it so. But we must get you and your son to safety first. Please, my lord. I will help you."

It took some coaxing for Rotri to comply, but eventually, Cristano took Domnall by the legs and Rotri held him under the arms. They moved him across the road and into a livery, one of the only buildings they hadn't burned because it was sheltering some of their horses. Once Domnall was lying on a bed of straw in a darkened corner, Cristano turned to leave, but Rotri stopped him.

"You and your cousins may serve me at Dordon and I will still give you all of the coin I have if you kill de Reyne," he said, his face swollen and wet. "He did this to my son."

"I know, my lord," Cristano said. "But I do not want your coin. I want something else."

"What is that?"

Cristano's dark eyes glittered in the dim light of the livery. "When de Reyne is dead, I want his wife," he muttered. "Robert de Tosni was an ineffective earl. De Reyne will not be the earl long enough to matter. But Stafford… It belongs to me. It has more of my blood and sweat in it than any de Tosni whelp. I will marry Lady Caledonia, take Stafford, and give you Tamworth. That's what you want… isn't it? Tamworth?"

Suddenly, Rotri didn't seem so despondent, as if Cristano's suggestion was enough to bring him some comfort. It was the perfect solution to their problem. He eyed the man, realizing that de Reyne's death would be a blessing in more ways than one.

"Aye," he said. "Tamworth was my brother's title. It should have been mine."

"It will be," Cristano assured him. "Do we have a bargain?"

"A marriage to my niece to secure Stafford?"

"I deserve it. More than that, I want it."

"Then we have a bargain."

As Cristano rushed off to collect his crossbow and find a place from which to hunt de Reyne, Rotri turned to his son lying dead upon the straw. Grief threatened to consume him as he gazed upon the only thing that had given him a reason for living. That reason was gone now. But his vengeance would be satisfied. In the end, Tamworth would still be his.

And that was all that mattered.

At that moment, something in him snapped.

Reality altered.

Lying in the straw at his feet, Domnall's right arm was over his head, his palm facing outward. He was waving at his father, encouraging him to go forth and see this plan to the end. That was logical, wasn't it? Domnall was *telling* him to continue. Stafford belonged to Cristano, but in order for the man to fully assume it, he needed to marry Caledonia. That elusive woman who had been forced into a marriage with de Reyne. It wasn't her fault, after all. She was a pawn. De Reyne and the king were the players. With de Reyne dead, she should thank Rotri for his intervention. Wasn't that what a good uncle would do?

Perhaps it was time to collect his niece. He knew where she was—all he had to do was go and get her. He was already out the door, heading for Stafford Castle. De Reyne would be here, at Millford, a victim for Cristano's crossbow. But Caledonia would be all alone, waiting for her uncle to save her.

She was finally his.

Once and for all.

CHAPTER NINETEEN

B Y THE TIME Thor and his men arrived at Millford, most of the village was nearly ash.

The first thing they saw, other than huddled and frightened villagers, was men on horseback riding up and down the burning roads and alleyways. There were two main roads in Millford and a variety of small pathways and alleys, most of which seemed to be full of smoke and fire.

"The raiders are still here," he said to the knights around him. "But I do not understand why."

Next to him, Darius' helmed head turned in his direction. "What do you mean?"

Thor pointed to a gang of raiders in the distance. "If they looted what they could and then burned the remainder, why are they still here?" he said. "They should have left long ago. Opportunists do not usually linger over their plunder."

"They do if they want to collect that which has not been burned," Darius said, keeping a tight rein on his excitable warhorse. "They are looking for anything of value in the ashes."

That made sense, and it didn't sit well with Thor. "Scavengers," he said with disgust. "Bully, you and True take half the men to the south side of the village. Your task will be to capture a couple of the men so we can interrogate them and find out who sent them. Darius and I will remain here with the rest of the men and flush them in your direction. Go around the village and not through it or you may drive them out before we can capture one of them."

Clayne and Truett took off, pulling about a hundred men with them as they went. They gave the village a wide berth by heading off toward the southeast, sweeping around the village as they headed for the southern side of the village. Thor and Darius gave them several minutes, during which a few of the soldiers questioned the displaced villagers as to who the raiders were. No one seemed to know. But the interviews were cut short when Thor gave the command to move into the village and chase any lingering raiders toward Clayne and Truett.

Thor and Darius split up once they entered the village. Thor took a group of men down the main road, forcing out some of the outlaws who were still lingering in the heart of the village. Most of them scattered, but a couple of them were cornered by Thor's men. They grabbed the raiders and began beating them as Thor moved forward, chasing men from their hiding places in burned-out cottages, forcing them south. But a few broke away and took off toward the east, sending Thor after them.

It was a senseless chase.

Thor pursued the men for a short time until he realized there was no logic to what they were doing. They weren't trying to flee. They were simply going up one alleyway and then down another. They weren't engaging the Stafford men for a fight and they weren't trying to run away from them. They were simply going in circles. The fires were smaller now, as the main street of the village had mostly burned, so there was heavy smoke in the air, muddling the senses of smell and sight.

But Thor didn't need to see these men to outsmart them.

He and his soldiers stopped chasing the particular group they'd been pursuing. Instead, they doubled back on their tracks because from the pattern of the fleeing men, they would be coming by them once again, and perhaps they could capture some of them, enough to find out who they were and where they had come from. Thor was disappointed because he hadn't even had the opportunity to fight one of them, a most undistinguished situation for *El Martillo*. He'd fought plenty of men in tighter quarters than this, but as he had observed, these men didn't want to fight.

They simply wanted to be chased.

It went on into the night. Eventually, Thor and more than half the men he'd brought with him had managed to clear out the alleys and cottages of any remaining raiders, driving them toward Clayne and Truett. In fact, the two knights had managed to capture about ten men, all of them being sequestered by Stafford soldiers, and although they hadn't interrogated them yet, they didn't need to. One of the Stafford soldiers recognized a former friend who had gone to serve Lord Dordon a few years earlier and that bit of information made it back to Clayne and Truett, who immediately relayed it to Thor.

As Caledonia had feared, her uncle and cousin were to blame after all.

Near midnight, all of the raiders had either run off or been captured. They had a total of thirty-three prisoners at this point, but no Rotri or Domnall de Wylde. All prisoners were being held near the southern end of town, just off the main road, where a gang of Stafford soldiers were guarding them. With the town now silent and the fires having finally died off, Thor gathered his knights for a conclave.

"It is time for answers," he said grimly. "This is the most disorganized, bizarre raid I have ever seen."

Darius, Clayne, and Truett heartily concurred. "They would not engage," Darius said. "Every time we would come close, they would run off like skittish children."

Everyone was nodding. "And in circles, no less," Truett said. "They ran around in circles, groups of them. I nearly collided with Bully at one point when our groups crossed paths."

Thor turned toward the village in smoldering ruins. "Did anyone notice that the raiders were carrying anything of value?" he said. "Did they even pillage, or did Dordon send them over here simply to burn?"

The knights shrugged, shaking heads, looking off at the village also. "I think they had some things of value that they were carrying," Truett said. "I thought I saw one of them with a sack of goods in his hands. Not even strapped to his saddle."

"I have a few men on foot patrolling the outskirts of the village," Darius said. "In case there are more men hiding. Their orders are to flush them out."

Thor's gaze lingered on the village before he returned his focus to his men. "Something doesn't feel right," he said quietly as he pointed toward the prisoners. "I do not care how you get the information out of them, but get it. Find out what their purpose was."

"You should do it, Thor," Darius said. "Blackchurch taught you how to interrogate a man the proper way. You should be the one to pull fingernails or break teeth."

That wasn't exactly what he did, but the gist of the statement was true. Thor had been taught interrogation methods that would make grown men squeamish. He'd had more than one occasion to use them, especially as a mercenary. With a shrug, he nodded his head.

"Then bring me one of the prisoners," he said. "I will show you how to do it right, you silly children."

There were grins all around because any one of those men could have interrogated a prisoner and done it quite ably. Perhaps with different methods than Thor would use, but ably nonetheless. Truett and Clayne were turning to collect a prisoner when one of the Stafford soldiers suddenly rushed up out of the darkness.

"My lords," the man, sweating profusely, said quickly. "You must come."

Thor looked at him with concern. "What's amiss?"

The soldier motioned to him almost frantically. "Come, my lord," he said. "You must see this."

He turned on his heel and began running, down a grassy slope toward one of the only un-burned structures in Millford. It was a livery, a long stone building, and no one had entered it because the sides were open. They could see what was inside—in this case, there were only a few horses tethered at one end. There were no men hiding inside that they could see. Thor, Darius, Clayne, and Truett entered the livery on the heels of the soldier, watching the man frantically point to a pile of dirty hay in one corner of the livery. It was in the shadows, tucked off in the darkness, but they could all see a pair of booted feet.

Expensive boots.

"I was walking patrol at Sir Darius' request," the soldier said breathlessly. "When I passed through the livery, I saw that man lying there. He is quite dead."

The knights moved over to the pile of hay and found themselves looking down at a well-dressed warrior who looked as if he'd been smashed into bits. It was quite dark in the livery and they couldn't get a good look at him, but what they could see—his clothing, his shoes—was well made.

Thor crouched down near the corpse, trying to get a good look at it, but it was impossible. He lifted a hand to the knights behind him.

"Find me a lamp or something for illumination," he said to anyone who could carry out the request. "Quickly."

Truett rushed off with the soldier, dashing to the Stafford men who were bearing torches against the dark night, and took one of them back to the livery. Truett handed it over to Thor, who held the torch over the body, trying to get a good look at the dead man's face. It took him about five seconds to realize whom he was looking at.

"Christ," he muttered. "That is the same bastard who tried to stop my marriage to Callie. That's one of the de Wylde men. The son."

Since no one else had ever seen Rotri or Domnall the day of the wedding, they had to take his word for it. "The uncle who has been trying to petition the church for a marriage between his son and Lady de Reyne?" Darius said. "Lord Dordon?"

Thor nodded. "The same," he said. He suddenly had a very, very bad feeling as he stood up, looking around. "If the son is dead, then *where* is the father? Was he part of the raid against Millford tonight?"

No one had an answer. They had a dead man, a burned village, and more than a dozen of the raiders as prisoners. But no Lord Dordon, who was clearly involved in some way. Thor couldn't explain why a sense of foreboding swept him, but he motioned to the soldier who had found the body.

"Find a few men and wrap him up," he said. "He goes with us."

With that, he headed out of the livery with his knights around him. Up the slope, they could see the Stafford soldiers gathered, as well as the small group of prisoners. But he was feeling jumpy, apprehensive, and he kept looking at their surroundings as if expecting Rotri to pop up out of the ashes. If the son's body was in the stable, he couldn't imagine that the father wouldn't be nearby.

It just didn't make sense.

"What's wrong, Thor?" Darius asked what they were all thinking. "What are you looking around like that?"

Thor could only shake his head. "Something is not right," he said. "We need to return to Stafford immediately. But we're taking the prisoners with us."

Darius and Clayne, who had served with Thor the longest, knew the man didn't panic without reason, but he was currently exhibiting a good deal of anxiety. Before Darius could ask him what his suspicions were, they all heard a high-pitched wail as it grew louder very quickly. Knowing what the sound was, as all fighting men did, the knights threw themselves onto the ground as a crossbow bolt sailed overhead. A second one came quickly on the heels of the first, slamming into the back of Truett's thigh as he lay on the ground.

Under attack, the Stafford men began to scatter for cover.

More arrows were flying, but they were big bolts, not the small ones meant for men. These were larger bolts, usually meant to take down horses or warriors with a good deal of protection. Realizing they were vulnerable to whatever was flying overhead, Thor rolled over to Truett, who couldn't sit up or move because the bolt had gone through the meaty part of his thigh and pinned him to the ground. Exposing himself after two more bolts landed close to them, Thor sat up, ripped the bolt out of Truett's leg, and pulled the man to his feet as they ran for cover.

Thor, Darius, and Truett made it back to the livery without being hit. Clayne went with the men, rushing into the smoking ruins for cover. That left the prisoners unguarded, and they began to scatter.

Thor watched them rush off into the darkness.

"Damn," he muttered. "We've lost our opportunity to find out what we're in the middle of."

"An ambush," Darius said. "This is clearly an ambush, Thor. Is it possible that the de Wylde son was going to warn us and they killed him for it? It looks as if he has been beaten to death."

Thor looked at him, pondering that question, before shaking his head in confusion. "I suppose anything is possible at this point," he said. "But I know who would know."

"Who?"

"Whoever is firing those bolts at us."

Darius nodded, understanding the implication. "Capture or kill?"

"I don't see that we have a choice unless we want to be pinned in the livery forever."

"How would you like to proceed?"

Thor could see the slope and the muddy area that formerly held the prisoners from one of the livery windows. "We need to draw them out," he said. "Someone must act as the decoy, and then those of us who are safely sheltered will see where the bolts are coming from."

"And then we move."

"Exactly."

"I'll go," Truett said, moving toward the livery entry with his bloodied thigh. "They already got me once. What is one more bolt?"

Thor grabbed his arm as he walked past. "Not you," he said. "You cannot move fast with that leg."

Truett pulled his arm out of Thor's grasp. "Watch me."

Thor rolled his eyes, grabbing at him again, but Truett was out of his reach. Resigned that the man was going to try to get himself impaled again, Thor and Darius moved to various vantage points near the livery windows that faced the village, and when Truett stepped out and made himself a giant target, the bolts began to fly again. Two zinged past Truett and, as he dashed back into the livery, the third one skimmed his left shoulder and tore his clothing.

"Good work, True," Thor said, peering at the torn shoulder to see that it was barely a scrape. "You survived."

"I told you I would."

Thor cast him a long look. "The night is not over yet."

As Truett agreed with a grin, Thor darted over to the north end of the livery, leaving Truett and Darius to follow. They had a fairly clear field of vision from this vantage point of the village, including a few stone outbuildings that hadn't burned.

"There were three bolts," Thor said, peering out into the darkness. "That means three men out there with crossbows. Remove your mail, your protection—anything that makes noise when you move or weighs you down. We have to find these men and move swiftly."

They began to strip down, all of them, as Clayne suddenly rushed in through the entry, tripping and rolling and ending up back on his feet again.

"God's Bones!" he exclaimed. "Whoever is firing is doing it with skill!"

Thor had his mail off, his helm off, and was going to work on repositioning his broadsword around his waist. "Indeed they are," he said. "And they have us trapped, so True and Darius and I are going to go after them, but we need your help."

"What?" Clayne asked, coming over to assist Truett with his broadsword strap. "What can I do?"

"Create a diversion," Thor said. "Distract them so they do not see us leave the livery. Have some of the soldiers scatter and create moving targets. It is dark enough that it will be difficult to hit them, so try to keep them safe as they move. But we need that diversion."

Clayne nodded, but he was watching Truett struggle with his injured leg. The man had had a bolt pierce his entire left thigh but pretended as if it didn't matter.

Clayne pointed at him.

"You are going to take True?" he said. "Look at him, Thor. He is injured. He cannot move swiftly. I'll go."

Truett ignored him as he tried to find a comfortable position for his left leg. "If you say another word about my capabilities, I'm going to load *you* into a crossbow and fire you," he said. "I'm perfectly capable, Bully. Go and do as Thor has asked."

Clayne looked at Thor beseechingly, but Thor simply shook his head. "You heard him," he said. "He will fire you into a tree if you persist. Besides, I need you with the men. Go, now. Do as I say."

Annoyed that he wasn't going to have the opportunity to take down one of the enemy crossbowmen, Clayne shot a nasty look at Truett, who caught it in his periphery and lashed out a fist, catching him in the chest. With the wind knocked out of him, and rubbing his sternum, Clayne headed over to the door that opened up to the slope and, beyond that, where the Stafford men were hiding. As he dashed out, the arrows began to fly.

Thor, Darius, and Truett made their move.

Thor was focused on the outbuilding that was about twenty yards in front of him. The building next to it had burned down, but the structure he had seen the bolts emerge from was stone. It was some kind of smithy shack, as those were usually built with stone because of the intense heat from the forges, so he crouched low to the ground as he moved, staying behind the burned-out shells of cottages, inching his way toward the stone building.

At one point, Clayne and the Stafford men began moving around because two more bolts flew out of the stone building, right at the group. That made Thor move more swiftly because he wanted to surprise the attacker and could only do that if the man was distracted. Reaching the stone building, he pressed himself flush against the wall, hearing someone moving inside. The door was closed from what he could see, so as Clayne created more of a diversion, Thor came away from the wall, braced himself, and kicked the door as hard as he could.

The panel collapsed and Thor charged in. Because it was such a small building, he didn't unsheathe his broadsword because he risked hurting himself in close quarters, so he produced a dagger that could easily slit a throat. The shack was very dark and he was aware of a body in front of him as he crashed into it, grabbing for a head so he could slit the throat.

But his opponent was skilled.

The moment he grabbed for the body, the person inside the

shack used the crossbow and cracked it right across Thor's forehead. The force of the blow was enough to stun him, but he kept his footing even as he could feel the blood running down his face. He dug his fingers into the man's hair—and he knew it was a man by this point—with the intent of dragging him out of the shack so he could have room to fight. He didn't want to fight in such a tight space because things could go wrong quickly. Heaving and yanking, he managed to pull the man to the door.

That was when the man began to seriously fight back.

Somehow, the dagger in Thor's grip was knocked away and it became a fistfight. Thor was big, and powerful, with hammer-like fists—hence the *El Martillo* moniker—and he put those knuckles to good use as he pounded the man who had been trying to kill him. He still had his broadsword strapped to his right thigh but didn't want to bring it out until he could get the man completely clear of the shack. The man wasn't going easily, however, and used his big feet to kick Thor in the right knee, bending it awkwardly. Grunting in pain, but furious at the blow, Thor didn't hold back.

The fists were flying.

They cleared the shack and began to beat each other soundly. Thor had the advantage of height and strength, and he used it. He also began to use his feet, sweeping the man's legs out from under him and them pouncing on him. But the man grabbed a fistful of dirt and smashed it into Thor's face, momentarily blinding him, and they both lost their balance. Together, they rolled down a slight incline onto a pathway below.

The fight continued.

Now that they were free of the confines of the shack, Thor

was determined to end the fight once and for all. Grabbing his opponent by the hair, he slammed the man's face into the rocky ground, several times, enough to stun him. Climbing off the man, he took several steps back and unsheathed his broadsword, taking an offensive stance as the man shook off the stars dancing before his eyes and rolled over onto his bum.

That was when Thor could get a good look at him.

His eyes widened.

"*De Lucera*?" he hissed in disbelief. "Cristano de Lucera? What in the hell are you doing?"

Cristano spat the dirt out of his mouth, touching a loose tooth before answering. "You are supposed to be dead, de Reyne."

Thor had to admit that he was a little stunned, but as he stared at de Lucera, things started to make sense just a little.

"*You* did this?" he said, gesturing to the village. "You instigated this… this raid?"

De Lucera sighed heavily and stood up. "Will you at least let me claim my broadsword and make this a fair fight?"

Thor held up a hand. "Wait," he said, more angrily. "Answer my question. You instigated this raid?"

De Lucera's gaze lingered on him for a moment. "I was not alone."

That comment brought the light of realization in Thor's mind. "De Wylde," he rumbled. "De Wylde and his son."

De Lucera shrugged. "You haven't said whether I can gather my sword."

"Why did you kill the younger de Wylde?"

De Lucera shook his head. "I did not," he said. "We do not know what happened to him. We found him that way, as if he'd been crushed or trampled."

"Where is his father?"

"I do not know, but the son's death drove him mad. He is probably off killing himself."

Thor's frustration was only growing with those answers. The truth of the situation was coming to him in pieces. "Start from the beginning and I may show mercy," he said. "Tell me what is happening here. Are you saying this raid was instigated by you and de Wylde to try to draw me out of the castle so you could shoot me down with a crossbow?"

"Let me collect my sword and I will tell you everything."

"Tell me everything and I may let you collect your sword."

De Lucera was at an extreme disadvantage and knew it. It wasn't as if he had much to bargain with. He thought that if he was honest with de Reyne, the man might let his guard down a little, which would help even the odds. Unless Adan and Benedicto were going to come to his aid against a superior opponent, he was on his own.

"After you exiled us from Stafford, we had nowhere to go," he said. "I have served Stafford for many years. I know the land; I know the people. I did not want to go far and start anew, so I went to Dordon. He is Lady de Reyne's uncle, after all. I asked him if he would consider accepting my fealty and that of my cousins."

Thor could only shake his head in disgust. "He is also my wife's enemy, and surely you must have known that," he said with skepticism. "Therefore, you went to him in the hopes that he would accept your fealty so you could remain close to Stafford and possibly cause problems for my wife and me. I would be more apt to believe that than any other explanation, so do not lie to me, de Lucera. I know you better than you know yourself."

De Lucera wasn't going to deny it. There was no point. "As it turns out, there is someone who hates you more than I do," he said, a glimmer of irony in his eyes. "When you married Lady Stafford, that sealed Dordon's hatred for you. While I was content to bide my time against you, Dordon was not. He wants you dead, de Reyne. With you gone, he is once again in control of his niece's destiny."

"He was never in control of her, not ever."

"Mayhap not, but with you gone, it makes the woman more vulnerable to his wishes."

Thor wasn't surprised to hear it. "So he moves beyond trying to marry his son to his niece," he muttered as the pieces of the puzzle began to come together. "Now, he simply wants to kill me so Caledonia will be alone again."

"That is correct."

"But even if I am dead, Caledonia is alive and he cannot have Tamworth if she is living," he said. "God, don't tell me… He wasn't going to try to marry her himself, was he?"

De Lucera shook his head. "Nay," he said. "I am going to marry her, assume Stafford, and give him Tamworth."

He said it so factually, as if it was nothing outrageous, but Thor found himself shaking his head in disbelief.

"Clearly, you two had a scheme," he said. "And that crossbow was meant to kill me."

"It was."

Thor had to wrap his mind around the whole plot. The poor village of Millford was caught in the middle of a power struggle and an attempted assassination while Cristano de Lucera sat calmly a few feet away. A man who had been promised Caledonia and Stafford Castle for his role in Thor's death.

It was astonishing.

"Something is not clear," Thor said after a moment. "Did de Wylde promise you this before his son's death? Because he wants Callie to marry his son, you know."

"He promised it to me after Domnall's death, if I would help him kill you," de Lucera said. "De Reyne, he was originally going to abduct you and ransom you back to your wife. But that changed at Domnall's death. After that, he simply wanted you dead. For the price of your life, he would demand the wealth of Tamworth."

"Then it is about the money?"

"It seems to be. Money and power are all that matter, are they not?"

Thor grunted. "There are a few more things worth living for."

"Like what?"

"A good woman."

It took de Lucera a moment to understand what he was saying. "Ah," he said. "You mean Lady Stafford."

Thor eyed the man in the darkness. "You saw what her marriage to de Tosni was like," he said. "You saw how he treated her. How he entrusted their children to that charlatan, Madam Madonna. Where is the woman, anyway? She left Stafford with you."

"She went with us to Dordon," de Lucera confirmed. "She did not stay, however. She wanted to return to Whitby Abbey, where she evidently came from, in the hopes that she could become a nurse for another noble family. She did not seem overly distraught about not returning to Stafford. She said that she would not serve under a whore."

He meant Caledonia, and it was a struggle for Thor to keep his temper at bay. "Lady Stafford is no whore, I assure you," he muttered. "Madam Madonna did not wish to return because she knew her reign of terror was over. She knew that Callie would not stand for her any longer. Hell, de Lucera, you served at Stafford. You saw how that woman treated the children."

De Lucera was unmoved. "It was not my concern."

That rubbed Thor the wrong way. Three starving little girls were not his concern? All of those adults at Stafford and no one could take responsibility for the children.

That disgusted him.

"So I see," he said, feeling that the conversation was at an end. "Let us sum up this situation, de Lucera—Madam Madonna has gone to prey on another family, the younger de Wylde is dead, and you are now my prisoner. But that leaves Lord Dordon."

"What about him?"

"*Where* is he?"

De Lucera shrugged. "As I said, his son's death drove him into madness," he said. "I do not know where he is."

That was probably the truth, but Thor had to make sure. "Would he have gone back to Dordon?" he asked.

"He was more concerned with seeing you dead. I do not think he would go home."

Thor was starting to get that bad feeling again. Off in the distance, he could see the Stafford army moving about and saw, distinctly, when Truett came into view dragging a body. Thor suspected it was one of the de Lucera cousins who, more than likely, were the ones shooting the bolts. If Cristano was, this surely his cousins were as well. Therefore, they had managed to subdue those who had caused the chaos at Millford, evidently for the sole purpose of killing the new earl of Tamworth and Stafford.

But they were missing one key player.

Rotri de Wylde.

That bad feeling grew worse.

"De Lucera," Thor said slowly, trying to keep his apprehension down, "I am going to ask you one question. Your answer will determine whether or not I kill you where you stand, so think hard and answer well."

Cristano sighed sharply and tensed, preparing for what was to come. "What is it?"

"Did you and de Wylde concoct this raid to draw me out of Stafford so de Wylde could get to my wife while I was busy fighting off the raiding army?" Thor asked through clenched teeth. "Does the fact that de Wylde isn't here mean he has gone to Stafford and to Caledonia?"

De Lucera shook his head. "That was not the original plan," he said. "But, as I said, the death of de Wylde's son did something to him. Even as Domnall lay at his feet, Dordon was demanding your death. I suppose it is possible that he has gone on to Stafford, knowing I would kill you and knowing we had made a bargain about your widow."

"Would it be fair to say that he has gone on to collect her?"

"Given how badly he wants you dead, I would say that is fair."

That was all Thor needed to hear. He moved to shout to his knights, but de Lucera took advantage of the distraction and grabbed for his broadsword. The entire situation deteriorated into chaos again, but when Thor finally got the upper hand, he didn't hesitate in doing what needed to be done.

De Lucera's head went rolling one way while his body fell the other.

Before Thor drew another breath, he was running for his horse.

CHAPTER TWENTY

S HE WANTED TO see her chicken.

That fluffy, soft chicken with the black feathers that had given her love and attention when no one else would. Even now, when she had plenty of attention and affection, Janet had not forgotten about her pet. She never would. She was deeply disappointed that the bed for her chicken hadn't been made. Darius had been given the task, according to Jane, but he was unable to finish it before he was called to duty by Thor because of the burning village to the east.

That meant Mary had no bed.

Sleeping in the big bed next to a softly snoring Joan, Janet was very worried for her chicken. The fowl had always come inside to sleep with her when she shared this chamber with Madam Madonna, though Madam Madonna had kicked the chicken once or twice when it annoyed her. But, surprisingly, she'd allowed the chicken shelter in the keep.

Caledonia, however, did not.

There was a difficult paradox there. Janet had come to love her mother. Caledonia was kind and patient and gave her hugs and food anytime she wanted it. She even let Mary come into the keep during the day, when they were having their lessons, as long as it didn't distract Janet from her learning—but at nighttime, Caledonia insisted that the chicken needed to go outside. Normally, that would have drawn Janet's ire, treating her chicken so poorly, but because she had come to love her mother, she was very torn about what to do.

She very much wanted her chicken inside.

Tonight, she'd been expecting the chicken bed, and when it hadn't come, she had tried not to weep. They'd had a lovely supper of bean stew with pork and carrots, plenty of bread and butter, and the milk that was left over when the butter was made. It was delicious. Janet had eaten until she could hold no more and gone to bed with a fully belly, but it didn't soothe her longing for her pet. Long after Jane and Joan had gone to sleep, Janet lay there and stared at the ceiling, wishing she had her chicken with her. Surely Mary was lonely out in the yard, now without a bed to comfort her.

Janet had to see her.

The keep was quiet at this hour and she knew exactly how to leave without being heard. She'd done it before, especially with Madam Madonna around. Not that the woman had ever cared what she did, but Janet had honed her silent skills on the nun. With both of her sisters sleeping heavily, Janet climbed out of bed, nearly falling to the floor, and made her way out of the chamber.

Her mother's chamber was next door to hers but the door was closed. That was the perfect situation for sneaking down to see her chicken. The door at the top of the stairs was bolted, so Janet quietly threw the bolt and opened the door. The darkened stairwell was beyond, and she made her way down, cautiously, until she was in the keep entry.

After that, it was simply a matter of slipping from the front door.

There were no servants around, which was fortunate because there was no one to question her. They were usually asleep at this hour, so Janet took advantage of that as she threw the big iron bolt on the front door and then lifted the wooden bar that braced the door shut. She pulled the panel open only to have it squeak a little, and she froze, looking around to see if someone had heard it and was coming to investigate. But the keep remained silent and, relieved, Janet slipped from the front door and down into the darkened bailey beyond.

CB

"I HAVE COME with a message for Lady Stafford. Quickly—admit me."

The soldiers at in the lower bailey weren't particularly wary of a single, unarmed man standing in the portcullis, but the sergeant in command did crowd up against the iron grate to ask some questions.

"What about the flames we saw?" he asked. "Were there raiders?"

"A few, but they have been subdued. Let me in because I bear a message for Lady Stafford."

The sergeant peered at him. "I don't know you," he said. "Are you one of de Reyne's royal soldiers?"

It took a split second for the man to realize that was the answer he should use. "Aye," he said. "I *am* a royal soldier."

The sergeant boomed for the portcullis to be lifted.

Rotri slipped in.

He had only been to Stafford once, for his niece's wedding, and that had been many years ago, so he didn't know the place at all. Even though Dordon wasn't too far from Stafford—perhaps a two-day ride—he'd never had any reason to go to Stafford.

Until now.

Now, he had every reason.

"Where is the lady?" he asked the sergeant. "She will be expecting this message."

The sergeant pointed to the keep high atop the hill. "There," he said. "Tell the gatehouse sentries that you come with a message. They will send for her."

Rotri thanked them and quickly moved toward the road that led up the motte. Stafford was lit up this night, awaiting their army's return, so he had plenty of light to find his way to the upper gatehouse.

I am a royal soldier.

It seemed strange that the sergeant had believed him, given that he wasn't wearing a royal standard, but he wasn't going to question the man's lapse. For once, he didn't let his pride lead the way. Normally, he would have announced himself as Lord Dordon, brother to the Earl of Tamworth, and demand to be admitted, but this time he didn't.

He didn't follow his instincts.

He was following his heart.

That greedy, small thing in his chest. The one that was shriveling, almost as dead as his son back at Millford. Domnall had told him to come, after all, and Domnall would have been clever about it. He would have scolded his father for not using any opportunity to gain access to Caledonia. That elusive niece, a woman they'd tried to snare for two solid years, was finally within his grasp because Rotri lied about being a royal soldier.

I'll claim her, Domnall. Wait and see.

He would make his son proud.

Up the narrow road to the upper bailey went Rotri. He had a good view of Stafford as a whole at this elevation, and it was an impressive place. Much more impressive than Dordon Castle. He could see now why Cristano wanted it. Truthfully, he didn't know Cristano well, and even though the man had promised him Tamworth, he could change his mind. Rotri would have to think about leverage, something forcing Cristano to honor his bargain. Perhaps he'd withhold the marriage to Caledonia until he had Cristano's promise in writing.

He was too close to his goal not to demand a guarantee.

The upper gatehouse loomed ahead, and the guards here had even less concern for Rotri's appearance than the sentries down in the lower bailey. They let him through with hardly a word, indicating the keep and telling him that they would send for a servant to summon the lady. No one seemed particularly interested in him, but they were concerned about the events happening in the town to the east. No one was sure what had happened other than a fire, and they didn't even really know which village had sustained damage yet, but their focus was on the event. Rotri could hear them talking about it. That only worked to his advantage because they weren't focused on him. They had believed him when he said he'd come with a message for Lady Stafford.

It was as simple as that.

In fact, no one had sent for a servant yet. They were still standing by the closed gate, talking about the distant action and the return of Stafford's troops. Hearing this, and realizing he wasn't being watched, Rotri began to casually wander toward the keep. It was dark and cold out this night, with a gust of wind every so often lifting the dirt and debris of the bailey. It was almost ghostly, as if the specters of Stafford were dancing around him. He could hear noises everywhere. Little by little, however, he edged closer to the keep.

Then he heard it.

A door opening.

Looking up, he could see that it was the entry door to the keep. A small child was coming down the steps. He stopped his advance, watching the child come to the bottom of the stairs. Dressed in what looked like a sleeping shift, she began to walk toward the eastern side of the bailey, but her gaze abruptly fell on him and she stopped. For a moment, they simply looked at one another until the little girl pushed her hair from her eyes and headed in his direction.

"Where are you going?" she asked.

Rotri didn't know what to say, and scrambled to come up with something. He wasn't entirely sure that if he didn't give the right answer, the child wouldn't raise an alarm. He briefly considered smothering her, but he held off. There was no need at the moment. But he would be ready to cut her off if he needed to.

"I… I am looking for Lady Stafford," he said. "I bear a message from her husband. Do you know where she is?"

The child nodded. "She is inside, sleeping."

Rotri looked up at the keep as if to see Caledonia through the walls. "I would like to see her," he said. "Will you send a servant for her?"

The little girl eyed him a moment, but she kept looking off toward the east side of the compound. "I came to find my chicken," she said.

Rotri looked off into the darkness, the same direction that had the little girl's attention. "Your chicken?" he repeated.

"Mary," the little girl said.

"And that is your chicken?"

"Aye."

"What is your name?"

"Janet," she said. "I live here."

"Are you a servant? What I meant to ask is if you tend the chickens."

She shook her head. "My mother is Lady Stafford," she said. "Who are you?"

That information filled Rotri with joy. He'd heard that his niece had children, but he hadn't known how many or what sex. He'd never really cared. But now, he had one of them in his grasp and wasn't going to let her go. *Leverage,* he thought.

He would use the child against the mother, if needed.

Fate had taken pity on him tonight.

"Will you take me to your mother, Lady Janet?" he asked politely. "I must speak with her."

Janet was indecisive. "But I must get my chicken."

Rotri held out a hand to her, a kind gesture if it had come from anyone other than him. But coming from Rotri, it was a deadly and possessive one.

"I will help you," he said. "We will find your chicken and then you will take me to your mother."

That was good enough for Janet. She grabbed his hand and practically yanked him back to the kitchen yard, where her chicken was sitting, quite comfortably, in a worn, woven basket that was used for many chores. She gathered up the fat black chicken and, with Rotri in tow, headed back the way she had come. He followed her all the way to the front door of the keep, where she suddenly stopped and turned to him.

"We must be quiet," she whispered. "And do not tell my

mother about the chicken."

He shook his head solemnly. "I will not, I swear it," he said. But then he looked up at the keep again, dark and forbidding against the night sky. "Is there anyone else in the keep?"

Janet nodded. "My sisters," she said. "And Nica, but they are all sleeping."

"Who is Nica?"

"My friend."

"Where does she sleep?"

Janet pointed up. "On the very top, in her own chamber."

That was enough chatter as far as Janet was concerned. Quietly, she took him inside, and Rotri shut the door behind them. The old hinges creaked, causing both to freeze in their tracks—surely the squeaking would alert someone—but several seconds passed and no one appeared. Relieved, Janet headed up the stairs with Rotri close behind her. Quietly, they took the stone steps, and Janet pushed open the door at the top of the stairwell.

It was as still and silent as it had been when she left. Leaving Rotri standing at the top of the stairs, she rushed into the chamber that she shared with her sisters and plopped the chicken on her bed, covering it up with the coverlet to hide it. Then she returned to Rotri, pointing to one of two closed doors on the landing.

"My mother is sleeping in there," she said. "I will wake her."

"Nay," Rotri said. "I will. Thank you for bringing me."

That was enough for Janet. She didn't question him. She was eager to get back to her chicken, so she simply left him and went back to her chamber, shutting the door.

That left Rotri alone on the landing.

Alone and ready to strike.

CHAPTER TWENTY-ONE

SOMEONE WAS CALLING her name.

In a deep sleep, someone was calling her name in a dream. *Caledonia.* She could hear them but couldn't see them. It was a male voice that she thought might be her husband, so she began to hunt for him in her dream. She was eager to see him, looking for him in the mist.

Caledonia!

It was louder this time. It felt as if it was right in her ear. In fact, it was so loud that it jolted her out of her sleep. She opened her eyes to a dark room except for the fire in the hearth that gave off some illumination—enough for her to see that there was someone else in the chamber with her. For a moment, she thought it was Thor and sat up with a gasp of delight, the cobwebs quickly clearing away. She was halfway out of bed before she realized that it wasn't Thor.

It was someone else.

Her eyes fixed on a living nightmare.

"Good," Rotri said. "You are awake. You and I must speak, Callie."

It took Caledonia a fraction of a moment to realize that her uncle was very real and standing in her bedchamber. When the awareness settled, she pealed a scream and threw herself to the opposite side of the bed, hysterical in her panic. She screamed again when she saw him move toward her, and she jumped over the bed in the opposite direction, rushing for a small alcove where she knew Thor kept some weapons. He had them in the keep, in the armory, in the hall, and a half-dozen other places around the castle because that was simply his way. He was always prepared for a fight. But Rotri caught her as she dashed for the alcove, and in her panic, she grabbed the nearest item— not even knowing what it was but seeing something in her periphery on a table—and smashed it right over his head.

Rotri was rocked by a blow from a broken pitcher as Caledonia darted into the alcove and made a grab for a dagger.

Shaking off the bells in his ears, Rotri was right on top of her.

"*Stop!*" he commanded, trying to force her to release the dagger. "Let go before you hurt someone!"

Caledonia was almost incoherent with terror. She tried to slash at him and managed to clip his right wrist, but he nearly broke her fingers forcing her to drop the dagger. As it clattered to the floor near the hearth, she screamed again and pulled away from him, running to the far end of the chamber, on the other side of a big table, and contemplated her next move.

Rotri stood near the alcove, inspecting the cut on his wrist.

"Now," he said decisively. "That will be enough of that. I did not come here to fight you."

Caledonia's breathing was coming in sharp gasps. "How did you get in here?" she demanded. Then she started smacking her hand on the table in a loud and commanding gesture. "Get out before I kill you!"

Rotri shook his head. He stood there, looking at her with both contempt and impatience, before sighing heavily and looking away. He appeared strangely weary as he sat down in the nearest chair, which was next to the hearth.

For a brief moment, the chaos in the room stilled.

It was quiet.

For now.

"Nay," Rotri said after a moment. "No more killing. There has been enough killing this night. Your cousin is dead, Callie. God help me, my son is dead."

She hadn't expected to hear that, so it threw her off guard a little. "Dead?" she repeated. "Domnall?"

Rotri nodded. "Domnall," he confirmed. "So is your husband. That is why I am here."

Caledonia sucked in her breath, her eyes widening. "Thor?" she gasped. "It's not true!"

"It is, I'm afraid. Killed in an ambush."

Those words hit Caledonia as heavily as a blow from a battering ram. She actually stumbled back, slamming into the wall, her hands flying to her mouth to hold back the hysterical screams.

"Nay," she breathed. "Nay, it cannot be. *It is not true!*"

She went from whispering the words to screaming them all in a split second, shouting at him as Rotri put up a hand to quiet her.

"I told you that it is," he said. "Your husband rode out to defend Millford, but my knights killed him. Now we must speak about your future, Lady Stafford."

Something happened to Caledonia at that moment. *Thor is dead?* She knew she shouldn't believe her uncle, but on the other hand, the only way he would be here, in a chamber with her, was if Thor was unable to prevent it.

Dead.

My husband is dead.

And with that, Caledonia started to scream. Her hands flew over her ears and she sank to the floor, screaming loudly enough for the entire castle to hear. Knowing this, Rotri ran out to the landing and locked the door at the top of the stairs to prevent anyone from entering to see what was amiss. It cut the floor off from the stairs. He didn't need any do-good soldiers trying to rescue Lady Stafford or, worse, the woman named Nica, as Janet had described her, interfering. He needed Caledonia's attention and was going to get it, because he had plans for the woman.

Finally, he had her where he wanted her.

"Callie, stop," he commanded as she huddled on the floor and screamed. "Do you hear me? *Stop!*"

She heard him, but she couldn't. She was in a quagmire of grief, deeper than anything she'd ever known, and her screams were meant for her husband to hear, wherever he was. Thor had to hear how badly she was taking the news because, in the short time that they had known one another, a love had been built that could not be broken. Not even by death. Perhaps her screams were meant to bridge the veil of death, to reach out to him to convey the depth and strength of the love between them.

He had to hear her.

But… oh, God… the pain.

Eventually, Caledonia fell over onto her left side and the screams faded to gut-wrenching sobs. Rotri had made his way over to her by this point, frowning as he gazed down upon her. He wasn't very tolerant of emotions or weakness. Infuriated, he pulled up a stool and planted himself on it as he yanked her into a sitting position.

"What is the matter with you?" he demanded. "Why do you weep for a man you were hardly married to? A man who was forced upon you?"

Caledonia couldn't answer him. She was leaning against the stone wall, her face turned away from him as she wallowed in grief.

"Answer me," he said. "Why do you carry on so for a man who simply married you out of greed?"

Caledonia suddenly lashed out a foot and caught him in the face, sending him toppling off the stool. "It was not out of greed!" she cried. "You are the only greedy bastard I know, and that is exactly why you are here! Greed has driven you to persecute me for the past two years, you vile son of a whore. Get out of here and leave me alone!"

Rotri wasn't bleeding, but it had been a good kick. Rubbing his sore nose, he reclaimed his stool and slapped her in the face when she tried to kick him again.

"Do not kick me," he warned. "The next time, my response will be more painful, so stop behaving like an animal and listen to me."

"Nay!" she shouted as she managed to squirm away from him and get to her feet. Sick, exhausted, and overwrought, she staggered away. "Get out of here, Rotri. I do not want to hear you."

Rotri stood up, tracking her as she stumbled out of his reach. "You have no choice," he said steadily. "You are going to listen to me because I have come to claim my due, something you have denied me since birth."

"I haven't done anything!"

Rotri cocked his head. "Untrue," he said. "Constantine was

the first. He is the one who truly stole my inheritance, but then you came along. You were a worthless female until your brother and father died, and then you became the heiress of everything that should have been mine."

She was over by the hearth now, glaring at him with tears and mucus streaming down her face. "I did not ask for it," she said. "I did not want it. If you want to blame someone, blame the king. Blame the laws. But do not blame me, because I never wanted it."

Rotri rubbed his sore nose again. "Be that as it may, it is yours," he said. "But I have waited long enough. You will marry Cristano so he can assume the earldom of Stafford, and he will give me Tamworth. I shall have what blood right should have given me long ago."

"Cristano?" Caledonia said with horror when she realized that was whom he intended to marry her to. "De Lucera?"

"Do you know another Cristano?"

"I will not marry that bastard and you cannot make me!"

"You will do as I tell you."

As the tears fading, a sense of self-preservation took hold. If what he said was true and Thor was dead, there was no way out for her. She was to be pushed from marriage to marriage because of her value as an heiress and nothing more. She was, once again, a commodity. *Déchet*, Robert had called her. She was back to being rubbish. From the days of heaven with Thor, it was back to the endless hell she had always endured.

But she wasn't going to endure it any longer.

"Nay," she said after a moment. "I will not do as you tell me. You are not my lord. You are nothing to me but a greedy, conniving fool who has lived in the shadow of my father his entire life. You are worthless, Rotri. You will never have

Tamworth because I am not going to let you have it. Once and for all, you will not have it."

With that, she bolted for the nearest lancet window, scrambling into it. The walls were thick, so every window had a wide ledge or even a stone seat. In this case it was a wide ledge, and before Rotri could stop her, she was clinging to the frame of a window that was high above the side of the motte. The plunge below, by the time she hit the ground, would be thirty feet or more. If the fall alone didn't break her neck, then the roll down the steep motte would surely finish her off.

Rotri could see that quite plainly.

"Nay!" he shouted. "Wait! Callie, *wait!*"

But Caledonia was pushing herself out of the window, barely holding on to the stone frame. "You will not have anything," she repeated, the tears returning. "The earldom of Stafford and Tamworth belongs to a de Reyne. It no longer belongs to the House of de Wylde. Therefore, if I die, Tamworth will revert to the Crown and you will be unable to get your filthy hands on it. Stafford belongs to my eldest daughter, but that isn't something you care about, thank God. You only want Tamworth, and I am going to put it out of your reach for good."

Rotri knew better than to try to grab her. All she had to do was loosen her grip and she would fall from the window. She would do that rather than let him get a grip on her, he was certain.

The tables were turning.

Now, he was the one panicking.

"Please do not jump," he pleaded. "Let us speak calmly. If you do not want to marry Cristano, then… then you do not have to. Please, Callie. Let us be reasonable about this."

The tears were coursing down Caledonia's face. "There is

nothing to discuss," she said. "My husband is dead. You have told me this. Is it true?"

Reluctantly, Rotri nodded. "I ordered him killed."

She winced when she heard the words, feeling the shock and pain all over again. "Then you have murdered a good man," she murmured. "It is true that the king forced us to marry. He did not want to do it, nor did I, and I went through great lengths to prevent it. But once I came to know him a little, I realized that he was a fine man. He was kind and considerate. He was attentive. He was everything I had been missing in my life, making me feel more loved and honored in just the short time we were married than I've ever felt in my entire life. I cannot face the prospect of life without him. I do not want to try."

"Callie, *please*—"

"Nay, Uncle," she said, cutting him off. "When you ordered him killed, then you murdered me, too. I will not let you taint his memory with your greed and deceit. Why men like you continue to live and men like Thor are allowed to die is something I must ask God when I see him, for I do not understand any of it. I do not understand why He allows such terrible things to happen. He sent me an angel only to take him away? He will have to explain that to me."

Rotri had his hands up in a supplicating gesture. "If you jump from the window and kill yourself, you will not be allowed to see God," he said, trying to use doctrine to get her out of the window. "You will not even be allowed to see Thor. You will suffer in the sulfur lakes for eternity. Think about what you are doing and understand the consequences."

That brought Caledonia pause. She, too, knew that church doctrine preached against suicide. But this wasn't suicide, was it? It was vengeance for Thor's death, punishment for Rotri's greed. Surely God would understand that.

But then there were her children.

She would be leaving Jane, Janet, and Joan without a mother. Again. And this time, there was no Madam Madonna to look after them, as poorly as the woman did it. She would be leaving her daughters to fend for themselves in a world that would just as soon eat them up like wolves upon lambs. They would end up in a foundling home, treated like rubbish for the rest of their lives.

Déchet, just like their mother.

As Caledonia crouched in the window, debating whether to live or die, she didn't see her chamber door open. She didn't see Jane stand in the doorway, observing her mother in the window ledge as a strange man tried to convince her to come away. When Rotri had bolted the door at the top of the stairs to prevent anyone from helping Caledonia, he had completely neglected the bedchamber with the young girls inside.

Eight-year-old Jane had heard everything.

Something had awoken her. It wasn't the screaming. It had been more of a whisper in her ear, telling her to rise. *Rise, child,* the voice had said. Perhaps it had been a dream, but it had been enough to get her up and hear almost all of the conversation in the next chamber.

Her mother was in trouble.

For a young lass who had been conditioned by a bitter old woman into believing that she had to constantly spread the word of God in order to get to heaven and that the woman who gave birth to her was the embodiment of the devil, the past two weeks had shown her something quite different.

Tenderness...

Understanding...

Love.

Jane had seen all of these things, things she had resisted, but she was resisting no more. Thor had spoken to her about the situation, and so had Darius. They insisted that Madam Madonna had lied about her mother, and the more time passed, the more Jane was coming to understand that. Earlier that day, she'd had the first lesson with her mother as Darius had sat next to her, helping her with her letters. It had been a glimpse into a world where people cared for her and nurtured her. For a child who had only known fear and neglect, it had been a pivotal moment.

But tonight, something bad was happening. Jane had heard the man in her mother's room speak of Thor being dead, which upset her. He had been so very kind, explaining things in a way she could understand even if she didn't believe it. One of the things he had told her, repeatedly, was how much her mother loved her. A woman that Jane had never given a chance until that afternoon. She didn't regret it. In fact, she wanted to do it again, but there would be no opportunity if her mother jumped from the window.

That frightened Jane.

She had to help.

Silently, Jane entered the bedchamber as the man and her mother were arguing. Over to her left, she could see a dagger on the floor where her mother had dropped it. It was long and sharp. After a moment of indecision, she collected the dagger and came up behind the man, who still hadn't see her. He was pleading with her mother to come out of the window, but Jane knew that the man had said some bad things. She knew there had been a fight and her mother had a bloody cut on her lip.

The man was bad.

Honor thy mother and thy father.

God wouldn't forgive her if she let something happen to her mother.

She lifted the dagger.

Oblivious to Jane's presence, Caledonia was pondering the future of her daughters without her when Rotri suddenly jerked and let out a gasp of anguish. He jerked two or three more times, bellowing in agony, before collapsing on the floor, facedown. As he fell, he revealed that Jane had been standing behind him, and Caledonia looked to see that the very dagger Rotri had forced from her hand was now protruding out of the small of his back. There were at least three other stab wounds, all quickly bleeding out. Something vital had been cut because the blood began to flow in rivers down to the floor.

When Caledonia looked at Jane, it was clear what had happened.

The child had blood on her hands.

Shocked, Caledonia came out of the window and ran to Jane, who suddenly threw her arms around her mother and began to cry. Overcome and distraught, Caledonia fell back onto her bum, taking Jane with her. She pulled the lass onto her lap, holding her so tightly that she was squeezing the life from her.

But Jane was squeezing just as tightly back.

"I'm sorry," she gasped. "I'm sorry, but he was wicked. He was going to hurt you and I... I heard what he said. I heard everything!"

Caledonia had her face in the side of the girl's head, smelling her firstborn's hair for the very first time. Her heart was beating so swiftly that she felt faint.

"You did not do wrong, my little angel," she said. "I swear, you did not do wrong. You saved me and I am so very grateful."

Jane loosened her grip enough to look her mother in the eye. "You… you are not angry?"

Caledonia smiled, kissing the child on the cheek. "Nay, sweetheart," she said. "You were very brave. You saved me."

"I had to."

"You did well, my angel."

Jane, perhaps a little overwhelmed by all of the affection and by the circumstances in general, simply nodded her head and held her mother tightly again. As tight as her little arms would hold her. It seemed that had finally come to terms with the woman who had given birth to her.

Her mother.

As Caledonia and Jane sat on the floor in a tight embrace, Nicola burst into the chamber followed by Janet and Joan. Nicola had had been awakened by the screaming, but with the stair door locked, she'd had to locate the key in order to get through. She found a chamber in shambles, a bloodied dead man on the floor, and Caledonia huddled with Jane. Nicola was so horrified that she stood there with her hand over her mouth as Janet and Joan crept over to their mother and sister. When Caledonia saw her younger daughters, she opened one arm to them, too, pulling them into her embrace.

And that was when Caledonia realized Janet was still holding her chicken.

That damn chicken.

Sitting on the floor, with her daughters crowding into her arms, Caledonia laughed until she cried, and when Thor barreled into the keep less than a half-hour later, that was how he found them.

Holding one another.

A family at last.

EPILOGUE

1279 A.D.
Edingale Castle

THE FLAGSHIP PROPERTY of the Earl of Tamworth and Stafford was abuzz with excitement tonight.

A baby was being born.

Gage eyed his son as the man stood in the solar near the elaborate Edingale-crested hearth, speaking to two of his daughters and his two eldest sons, Thorne and Kirk. The youngest, Reed, was still a toddler and his grandmother, Wynter, had charge of him. Reed had a runny nose and a cough, so Wynter was trying to get him to sleep. The eldest daughter, Jane, was in the chamber where her mother was currently giving birth to her seventh child, and from what Gage could hear, the other daughters wanted to know why they could not be included in the miracle of childbirth. He had to suppress a smile at the answers Thor was giving because it seemed to be a losing battle.

He thought he'd better save the man.

"Thor," he called over to him. "Come here a moment. There's something I forgot to tell you."

Thor tried to move away from Janet and Joan, who were growing into beautiful young women and already had their share of admirers, much to Thor's distress. Janet, in particular, had developed a large bosom at a young age, something that gave Thor heart palpitations, as grown men were starting to notice his still-young daughter. Joan, around twelve years of age now, was still petite and underdeveloped, but had fortunately learned to speak quite articulately. She was the chatterbox in the family, strangely enough.

And Thor couldn't break away from them.

"Thor!" Gage called again. "Attend me."

"Do you see what you've done?" Thor said to Janet, Joan, Thorne, and Kirk. "You have made your grandfather angry with me. Now he is shouting at me."

Joan wouldn't be put off. "But, Papa, we—"

"*Not* now," Thor said, interrupting the girl by patting her on the cheek and giving her a kiss on the forehead. The older girls, even if they were of de Tosni blood, had been calling him *papa* for many years now. "I told you that your help was not needed. If it is, the midwife will ask. At this moment I would like for you to take charge of your brothers. The hour grows late. See that they have supper and get to bed. Will you do this, please?"

Tending younger brothers who were almost as big as they were wasn't something that thrilled Janet or Joan. They loved the dark-haired, blue-eyed lads in Thorne and Kirk de Reyne-Wylde, but the boys were often uncooperative and they didn't have Jane with them to lower the hammer if they got out of hand. But they'd agreed, begrudgingly taking charge of a seven-year-old and a four-year-old boy.

Thor could hear them squabbling as they headed toward the

hall for a bit of supper.

"Christ," he muttered, plopping exhaustedly next to his father. "How in the hell did you manage to keep your sanity when we were younger? The older they become, the more difficult they become."

Gage grinned. "They do not become difficult," he said. "They simply become more challenging because your children are smarter than you are by the time they are ten years of age. You and Brian were, for certain. Taite was. He was stronger than I was, too. Hart was smarter than I was the moment he was born. But Johnny and Keats… They were very easy to control. They have a more malleable side that you and your brothers don't."

Thor smiled, thinking of his younger brothers. "I saw Taite recently when I visited Narborough Castle," he said. "He and Darius make a formidable command team. I'm envious."

"They do," Gage said. "Honestly, I'd always hoped that Taite would return home someday, but he has integrated himself into the de Winter war machine so much that I do not think they can do without him."

"He loves it there."

"He does."

"But they took Darius away from me," Thor said, frowning. "I had hoped he would remain with me forever."

"I know," Gage said. "And he did for a time after he married your sister, but when his father died, he had to return home and assume his place."

"I miss him."

"I know you do, but he and Nicola are very happy at Narborough."

Thor knew that, but that didn't change the fact that he

missed Darius after the man returned home four years ago. Clayne and Truett still remained with him, and Truett even had a local lady he had his eye on, but there were times when Thor missed Darius' companionship as well as his counsel.

But life moved on.

"What did you want to tell me?" he asked his father, remembering that the man had summoned him. "Or was that simply to get me away from the mob?"

Gage snorted. "I really did have something to tell you," he said. "I've been waiting for the right moment and it seems this is it. We are finally alone, waiting for a new life to make an appearance."

Thor eyed his father, mildly curious, but his attention was mostly on the bedchamber over his head where his wife was laboring to bring forth her seventh child. Her previous six pregnancies, according to Caledonia, had been very easy, but this one had seemed to tax her a great deal. She had struggled through it.

And that had her husband worried to death.

"I have been through childbirth with Callie three times already," he said. "I swear to you, the wait does not become easier with each pregnancy. It becomes worse. I want to go upstairs and be with her in the worst way."

Gage patted him on the arm. "You would only be in the way," he said. "She has the finest midwife. When your mother is finished tending the little monster you call your youngest son, she will be with her as well. There is nothing you can do, so you may as well wait here with me."

Thor knew that. This wasn't the first time his father had sat with him, waiting for a grandchild to be born.

"You're right," he said, resigning himself to the wait. "Now, what is it that you wished to tell me?"

Gage sent a nearby servant for wine before answering. "The subject of Madam Madonna is about to rear its ugly head again," he said. "You have not forgotten about her, have you?"

Thor looked at him in mild surprise. "I have not heard that name for a couple of years, at least," he said. "Of course I haven't forgotten about her. What about her?"

Gage nodded. "You tasked me with finding her years ago," he said. "You told me you wanted to find Madam Madonna, and if she happened to be serving another family by tending their children, you wanted to warn them."

"I did and I still do," Thor said. "Where is she?"

Gage waggled his eyebrows. "That, my son, is quite a story," he said. "When we first started looking for her, it was at Whitby Abbey because you were told that she had returned there."

"Aye, I had."

Gage snorted softly. "It seems so long ago now," he said. "At least eight years ago when we started looking for her."

Thor nodded. "As I said, I hadn't heard the name in a couple of years," he said. "What about her?"

Gage looked at him. "You will be happy to know that our patience has come to fruition," he said. "If you recall, I put a man on this, a mercenary who used to serve with Uncle Varro years ago."

"I remember," Thor said. "How is Uncle Varro, by the way?"

Gage shrugged. "Very old and very much in love with my mother-in-law, your grandmother, which I still find disturbing."

Thor started laughing. "He and Grandmother Maryann have been married for over twenty years," he said. "Why does their relationship disturb you so?"

Gage shook his head. "I do not know, but it does," he said. "Uncle Varro is a mercenary leader, not a lover."

"He is apparently both," Thor said, still grinning at his father, who pretended to be upset that his uncle had pursued his wife's widowed mother those years ago. "But we are getting off topic. What about Madam Madonna?"

"Right," Gage said, focusing. "You recall that the mercenary tracked her to Newcastle, where she took a ship to Amsterdam. Somehow, she had found a position with a Flemish count and his family."

"I remember."

"But she was dismissed, for neglect, we were told, and we lost her trail."

"I remember all of this."

The servant picked that moment to return with wine, leaving it on the table with bread and cheese before retreating. Gage poured his son a full measure and handed him the cup.

"About six months ago, we picked up her trail again," Gage said. "This mercenary is now working a private position for a wealthy merchant in Portsmouth, guarding the man's shipments, and he heard from a serving wench who works for the merchant that there was recently a great scandal in town. It seems that a woman who called herself Sister Madonna had started a foundling home with the sponsorship of the local church, only Sister Madonna was taking in children but leaving them to starve. She was using the money for herself, living like a queen, while her charges suffered. When the local priest figured that out and confronted her, she ran off and evidently jumped into the sea to avoid an angry mob of townspeople. She was swept out to sea and is presumed drowned."

Thor's eyebrows lifted. "God's Bones," he said. "Are you serious?"

Gage nodded. "Of course, I do not know if this woman was, in fact, your Madam Madonna, but the clues are there."

Thor was stunned. "It sounds exactly like her," he said. "She did the same thing to Janie and Janet and Joanie when they were very small. Nearly starved them to death while she lived rich and satisfied. Good God, who was stupid enough to trust that woman with a foundling home?"

"A very remorseful priest, evidently," Gage said. "In any case, I think we can safely say that the mystery is solved. The woman will never harm any children again. It sounds as if she received what she deserved."

Truer words were never spoken. The first few years after Thor and Caledonia married, he and his father had spent time and money searching for Madam Madonna. Thor wanted to bring her to justice for what she'd done to Caledonia's children, and for some time he was determined to do it. But the trail had grown cold and he'd all but given up, as he'd told his father.

This news was as shocking as it was welcome.

"Incredible," he finally said. "I know that Callie will want to hear this."

"How do you think she will react?"

Thor shrugged. "I think she wanted to punish the woman herself," he admitted. "But to know she received a harsh punishment at the hands of others... I think she will accept that. As long as Madam Madonna isn't harming other children, I think she'll be satisfied."

Gage shook his head sadly. "Callie had a difficult life until she married you," he said. "If we can at all right the sins of the past, you know we will try."

Thor smiled at his father. "I know," he said. "Your help with Madam Madonna meant a good deal to her. But those who have sinned against Callie in the past are largely gone now—de Tosni, Rotri and Domnall de Wylde, and now Madam Madonna. If there was anyone else, she hasn't told me. I think living the life we have for the past eight years has eased the memories of the horrors and has also tamed her wild streak. No more wandering, no more taverns or inns or drinking. All of that has stopped. We only look ahead these days. We do not look back."

Gage put his hand on Thor's shoulder. "Wise words, lad," he said. "But what about Gomorrah?"

"What about it?"

"That was her favorite place, once. Does she ever talk about it?"

Thor shook his head. "She does not because I told her that if she so much as entertained the idea of ever returning, I would burn the place to ash," he said firmly. "She promised me she would never go back. But then she laughed, so I do not know if she was serious or not."

Gage chuckled. "You married a headstrong woman, lad," he said. "I would be on my guard, always."

Thor joined in his father's laughter, but before he could reply, Jane suddenly appeared. Tall and elegant, with her mother's white hair and dark green eyes, she took one look at Thor and broke out into a smile that nearly split her face in two.

"The baby is here," she announced happily. "It is a girl!"

Thor broke down laughing. He was so happy that he simply couldn't help it. "Finally," he said as his father slapped him on the back. "A lass after all of those boys. How is your mother? Is she well?"

Jane rushed forward, grasping him by the hand and pulling

him to his feet. "Mother is very well," she said. "She says that you must come right away and see your black-haired daughter."

Grinning, Thor and Gage followed Jane to the master's chamber on the top level of Edingale's keep, a vast and lavish chamber that seemed to be full of people. There were midwives, a physic, and servants milling about. Thor also caught sight of his mother over near the bed, fawning over a small bundle in Caledonia's arms. When Caledonia looked up and saw her husband, the smiles of love and adoration that passed between them were tangible.

Thor had eyes only for his wife.

"My love," he said as he came to the bed and kissed her gently on the mouth. "Are you well? How do you feel?"

"Exhausted," Caledonia admitted. "Your daughter did not want to come forth. She was quite happy in my belly."

Thor could see a little face and tufts of dark hair peeking out from the swaddling. He tried to reach for her but realized that Jane was still holding his hand. She hadn't let him go. He smiled at the young woman he very much considered his daughter and gave her hand a squeeze.

"Have you held your sister?" he asked her.

Jane shook her head, but her gaze was on the baby. "Nay," she said. "Mother said you must hold her first. She promised I can hold her next."

Thor had to pry his hand out of Jane's so he could collect the infant from his wife's arms. He held the baby with a good deal of confidence, cradling her against his chest as Jane tried to get a look. He finally peeled back the swaddling so she could see the infant. The big sister was quite thrilled with her.

"Well?" Caledonia said, smiling wearily at her husband and eldest daughter. "We had planned on a lad, but I do not wish to name my daughter Lance. What shall we name her?"

Thor shrugged, looking at Jane. "Do you have any suggestions?"

Jane nodded hesitantly. "I must confess something," she said, looking between her parents. "I prayed for a sister. I love my brothers, but I did not want them to outnumber the girls, so I prayed very hard for a sister."

Caledonia chuckled. "God heard your prayer," she said. "It seems to me that since you prayed for this child, you should name her."

"I agree." Wynter, Lady Ashington, spoke up. Standing on the other side of the bed, the beautiful woman with the red hair was watching the touching scene with a great deal of delight. "Janie, what name shall the baby have?"

Jane's gaze moved to the infant, who was starting to squirm. "I… I like the name Julianna," she said. She looked up at Thor. "Do you like the name? Julianna?"

"I love the name," he said. "Well done, Janie. Would you like to hold Julianna now?"

Thrilled that her parents liked the name, Jane nodded eagerly and rushed to sit down next to her mother on the bed. Thor placed the baby carefully in her arms, and Jane gazed at the baby for a moment before bursting into quiet tears. As Caledonia and Wynter comforted the emotional young woman, Thor stood back by his father, watching the tender scene.

"Sometimes I have trouble believing just how rich my life really is," Thor murmured. "Do you remember that moment, years ago, when Henry forced me into this marriage?"

"Well I do."

Thor looked at him. "I never had the chance to thank him before he died," he said. "I have always regretted that."

A smile played on Gage's lips. "He went to his grave thinking we were both angry with him."

Thor snorted softly. "I once told him that I did not think I would make a very good husband."

"I remember."

"Have I?" Thor turned to his father, tears suddenly in his eyes. "Have I been a good husband, Papa? A good father? I've so wanted to emulate you in everything. I hope I have made you proud. I know that I added Wylde to my name, to honor my wife's family and the Tamworth line, and I have always been afraid that, secretly, that has disappointed you. Has it?"

Gage put his arm around his son's shoulders. "Of course not," he said. "You are simply making your own mark, creating your own dynasty. Some say that the measure of a man is upon the field of battle, or in the political arena. But I've come to think that the true measure of a man is how much he is loved by his family and friends. You took a broken woman and her equally broken children and created something fine and whole. Henry was right when he said you deserved more than being a garrison commander for your father. He was right and I was wrong."

Thor smiled weakly, wiping at the tears in his eyes. "I think we were both wrong," he said. "I will have to name a son after him as penitence."

"Wherever Henry is, I am certain that will please him."

"So long as I please you, that is all I am concerned with."

Gage gave Thor a squeeze, but Caledonia was calling to him, so he stood back as Thor joined his wife. He leaned over Jane, still holding the baby, as Caledonia pointed out a dimple on the baby's chin.

Just like her father.

Those years ago, Gage had indeed been wrong when it came to fighting the idea of his son, his greatest son, marrying a widowed countess. He was grateful that he'd been wrong, because what Thor had with Caledonia was nothing short of magical. As Gage had said, Thor had taken a broken woman and her broken children and made something whole and wonderful out of them.

And they made something whole and wonderful out of him, too.

Thorington de Reyne-Wylde, Earl of Tamworth and Stafford, had turned out to be a remarkable warlord in his own right. He had indeed made his own mark by taking on his wife's surname, bringing a Wylde streak to the Aragon mercenary and Visigoth blood that already flowed in his veins.

One Wylde knight, indeed.

And Gage couldn't have been prouder.

Cଔ THE END ଚ୦

Children of Thor and Caledonia de Reyne-Wylde

Robert's daughters:
Jane
Janet
Joan

Thor's children:
Thorne
Kirk
Reed
Julianna
Lance
Justina
Jeniver
Henry
Gray

Kathryn Le Veque Novels

Medieval Romance:

De Wolfe Pack Series:
Warwolfe
The Wolfe
Nighthawk
ShadowWolfe
DarkWolfe
A Joyous de Wolfe Christmas
BlackWolfe
Serpent
A Wolfe Among Dragons
Scorpion
StormWolfe
Dark Destroyer
The Lion of the North
Walls of Babylon
The Best Is Yet To Be
BattleWolfe
Castle of Bones

De Wolfe Pack Generations:
WolfeHeart
WolfeStrike
WolfeSword
WolfeBlade
WolfeLord
WolfeShield
Nevermore
WolfeAx
WolfeBorn

The Executioner Knights:
By the Unholy Hand
The Mountain Dark
Starless
A Time of End
Winter of Solace
Lord of the Sky
The Splendid Hour
The Whispering Night
Netherworld
Lord of the Shadows
Of Mortal Fury
'Twas the Executioner Knight
Before Christmas
Crimson Shield
The Black Dragon

The de Russe Legacy:
The Falls of Erith
Lord of War: Black Angel
The Iron Knight
Beast
The Dark One: Dark Knight
The White Lord of Wellesbourne
Dark Moon
Dark Steel
A de Russe Christmas Miracle
Dark Warrior

The de Lohr Dynasty:
While Angels Slept
Rise of the Defender
Steelheart
Shadowmoor
Silversword

Spectre of the Sword
Unending Love
Archangel
A Blessed de Lohr Christmas
Lion of Twilight
Lion of War
Lion of Hearts

The Brothers de Lohr:
The Earl in Winter

Lords of East Anglia:
While Angels Slept
Godspeed
Age of Gods and Mortals

Great Lords of le Bec:
Great Protector

House of de Royans:
Lord of Winter
To the Lady Born
The Centurion

Lords of Eire:
Echoes of Ancient Dreams
Lord of Black Castle
The Darkland

Ancient Kings of Anglecynn:
The Whispering Night
Netherworld

Battle Lords of de Velt:
The Dark Lord
Devil's Dominion
Bay of Fear
The Dark Lord's First Christmas
The Dark Spawn
The Dark Conqueror
The Dark Angel

Reign of the House of de Winter:
Lespada
Swords and Shields

De Reyne Domination:
Guardian of Darkness
The Black Storm
A Cold Wynter's Knight
With Dreams
Master of the Dawn
One Wylde Knight

House of d'Vant:
Tender is the Knight (House of d'Vant)
The Red Fury (House of d'Vant)

The Dragonblade Series:
Fragments of Grace
Dragonblade
Island of Glass
The Savage Curtain
The Fallen One
The Phantom Bride

Great Marcher Lords of de Lara
Lord of the Shadows
Dragonblade

House of St. Hever
Fragments of Grace
Island of Glass
Queen of Lost Stars

Lords of Pembury:
The Savage Curtain

Lords of Thunder: The de Shera Brotherhood Trilogy
The Thunder Lord
The Thunder Warrior

The Thunder Knight

The Great Knights of de Moray:
Shield of Kronos
The Gorgon

The House of De Nerra:
The Promise
The Falls of Erith
Vestiges of Valor
Realm of Angels

Highland Legion:
Highland Born

Highland Warriors of Munro:
The Red Lion
Deep Into Darkness

The House of de Garr:
Lord of Light
Realm of Angels

Saxon Lords of Hage:
The Crusader
Kingdom Come

High Warriors of Rohan:
High Warrior
High King

The House of Ashbourne:
Upon a Midnight Dream

The House of D'Aurilliac:
Valiant Chaos

The House of De Dere:
Of Love and Legend

St. John and de Gare Clans:
The Warrior Poet

The House of de Bretagne:
The Questing

The House of Summerlin:
The Legend

The Kingdom of Hendocia:
Kingdom by the Sea

The BlackChurch Guild: Shadow Knights:
The Leviathan
The Protector

Regency Historical Romance:
Sin Like Flynn: A Regency Historical Romance Duet
The Sin Commandments
Georgina and the Red Charger

Gothic Regency Romance:
Emma

Contemporary Romance:

Kathlyn Trent/Marcus Burton Series:
Valley of the Shadow
The Eden Factor
Canyon of the Sphinx

The American Heroes Anthology Series:
The Lucius Robe
Fires of Autumn
Evenshade
Sea of Dreams
Purgatory

Other non-connected Contemporary Romance:
Lady of Heaven

Darkling, I Listen
In the Dreaming Hour
River's End
The Fountain

Sons of Poseidon:
The Immortal Sea

Pirates of Britannia Series (with Eliza Knight):
Savage of the Sea by Eliza Knight
Leader of Titans by Kathryn Le Veque
The Sea Devil by Eliza Knight
Sea Wolfe by Kathryn Le Veque

<u>Note:</u> All Kathryn's novels are designed to be read as stand-alones, although many have cross-over characters or cross-over family groups. Novels that are grouped together have related characters or family groups. You will notice that some series have the same books; that is because they are cross-overs. A hero in one book may be the secondary character in another.

There is NO reading order except by chronology, but even in that case, you can still read the books as stand-alones. No novel is connected to another by a cliff hanger, and every book has an HEA.

Series are clearly marked. All series contain the same characters or family groups except the American Heroes Series, which is an anthology with unrelated characters.

For more information, find it in **A Reader's Guide to the Medieval World of Le Veque**.

ABOUT KATHRYN LE VEQUE

Bringing the Medieval to Romance

KATHRYN LE VEQUE is a critically acclaimed, multiple USA TODAY Bestselling author, an Indie Reader bestseller, a charter Amazon All-Star author, and a #1 bestselling, award-winning, multi-published author in Medieval Historical Romance with over 100 published novels.

Kathryn is a multiple award nominee and winner, including the winner of Uncaged Book Reviews Magazine 2017 and 2018 "Raven Award" for Favorite Medieval Romance. Kathryn is also a multiple RONE nominee (InD'Tale Magazine), holding a record for the number of nominations. In 2018, her novel WARWOLFE was the winner in the Romance category of the Book Excellence Award and in 2019, her novel A WOLFE AMONG DRAGONS won the prestigious RONE award for best pre-16th century romance.

Kathryn is considered one of the top Indie authors in the world with over 2M copies in circulation, and her novels have been translated into several languages. Kathryn recently signed with Sourcebooks Casablanca for a Medieval Fight Club series, first published in 2020.

In addition to her own published works, Kathryn is also the President/CEO of Dragonblade Publishing, a boutique publishing house specializing in Historical Romance. Dragonblade's success has seen it rise in the ranks to become Amazon's #1 e-book publisher of Historical Romance (K-Lytics report July 2020).

Kathryn loves to hear from her readers. Please find Kathryn on Facebook at Kathryn Le Veque, Author, or join her on Twitter @kathrynleveque. Sign up for Kathryn's blog at www.kathrynleveque.com for the latest news and sales.

www.ingramcontent.com/pod-product-compliance
Lightning Source LLC
Chambersburg PA
CBHW060427310726
48977CB00001B/82

* 9 7 8 1 9 6 3 5 8 5 5 8 2 *